A blessed event

Brittany, Rose and Irish
are about to encounter
the miracle of birth.

Michael, Sullivan and Max
are about to encounter
the women of their dreams.

A baby will bring them together,
but can love convince them to stay?

Strange things can happen when there's a

Baby on the Way

Relive the romance...

by Request™

Three complete novels by your favorite authors!

About the Authors

DALLAS SCHULZE

loves books, old movies, her husband and her cat, not necessarily in that order. She's a sucker for a happy ending, whose writing has given her an outlet for her imagination, and she hopes that readers have half as much fun with her books as she does! Dallas has more hobbies than there is space to list them, but is currently an avid quilter.

LINDA TURNER

began reading romances in high school and began writing them one night when she had nothing else to read. She's been writing ever since. Single and living in Texas, she travels every chance she gets, scouting locales for her books.

CAIT LONDON

a.k.a. Lois Kleinsasser, is having the time of her life. The mother of three daughters (three is her lucky number), she is a national bestselling author in contemporary and historical romance. She travels and researches the historical trails of the West.

Baby on the Way

Dallas Schulze
Linda Turner
Cait London

Silhouette Books

Published by Silhouette Books
America's Publisher of Contemporary Romance

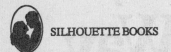

SILHOUETTE BOOKS

by Request—Baby on the Way

ISBN 0-373-20104-4

This edition published by arrangement with Harlequin Enterprises B.V.

Printed in U.S.A.

CONTENTS

A Note from Dallas Schulze

Babies are magical beings. They're tiny. They're helpless. Yet they have the ability to change the lives of those around them. From the moment a couple finds out they're going to have a baby, their lives are forever changed. For good or for ill, for better or for worse, nothing is ever quite the same again.

In "The Vow," I chose to tell a story of two people who are brought together by a baby and whose lives are changed in ways they could never have anticipated. It's about love and marriage and how you sometimes don't see what's right under your nose. And, of course, it's about a baby on the way.

Dallas Schulze

THE VOW

Dallas Schulze

Chapter 1

"We are gathered here today to say farewell to two people, a father and his son, who meant a great deal to all of us. Larry Remington was a respected member of our small community. His passing will leave a gap in many lives. And Dan Remington, a true son of Remembrance, was born into our town, spending all of his tragically short life among us."

Michael tuned out the pastor's voice. He didn't need someone else to tell him how great his loss was. Dan had been his best friend. His absence was like a knotted fist in the pit of his stomach. It just didn't seem possible. Plane crash in Central America or no, Dan simply couldn't be dead.

But he was. No survivors. Dan, his father, the whole archaeology team gone in an instant. The pilot had managed to radio their coordinates as the plane was going down. They had served only as a guide to the burned-out wreckage.

Michael stared at the back of the seat in front of him. The pastor was droning on about Dan's life, his career aspirations. Why the hell did they always have to talk about what could have been at these things? Was it supposed to make it easier for everyone to hear a litany of everything that would never happen?

He glanced across the aisle and felt the knot in his stomach tighten. Brittany. What was she thinking? Feeling? As he watched, she reached up, her fingers grasping the gold heart pendant that was her only jewelry. Dan had given her that last Christmas. Michael remembered him picking it out, laughing that it was certainly more decorative than wearing his heart on his sleeve.

His eyes traced the delicate lines of her profile. She looked so fragile, so helpless. Her thick black hair was drawn back in a simple knot, baring the slender length of her neck. Her skin was so pale it seemed translucent. He wanted to go to her, put his arm around her and tell her that everything was going to be all right. The intensity of his desire to soothe her pain made him uneasy, and he looked away.

Dan had been his best friend. Brittany was the woman he'd loved. It was an extension of Michael's friendship that made him want to comfort Brittany. Besides, he liked Brittany for her own sake. Had liked her since the moment Dan had introduced them. In fact, if Dan hadn't— He shrugged the thought away. Brittany had clearly thought the sun rose and set on Dan Remington. Her pain must run deep.

His eyes were drawn to her again. She really was lovely. She seemed to feel his gaze, for her eyes lifted, meeting his. They were almost the same gray as her dress. Michael had never thought of gray as a warm color until he'd met Brittany and seen how full of life and fire her eyes were. Now the fire was quenched, the life dulled, her pain obvious. He gave her a crooked smile. The corners of her mouth lifted in acknowledgment before her eyes dropped back to her hands.

Michael was more or less successful in blocking out the majority of the service. When it ended at last, he stood, hunching his shoulders against the ache that had settled in the middle of his back. The other mourners were filing into the vestibule at the front of the church. There would be food set out, sustenance for those left behind.

The last thing Michael wanted to do was nibble stuffed mushrooms and make small talk about what a terrible tragedy this had been. His grief was a private thing, not something he wanted to share over tea and crumpets. He turned, planning to make his exit out another door. Catching a glimpse of pale gray, he hesitated. Brittany's full skirt disappeared into the vestibule.

There was nothing he could say to her, no comfort he could offer, which didn't explain why he changed his plans and followed her into the other room.

Everything was just as he'd expected. People stood around in small groups, talking quietly, sipping coffee and fruit juice from paper cups and shaking their heads over the tragic waste of it all.

"If only Larry hadn't been so determined to go on this foolish trip.... Well, yes, it had been a dream of his for years, but he'd certainly been well past the age of going on wild-goose chases. And to take Dan with him.... True, Dan had been as excited by the idea of an archaeological expedition as his father. But look where it had gotten the pair of them. And there was poor Clare, left alone. And at her age."

Michael made his way through the gathering, careful to meet no one's eye, his face set in an expression that did not invite approach. His blue eyes skimmed the group.

"Michael Sinclair. I didn't realize you were here."

He stiffened and then turned reluctantly. Merideth Wallings was quite possibly the worst gossip the world had ever known. She was also shallow, grasping and generally unpleasant. Unfortunately, her family owned half of Remembrance, and she'd grown accustomed to the deference this tended to purchase for her.

"Mrs. Wallings." He nodded, trying to look as if he had other places to go. Merideth didn't notice.

"Isn't this just the most awful tragedy?" She took a bite of a cracker, her dark eyes snapping with excitement. "It's just impossible to believe that they're dead. Poor Larry. And poor Dan, in the prime of life. You and Dan were quite close, weren't you?"

"We were good friends," Michael said repressively.

"It's just terrible. I don't know how poor Clare is going to manage."

"It will be difficult. If you'll—"

"I don't see your parents here today." Merideth craned her neck as if expecting to see Donovan and Beth lurking in a corner.

"They're on a cruise. I called them with the news, but they couldn't make it back in time for the services."

"That's right. Poor Beth. How is she doing?"

"She's doing just fine."

"It must have been so hard for her to lose the baby."

"These things happen."

"Yes, but it's harder when you get to her age." Merideth crunched a carrot stick.

"She's fine." Michael's eyes grew frosty. A lesser person might have taken notice that she was stepping on shaky ground. Merideth was made of sterner stuff.

"Well, of course, Beth always has been the sort to put up a brave front. You know, at her age, it was risky to try a pregnancy to start with. We can't stay young forever, you know. I could have told her, if only she'd asked me, that it was a mistake to try for a child at this late date. It's just too dangerous. It's a shame Donovan—" She broke off, shaking her head, her mouth turned up in a grimace she appeared to think was an indulgent smile. "But then, men can be so foolish about this sort of thing. They just don't think about the risks we women take."

"Mrs. Wallings, this child was something *both* my parents wanted. Its loss was something they both felt."

"I'm sure it was, Michael. I certainly didn't mean to imply that it wasn't. It's just that these things are always felt more keenly by the woman. After all, we are the ones who carry the child beneath our hearts. I know just how Beth must be feeling right now."

"I seriously doubt that," Michael told her bluntly, annoyance and distraction overtaking him. "Excuse me." He walked away, leaving her with her mouth agape.

He'd spotted Brittany near the window, though even without that excuse, he couldn't have tolerated another minute of Merideth Wallings's sanctimonious claptrap. He moved through the crowd as quickly as politeness allowed, slowing a few paces from Brittany.

Now that he was so close, he suddenly doubted the wisdom of approaching her. After all, they didn't know each other all that well. Dan had been their connecting link, and now that link was gone. She was staring out the window, unaware of him. He could just leave.

But she looked so alone. Her slender figure seemed dragged down by the weight of her simple dress. He had the feeling that the slightest touch might shatter her into a million pieces.

"Brittany." He said her name softly. She started but didn't immediately turn.

"Michael." His name held a wealth of pain, making him wonder if his presence was too great a reminder of her loss. But she reached out, her hand seeking his. Michael took it, feeling the delicacy of her fingers against the callused strength of his palm. He joined her at the window.

Hot summer sunshine blazed down outside, incongruous in the face of the reason they were here. It should have been pouring rain. Brittany must have felt the same thing.

"They shouldn't have funerals in the middle of summer," she said quietly. "Funerals should be for winter, when everything is all cold and grim."

"It does seem wrong, doesn't it?" They stood without speaking for a few moments, their hands still linked.

"It doesn't seem possible," Brittany said, drawing her hand from his to wipe a solitary tear from her cheek.

"No, it doesn't." He wanted to reach out and pull her into his arms, let her cry her grief out on his shoulder. Instead, he pushed his hands into his pockets, reminding himself that it wasn't his place.

"How are you doing?" he asked instead. For the first time, she looked at him.

"I don't really know." Up close, he could see the smudgy gray shadows beneath her eyes. "And you? Dan always said you two were like brothers. It must be very hard for you."

"Yeah." Michael looked away, gritting his teeth against the ache in his throat. "I'm doing okay."

"No, you're not. Not any more than I am. None of us are." Her voice rose, drawing a few eyes in their direction. She gulped, fighting for control. "It's not fair Michael. It's just not fair."

"I know." He glanced around, noting the attention they were getting. "Come on, let's get out of here." He set his arm around her shoulders, ignoring the questioning looks as he drew her to the door.

Outside, the hot Indiana summer enveloped them, but it couldn't banish the chill of loss. Brittany leaned against him, letting him lead her toward the narrow lawn next to the church.

"Did you bring your car?" he asked.

"No. I got a ride from a friend."

"I'll drive you home."

"Michael." The sudden urgency in her voice brought him to a stop. "I'm going to be sick," she said thinly. One look at her pale face told him that she wasn't kidding and that there was no way she could make it back inside. He steered her around the corner of the church into the relative privacy of a group of bushes.

"Go away," she ordered, the impact lost in the quavering tone of her voice.

"Don't be an idiot." The look she flashed him showed annoyance, but she didn't have a chance to argue. Michael held her head, supporting her trembling body with the strength of his own.

Once the sickness was over, several minutes passed before she gathered the strength to push him away, standing waveringly on knees that clearly weren't too keen on supporting her.

"You should have left me alone."

He might have showed some penitence if she hadn't had to clutch at his arm when her knees threatened to buckle. He slid an arm around her waist, guiding her shaky footsteps to the scarred water fountain that stood next to the church.

Brittany rinsed her mouth, then she drank thirstily of the cool water. When she was through, Michael dampened his handkerchief and wiped it across her moist forehead. It was a measure of her exhaustion that she didn't protest, closing her eyes and leaning against him as the cool cloth soothed her clammy skin.

"I'm sorry," she murmured.

"Don't be an idiot."

Her eyes came open. "You keep telling me that." Her smile flickered and then broke, her eyes filling with tears. "Maybe I can't help it."

He glanced over his shoulder as the church door opened and several people walked out. "Come on. Let's get out of here."

They didn't speak again until he had his old Mustang on the road, heading away from the church.

"I always liked this car," Brittany said.

Michael barely glanced at the gleaming black paint and immaculate upholstery. He'd spent his last two years in high school working on the junk heap the car had been, restoring it to pristine condition. Right now, he had more important things on his mind.

"How are you feeling?"

"Stupid. Embarrassed."

"There's nothing to be embarrassed about. Are you all right now?"

"Sure." She laughed, a bitter tone in the sound. "I'm just great if you—" She broke off, shaking her head. "I'm fine."

"What were you going to say?"

"Nothing. It's not important." The set of her chin told him he wasn't going to get anything out of her unless she chose to allow it.

He braked for a red light near the center of town, casting a quick look in her direction. She was staring out at the downtown bustle, but he knew she wasn't seeing it. Her gaze was turned inward. There was something wrong—he understood her sense of loss, but her introspection seemed to go beyond Dan's death.

"Brittany." She turned to look at him as the light changed to green. He put the car in gear, half-glad for the excuse not to look at her. Looking at her could easily become a habit. "What's bothering you? There's something more than Dan's—" He stopped, unable to say the word.

"No. No, there's not. At least, nothing that you can help me with. Did I tell you that I'm staying with my parents for a couple of days? You don't have to drive me all the way to Indianapolis."

Michael hesitated. Instinct told him to push her, to make her tell him what was wrong. Good manners dictated that he back off. If she didn't want to tell him, there was no law that said she had to.

"Where do your parents live?"

He followed her directions to a small development on the far edge of town. It was the first tiny square of tract homes to have gone up in Remembrance, back in the fifties. As such, he supposed it had some vague historical significance. But the architect in him winced at the rows of little square houses. The years had given them some individuality, but stripped of the minor changes, they were all identical, all without character.

He pulled up before the house she indicated, a plain white box even more stark than its neighbors. The immaculate lawn looked as if it had been mowed by a surgeon, the trees precisely pruned, the flower beds meticulously edged. The effect should have been lovely. Instead, it was too symmetrical, too perfect.

He turned to Brittany, but she was talking before he could open his mouth. "Thank you for the ride home. I hadn't even thought about how I was going to get back."

"I'll walk you up to the door."

"That's not necessary." But he was already out of the car, coming around to her side to open her door. She took his hand reluctantly, letting him help her out of the car before releasing it.

They walked up the neat brick path in silence. Brittany fumbled in her purse as they stepped onto the narrow porch, Michael's shoes echoing on the wooden floor.

"Got it." She smiled nervously as she pulled out a key and inserted it into the lock. "I'm all the time losing keys. It's a good thing I have a roommate at school who can let me in.

Otherwise, I'd probably have to set up camp in the library—"

"Brittany." Michael's quiet voice broke into her babbling. She stopped, sucking in a breath that came near to a sob.

"Michael, please. I can't take much more today."

"I'm not trying to cause you more grief. But I know there's something wrong. Now that Dan isn't here, I hope you know you can come to me."

"Oh, Michael." Her shoulders slumped for an instant before she straightened them. She looked up at him, her eyes glistening with tears but her chin set. "There's nothing wrong. I'm just trying to deal with what's happened."

Michael didn't believe her for a moment, but he couldn't force her to talk to him. He shoved his hands into the pockets of his suit pants. "You'll call me if you need anything?"

"Of course. Thank you." She turned away, flipping the lock open. It was dismissal, polite but firm, and there was no arguing with it. Michael turned, taking a step away, every instinct screaming that all was not right, that he shouldn't leave her like this.

He turned back, uncertain of what he was going to say but knowing he had to speak up. Only it wasn't necessary. Hearing him approach, Brittany started to turn from the half-open door. She stopped, wavered and lifted a hand to her forehead, her skin suddenly dead white. Michael caught her as her knees buckled.

She sagged against him, unconscious. He lifted her into his arms, feeling his heart jump with fear. She was so pale. Pushing the door open with his shoulder, he carried her inside, kicking the door shut behind him. They were in the living room, a plain room with furniture that looked as if it had been moved in when the house was built and hadn't been shifted so much as an inch since.

Carrying Brittany to the sofa, set rigidly in place between two end tables, Michael laid her down. She stirred, moaning faintly. Not knowing what else to do, he crouched next to her, taking her hand in his, patting it gently. Her lashes lifted slowly, and she stared at him, dazed.

"You fainted."

"Did I?" she asked, lifting her free hand to touch her forehead, as if not sure that either still belonged to her.

"I think I should call a doctor."

"No!" Her fingers tightened over his, her eyes frightened. "I don't need a doctor."

"Brittany, you fainted."

"It's been a rough day." She struggled up, obviously determined to put the incident behind her. Michael helped her sit up and then sat next to her, still holding her hand.

"You're as pale as a ghost, and your pulse is faster than it should be."

She tugged her hand from his, shooting him a resentful look from under sooty lashes. "I thought you were an architect, not a doctor."

"I thought I was a friend."

"You are, Michael. You know you are." She was distressed that he would think otherwise.

"Then why won't you tell me what's troubling you?"

"Because, there are some things that you just can't help with."

"Try me." A vague suspicion was forming in the back of his mind.

"I can't," she whispered, shaking her head.

"Brittany." He stopped, staring at her bent head. This was none of his business. She was Dan's girl. But as Dan's best friend, didn't he have an obligation to look after her? Isn't that what Dan would have wanted? But if she didn't want his help... In the end, it wasn't a matter of logical argument. He simply couldn't leave her like this.

"Brittany, are you pregnant?"

She jumped as if he'd cracked a lash across her shoulders, her head jerking up, wide gray eyes meeting his.

"No, of course not." But the truth was in her eyes, and Michael felt a hardness in his chest that was impossible to define.

"Did Dan know?" he asked tightly. If Dan had known and left her alone...

"I told you, I'm not—" She broke off, reading the hopelessness of the lie in his look. Her shoulders slumped and she dropped her gaze to her clasped hands. "No. He didn't know."

Michael drew in a deep breath. Dan hadn't known. The idea that he could have known and abandoned Brittany had been insupportable.

"You didn't know?" he questioned.

"I knew. I should have told him. If I had, maybe he wouldn't have gone, and he'd still be alive." She waved a hand, forestalling his protest. "I know it's stupid to think that way, but I can't help it."

Michael reached out, catching her hand in his. "Why didn't you tell him?"

"We fought. I wanted to get married, and he said it was stupid to get married while I was still in school. He said we'd talk about it when he got back. Only now he won't be coming back," she ended starkly.

"If you'd told him..."

"I know. I know. If I'd told him I was pregnant, he'd have married me. But then how would I ever know if he married me because he wanted to or because he *had* to?"

"Dan was crazy about you," Michael protested.

"Maybe. But I'd never have known for sure."

There didn't seem to be anything to say. Michael stared at their linked hands. What was he supposed to do now? What would Dan have wanted him to do?

"What are you going to do now?" he asked finally, feeling hopelessly inadequate.

"I don't know. There hasn't been much time to think since I got the news about Dan."

He stood up, moving away restlessly. "Are you going to have the baby?" The question came out too abruptly, and he shook his head. "Forget it. It's none of my business."

"It's all right." Now that the truth was out, Brittany seemed much more calm. "I'm going to have it. This is my child, mine and Dan's." Her fingers touched her still-flat stomach as if she could feel the tiny life she carried. "It's a part of us—all that's left, in a way."

"Is there anything I can do?" he asked, feeling awkward and uncertain. "Anything you need?"

"No. I'm going to be just fine." She lifted her chin, drawing her shoulders straight. "I fell apart today, but that won't happen again."

"Are you sure? Anything at all. I'm not just asking because you're carrying Dan's baby."

She half smiled but shook her head again. "Thank you. After the way I dissolved all over you, I'm surprised you didn't run for cover ages ago."

"Today was rough for all of us," he said.

"I know. I don't know what I'd have done without you. Thank you, Michael."

"No big deal." He shrugged her thanks away. He didn't want her gratitude.

"It was a big deal to me." She stood up and crossed the short distance between them. Michael looked down into her eyes, feeling an odd wariness he couldn't quite define. She raised up on her toes, balancing herself with a hand on his arm as she placed a kiss on his cheek.

Her mouth felt soft on his beard-roughened skin. Her scent was soft also, a mixture of lavender and sunshine. It drew him, making him want to put his arms around her and bury his face in her hair. Maybe then he could forget the aching sense of loss that gnawed at him. With Brittany in his arms, surely anything would be possible.

The feeling was so strong that he took a step back, the movement too quick so that she almost lost her balance. He put a hand to her waist, steadying her for an instant before withdrawing even that small contact.

It was safer if he didn't touch her. Safer in what way, he couldn't have said.

"You must be tired," he muttered.

"I am." If she noticed anything odd in his behavior, he couldn't tell. She pushed a straying lock of hair back.

"Your parents, they'll help you?"

"They'll be pretty upset, but I believe, when it comes right down to it, they'll do everything they can."

"Well, if there's any problem, call me."

"I will."

The pause threatened to grow awkward. He should leave. He'd said everything he could. She was probably hoping he'd go. But still he lingered, reluctant to leave her.

"Are you sure there isn't something I can do? There must be something you want or need."

"No, really Michael, I'm doing okay."

"You'll call me if you need anything?" He edged toward the door, torn between his concern and his need to put some distance between them.

"I'm not going to need anything."

"Promise you'll call me," he insisted again.

"I'll call you."

He reached out, unable to resist the urge to smooth back that errant lock of hair. "We're not going to lose touch," he told her firmly. "If you don't call me, I'm going to come looking for you."

"Okay." Tears trembled on her lashes, but she managed a wavering smile. "We won't lose touch."

Courting fire, he bent and kissed her cheek. When his head lifted, their eyes met for a long, silent moment before he turned and left without looking back.

Long strides carried him down the walkway, but once in the Mustang, he just sat, staring out the windshield. A vague headache throbbed behind his eyes. The days since the news had come about the plane crash blurred together in one indistinguishable gray fog. The memorial service was already half-forgotten.

Dan was gone. It was a fact that had to be accepted. Only Dan wasn't really gone. Brittany was carrying his child. The headache intensified. He should be glad that something of his friend would continue in the world. So why was it that all he could think of was that if Dan were to appear in front of him right at this moment, alive and unhurt, his first urge would be to punch him in the teeth?

Chapter 2

Brittany watched Michael go, feeling as if a lifeline were vanishing. After shutting the door behind him, she had to bite her lip to keep from calling him back.

"Don't be stupid," she muttered to herself. She didn't have anything to worry about. She was young and healthy. The doctor had told her that there was no reason to expect any problems with the pregnancy. Lots of women went through a pregnancy alone these days. There was no reason in the world why she should cling to Michael Sinclair.

She sat down, linking her hands together in her lap, fingers tense. She was going to be fine. The low growl of the Mustang's engine brought her to her feet. Standing at the window, she watched as it pulled away from the curb and disappeared down the street. She bit her lip, weak tears filling her eyes. He was gone. She hadn't realized how desperately she'd wanted him to come back. His arms had felt so strong, as if he could protect her from anything.

For the first time since Dan left, she'd felt secure. The future hadn't seemed quite so frightening. She'd tried to be positive with Michael, telling him that everything was going to be all right. What she desperately needed was someone to convince her of that.

Brushing impatiently at the dampness on her cheeks, she drew in a deep breath, then she turned away from the window and the empty street outside. She was behaving like a die-away heroine in a Victorian novel. She'd felt safe with Michael Sinclair, but that was probably because he reminded her of Dan. Not that the two men were anything alike, but they'd been best friends. Being with Michael almost made her feel as if Dan couldn't be far away.

Dan. Tears filled her eyes again. It just wasn't possible that he wasn't coming back. He'd always been so vibrant, so strong. Not the kind of quiet strength Michael had. Dan's had been a more boisterous, outgoing kind of strength.

Michael seemed to think things out before he acted. Dan hadn't thought anything out. He'd been quick to laugh as much as he'd been quick to anger—whichever, he was always gloriously alive.

If only she'd told him about the baby that last night. If he'd known she was pregnant, he'd never have left her. But she hadn't told him. Her stupid pride had demanded that he want to marry her without knowing about the child. They'd quarreled, then Dan had stormed off for Los Angeles, where the team was gathering. He'd never known about the baby. She'd thought that there'd be time to tell him, time to make up. Only they'd run out of time.

Brittany rested her hand on her flat stomach. The child she carried was all she had left of him. There was no outward sign yet, but she could feel the changes in her body. Inside, a new life was growing, one that would be a part of her and Dan and yet wholly its own. She didn't have time to wallow in grief and self-pity. She had to go on. Dan would have expected it of her, and more importantly, she owed it to the child—her and Dan's.

She reached out to straighten a doily on an end table. There was no sense in dwelling on the past. It couldn't be changed. The future was what counted now. And she had the best reason in the world to focus on the future.

Glancing at the clock, she figured her parents would be home soon. They'd gone to the golf course as they had every Thursday afternoon since her father retired. They didn't know about the baby, barely even knew about Dan. She'd tell them this afternoon.

She'd given a lot of thought to the future—her future and her child's. It wouldn't be easy, but she thought she could manage the first semester of the year during her pregnancy. After that, she'd have to take some time off. But once the baby was a few months old, she could finish school, get her degree and then get her teaching credentials.

Once she got a job, she'd be able to start creating a home for herself and her son or daughter. Her plan would work. She knew it would. But it was going to require a lot of help from her parents. She could count on them—couldn't she? Despite her determination to stay positive, she felt a chill. They weren't likely to take the news well.

Like the house, her parents hadn't changed with the times. She'd been born late in both their lives, a not entirely welcome surprise. They'd done their best, but their lives had already been neatly and precisely established when she was born, and they hadn't seen any reason to make more than the absolutely necessary changes.

Brittany had always accepted the fact that she was somewhat of an intruder in her parents' lives. It wasn't that they didn't care about her. It was simply that there wasn't really a place for her. In a way, she admired them. The rest of the world might be embracing flexible morals and ethics that could be tailored to any situation, but in the Winslow household, right was still right and wrong was always wrong. Things were black-and-white, never muddy gray.

Good people went to church on Sunday, voted in every election and minded their own business. Men held jobs and supported their families. Women stayed home and raised the children.

They'd reluctantly conceded that perhaps the world had changed somewhat in this respect. It might not be a bad idea for a woman to have a way to earn a living, which was why they'd agreed to finance her education. Brittany suspected it was the thought of having her dependent on them that had swayed them.

One thing she was sure they hadn't changed their views on was that a good girl did not sleep with a man before marriage. She'd half agreed with them until she met Dan. With Dan everything had been different.

She sighed, wrapping her arms around her waist. She had to tell her parents about this. She needed their support, financially and emotionally. They loved her. They might be hurt, disappointed in her, even, but they'd be able to set that aside. Wouldn't they?

"How could you do something like this?" It was her father who spoke, but looking from one accusing face to the other, Brittany knew that it could have come from either of them.

"It wasn't something I planned, Dad. It just happened."

"This sort of thing doesn't 'just happen' to girls who don't do things they shouldn't." That was her mother, her plain features drawn into distressed lines as she looked at her daughter.

"Mom, I—" She broke off, searching for words. How did she explain her relationship with Dan, that being with him had seemed the most right thing in the world? Her mother couldn't even say the word *sex*, let alone understand the needs she'd felt in Dan's arms. Brittany had often thought her own conception a miracle.

"What about the father? Is he willing to do the right thing by you?" her father demanded sternly.

The question sent a stabbing pain through her, and it was a moment before she could answer. The loss was still so fresh.

"I told you, Dad. Dan died in a plane crash last week," she said quietly. *How could they have forgotten that?* "If he were here, yes, I think he'd want to marry me."

"You *think* he'd want to marry you?" Her father glared at her from the depths of his wing chair. "You *think*? You did *that*—" his tone made the simple word an obscenity "—with a boy whom you only *thought* would marry you?"

Brittany immediately felt as if she'd been branded with a scarlet letter. *S* for slut. Color rose in her cheeks, and her eyes stung.

"Things are different now, Dad. It isn't considered a crime to sleep with a man before you get married. And I love...loved Dan." She bit her lip against the pain of using the past tense.

"Things aren't different in this household, young lady. I thought we'd raised you to a better standard than that. That's the trouble with the world today. Too many young people going out and doing just what they want to do without a thought to right or wrong."

"George, I think it's best if we don't get distracted from the matter at hand." His wife pulled him away from a lecture Brittany had heard many times in the past. "We need to decide what we're going to do about her."

"Her?" Brittany said. "You don't have talk about me as if I'm deaf, Mom." She tried a wavering smile, but her hand was clenched on the arm of the sofa.

This wasn't what she'd expected. This attitude that she'd committed a capital crime. She'd known that they'd be disappointed, angry, hurt, but she hadn't been prepared for the coldness. My God, they were looking at her as if they disliked her.

"I'm sorry if I've hurt you. I never intended to hurt you. But I need your support now. More than ever before."

Despite the naked plea in her voice, there was no warming in the eyes turned toward her, and a cold lump of fear settled in the pit of her stomach.

"Our 'support'?" her mother questioned. "How can we support what you've done?"

"It's not like I killed anybody. I made a mistake."

"I think the problem, Brittany, is that you think the mistake is in turning up like this...." Her father waved his hand in her direction, unable or unwilling to say the actual word. "The real mistake was in being . . . intimate with this young man to start with. This is your punishment for your immoral actions."

Brittany stared at him as if seeing him for the first time. How could he sit there and pass judgment on her like this?

"I don't think I want to think of my baby as a punishment for my—actions."

"Perhaps not, but that's what it is," her mother said.

"So what's the bottom line here?" Brittany asked, anger lending a challenging edge to her voice. "Are you going to cast me from your home, refuse to acknowledge my existence?"

"Certainly not." Ann Winslow arranged her full skirt more neatly around her knees, fussing with it until it fell into precise folds. "Your father and I would never do such a thing."

Brittany drew a deep breath, feeling the tears—so quick these days—start to her eyes. For a moment she'd been facing a very bleak future.

"I knew I could count on you."

"Naturally. We *are* your parents. We've always done our best by you. You have no reason to think that we wouldn't this time, also."

"Thank you. I know this is very hard for both of you."

"It would have been nice if you'd thought of that before you did what you did," her father said repressively.

Brittany bit her tongue, holding back the urge to tell him that this might just be a little harder on her than it was on them.

"George, there's no sense in recriminations now. What's done is done."

Brittany allowed some of the tension to ease from her muscles. It was going to be all right. They were upset. It had been foolish of her not to realize just how upset they'd be. But it was going to be all right now. They'd had a chance to absorb the shock. Her mother would calm her father's indignation, and they'd work things out. It might be a while before they forgave her completely, but once they saw their grandchild, all this would seem so unimportant.

"What's important now is to decide just how we're going to handle this." Brittany brought her attention back to the conversation as her mother continued, the relief making her feel almost light-headed.

"I'd like to finish college," she said. "I know it won't be easy, what with the baby due in the middle of the school year, but I think it's important."

"Brittany, please don't interrupt. This is something your father and I will have to give some consideration."

"Isn't my input important?" Her half smile went unanswered, and a small chill settled in her chest. Things were going to be all right, weren't they?

"I believe you have already proved that your judgment is less than sound," her mother said coolly. "I suggest you let your father and I come to some decisions regarding your future."

"Since *we* are discussing *my* future, I'd like some say in any decisions that are made."

"Very well. Your father and I haven't had a chance to discuss it yet, of course, but I think the appropriate path is quite clear. You should go to your aunt and uncle in New York. They have a house in the upstate area, and I'm sure they won't mind having you stay with them.

"You can stay there until the child is born, at which time it can be put up for adoption, then you can come home."

Brittany heard the last words as if they were coming to her through a long tunnel. She lifted a hand to her throat, her fingers were shaking.

"You're not serious," she finally managed to get out.

"Certainly I'm serious," her mother said, as if what she'd proposed wasn't the most horrible thing Brittany had ever heard in her life.

"This is my child you're talking about. Your grandchild."

"This child is an embarrassment to the family," her father said. "What would the neighbors say?"

"'What would the neighbors say?'" Brittany repeated incredulously. "You're actually worried about what the neighbors might think?"

"Naturally. We have to live among these people."

"And what they think is more important to you than your grandchild. You're more concerned with their opinions than the fact that the man I was in love with is dead."

"Don't be melodramatic, Brittany." That was her mother, her tone soothing. "Naturally, we're very sorry that he's dead."

"But only because he can't make an honest woman of me now. Right?" Brittany shot to her feet. She felt as if she were seeing her parents for the first time. Their narrow little world was no longer just an odd quirk—it was a smothering reality. It had choked the life out of them a long time ago, and now it was threatening to reach out and swallow her. "The truth is that you don't care about anything quite as much as you care about what other people might think.

"Well, I'll solve your problem for you. I'll go away. But I'm not going to hide my shame two thousand miles away. I'm not ashamed of what I did, and I'm not ashamed of my child. We'll manage just fine without you."

She turned and stalked from the room, ignoring her mother's startled look and her father's command that she come back. Taking the stairs two at a time, she sought the thin sanctuary of the room she'd had since childhood, slamming the door shut. She leaned back against the door, her heart pounding as if she'd run a marathon.

How could they talk like that? Look at her like that? This was a child she was carrying, not an embarrassment to be quickly swept under the carpet. Didn't they have any feeling for the baby? For her?

She wrapped her arms around her middle, suddenly feeling very cold. All her life she'd been the intruder in their lives, the interruption they hadn't planned or truly welcomed. And she'd accepted that. They loved her in their own way, perhaps not as she'd have wished but as much as they were capable of. She'd never doubted that.

Now, she was seeing how foolish she'd been. They didn't love her. They couldn't. If they loved her, they could never have sat there talking to her like that, suggesting that she give her baby away as if it were an unwanted bundle.

She didn't have to stay here. She *wouldn't* stay. She would go somewhere else, build a life for herself and her son or daughter. Determination carried her as far as dragging her suitcase from the closet. As she placed it on the bed, the reality of her predicament began to set in.

Just where was she supposed to go?

She sat down next to the open suitcase, staring at it blankly. She had some money but only a few hundred dollars. The new school year seemed so far away. The friend she roomed with then was in Boston with her relatives, and they'd sublet their tiny apartment for the summer. Even if Janie was around, she couldn't support the two of them.

There was a baby on the way. Having babies was not cheap. She'd counted on the fact that her father's insurance might cover the hospital costs. And after the baby was born, what was she going to live on then?

Tears burned her eyes, but she blinked them back. She'd cried enough today, cried enough to last a lifetime. Tears weren't going to solve any of her problems. She couldn't stay here. That much was clear. It was also clear that there'd be no going back to college in the fall.

She got up and moved to the dresser, grabbing a handful of lingerie at random. Dropping it into the suitcase, she moved to the closet, lifting out a stack of hangers. In a few months, none of her clothes would fit her. Where was the money going to come from for new ones?

A soft tapping at the door interrupted the panicked circle of her thoughts. She stiffened, staring at the door warily.

"Yes?"

"Brittany, I'd like to talk to you." Her mother's voice was muffled. Brittany hesitated. The pain she'd felt downstairs was still fresh. If her mother was going to try to talk her into giving up her baby, she didn't want to hear it. On the other hand, maybe they'd realized what a mistake they were making.

"Come in."

She didn't look at her mother as the door opened and then shut. Carrying the stack of clothes to the bed, she began stripping them from the hangers, folding them as neatly as her shaking hands would allow, conscientiously arranging them in the suitcase.

"You're leaving."

"You don't expect me to stay here, do you?"

"Where are you going?"

"I don't know. A motel for a day or two until I can figure out what to do. Do you care as long as the neighbors don't find out I'm pregnant?" Her eyes met her mother's challengingly, and Ann's dropped first.

"Naturally, I care. You *are* my daughter."

"What would people think if you didn't care?" Brittany said with a sudden flash of insight. Harsh spots of color appeared in her mother's thin cheeks, and she didn't lift her eyes. Brittany hadn't thought she could be hurt any more, but she felt a sharp stab of pain at the guilt she read in her mother's silence.

"Oh, Mom. Is that why you came up here? Because you're worried about what your friends will think if you don't try to talk me out of this?"

"Of course not." But the denial came a little too late to be completely believable. She lifted her head, reading the accusation in Brittany's eyes, her flush deepening. "You act as if what people think of you isn't important. That's easy to believe at your age. When you get a little older, you realize that people's opinions can reflect on every aspect of your life—the kind of job you can get, where you live, who your friends are. If people don't think well of you, respect you, then life isn't very pleasant."

Brittany looked at her mother and felt a deep pity. All these years she'd thought that maybe there was something wrong with her that her parents couldn't love her the way other people loved their children. But it hadn't been her at all.

"I didn't say that it isn't important to consider other people's opinions," she said gently. "But you can't live your life by them. There are things that have to come before that, things like love and family."

For a moment she thought she saw a flicker of uncertainty in her mother's eyes, as if maybe she was getting through. Mother and daughter faced each other across a chasm so wide neither could quite see how to cross it. There was a moment, a moment only, when they almost reached out, but then Ann looked away, and Brittany knew then that nothing had changed. Maybe it was too late for her mother to change.

"Naturally, you're entitled to your opinion. Your father and I have tried to be good parents. We cannot do more than that."

"No, I guess you can't." Brittany went to the closet and reached for another handful of hangers, tears blurring her vision. She carried the clothes back to the bed and began pulling them off the hangers, folding them roughly and stuffing them into the suitcase. Her mother watched silently, obviously feeling that she should say something or do something and obviously at a total loss as to what.

"We only want what's best for you, Brittany," she tried at last. "You think we're being very harsh, but a child is an enormous responsibility."

"Well, you don't have to worry about that. It will be my responsibility, not yours." Brittany swept a handful of bottles off the dresser, dumping them in on top of her clothes with a rattle of glass.

"If you're determined to do this, there's nothing we can do to stop you."

"I'm determined."

The flat answer seemed to leave her mother momentarily without words. "At least wait until morning. Sleep on this decision."

"I don't need to sleep on it." She pushed the top of the suitcase closed and flipped the latches.

"Wait until morning, anyway. It's getting dark. There's no sense in you trying to find a place to stay tonight."

Brittany's first instinct was to refuse to spend another minute under this roof, but she hesitated. The events of the day had been more than a little draining. She was running on adrenaline now, but she knew that when it faded, exhaustion was going to hit her. She got tired so much quicker these days. Besides, if she stayed here tonight, she could save the money a motel would cost her. Pride had its place, but she had more than herself to consider now.

She nodded slowly. "All right. I'll wait till morning." She dragged the suitcase off the bed, setting it on the floor with a thump before turning to look at her mother. "I'm not changing my mind about this. But you're right, it would be foolish to leave now. I'll stay tonight."

"Good." Ann nodded briskly, turning to leave. She stopped, her hand on the doorknob, her back to her daughter. "It's not that I don't care, you know." Her voice was so low, Brittany had to strain to hear it.

"I know." That seemed to be all her mother needed. She left the room, closing the door behind her, leaving Brittany to stare at the blank panel of wood.

She felt numb. The day had been full of too much emotion, too much stress. She was physically and mentally exhausted. She wanted to crawl into bed and pull the covers over her head. She wanted to cry and scream and demand that somebody make things right again. But there was nobody who could. Most of all, she wanted somebody to lean on, just for a little while. But there was nobody for that, either.

Except Michael Sinclair.

The thought popped into her head unbidden. Michael had been there for her this afternoon. For a few wonderful moments, she hadn't been so completely alone. He'd been Dan's best friend. She could call him. He'd come get her, find her a place to stay. She knew he'd help her.

But what right did she have to drag him into this? True, he'd said to call him if she needed anything, but that was one of those polite gestures people made, never expecting you to take them up on it. Remembering those dark blue eyes, she found it hard to believe that Michael Sinclair ever said anything he didn't mean.

Still, even if he *had* meant it, he'd been thinking in terms of something small. She couldn't call him up and tell him she needed money, a place to stay and a job, and gee, could he do anything about it?

Pride forbade it.

She couldn't afford pride right now. Or was it that pride was all she could afford?

She rubbed at the ache in her temples. She was so tired. Kicking off her shoes, she turned back the covers, crawling under them fully dressed. She'd just lie down for a few minutes. When she woke up, things would be more clear.

The pillow had never felt softer as her head sank into it. She couldn't remember ever being so achingly tired. The memorial service, the scene with her parents, the aching loss that nagged at her heart, all blurred into a gray fog as her eyes drifted shut. Just a little rest and she'd feel much better.

She fell asleep with her thoughts still a tangled mess. She dreamed—vague, amorphous dreams in which the only thing that was clear was the presence of a tall man with tobacco-brown hair and eyes the color of a summer sky. In the dreams, he held her close, protecting her from the shadows that tugged at her. And she felt safe.

Chapter 3

Michael slowed the Mustang to a near crawl as he turned the corner onto the quiet street. He still wasn't sure about the wisdom of coming here. He should have just called. He could have found out how Brittany was doing over the phone.

But he wanted to see her. If he was honest with himself, he'd been wanting to see her since about thirty seconds after he'd walked out the door after the memorial service. He'd been fighting the urge for weeks, and he'd finally lost the battle.

He pulled up to the curb in front of the house and got out. It was early October now; the trees, though still green, were beginning to look worn and pale. It wouldn't be long before they'd start turning, then the leaves would fall, a soft prelude to winter's snow.

The neighborhood was as overly structured as it had been the first time he saw it. He hunched his shoulders beneath the soft flannel shirt, feeling constricted. Everything was so tidy, so square. Each house aligned precisely with the ones beside it. Each path leading directly from the street to the front door.

Shoving his hands into the pockets of his jeans, he stared at the house in front of him. He should have called or come to see her ages ago. There hadn't been a day when he hadn't thought about her, wondered how she was doing.

The very intensity of his desire had kept him away. Brittany had been Dan's girl. When it came right down to it, he didn't even know her all that well. Maybe his desire to see her was some tangled way of trying to hold on to Dan. And maybe it wasn't.

He muttered a curse under his breath as he started up the walkway. He didn't normally spend this much time analyzing his reasons for doing something. And he was an idiot to do it this time. He was concerned about Brittany because his best friend had been in love with her, was the father of the child she carried. There was nothing wrong with wanting to make sure she was all right. He was doing this for Dan, that's all.

His boot heels echoed on the wooden porch, announcing his presence even before he rang the doorbell. He could hear the bell ringing inside the house, a dignified two-tone sound as dull and uninspired as the neighborhood.

"So what did you expect, 'Yankee Doodle Dandy'?" he muttered under his breath.

The woman who opened the door bore enough resemblance to Brittany to make their relationship apparent. Her hair was streaked with gray, but the color underneath was the same deep black as her daughter's. Her eyes were gray, also like Brittany's, but it was a dull color, not the warm shade that made Brittany's so striking.

"Mrs. Winslow?"

She eyed him through the screen without warmth.

"Yes."

"I'm Michael Sinclair. I'm a friend of Brittany's." That got a flicker of reaction, but it wasn't welcome.

"Yes." There was nothing added to the single syllable. Michael drew a deep breath, wondering if there was something wrong with the woman.

"Is Brittany here?" He tried a smile, but it didn't seem to help.

"No, she's not."

Something more than one syllable. They were making progress.

"Do you expect her soon? I'd like to talk to her."

The pause stretched until he began to think she wasn't going to answer.

"She doesn't live here anymore."

"She's moved out?" He felt a twinge of uneasiness. It seemed an odd time for her to be moving out, unless... "Did she go back to school?"

"I couldn't say." The flat statement was not encouraging, but he tried anyway.

"I don't mean to be rude, but I really would like to see her. I'm not an insurance salesman or anything. I was a friend of Dan's."

This time there was no mistaking the chill in her eyes. "If you wish to see her, you'll have to look for her. I'm afraid I can't help you. Good day."

The door shut quietly but firmly, leaving him staring at it. He waited, half expecting it to open again, unable to believe that the conversation had been concluded so abruptly. But the door didn't open. After a moment, he turned and walked off the porch, going over the conversation in his mind, trying to find a reason for the hostility she'd clearly felt.

There'd been caution when she opened the door, which was understandable. Even in Remembrance, people were a little hesitant to open their door to a stranger these days.

When he'd said he wanted to see Brittany, the caution had taken on an uneasy edge. It was Dan's name that had seemed to bring out the hostility.

Michael frowned as he slid into the Mustang. He supposed he could understand why Brittany's parents would feel some anger toward Dan. He'd left her alone and pregnant. Even though it was hardly his fault that he hadn't come back, maybe her parents couldn't be expected to see the more logical side of the situation.

He started the engine and pulled away from the curb. But her mother had acted as if she didn't even know where Brittany was. At a time like this, wouldn't she have wanted to stay near her family? Surely she'd need their support, in more ways than one.

If she wasn't with her family, where was she? She could have gone back to school. Maybe her mother was the secretive type and hadn't wanted to tell him where Brittany was.

He braked at the light on Main, his eyes unfocused as he waited for the light to change. There was an uneasy feeling in the pit of his stomach, a feeling that something wasn't right. If Brittany was in trouble, wouldn't she have called him? But why should she? He hadn't called her all these months; she probably thought he wouldn't want to hear from her.

The driver behind him tapped his horn impatiently. Michael blinked, realizing that the light was green and had been for some seconds. He turned right and then coasted the car to a stop next to the curb, oblivious to the fact that he was in a red zone. He wasn't parking, anyway; he was thinking. He left the engine idling, his fingers tapping on the wheel.

Ten to one, Brittany was fine. She'd probably think it was pretty peculiar if he went to a lot of trouble to find her. But what if she wasn't fine, as his instincts were screaming? He had to know. If he had to justify it, then he owed it to Dan to make sure she was all right.

So how was he going to find out if his instincts were right? Her parents were a dead end. They either genuinely didn't know, which he found appalling, or they weren't going to tell him.

If Brittany had gone back to school, she'd probably gone back to the little apartment she'd shared with that other student. What was her name? He'd only met her once, a pretty girl with red hair. Jenny? Gerry? Janie. That was it. Janie. She was probably safe and sound with Janie.

He glanced at the wide gold watch on his wrist, a frown hooking his dark brows together. He was supposed to be on the Adams site in less than an hour. His parents had come back from their cruise weeks ago and Donovan was back in the office, but the Adams project was his design and his responsibility.

When he got back to the office this afternoon, he could see if there was a phone listed under Brittany's name in Indianapolis. And if there wasn't? The phone could be in her roommate's name, though he hadn't the slightest idea what Janie's last name was. He knew where they lived. He'd gone with Dan once to pick Brittany up, and he knew he could find the apartment again.

Was he actually thinking of driving into the city just because he felt a little uneasy? Brittany would think he was crazy if he showed up on her doorstep out of the blue. He'd call her this afternoon. If he couldn't find her number, *then* he'd think about the next step.

He flipped on his turn signal, watching for a break in traffic before pulling out. Maybe Dan's death had left him a little paranoid. There was no reason why Brittany should have kept in touch with him, no reason why he should feel this knot in his stomach.

Approaching the highway, he moved into the right lane. He'd go out to the Adams site, talk with the foreman, meet with the inspector and do all the things an architect was supposed to do. When he got back to the office, he'd get Brittany's number and give her a call, then he could see how foolish he'd been to worry. That was the only sane, logical thing to do.

Horns blared behind him as he abruptly switched lanes, gunning the engine to cut through a gap in traffic and turn left onto the highway. He could call the site from the city and reschedule. First, he had to know that Brittany was all right. He lowered his foot on the accelerator.

Finding the apartment wasn't hard. It wasn't a large building or particularly elegant, but it was well kept and close to the university. It was the latter attribute that guaranteed the owners a full roster of tenants.

He parked down the street from the building. Now that he was here, he felt like an idiot. He'd canceled a business appointment and made a two-hour drive without a shred of evidence that there was anything to worry about. He wasn't even sure what he was going to say to Brittany once he saw her. *Just happened to be in the neighborhood and thought I'd drop by?*

Not too likely. He could hardly tell her that he'd driven all this way just because he had a feeling that something was wrong. She'd think he was crazy. Which was exactly how he felt. He hunched his shoulders, glaring at the modest building as he approached. For two cents he'd turn around and go home. Except that he knew he wouldn't feel easy until he'd seen her, assured himself she was all right. It was the least he owed Dan, he told himself.

The apartment was upstairs, and he found himself measuring the stairs as he climbed, trying to judge how difficult they'd be for a pregnant woman to manage. He was not happy with the results. The steep stairs would be a hazard.

He frowned as he stepped out onto the landing and started down the hallway. The image of Brittany heavy with child brought mixed emotions that he still hadn't been able to sort out. Concern, he understood. The anger that tugged at him when he thought about the child she carried was something else again.

He stopped in front of the door, staring at the blank panel for a long moment before ringing the bell. He was just going to say hello, assure himself that she was doing fine, then he'd leave.

He waited and when no one came to the door, he rang the bell again. There was still no response. He leaned heavily on the bell, though it was obvious that nobody was home. In all his mental arguments, he hadn't thought of the simple possibility that nobody would be here.

Now, faced with the unresponsive door, he was nonplussed. Should he leave a note or wait in the car until someone came home? Since the whole purpose of this visit was to assuage his overactive imagination, leaving a note was not going to do much good. On the other hand, sitting in the car like a lovesick teenager didn't hold much appeal, either.

He gave the bell one last irritated jab. This had started out earlier as a simple visit. He should have been on the Adams site hours ago instead of standing here in this drafty hallway feeling like an idiot. Disgusted, he turned from the door.

He was halfway to the stairs when he noticed the girl coming toward him. Even in the dimly lighted hall, that red hair was unmistakable.

"Janie?"

He spoke too loudly, his voice echoing in the hallway, and she jumped, dropping two books from the stack she carried. She looked at him warily, glancing over her shoulders as if judging the distance to the stairs.

"Sorry. I didn't mean to scare you," he apologized as he bent to scoop up the books. "Michael Sinclair. We met about six months ago. I'm . . . I was a friend of Dan Remington's."

The tension left her shoulders and she smiled, reaching out to take the books he was holding. "Sure. Sorry I didn't recognize you at first. The light in here is lousy. We keep nagging the manager, and she keeps saying she'll change it, but she never does." She was moving down the hall as she talked, digging in her purse for her keys. "Come on in."

Michael followed her into the apartment, pushing the door shut behind him. Janie dropped the stack of books on a table, then she kicked off her shoes before turning to look at him.

"I was really sorry to hear about Dan. I didn't know him all that well, but Brittany was crazy about him. Seems incredible, doesn't it?"

"Yes, it does." He wasn't here to discuss Dan. That wound was still too raw to bear any probing.

"I guess it just goes to prove that you can't count on anything. Can I get you something to drink? I've got some soda, milk if you're the healthy type, or there may be some cheap wine left over from the weekend, but you drink at your own risk."

"No, thanks." Michael reined in his impatience, but perhaps he didn't do a very good job. Janie glanced at him and grinned, her rather ordinary features lighting with amusement.

"I guess you didn't come all this way for idle chitchat."

"Sorry. I didn't mean to be rude."

"Not rude, exactly. But you look like you might start pacing at any moment. To save wear and tear on the carpet, why don't we cut to the chase?" She leaned back against the breakfast counter, which separated the kitchen from the living room. "What can I do for you?"

"I'm looking for Brittany."

"I thought you might be. She isn't here."

"You mean she isn't home?"

"No, I mean she doesn't live here anymore." She hitched herself onto a tall stool, settling her feet on the top rung.

"When did she move out?"

"Right before classes started."

"Where is she? Is she all right?" The questions came out with a sharp edge. All the uneasiness he'd felt earlier returned a hundredfold.

Janie gave him a long look as if weighing how much to say. "She's all right. At least she was a couple of weeks ago, which was the last time I saw her."

"Why did she move out? Is she still going to school? Where is she living?" He fired the questions at her, leaning forward as if prepared to shake the answers loose.

"Slow down." She leaned her elbows on the counter behind her, cocking her head to one side. "I guess you really are concerned about her. She moved out because her parents refused to continue to pay her tuition. No, she's not going to school."

"Where is she?"

Janie told him and Michael's uneasiness blossomed into full-fledged panic. The area she'd named was not a part of town where anyone lived by choice, especially not a woman alone.

Janie shrugged. "I told her she could stay here. My parents would have coughed up enough to cover the full rent. But she refused. She found this dinky little room, insisting it would be just perfect for her and the baby. You do know about the baby, don't you?"

"I know." He thrust his fingers through his hair. "Why didn't she call me? She can't stay there. It's not safe."

"That's what I told her, but she can be pretty stubborn."

"Stubborn? This isn't stubborn. This is insane. I need the address." There was an edge of anger in his voice that boded ill for Brittany when he found her.

Janie grinned as she turned and lifted a basket off the counter, shuffling through the stacks of paper that filled it to overflowing. "I tried to talk her out of it. Here it is."

Michael snatched the paper from her fingers, unconcerned with manners. "Thanks."

"I was going to copy it down for you," she commented mildly as he stuffed the paper into his shirt pocket. "That way I could keep it in my address file." She lifted the basket.

"You're not going to need it, because she's not going to be staying there."

"Well, I wish you better luck than I had in talking her out of it."

"I'll carry her out bodily if I have to," he promised. "Thanks for the help."

"You're welcome." But she was talking to the door as it shut behind him. She stared after him for a moment, a slow grin widening her mouth. She had the feeling that things were looking up for Brittany.

Michael found the address without trouble. If he'd considered it, he might have thought it a miracle that he could even read street signs through the fog of anger that all but blinded him.

What the hell was she thinking of? He parked the Mustang next to the curb, wedging it between two cars whose bodies were so rust pocked it was a miracle they didn't simply dissolve into piles of dust. Half a dozen children ranging from six to thirteen or so stopped their desultory game of kickball to stare at the shiny black car.

Michael noticed their interest and paused. At this point, he couldn't have cared if they stripped the car to the frame. On the other hand, it would delay his plans to get Brittany out of here immediately. He waved the oldest child over, a lanky boy with a shock of white-blond hair and a face much too old for his years.

"How would you like to earn fifty bucks?" The boy's eyes lighted with interest, but life had already taught him caution.

"Doin' what?"

"Keep an eye on my car for me. I'm going to be in there for a while. And if my car is still here and untouched when I come out, there's fifty bucks in it for you."

The boy's eyes flickered over the car. "I could get more than that for the hubcaps."

"Yeah, but then you'd have me to deal with." Their eyes met, each measuring the other. Finally, the boy nodded slowly.

"Okay. But how do I know you've even got fifty on you or that you'll give it to me when you come out?"

"So young, yet so suspicious," Michael chided, reaching for his wallet.

"Just practical, mister."

Michael pulled a fifty-dollar bill out of his wallet, tearing it neatly in two. He handed the boy one half and tucked the other back into his wallet. The boy looked at the half bill, then grinned.

"That's a pretty neat trick, mister. This won't do me no good if your car is gone. I'll take care of it for you."

"Thanks." Michael turned away, the momentary distraction forgotten as he walked up the cracked steps and pushed open the door of the apartment building. The entryway smelled of urine and despair. The carpeting was worn to the bare floor in places, creating traps for unwary feet. A row of brass-colored mail boxes lined one wall, the doors on several standing drunkenly open.

A steep flight of stairs rose along the left wall, and Michael picked his way over to them. An old man slept on the bottom stairs, hardly more than a bundle of rags and bones.

Michael's anger mounted with every step he took. The thought of Brittany living in a place like this was intolerable. Why hadn't she called him? She must have known he'd do anything to help her, anything at all.

How could she have known, you jerk? You didn't get in touch with her. He stepped around a carton whose contents had seeped onto the second-floor landing. Well, he was here now, and he wasn't leaving until he took Brittany with him. She wasn't spending another night in this place, not even if he had to drag her bodily from it.

Four doors faced onto the landing, each more battered than the last. He was unsurprised to find that Brittany's door was the most battle scarred, though it looked as if someone had made an effort to wash the worst of the grime from the peeling surface.

He drew a deep breath, controlling the urge to simply kick the door in and snatch her away. He'd stay calm and rational. And if that didn't work, there was always kidnapping.

He rapped on the door, the sound echoing off the low ceiling. He heard the door behind him open, but he didn't turn. Her neighbors were welcome to their curiosity. He was about to knock again when he heard a stir of sound from inside and then Brittany's voice, hesitant and holding a note of fear.

"Who is it?"

Relief surged through him, stealing his voice for an instant. Until he heard her voice, he hadn't realized just how much he'd feared that something might have happened to her. He cleared his throat.

"It's Michael." There was a long silence.

"Michael?" Her voice came from just the other side of the door. "Michael Sinclair?"

"No, Michael the ax murderer," he said drily. "Open the door, Brittany."

"I. . . Just a second." He heard her fumbling with the locks, and then the door opened slowly. She stood there, looking at him, her eyes uncertain, as if she could hardly believe that he was there.

Michael couldn't have believed that she could be even more beautiful than he remembered, but she was. She was paler, a little thinner. Dark circles created smudgy patterns under her eyes. But she was still hauntingly beautiful. His eyes skimmed over her, seeking reassurance that she'd come to no harm.

"Michael." She reached up, shoving the thick fall of her hair back self-consciously. "I wasn't expecting anybody. The place is a mess. *I'm* a mess."

"You look fine." He arched his brow questioningly when she continued to stand in the doorway. "Can I come in?"

"Oh. Sure. I'm sorry. I don't know where my manners are today." As she stepped back, he wondered if it was his imagination that she seemed reluctant to let him in. "Like I said, the place is a mess. Careful of that spot in the rug. It's inclined to trip people up."

Michael stepped over the torn place in the rug and into the living room. The apartment hadn't been an inspired creation when it was new. There were no interesting details to soften the boxy lines. Any charm it might once have had had been ground away by age and neglect.

One pane of window glass was broken and had been replaced with a sheet of plywood that looked as if it had been there for decades. The paint might once have been cream colored. Now it was a sad gray, showing too many years of wear.

The furniture was only marginally better. There was a sofa that sagged in the middle. Brittany had thrown colorful pillows over it, but nothing could disguise its age. Matchbooks propped up one leg of the scarred coffee table. An easy chair that looked as if it might or might not bear weight sat beside a lamp with a shade that had been wired into place.

Nothing Michael saw did anything to assuage the anger he felt at finding her here. He wanted to shake her. He wanted to snatch her up and carry her out of this place.

"Would you like something to drink?" She moved around him, fussing with the pillows on the sofa, picking up a blouse that had been draped over the back of it. "I guess you can tell I wasn't expecting anyone. The place never looks great, but it doesn't usually look this bad. I was going to clean house today. Not that there's a whole lot to clean." Still talking, she tossed the blouse through a door he assumed led to the bedroom.

"When in doubt, throw it in the bedroom. It's a good thing you can't see how bad it looks in there. I'm afraid my housekeeping skills only extend to the public areas. The bedroom always looks like a bomb just exploded in it. You never did say if you wanted something to drink. I don't know exactly what I have. Milk. I've been drinking so much milk I expect to start mooing any time now. There might be some soda. Janie brought some over last time she was here. Janie can't survive without soda. And I think I have some instant coffee. Of course, not everyone likes instant."

"No, thank you." His words stopped her as she reached the kitchen door.

" 'No, thank you'?"

"I don't want anything to drink."

"Oh."

His refusal seemed to leave her uncertain. She hovered in the doorway to the kitchen, looking as if she didn't know what to do. The silence stretched. Outside, children shouted in play. Someone started a car, the engine knocking and banging in protest. The smell of cooking onions drifted from somewhere nearby.

It was Michael who finally broke the silence.

"Why didn't you call me?"

Why hadn't she called him? Such a simple question. If only the answer was as simple. Brittany pleated the tail of her shirt, left out to conceal the fact that she could no longer button her jeans. Her fingers were trembling. She'd thought of calling him. There hadn't been a day that went by that she hadn't thought about it.

Now, seeing him here in this shabby room, she knew why she hadn't called. Pride. She'd wanted—needed—to do this on her own. Now that he was here, she knew she'd never been so glad to see anyone in her life. She sifted her hand through her hair, aware of the exhaustion that was never far away these days.

"I don't know," she answered him at last. "It's not really your problem, is it?"

"Not my problem," he repeated. "Did you think I wouldn't care?"

"No, of course not. I knew you'd care."

"But you didn't call."

"There was really no need. I'm managing all right." He flicked a contemptuous look around the shabby apartment, and she flushed. "Okay, so this is hardly a Sinclair and Associates design, but it's not that bad."

"It's a pit," he said bluntly.

"How did you find me?" She couldn't argue with his opinion, so she changed the subject.

"I went to see your parents." Her eyes flashed to his, and though he wouldn't have thought it possible, she seemed to pale a bit more. She looked away, staring at the faded carpeting.

"What did they say?" She poked at a threadbare patch with her toe.

"Not much. I spoke with your mother...asked to see you. She didn't seem to know where you were."

"I sent them my address. I bet they burned it for fear the neighbors would find out where I was living."

There was a wealth of bitterness in her words, and the picture Michael had been trying to piece together became a little more clear.

"I gather they didn't take the news about the baby very well."

She laughed but there was no humor in the sound. "They wanted me to go off somewhere to have it and then give it away. They were afraid that the *neighbors* might find out about it."

"Why would the neighbors care?"

She laughed again, ending on a half sob. "That's the funny thing. They wouldn't. But my parents are convinced that my having an illegitimate child—a bastard—could ruin them. Dammit" She scrubbed angrily at the tears that spilled down her cheeks.

She looked so small, so forlorn and so proud. Michael wanted to take her in his arms and hold her, promise her that nothing was going to hurt her again.

Instead, he shoved his hands into his pockets, looking at the wall behind her, giving her a chance to compose herself.

"I'm sorry." She sniffed, wiping the moisture from her eyes. "It's not worth crying over."

"You should have called me."

"It wasn't your problem."

"I thought we were friends. And if that isn't enough, Dan was my best friend. That makes it my problem."

"Well, thank you." Her sarcastic tone made it clear that gratitude was not what she felt. Anger dried the last of her tears. "I'm so flattered to know that you consider me one of your problems."

"That's not the way I meant it."

"Just how did you mean it?" She tucked her hands into her pockets, her elbows hugging her sides. Just having him here created a roiling sensation in the pit of her stomach. She'd felt so many emotions since she'd heard his voice on the other side of the door—relief, joy, shame, anger. They were all tangled up inside. She wanted him to go away. She wanted him to stay. She wanted him to see that she could take care of herself. And she wanted him to put his arms around her and promise to take care of her.

"Look, I didn't mean to start a quarrel," Michael said. He thrust his fingers through his hair, his expression rueful. "I just don't understand why you'd choose to live like this—" his gesture encompassed the worn room "—when you must have known I'd gladly help you."

Her chin inched up a notch. "I've managed all right."

"Sure. You're doing just great. You're living in a building that should have been condemned ten years ago in a neighborhood Rocky would be afraid to walk through without an Uzi for protection. God knows what you're doing for money."

"My parents gave me the money they would normally have given me for my first quarter at school, and I've got a job."

"Doing what?"

"I'm a waitress at a perfectly respectable restaurant."

"What restaurant? That fleabag hangout down the street?" She didn't have to answer him. He could read it in her eyes. "Are you crazy? That place is probably frequented by every pimp and drug dealer within a fifteen-block radius. I bet you get more propositions than tips. And I suppose you walk there and back. Do you know what could happen to you on the street?"

"Nothing has happened to me." She knew it was a thin defense. The problem was that everything he was saying was true. It wasn't as though she hadn't had the same thoughts a hundred times herself. But it hadn't seemed as if she had a choice.

"You look like you haven't had a decent meal in weeks." Critical blue eyes raked her from head to foot. Brittany tugged defensively at her clothes.

"I've eaten."

"When? When did you eat last?"

"I...this morning," she finally got out. The truth was that she hadn't felt like eating for the past couple of days. Even as careful as she'd been, money was stretched thin. Worry and lack of sleep had drained her appetite.

"You're lying."

The flat statement stole her breath. She stared at him, searching for the words to protest, to argue, to say anything at all. He looked so angry. Why was he so angry with her? He was looking at her as if he hated her.

She blinked furiously against the tears that burned in her eyes. She wouldn't cry again. She would not cry. Pressing the back of her hand to her mouth, she struggled for control. She'd shed too many tears these past few weeks. But she lost the battle as the first salty drop found its way down her cheek. Furious with him, with herself, she turned away, holding her breath in an effort to grab hold of her dissolving control.

"I'm sorry." She hadn't heard him move, but suddenly he was right behind her, his hands on her shoulders. "I'm acting like a bastard. Don't cry, Brittany. I'm sorry."

If his anger had started her tears, it was his gentleness that caused them to overflow. Her breath left her on a sob as she bent to press her face into her hands.

"Damn." It was impossible to guess whether the mild curse was directed at her or at himself. She was beyond caring. When he turned her toward him, she didn't resist. It had been so long since she'd been able to lean on someone. She'd felt so abandoned and so scared.

She pressed her cheek against the soft flannel of his shirt. His arms were strong around her, just as she'd known they would be. For a little while, she could feel safe again.

Holding her, Michael fought to remember why he was here and just what the situation was. This was Brittany, his best friend's girl. She carried Dan's progeny. He was only holding her, comforting her because of Dan. He couldn't help Dan anymore, but he could make sure that the girl he'd loved, his child, were safe.

"Don't cry anymore. It's not good for you."

Brittany took a deep breath, choking off the next sob. It felt so good to lean on him, but she didn't have the right to do that. She drew a shuddering breath, pushing herself away, wiping at her eyes.

"I'm sorry." Half sobs broke the words. "I'm not usually such a crybaby. Hormones, I guess."

"I'm the one who should apologize." He handed her a handkerchief, watching as she dried her eyes and then blew her nose, a prosaic little gesture that seemed oddly touching. "I was a total bastard, and I'm sorry."

"Well, you weren't very nice," she agreed, staring at the handkerchief for a moment before stuffing it into her pocket.

"I had no business jumping all over you like that, but when I saw you living like this—" A quick gesture finished the sentence. Brittany looked around the room, seeing it through his eyes. She'd grown so accustomed to it that she'd almost forgotten how seedy it really was.

"It's the best I could manage." But the defensiveness had left her voice. She'd been trying to convince herself that she was managing okay, but he'd forced her to see that pride could only carry you so far. Still, she couldn't admit failure without a struggle.

"Do you have a better suggestion?" she asked, meeting his eyes challengingly.

"Yes, I do."

"Well, what is it?" she prodded when he didn't continue.

"You can marry me."

Chapter 4

"What?" She'd never read anything that said that pregnancy caused auditory hallucinations, but that must be the case. It wasn't possible that he'd just said what she thought she'd heard.

"I want you to marry me."

There. She'd heard it again. If she was hearing things, would she have heard the same thing twice?

"You're kidding, right?"

"I'm not kidding," he said coolly, looking as if what he was suggesting wasn't the most incredible thing she could imagine.

"You have to be kidding," she told him a little desperately. She groped behind her for the dubious support of the stuffed chair. This was not a conversation to be had while standing.

"Why?"

"'Why?'" The simple question sent her thoughts stumbling. *Why* There were a thousand reasons, and she couldn't think of any of them.

"Why do I have to be kidding, Brittany? It's the perfect solution." He sat on the edge of the sofa, leaning toward her.

"It's not perfect. It's insane."

"Why?"

"Would you stop asking that," she snapped. "It's perfectly obvious."

"Not to me. You need a place to stay. You need help with the baby. No matter how much pride you have, you've got to see that you can't stay here. Is this where you want to raise your child?"

"Of course not. This was only temporary."

"Until what? How are you going to get out of here?"

"I don't know," she admitted reluctantly. Hadn't she spent sleepless nights wondering just that?

"If you marry me, you'll have a place to stay. I've got a place outside Remembrance. It's not very big, but it's certainly better than this."

"Michael, you haven't thought this through. It doesn't make sense."

"Tell me what's wrong with the idea." His jaw set in a way that told her it wouldn't be easy to convince him of what should be obvious. And how did she go about convincing her foolish heart, which fairly leaped at the idea of having someone to share her burden? She tried to marshall her arguments, her fingers twisted together in her lap.

"I can't say that I'm not tempted," she began carefully. "I mean, it's pretty obvious that I'm not managing all that well on my own. I guess people with part of a degree in English aren't all that in demand."

She stopped but Michael said nothing. He only waited, as if confident that things were going to go precisely as he thought they should. Brittany felt a spurt of irritation at his confidence, but she was too tired for it to last long. She sighed.

"There's nothing in this for you, Michael. Maybe I've got an excess of pride, but I'd have to have none at all to accept what you're offering."

"I appreciate you looking out for my interests, Brittany, but I'm capable of doing it myself. And you're wrong. I would get something out of this marriage."

"What?"

"Peace of mind. I'd know that you were cared for. I wouldn't have to worry about you turning up in some worse dive than this."

"Why should you care so much?" she asked tiredly, leaning her head against the back of the chair. He hesitated, his eyes dropping to the tattered carpet.

"Dan was my closest friend, almost a brother to me. If the only thing I can do for him is take care of you, then I'd like to do it...if I can get some cooperation from you." He glanced at her, half smiling.

She didn't return the smile. She looked at him, her eyes searching. She wanted to say yes. She wanted to say yes to this whole insane proposal and know that she wasn't alone anymore.

"You can't base your whole life on doing what you think Dan would want."

"Not my whole life. Just until the baby is born and you've had a chance to get on your feet. What do they call it in all those romance novels? A marriage of convenience. It'll be temporary."

Brittany closed her eyes, shaking her head slowly against the temptation. How quickly all her determined independence faded when she was offered an alternative.

"No," she said at last, opening her eyes to look at him. "There's just not enough in this for you. If you want to help me, I'm not so stupid that I won't let you, but you don't have to marry me."

"But marriage is the most practical way to go."

"Practical?" She laughed, feeling a touch of hysteria. "You're telling me this is practical?"

"Have you thought about what it's going to cost to have the baby?"

"Yes." She'd thought of little else the past few weeks.

"If you're my wife, my insurance will cover you and the child. Even once we're separated, the child will still be covered."

She wavered. He made it sound so reasonable, so logical. In her heart, she knew it was crazy, impractical, but oh, how she wanted to agree.

"I don't know," she muttered.

Michael reached out to catch her restless hands in his. "This is something I want to do, Brittany. Stop worrying about me and think about the baby. He'd have everything he needed, the best of care. You can't give him that if you're worried sick all the time."

"It might be a girl, you know."

"Then marry me and let me take care of you and *her*. You're not even eating right, now."

"I'm eating okay," she said fretfully, staring at their linked hands.

"Shall I go inventory your kitchen?"

"No." She sighed, knowing what he'd find. A jar of peanut butter, a box of saltines and a half a carton of milk weren't likely to convince him that she was following a nutritionally complete diet.

"Look, I'm not trying to make you feel like you've failed. I just want you to see that you need some help. There's nothing wrong with that."

"I just don't see that you'd be getting much out of this." But she was weakening. She could hear it in her own voice, and she knew Michael could, too.

"Let me worry about that. Let me take care of you, Brittany." She felt tears start to her eyes. Did he know how much she wanted to say yes? She was so tired, so awfully tired.

His hands felt strong on hers. His palms were rough with calluses. Dan had told her once that Michael was just as likely to work at framing a wall as he was at designing the building it went in. They were good hands, the kind of hands you could put your future into.

"I don't know," she whispered.

"I do." His fingers tightened over hers. "Come on, Brittany. Say yes. This is my first marriage proposal. You don't want to blight my life by turning me down, do you?"

Her mouth trembled over a smile. He made it seem so reasonable. He could even joke about it. Would it really be so terrible of her to agree? As he said, it would only be for a few months. And she had to think of her child. Michael was right about the marriage offering some definite advantages to the child. Did she have a right to put her pride over the welfare of her baby?

"Are you sure about this? Really, really sure?"

"I'm really sure."

Her eyes searched his, looking for the doubts he had to be feeling. But there was nothing but confidence to be seen in those clear blue depths. It was a mad idea.

"It would only be for a few months," she said, more to herself than to him.

"Just until you get on your feet," he promised.

"I can't believe I'm considering this!" She pulled her hands from his, standing up, needing to put some distance between them. It was too hard to think when he was sitting so close, making it all seem so plausible.

"It's a little unconventional, maybe, but it doesn't have to be forever."

She heard him stand up, but she didn't turn to look at him. Staring out the window, she tried to sort her thoughts. Twilight had fallen while they talked. She hadn't even noticed the fading light. Lights shone in the windows of the apartment building across the alley.

Darkness should have been kind to the shabby neighborhood, but it wasn't. The lack of light only seemed to emphasize the dinginess, the hopelessness that walked the streets.

Behind her, Michael snapped on a lamp. Brittany's fingers clenched on the windowsill as the light spilled out behind her. Maybe it was symbolic. She had to decide between the darkness she faced or the light Michael was holding out to her.

If it was wrong, she didn't want to know it. She was just too damned tired. She closed her eyes, leaning her forehead on the cool glass.

If Dan had still been alive... If Dan had been alive, none of this would be necessary. Things would have been the way she'd dreamed of them being. But Dan was dead and so were the dreams they'd shared.

She had to get on with her life as best as she could. Michael was offering her a way out.

"Brittany? Is it really so hard to decide?" His question held a note of uncertain humor. She turned away from the window, startled to find that he was standing right behind her. The light was behind him, leaving her in shadow.

"No. No, it's not so hard," she said softly. Drawing in a deep breath, she lifted her eyes to his, searching for some doubt. There was nothing there but confidence, something she dearly wished she had more of at this point. "Are you truly sure?"

"I'm truly sure," he told her gently. He reached out, tucking a stray lock of hair behind her ear. It took all Brittany's willpower not to close her eyes and lean into that touch. "Brittany, this is as much for me as it is for you. I *want* to do this."

He was so close his scent filled her nostrils, warm and male. How could he be so sure? She wanted to believe him—needed to. She was too tired to fight anymore.

"Yes." The word was barely a whisper, and Michael leaned closer, bending his head over hers.

"What?"

"I said yes. I'll marry you."

A quick intake of breath was the only sign of reaction for the space of several slow heartbeats. Brittany stared at the base of his throat, left bare by his open shirt. Why didn't he say something?

He touched her hair with gentle fingers, and she looked up at him, half-afraid of what she'd see. Was he regretting it already? His face was in shadow, making it difficult to read his expression, but she didn't think it was regret she saw there.

"Thank you."

"I think it should be the other way around. I should be thanking you," she said tiredly, finally giving in to the urge to lean her face against his hand. There was such strength in him. And she needed that strength right now. "I feel as if I'm using you. If it wasn't for the baby..."

"If it wasn't for the baby, the situation would be completely different," he agreed. "But that isn't the case. There's nothing wrong with taking help from a friend."

She laughed, barely holding back the sob that threatened to escape. "I think this is going a little above and beyond the call of friendship, but I can't argue anymore."

"How long will it take you to pack your things? I want you out of here tonight."

"Tonight?" She stepped away from him, looking around the shabby apartment. It wasn't that she'd been happy here, but it *had* been more or less home for the past weeks. "Where would I stay?"

"I'll take you to my parents. You can stay with them until I can make arrangements for us to be married. You don't *want* to stay here, do you?"

"Of course not. It's just that everything is happening so quickly. You can't show up on your parents' doorstep with me in tow. I mean, wouldn't you like a chance to prepare them?"

"I'm not leaving you alone here another night. Besides, my parents love surprises."

"Donovan, have you seen my gray blouse?" Beth's voice was muffled by the closet doors as she searched for the item in question.

Donovan stepped out of the bathroom, toweling his hair dry, another towel wrapped low on his hips. "Have I seen what?"

"My gray blouse. I can't find it."

"The one with the fancy buttons?"

"That's it. I was going to wear it tonight."

"Why don't you just wear what you have on?" He leaned one shoulder against the wall, admiring the view as Beth backed out of the closet. He couldn't put a name to what she was wearing, but he could describe them in one word. Sexy.

"Sure. That's a great idea. Go to the opening of a new restaurant wearing a camisole and tap pants."

"Is that what you call those things?"

"These *things* are pure silk and cost enough to balance the national debt."

"I guess I'll have to build another house to pay for them," he said lazily, reaching for her.

"Stop it." She leaned away from him, her hands on his chest, half laughing as he nuzzled the sensitive skin of her neck. "Donovan Sinclair, I want to go out tonight."

"I could make staying home an interesting proposition," he promised, his hand splayed across her upper back to hold her still for his exploring mouth.

"I'm sure you could," she said breathlessly. "But we promised Carol we'd be there."

"She'll be so busy she won't even notice whether we're there or not."

"You know she'll notice." Beth made the mistake of turning to look at him, and Donovan pounced, his lips catching hers. Beth melted, her arms stealing around his neck. The bedroom was silent for several long seconds. Beth gathered all her resources and wrenched her mouth from his, shoving at his shoulders until she could get enough room to breathe.

"Behave yourself," she ordered him.

"I thought you liked it when I misbehaved," he murmured, a wicked green light in his eyes.

"I mean it, Donovan."

"So do I."

"This is important to Carol. After all, she sold the nursery to buy this place. She really wants to make a success of it."

"Didn't I personally help her renovate it?" he asked in a injured tone, finally giving in and releasing her.

"Yes, you did a wonderful job, but this is her big opening night, and I think she needs our support."

"I think she's nuts," he grumbled, retreating into the bathroom to dispose of both towels. "The last thing this town needs is another restaurant."

"Carol thinks this one will be unique enough to attract business."

"With a name like El Gato Loco, the only thing it's going to attract is linguistics majors."

"I don't think it's that difficult to translate," Beth defended. "And I think The Crazy Cat is a great name for a restaurant with authentic Mexican food."

"I think she's going to lose her shirt." Donovan walked back into the bedroom, sans towel, and Beth felt her knees weaken.

He was so magnificently male. After all these years, just looking at him made her heart beat a little faster. He walked to the bed, reaching for his shorts before turning to see her watching him. Catching the look in her eyes, he grinned.

"Too late. You had your chance and you spurned me. Carol is expecting us."

"Well, we could be late."

"Certainly not. Wouldn't dream of it." His grin widened at the faint pout she affected. "We'll make up for it later."

"Promise?"

"Most definitely." He stepped into the shorts, and Beth returned her attention to the closet, finding the missing gray blouse hiding behind a rust-colored jacket. Shrugging into it, she moved over to the mirror, checking her makeup.

"Did Michael say whether or not he was coming tonight?"

"I didn't talk to him about it." Donovan's voice held a repressive note.

In the mirror, Beth could see him frown as he tucked his shirt into his slacks. "Problems?" she asked as she turned away from the mirror and picked up her skirt, a swingy affair of bright blue.

"I don't know. He was supposed to meet with some people at the Adams site today. He called, canceling at the last minute."

"He must have had a good reason."

"He said something about personal business."

"Well, it must have been important. That house is his pet project. He wouldn't have canceled on it for nothing."

"Well, I'd still like to know the reason. Adams called me, demanding an explanation."

Beth tugged the zipper up on her skirt. "It's been rough for Michael since Dan was killed."

"I know."

"And it didn't make it any easier that I lost the baby right before that. We weren't even here for him."

Donovan drew her into his arms, pressing his cheek to the golden softness of her hair. "It was bad timing all around, but I want you to stop acting like it was all your fault. The doctor said there was nothing anybody could have done to stop the miscarriage."

"I know." Her voice was muffled, and he knew she was fighting back tears. In those first few weeks after the miscarriage, she'd never cried—not once. She'd held in all the grief and pain, growing pale and quiet, as if losing the baby had stolen a part of her soul. It wasn't until he'd taken her away, bullying her into going on the long cruise, that she'd finally begun to deal with the loss.

"But if I hadn't been such a dope about losing the baby, we would have been here when Michael got the news about Dan, instead of being out in the middle of the Pacific, where we couldn't do him any good."

"You weren't a dope. It was just one of those things. I don't know that we could have done much for him even if we had been here. It's been a long time since he came looking for us to get him through bad times."

"I still think it would have helped." She pushed back until she could meet his eyes. "He's been so quiet."

"Dan was his best friend. Michael will be okay. He just needs time."

"I guess." She sighed, her eyes still worried. "It's hard to remember that he's not a little boy anymore."

“He hasn’t been a little boy for a very long time, love.”

“I know.” She shook her head, forcing a smile. “I’m just being silly.”

“That’s how I like you best.” Donovan’s eyes held a tender light that never failed to make her feel loved and protected. “Come on. If you’re going to make me go to this shindig, let’s get it over with.”

He released her to walk across the room, and Beth felt a familiar twinge of regret at the limp that had forever replaced his old, powerful stride. It just didn’t seem fair, but then it could have been much worse. So much worse, she reminded herself. She bent to slip on her shoes, remembering that rainy night, Michael’s call from the hospital and later, much later, seeing the wreckage of that damned motorcycle and knowing how close she’d come to losing both husband and son.

“Beth? Are you coming?” Donovan turned at the door, arching one dark brow in question.

She crossed the room to him, linking her arm with his and leaning her head on his shoulder for an instant.

“I love you, Donovan Sinclair.”

“I love you, too.”

They were halfway down the stairs when they heard the sound of a key in the front door.

“Michael.” Beth hurried down the stairs to greet her son. Donovan followed at a more leisurely pace, noting that Michael was not alone.

“Mom.” Michael returned her hug, looking over her shoulder to meet his father’s eyes. He released Beth, turning to draw Brittany forward. She’d hung back, her reluctance to be noticed obvious.

“You remember Brittany Winslow, don’t you?”

“Of course.” Beth held out her hand, her smile friendly. “You came to our Fourth of July party, didn’t you?”

"Yes. I'm sorry to drop in on you like this, Mrs. Sinclair."

"Call me Beth, please."

"Thank you." Brittany's eyes dropped to the floor and stayed there. Donovan joined the group by the door, breaking the pause that threatened to stretch to awkward lengths.

"Hello, Michael. Brittany, nice to see you again."

"I'm sorry we've sort of popped in like this, but I'd like to talk to you, if you've got a few minutes."

"Of course." Beth hadn't been a mother all these years without learning to recognize the strain in her son's voice.

"It looks like you were going out," Michael said.

"Nothing that can't be postponed," Donovan said. "Why don't we go into the living room and sit down?"

Michael took Brittany's arm, feeling her tension as he led her into the living room. She'd argued all the way here that he couldn't just drop her *and* the news that they were getting married on his parents all at once. And he'd told her over and over again that there was nothing to worry about.

Now that he was here, he wasn't quite so sure. It *was* an awful lot to absorb. On the other hand, he didn't really have a choice. If he and Brittany were to be married as soon as possible, then he could hardly delay letting his family know about it.

Brittany sat on the edge of a chair, her feet precisely together, her hands clasped in her lap. She looked as though she were on the way to her own execution. Michael chose to sit on the arm of her chair, half-afraid that if he didn't stay close, she might bolt for the door.

Beth settled onto the sofa, and Donovan chose a stance near the fireplace, leaning one arm on the mantel. Once they were all comfortable, no one said anything for the space of several seconds. Donovan's eyes seemed watchful, Beth's curious.

"What did you want to talk to us about?" Donovan finally asked.

Michael felt Brittany start. He cleared his throat. "Actually, I've got a bit of a surprise for you both." *Wrong tone, idiot. Don't sound so jovial. You sound like Ed McMahon about to announce a new winner in a sweepstakes.*

"A surprise?" Beth's smile was intact, but the look she gave Donovan was uneasy.

"Brittany and I are getting married. Immediately."

The words came out stark and unadorned. They seemed to lie in the air as if painted in flaming red. No one said a word. Donovan didn't move, didn't by so much as a flicker of an eyebrow reveal his reaction to the news. Beth opened her mouth, closed it, opened it again, then she sat back on the sofa without speaking, her wide blue eyes fixed on her son.

Brittany, glancing down at the floor, looked as though she were going to faint. There wasn't a trace of color to be seen in her face, and her fingers were knotted together in her lap. He felt a surge of protectiveness, a feeling that was rapidly becoming familiar.

He dropped his hand to her shoulder, telling her silently that everything was going to be okay. His eyes took on a faint challenge when he looked at his parents.

"I realize this must be a surprise to you."

"Well, yes, it is rather." Beth glanced at Donovan as if trying to read something in his expression. He returned her look with an arched brow.

"Don't look at me. I had no idea."

"No one did. We just decided this afternoon. I was hoping Brittany could stay with you until I can arrange for us to be married."

"I... Well, we..." Beth trailed off, staring at him helplessly.

"What your mother is trying to say is that we're both still a little dazed by this news. We didn't even know the two of you were seeing each other."

Brittany reached up, clutching at Michael's hand. He returned the pressure with a reassuring squeeze.

"Like I said, it's been a little sudden for us, too."

"Are you sure this is what you want to do?" Beth asked worriedly.

"We're certain."

"But why rush things? Why not take your time to plan a wonderful wedding?"

"We've got a good reason for rushing things," Michael replied. Brittany's fingers tightened over his, a silent plea in the gesture. But his parents were going to have to know. "Brittany is pregnant, Mom."

"Pregnant? But I thought you and Dan—" Beth broke off, color flooding into her face. "I'm sorry. I didn't mean to... I just..." She trailed off weakly.

Michael drew Brittany closer, the possessiveness of the gesture clear. "I'm very excited about the baby," he said firmly.

"No one said you shouldn't be, Michael." That was Donovan, his voice calm, though his eyes reflected his shock. He came forward, placing his hand on Beth's shoulder. "We just weren't expecting—"

"No." Brittany's protest cut into words. It was the first thing she'd said since the conversation began. She straightened away from Michael's supporting arm, drawing in a deep breath. There was not a trace of color in her face, but her chin was set with determination.

"Brittany—"

"No, Michael. I want them to know the truth."

"I think we'd all like that," Donovan agreed.

"This isn't Michael's baby. It's Dan's. Michael told me that I didn't have to tell you the truth, but I think you should know."

"Thank you," Beth said weakly. She reached up to catch Donovan's hand, clinging to it as if to a lifeline.

"I'm sure you can see why we want to get married right away." Michael's eyes held a cool challenge.

"Well, actually..." Beth began, but Donovan squeezed her hand, cutting off her protest.

"Look, I hate to sound terribly old-world and chauvinistic, but do you think I could talk to Michael alone, Beth?"

She looked up at him, reading the plea in his eyes. Every instinct cried out that she had to talk to her son, had to try to understand what was going on here. But maybe Donovan was right. The two of them had always been close. Maybe this was something better worked out between them.

"All right." She drew a deep breath and stood up, forcing a smile as she looked at Brittany. "Would you like a cup of tea?"

Brittany hesitated, glancing up at Michael before nodding. "Thank you."

Michael rose as Brittany stood up, watching her leave the room with his mother.

"Your mother isn't going to put arsenic in her tea," Donovan said drily.

"I know. It's just that Brittany is rather fragile at the moment."

"Aren't we all," Donovan muttered. "You want to tell me the full story?"

Michael shrugged. "There's not really all that much to tell. Brittany needs someone to take care of her until the baby is born."

"I can appreciate that. But marriage? Can't you help her without marrying her?"

"This is the best way. She and the baby will qualify for my insurance coverage. She'll have a place to stay, someone to look out for her."

"What about you?" Donovan asked quietly. "What is this going to mean to you?"

Michael took his time with the answer, trying to find the words to explain something he didn't entirely understand.

"Dan was my best friend. He loved Brittany and I think he would have married her had he known the circumstances. It sounds corny, but I feel as I owe him this much by stepping in."

"It's not going to be easy. Marriage is tough enough, but when you add a baby into it..." Donovan shook his head, remembering the early days with Beth, the strain, the pressure.

"I don't expect it to be a walk in the park. But you and Mom managed it. I don't see why Brittany and I can't do the same."

"Your mother and I loved each other. Can you say the same?"

"Do you use sugar?"

"Yes, thank you." The short exchange was the first thing either of them had said since leaving Michael and Donovan.

Brittany watched as Beth moved around the kitchen, preparing tea. The other woman's movements were stiff, reflecting her distraction. Tea was the last thing on either of their minds. Beth set a cup of steaming liquid in front of her. Brittany lifted the sugar spoon, but her fingers were trembling so much she ended up with at least as much sugar on the table as in her cup.

"I'm sorry." She dabbed at the spilled sugar, fighting the burning sensation in her eyes.

"It's all right." Staring at the girl's downcast head, Beth felt a wave of sympathy. She'd been younger than Brittany when Michael was conceived, but the experience of finding yourself with an unplanned pregnancy couldn't be easy at any age. "I won't bite, you know."

"I know." Brittany's voice shook, and she refused to lift her head. "You must think I'm the most awful person."

"I don't think you're awful at all. I am worried," she said carefully. "Marriage seems . . ." She waved her hand, lacking the words to explain what she was thinking.

"It was Michael's idea. In fact, he insisted. I suppose I should have been stronger." She stared at her teacup. Beth waited, sensing there was more to come. Brittany looked up suddenly, her eyes catching Beth's.

"I've been so frightened. After Dan died, I was alone. Michael is so strong and I . . . I need that strength. I know I shouldn't let him do this, but I . . ." She stopped, her eyes dropping away. Her voice shook when she went on. "Have you ever been all alone and so scared you could hardly breathe sometimes? If it was just me, I'd have been all right. But there's the baby."

"What about your parents?" Beth asked softly. Despite herself, she was moved by Brittany's pain. "Couldn't they help you?"

"My parents." Brittany laughed, a short, harsh sound. "When I told my parents about the baby, they wanted to send me off somewhere to have it and then give it away. They were worried about what the neighbors might think if their daughter had a child out of wedlock."

"Your poor thing." Beth remembered how frightened she'd been when she told her father she was pregnant. Looking back, she could see that he must have been angry and scared for her, but there'd never been so much as an instant when he'd made her feel less than loved, less than wanted. What must it be like to have your own family turn their backs on you? "It must have been just awful for you."

Brittany blinked back tears. The concern in Beth's voice was everything she hadn't gotten from her own mother.

"I know you must think I'm awful to let Michael do this for me. But it's only until the baby is here."

"You make it sound so simple, Brittany. A marriage, for any reason, is very complex." Beth shook her head, maternal concern warring with compassion for the girl across the table.

"You don't get married and simply remain two people living together. There's you and your husband, and then there's this third entity that's the marriage. It takes on a life of its own. You've got a whole new set of loyalties, new ties, new demands."

"I know it might not be as easy as it seems now," Brittany said slowly. "But I think if we're careful, we can make it work. Michael seems to feel that he needs to do this for Dan's sake, and I don't want to struggle on my own anymore. I want—need—what he wants to give. I won't hurt him. I promise you that. I won't hurt him, no matter what."

Beth looked at her, seeing the sincerity in those big gray eyes, the fragility in the delicate bone structure. She was so young. When you were young it was easy to make promises about not hurting someone. And you believed them. Life had a way of interfering with promises like that.

She sighed, feeling suddenly very old. "I won't fight you on this, Brittany. I honestly don't know if you're doing the right thing or not. But I know Michael well enough to know that he's made up his mind, and I'll just have to trust his judgment."

"Thank you. Beth." The name came as an awkward afterthought. She smiled, a hesitant expression that lighted her pale face with genuine beauty. Beth looked at her, wondering how it was possible that Michael wouldn't get hurt.

Chapter 5

The wedding was held in Donovan and Beth's home. Besides the bride and groom and justice of the peace, the only guests were Beth and Donovan and Brittany's friend Janie. Brittany didn't throw her tiny bouquet of white roses and baby's breath, nor did anyone toss rice at the newlyweds.

Brittany listened to the solemn words of the ceremony, her head bent, her eyes focused on nothing in particular. This wasn't the way it was supposed to be. This wasn't the way she'd dreamed of her wedding. There should have been laughter and lots of guests, and she should have been wildly happy.

And Dan should have been standing beside her.

She stared at her fingers lying in Michael's. His hand was so much larger than hers. There was strength there. And compassion.

"Do you, Michael Patrick Sinclair, take this woman to be your lawfully wedded wife? To have and to hold, to love and to cherish from this day forward as long as you both shall live?''

''I do.''

How could he sound so confident, so calm? It was all a lie. They weren't going to love and cherish or have and hold. Those words were meant for other couples, couples who were in love, who were marrying for the right reasons.

''Brittany?'' The minister's quiet voice broke into her circling thoughts, calling her back to the matters at hand. She realized it must be time for her response. She couldn't do it. She just couldn't promise those things.

Michael's hand tightened over hers, and she looked up, meeting his eyes. She could lose herself in those eyes, clear blue and as deep as the ocean. His eyes promised her that everything was going to be all right. He'd make sure of it. She looked into his eyes and clung to his hand.

''I do.'' The response was hardly a whisper, but it was enough.

She didn't hear the rest of the ceremony, was barely aware of the minister pronouncing them man and wife. She never took her eyes off Michael's, feeling as if they were the only lifeline she had. Michael's head lowered, his hand gently squeezing hers. This must be the part where he was supposed to kiss the bride.

She felt a momentary panic, as if, in some way, having him kiss her were more frightening than the ceremony itself. His free hand came up, his palm slightly rough against the softness of her cheek. She closed her eyes as his mouth touched hers. It was a gentle kiss, given without demands. His mouth was warm against hers, and she found herself relaxing, returning the kiss in the same spirit.

Her lashes came up as he lifted his head. There was something in his eyes she couldn't quite read. A question? A need? The expression was gone so quickly, she half thought she'd imagined it.

"Congratulations." Beth was the first to come forward, her smile contrasting with the worry in her eyes. Brittany returned her hug, grateful for the show of support. In the few days since Michael had brought her here, she'd found his parents to be warm and supportive.

They might not agree that marriage was the best thing but, having accepted the reality of it, they'd gone out of their way to make Brittany feel comfortable.

It had been Beth who had insisted that Brittany have a wedding gown. And Beth who'd taken her shopping, helping her choose the simple ivory dress she now wore.

"Welcome to the family," Donovan said, and Brittany lifted her cheek to accept his kiss. Donovan wasn't as easy to know as Beth. There was a reserve about him that reminded her of Michael. But there was an underlying warmth, too.

"Congratulations, Brittany." Janie's words were a little hesitant, as if she wasn't quite sure whether or not congratulations were in order.

"Thank you." Brittany glanced at her friend, then she returned her gaze to the small bouquet she held. Donovan had handed her the bouquet just before the ceremony, his smile kind, as if he'd sensed the panic she was feeling. She smoothed a rose petal with one shaking finger, thinking of her own parents.

"Well, I think we should have some champagne to celebrate," Beth said, her tone hearty.

Despite the effort everyone put forth, the mood could not have been called exactly jovial. Odd little silences were prone to fall and then be broken just as suddenly. Beth sat very close to Donovan, as if needing the support of his nearness.

Brittany said very little. She couldn't seem to get words out past the tightness in her throat. None of this felt real.

She felt like an actress in a play, only she couldn't quite remember her lines.

Janie left as soon as was polite. Brittany saw her to the door.

"You keep in touch," Janie told her, giving her a rather fierce hug.

"Of course I will." Brittany returned the hug, feeling a tiny crack in the wall that separated her from the rest of the world.

"I think your Michael is terrific. Give him a chance, Britt."

She was gone before Brittany could say anything, hurrying down the steps. Brittany watched her go, her fingers tight around the edge of the door. She was oblivious to the cool evening air as she watched the taillights of Janie's little compact disappear. She felt as if she were seeing the last trace of her old life vanish—the life she understood.

Stupid. That life had ended when the child she was carrying was conceived. And Dan's death had made her realize she couldn't go back. Not ever.

Her Michael? He wasn't *her* Michael. Or at least, if he was, it was only temporary. As if he were on loan. Like a library book. She giggled at the thought. The hysteria underlying the sound startled her, and feeling self-conscious, she put a hand over her mouth.

"Brittany?" She jumped at the sound of Michael's voice. "Are you okay?"

"I'm fine." She shut the door carefully before turning to look at him. "Just a little tired, I guess."

"We can go home now, if you'd like."

She pushed back a tendril of hair that had fallen loose from her chignon, suddenly aware of how tired she really was. It had been so long since she'd been able to rest without some worry nagging at her—since she'd realized she was pregnant.

"I'd like that, if your parents wouldn't think it was too rude."

Michael gave her a crooked smile. "I don't think this has been any easier on them than it has on us. They'll probably be glad to see us go."

Michael's house was on the outskirts of Remembrance, backed by rolling fields. It was land he'd bought from his father. He'd built the house himself, much of it with his own hands.

Approaching it in the darkness, Brittany could make out only the shape of it. A high peaked roof outlined against the night sky, wide windows that reflected the headlights as they pulled into the driveway. Michael shut off the engine, and silence suddenly became a third presence.

He didn't say anything or seem to expect her to. He thrust open his door, coming around to open hers while she was still staring at the house. Brittany took the hand he held out to her, feeling, as always, the strength of him. This time, it sent a shiver up her spine. Staring up at him in the darkness, she could make out nothing beyond the shape of him—tall, broad shouldered.

Why hadn't she ever noticed how big he was? Maybe even an inch or two taller than Dan's six foot. He seemed to tower over her in the darkness.

What had she done? She barely knew this man. Oh, she knew he'd been Dan's friend, the quiet one of the duo. And she knew he'd been kind to her. But she didn't really *know* him.

And she'd just married him.

She shivered and Michael felt it through the hand he still held. Mistaking the reason, he drew her closer.

"I guess autumn is really here. It's chilly after the sun goes down. Let's get you in the house. I can get your suitcase later."

Brittany let him lead her toward the house simply because there was nowhere else to go. She was overwhelmingly aware that she'd just made a major commitment to this man—a near stranger.

Michael unlocked the door, flipping on a light as they stepped through.

"The living room is through here."

Brittany went in the direction he pointed, stepping onto thick carpeting. A huge stone fireplace dominated one wall; the rest of the room was almost stark in its simplicity. It was a man's room—heavy leather furniture designed for comfort, a few paintings and none of the quirky little touches a woman might have added. Brittany felt like an alien presence.

"It's pretty austere, I suppose." She turned to see Michael frowning as he looked around the room, as if trying to see it through her eyes.

"Oh no. It's beautiful, really."

He shrugged. "I furnished it for comfort, not style. You're welcome to make changes if you want."

"Oh no. I wouldn't dream of fiddling with your home."

"Brittany, it's your home now. Even if it's only for a while. I want you to be comfortable here. Besides, the place could probably use a little sprucing up."

"Home," she repeated, looking around the big room. Home. It didn't feel like home. But then, she couldn't imagine what would right now.

"I didn't know you played guitar."

Michael followed her gaze to the guitar that sat propped in a corner. "I don't. At least not very well. It's something I like to relax with once in a while. You can let me know if it bothers you."

He crossed to the fireplace, kneeling to set a match to the wood pile that already lay there. Flames devoured the crumpled newspapers and licked up through the stack of kindling before reaching the small logs.

"It's a little early in the year for a fire, but I like the look of it." He stood up, dusting his hands together as he stared down into the small blaze.

"I guess it's just now occurring to me what a disruption this is going to cause in your life," Brittany said slowly.

He turned, arching a brow when he saw that she was still standing in the middle of the floor. "There isn't a whole lot to disrupt, believe me. Have a seat. You look like you're getting ready to leave. You want something to drink or eat? You didn't eat much at supper."

Brittany sank onto the sofa, her eyes skimming the room again, trying to develop a picture of the man she'd married a few hours before. She'd given so much thought to what this marriage was going to mean to her and so little to what it was going to mean to him.

"You know, I never even asked if you had a girlfriend who might object to this arrangement."

"I don't."

"But I should have asked," she insisted. "I've only been thinking about how this is going to affect my life. I've given hardly a thought to what it's going to do to yours."

"I told you before, I'm perfectly capable of looking out for my own interests. You don't have to worry about me, Brittany."

"But I should have thought about it." Her eyes reflected her distress. Michael came and sat on the huge glass-topped coffee table in front of her. In the dim light cast by the fire, his eyes appeared midnight blue.

"I don't want you to worry about anything but yourself and the baby. The whole purpose of this is to make sure that the two of you are okay."

Her eyes dropped to where her fingers were restlessly pleating the ivory silk of her dress. "I can't just not think about it. You're doing so much for me."

"I told you before that this is something I *want* to do." He reached out, catching her hand in his. "I want to do this for Dan."

It was the first time either of them had mentioned Dan's name in days. Reminded of her loss, Brittany felt the familiar wave of grief wash over her. But it was gentler now, more a deep sadness than raging pain. Without realizing it, she was coming to terms with the loss.

Perhaps Michael felt the same rush of pain. His fingers tightened over hers for an instant. The only sound in the room was the crackle of the fire. Outside, an owl called mournfully as if seeking something forever lost. Michael drew a deep breath, forcing a light note into his voice.

"Besides, you make it sound like I've sentenced myself to hard labor. I can think of worse fates than to be married to a beautiful woman. I'll be the envy of all my friends."

Brittany withdrew her hand from his, reaching up to tuck a loose strand of hair back. Her smile might be a little wavery around the edges, but she was determined to follow his lead.

"In a few months I'm going to look like a water buffalo. I don't think your friends are going to be terribly envious then."

"Sure they will. None of them have a water buffalo in the house."

She glanced up, catching the teasing light in his eyes. Her mouth curved up in the first genuine humor she'd felt in weeks. The movement felt rusty.

"Thanks. Just wait till you have to install a hoist to get me out of the tub, and then see how you feel."

"I'm sure I'll cope." He stood up abruptly. "I'm going to make some cocoa."

"Cocoa?"

"Sure. The perfect thing to sip by the fire. Besides, aren't pregnant women supposed to drink lots of milk?"

He was on his way out of the room as he spoke, apparently feeling that a reply wasn't essential. Brittany looked after him, wondering if she'd said something to upset him.

In the kitchen, Michael pulled open the refrigerator door with such force that a bottle of salad dressing tumbled out, cracking on the tile. Muttering a curse, he took out the milk, pouring it into a pan and setting it on the stove before grabbing a towel to mop up the mess on the floor.

This wasn't going to be as easy as he'd thought it would be. He'd had it all planned. They'd live together, but it would be more in the nature of a platonic friendship than husband and wife. He'd make sure that she got the care she needed—the only thing he could do for Dan.

In a year or so their lives would go in different directions. Sure, there'd still be ties, but this would just become a rather peculiar interlude in both their lives.

It had only taken Brittany's joking words to tell him that it wasn't going to be as easy as he'd tried to believe. The thought of her in the bath created vivid and unwelcome images in his mind. Her skin would be moist, little drops of water pearling on her shoulders and breasts.

It would be a bubble bath in which the fluffy white foam would float over the surface of the water, offering tantalizing glimpses of creamy skin. She'd have her hair up in one of those casually twisted knots on top of her head, but several tendrils would be loose, caressing the nape of her neck.

She'd look up at him, those wide gray eyes all soft and wanting. And her mouth—her lower lip would be just slightly thrust out in anticipation of his kiss. He'd kneel beside the tub and—

A stab of pain slashed through the image. With a curse, he dropped the piece of glass, staring at the blood welling up at the base of his thumb. Standing up and moving to the sink he thrust his hand under a stream of cold water. What he really needed was a cold shower.

What was happening? He had no business conjuring erotic fantasies about Brittany. She was Dan's girl.

And your wife.

But that was just an arrangement to take care of her. It was temporary.

But you never discussed the sleeping arrangements with her.

They didn't need to be discussed. He'd already cleared out a bedroom for her. He shook his head, wishing he could clear out his mind as easily.

The wedding today hadn't been quite what he'd expected. When they'd decided to get married, he'd looked on it as a necessary step. He hadn't given any thought to the actual marriage. Although, if he had thought about it, he wouldn't have expected the ceremony to have any effect on him. It was just a minor detail—something that had to be done before they could go on to more important things.

Then he'd seen Brittany in her wedding dress. It wasn't a real wedding dress, with yards of lace and ten feet of train. There'd been no veil, no ruffles. Just plain ivory silk, high at the neck and long sleeved, with a full skirt that fell to past her knees.

When he thought about it, there was nothing spectacular about the dress. Yet, in the first moment that he'd seen her coming down the stairs, she'd taken his breath away.

During the ceremony, he'd found his eyes drawn to her. The words the minister was saying, words he'd more or less expected to ignore, had suddenly seemed full of meaning. To love and cherish, to have and to hold. They were just words, but he couldn't deny that he'd felt guilty at taking the vows, knowing that there was no truth in them.

Angry hissing made him jerk his hand out of the water and turn toward the stove. Milk foamed over the top of the pan, bubbling onto the stove top with evil pleasure, there to burn to brown crust. Michael's hand was numb from having rested under the cold water so long, but it wasn't so numb that he couldn't feel the pain when he unthinkingly grabbed the pan's handle with his bare hand.

He yelped, jerking back, upsetting the pan, thus creating the final disaster as it tipped, spilling scalding milk down the front of the stove. Nursing his wounded hand, he stared at the mess. This was his punishment for having lascivious thoughts about a woman he had no business having such thoughts about.

"Wages of sin," he mumbled, thrusting his uninjured hand through his hair. By now, Brittany was probably wondering if he'd had to milk a cow to get the milk for cocoa.

When Michael stepped into the living room, prepared to tell her that the only way she was going to get cocoa was if she wanted to go to the all-night café a few miles down the road, he saw that explanations weren't necessary.

The fire still burned, sending tongues of flame up the chimney, but Brittany wasn't watching it. She'd kicked off her shoes, curling her legs under her. Her head was propped rather awkwardly against the arm of the couch, and she was sound asleep.

Looking at her, Michael felt a wave of emotion he couldn't quite define. She looked so small and vulnerable. He wanted to protect her, keep her safe.

"A lousy protector you'd make," he muttered jeeringly. "You just about killed yourself in your own kitchen."

But the feeling persisted, irritating him. He reached out to shake her awake but drew back without touching her. She looked so tired. The past few months seemed to have drained all the energy from her.

Mumbling at his own stupidity, he bent and scooped her up into his arms. She stirred as if waking and then settled more comfortably against him, turning her face into his neck. Her weight seemed insubstantial as he carried her into the bedroom. She was going to have to start eating more. He didn't know much about pregnant women, but he was willing to bet that Brittany hadn't been eating the way she should.

Michael sat her on the bed and then straightened up. Looking at her, he hesitated. She wasn't going to be very comfortable the way she was.

"Brittany?" He called her name quietly, giving one shoulder a gentle nudge. She mumbled in her sleep but didn't wake. "Brittany?" He tried again but it was clear it was going to take more than that to wake her. Even when he clicked on the bedside lamp, she didn't twitch. In this light, the smudgy purple shadows under her eyes were easy to see.

With a sigh, he turned her until he could see the row of buttons at the back of her dress. Manipulating the tiny globes through loops that seemed one size too small, he tried not to think about what he was doing. He didn't need to remember that it was his wife he was undressing or that this was their wedding night or just how beautiful she looked when she smiled.

Unbuttoned, the dress was not difficult to ease off, leaving her clad in a pale slip and panty hose. Michael hesitated only a moment before deciding not to push his luck. The hose could stay precisely where they were. Rolling Brittany to one side, he pulled back the covers before lifting to lay her against the sheets.

She stirred as the cool cotton touched her bare shoulders, her mouth curving in a smile of sensual sweetness. Her eyes still closed, her hand lifted, seeking. Michael caught it, feeling the fragility of her fingers against his.

"Mmm?" This time her murmur held a questioning note, and her lashes stirred as if she were trying to wake.

"Go back to sleep." He brushed her hair back from her forehead with his free hand, wondering at the softness of the tendrils that clung to his fingers. "Go to sleep," he whispered.

The sound of his voice seemed to relax her. As she sank deeper into the pillow, her mouth remained tilted up at the corners. She sighed.

"Dan."

Michael's fingers froze against her forehead. For a slow count of five, he didn't move. Then he slowly lowered her hand, tucking it carefully under the covers. His face was without expression as he reached out to snap off the lamp and left the room, shutting the door behind him.

The fire still flickered in the living room, though it was burning low. Crossing the room to a shallow cupboard built against one wall, he took out a bottle of whiskey and poured a shot into a small glass, then without hesitation, knocked it back neat. It burned in his throat before settling in a warm lump in his gut. He poured another shot before capping the bottle and putting it away.

Carrying the glass over to the fire, he stumbled over one of Brittany's shoes. Sinking into a chair, he reached down to pick it up. Such a tiny foot.

Dan.

He took a swallow of whiskey. *Whose name did you expect her to say, dope? Yours? Not bloody likely.* Besides, he didn't want her muttering his name in her sleep, anyway. This whole arrangement was temporary. It would soon be over. It wouldn't do to forget that.

It also wouldn't do to forget that the only reason Brittany had agreed to marry him was because the alternative was even worse than the solution. As soon as she'd had the baby and gotten on her feet, she was going to be out of the marriage as fast as you could say divorce. Or annulment. Hell, he didn't even know which it would be.

He took another swallow of whiskey, frowning at the shoe in his hand. Right now, she needed him. When she didn't need him anymore, she'd be gone. Which was exactly the way he wanted it.

He tossed back the last of the whiskey, then he set the glass down with a thump. Everything was going to work out just the way he'd planned it. He'd help Brittany for Dan's sake, a last favor for a friend. That's all there was to it.

Dan.

The shoe hit the far wall with a satisfying thump before bouncing back onto the carpeting. Michael glared at it, wishing he had another whiskey.

The first thing Brittany was aware of was feeling rested, something she hadn't felt in a long time. She kept her eyes closed, snuggling deeper into the pillow. The bed had never felt better. She wanted nothing more than to lie just where she was, eyes closed, the rest of the world a distant annoyance.

But once awake, there was no coaxing sleep back. With a frown, she buried her face in the pillow. Memories were intruding on the sleepy content she was trying to cling to. The bed, though comfortable, was unfamiliar. The light came from the wrong direction.

Michael. With a groan, she turned over, opening her eyes. She'd gotten married yesterday. She was in Michael's house—her husband's house. The ceiling was open-beamed pine, giving the room a feeling at once rustic and airy. The furniture was also pine. The overall motif was country without being cutesy.

Pulling herself upright against the pillows, she pushed her hair back from her face, trying to piece together how she'd gotten here. The last thing she remembered was Michael going off to make cocoa. She'd been staring into the fireplace, too tired to even worry about the huge step she'd taken. That was the last thing she could remember. She must have fallen asleep on the sofa, and Michael had brought her in here.

Spotting her dress draped over the back of a chair, she realized that that wasn't all he'd done. She pushed back the covers, relieved to find that he'd stopped with the dress. The thought of Michael undressing her was disturbing. It seemed so intimate. She shook her head. Her full slip was more modest than a lot of things women wore on the street.

Sitting up straighter, she swung her legs over the side of the bed, waiting for the vague queasiness to subside before she tried to stand up. She'd been lucky so far. Morning sickness hadn't been a problem. Hopefully, it would stay that way.

There was a bathroom connected to the bedroom, where Brittany took time to wash her face and comb her hair before venturing back into the bedroom in search of clothes. There was no sign of the suitcase she'd brought from Beth and Donovan's after the wedding, but the boxes in the corner held the rest of her things. Michael had brought them over two days ago.

It didn't take long to slip into a pair of jeans and a shirt. She wore the shirt out, letting the long tails hide the fact that she couldn't snap her jeans anymore. She was going to have to buy some new clothes. She frowned as she finished buttoning the shirt. Finances were another thing she and Michael hadn't discussed in detail.

In fact, it was only now—after they were married—that she was realizing just how few things they *had* discussed. Brittany frowned at her refelction in the mirror as she pinned her hair back off her face. Maybe accepting the idea that she was going to marry him was all she'd been able to deal with at first. Now that that was a reality, she was starting to wonder about the details of this arrangement.

The first thing to do was to get up the courage to leave the sanctuary of the bedroom and face Michael. Her husband. Michael was her husband. She was his wife. No matter how she phrased it, she couldn't make it seem real. The ceremony the day before was already vague, dreamlike, as if it were part of someone else's life.

Only it wasn't. She, Brittany Winslow, was now Brittany Sinclair, and she might as well get used to the idea. Drawing a deep breath, she opened the door and stepped into the hallway.

Sunlight spilled through a bank of high, narrow windows along one wall, making the hallway much brighter than might have been expected. There was a door at the far end that she assumed must lead to Michael's bedroom. From the stillness of the house, it appeared that he was still sleeping.

As it turned out, he was asleep but not in his bedroom. Brittany was halfway across the living room before she realized that she wasn't alone. Michael was sprawled in the wide leather chair in front of the fireplace, his long legs draped awkwardly over the arm, his neck at an impossible angle.

Her first urge was to retreat to the bedroom, which already seemed a haven. She squelched it immediately. She couldn't run every time she saw Michael. Besides, he didn't even know she was here. Despite herself, she was drawn closer, studying his sleeping face.

He looked younger. Sleep eased the maturity from his face, leaving him vulnerable. Odd, she'd never really noticed just how handsome he was. She'd always been vaguely aware that he was attractive, but all her attention had been for Dan.

If she'd been asked, she'd have said that Dan's sandy-brown hair and light blue eyes were surely the epitome of male beauty. Yet, there was something appealing in Michael's darker good looks.

A lock of tobacco-brown hair had fallen across his forehead, and she reached out to push it back, surprised by the silky feel of it against her fingers. She drew her hand back, oddly disturbed. She wasn't sure she wanted to see him like this—soft, vulnerable, more human, somehow.

She'd had this vague idea that, even after they were married, they'd remain somewhat distant from each other. She hadn't thought about what it was going to be like to live with him, to see him across the breakfast table, to bump into him after a shower, to see him vulnerable as he was now.

Brittany turned away, uncomfortable without being able to put a precise name to what it was that bothered her. She was just imagining things. Weren't pregnant women supposed to be prone to flights of fancy? So she'd seen Michael asleep. So what?

All it took was seeing the kitchen to bring her solidly to earth again. It was basically a rather nice kitchen. Compact but designed so that it looked bigger than it actually was. It wasn't the decor that brought her to a halt.

On the floor in front of the refrigerator was a puddle of blue cheese dressing, a broken bottle floating forlornly in the middle. On the counter were two cups and a box of cocoa. On the stove was a pan, and all over the stove was what must have been the contents of the pan.

She was on her knees mopping up the dressing when a small sound made her glance up. Once Michael came around the corner, he stopped dead, obviously surprised to see her.

"Brittany." He thrust his fingers through his hair, rumpling it into soft brown waves. "I thought you'd still be asleep."

"I've been up a few minutes." She returned her attention to the dressing, picking pieces of broken glass out of the mess and dropping them into the dustpan she'd found behind the door.

"Here, you don't have to do that. I should have cleaned it up last night." He crouched beside her, reaching for the dustpan, but she moved it out of reach.

"I'll do it."

"I'm the one who broke the bottle."

"And let the milk boil over." She looked up in time to see his guilty glance at the stove.

"Things didn't go so well last night. It's just as well you fell asleep. But I didn't leave the mess for you to clean up. I was going to do it myself."

"But you fell asleep."

"Well, I'm awake now and I can take care of it."

Brittany reached for a roll of paper towels and started to sop up the sticky dressing, ignoring Michael's halfhearted attempt to take paper towels away from her.

"You know, I was actually rather relieved to see the kitchen like this."

"Relieved?" He said, looking surprised. "You like filthy kitchens?"

"Not particularly." She threw the wet towels into the trash can and sat back on her heels, looking at him. "But it was nice to find out that you aren't entirely perfect."

Surprise flared in his eyes. "You must be thinking of someone else," he said at last. "'Perfect' is not a word even my own mother would apply to me."

"Well, these past few days, you've been so calm. In complete control. It can be a little intimidating."

He reached out to catch her hand when she moved to stand up. "Do I intimidate you?"

Brittany stared at their linked hands. The plain gold wedding band on her third finger caught the sunlight pouring in through the window over the sink.

"Not 'intimidate,' precisely," she said quietly.

"What 'precisely'?" he pressed.

"You seem to know exactly where you're going and exactly what you want. I feel like I've been floundering for the past couple of months. Since...since Dan's plane went down, I haven't been able to focus on much of anything."

"I think that's understandable." His thumb rubbed the wedding ring. "You've had a lot to wade through."

"I suppose." She sighed, looking up at him. "Why do I have the feeling that, if you were in my shoes, you would have managed better than I did?"

"If I were in your shoes, I'd have been in every medical journal in the country."

He said it so seriously that it took a minute for his meaning to sink in. When it did, she felt a smile crack, and then laughter welled up. The sound was rusty but it was definitely a laugh. It felt wonderful. As if she'd been only half-alive for a long time. Now life was pouring back into her veins.

Kneeling there on the kitchen floor, her hand still in Michael's, their shared laughter mingling in the morning air, Brittany felt a surge of optimism. Life *did* go on. Maybe it could even be good again.

Chapter 6

The next few weeks were full of adjustments. Adjusting to marriage, adjusting to each other and, for Brittany, adjusting to all the changes in her body. The past was pushed into the background by the necessity of figuring out the present.

Brittany still wore the locket Dan had given her, but she thought about him less often. There was so much to deal with in her life right now that she didn't have time to think about her loss. When she did think about it, she found the pain growing less acute.

Michael did everything he could to make her life comfortable. He bought her a car, used but reliable, so that she wouldn't have to rely on him for transportation. When she protested that he was spending too much money on her, he shrugged. But the car stayed in the driveway, and the keys stayed on the hall table.

When he opened a bank account for her, she argued vociferously.

"I don't need your money, Michael. I still have some left of what my parents gave me."

Michael glanced up from the stack of papers he'd been making notations on. "It can't be all that much. You'll need more."

"You've given me so much already," she protested. "I don't need the money."

"Use it to buy things for the baby, then. Aren't babies supposed to need all kinds of terribly expensive things?" he suggested vaguely, his attention drifting back to the paperwork at his elbow.

Brittany opened her mouth to continue the argument and then shut it again, fuming silently. In the month since their marriage, she'd learned that arguing with Michael was one of life's more frustrating exercises. He never got angry. He simply stated his viewpoint and then dropped the subject, as if leaving the decision up to her. There was no pressure, no demands. So why did she have the feeling that she was going to end up doing exactly what he thought she should do?

He shut the folder he'd been studying, then he pushed his chair back from the table, reaching for his plate.

"I'll get that," Brittany said.

"It's no bother," he said, intercepting her. "I've got to go check a couple of sites, and I've got some paperwork that will probably keep me in the office most of the afternoon. Is there anything I can get you while I'm in town?"

"No, thank you. I have everything I need." Brittany trailed after him into the kitchen, vowing to break every plate in the house if he tried to wash the dishes before he left. To avoid the necessity for violence, she all but snatched the plate from his hand, standing in front of the sink like a soldier guarding a nuclear power plant.

"I'll take care of the dishes," she said firmly.

Michael's brows rose as if he thought her attitude a little odd. "Okay. I guess I'll get started, then. If there's anything you need—"

"I know. I can call the office and they'll get hold of you. I'm pregnant, Michael, not dying."

"Sorry. I didn't mean to sound like I thought you couldn't take care of yourself." He hesitated a moment and then gave her a half smile. "I'll see you later. Take it easy."

Brittany still hadn't moved when she heard the door shut behind him. Her shoulders slumped as she wandered back into the dining room. The checkbook still lay in the middle of the table.

Why did she argue with him? It was true that the baby was going to need a lot of things. She was going to have to buy some clothes for herself. She was down to one pair of pants she could get into, and those wouldn't even zip all the way up. The few hundred dollars she had left in her own account wasn't going to go very far.

It was just that when she'd married him, she hadn't expected to become an instant parasite, which was what she felt like. The problem with Michael Sinclair was that he was so damned self-sufficient. He didn't *need* anyone or anything.

He didn't need her to cook or to take care of the house. He was capable of doing those things himself. He didn't seem to expect anything of her. He treated her like a cross between a porcelain doll and an old school chum. Friendly, casual and very careful.

In a fit of annoyance, Brittany picked up the checkbook, then threw it against the wall, feeling a twinge of satisfaction when it bounced onto the floor near her feet. If she'd thought about it at all, she would have assumed that there'd be something she could do so that she felt like more of a partner in this arrangement.

Only Michael didn't need her to do anything. She sighed, her anger replaced with a vague depression. Touching the slight rounding of her belly, she bent down and picked up the checkbook. Rather than spend another day staring at the television, she might as well go and get some clothes that fit.

She was really an ungrateful wretch, she thought remorsefully. He had put his entire life on hold for her, and she resented the fact that he didn't seem to need her help. He provided her with a nice home, a car, money. He was polite and never acted as if he expected gratitude from her, and she snapped and snarled at him.

"It's just that he's *so* polite," she mumbled, picking up the rest of the dishes and carrying them into the kitchen. "Doesn't he ever get angry?"

His calm control was so different from Dan's volatility that it was hard to remember that the two of them had been friends. Didn't he sometimes resent her presence? Didn't he sometimes regret what he'd done?

She rinsed the dishes and set them in the dishwasher, her expression thoughtful. Maybe he was trying to avoid making her feel as if she owed him something. Maybe he was trying to make it clear to her that his help came without strings. And here she was bitching and moaning as if he were making her life a misery.

Guilt clutched at her. She'd have to make it up to him. Tonight, she'd cook him a special dinner.

Michael rolled his head against the ache that had settled in the back of his neck. Too many hours spent over a drafting board, too many arguments with contractors who thought they understood the design better than the architect, and too many nights spent lying awake, thinking about Brittany sleeping just down the hall.

He shut the door of the Mustang behind him with a little more force than necessary. It was dark already, and the evening air was chill with a promise of winter to come. The holiday season was just around the corner, and he couldn't remember a year when he'd felt less like celebrating.

He hunched his shoulders inside the sheepskin-lined denim jacket, staring at the lights that spilled from the windows of the house. His house. His home. His wife. Only he couldn't really think of her that way. She was only sort of his wife.

So why was it that he was beginning to feel a definite possessiveness about her? Why was it so hard to remember that she'd only married him because she was carrying his best friend's child?

Mumbling irritably under his breath, he stalked across the lawn to the door. His key was only halfway to the lock when the door was opened from inside. Light and warmth poured out in a welcoming flood. Brittany stood just inside the door, wearing a loose dress in a color he couldn't quite describe, something between gold and green with overtones of both.

"Hi," she said. He blinked in the brilliance of her smile.

"Hi." Still he hesitated on the doorstep, feeling oddly wary.

"Are you going to come in, or are you going to eat your dinner on the porch?" Her question was light and teasing.

"Sorry." He stepped into the hallway, shrugging out of his jacket. Brittany took it from him before he had a chance to turn toward the coat closet. "Dinner?"

"Don't tell me you're not hungry," she said brightly, shutting the closet door before turning to look at him. "I spent the past two hours in the kitchen."

"I told you I didn't want—"

"I know, I know. You didn't want me to feel like I had to cook for you. But I wanted to do this. I thought we could celebrate tonight."

"'Celebrate'? Celebrate what?" He followed her into the dining room, feeling his wariness grow. They'd achieved a sort of balance the past few weeks. They didn't get too close, didn't rock the boat. He had a feeling that whatever Brittany had planned was going to rock the boat with a vengeance, and he wasn't sure he liked the idea.

"Oh, I don't know. We can celebrate my new wardrobe." She turned from the table, holding out a glass of wine, sweeping her other hand over her dress at the same time. "I have now officially joined the ranks of pregnant people. I bought maternity clothes today."

"You look very nice," he said slowly. She looked more than nice. She looked beautiful. He took a sip of wine, wishing he didn't have to notice just how beautiful she was.

"Or we could celebrate the fact that fall is almost over," she offered, reaching for her own wineglass.

"I didn't think the end of fall was something that people celebrated. Are you supposed to be drinking?"

A flash of irritation showed through the determined good cheer. "Apple juice." She held the glass up to the light so that the golden color was obvious. "I'm taking good care of myself," she said brightly.

"Good." Michael sipped the wine without tasting it. There was something in her mood that made him uneasy. It was as if she were trying too hard to be bright and cheerful.

"How was your day?"

"It was fine." The look she flashed him told him he was hardly carrying his end of the conversation, and he forced a smile, trying to relax. "How was your day?"

"It was great." If she'd smiled any wider, her cheeks would surely have split. "Not only did I buy some clothes better suited to my girth, I also went to the supermarket and got some groceries."

"You didn't have to do that. I told you I could handle the shopping. I don't want you carrying a lot of heavy bags."

Her smile seemed a little rigid, but it stayed in place. "I made sure none of them were too heavy."

"Good." He stared at his glass. He seemed to be saying "good" an awful lot tonight. It was obvious Brittany was trying to accomplish something with all this good cheer, but he wasn't quite sure what it was, and any disturbance in the status quo made him uneasy.

"I hope you like beef Wellington. I've always wanted to try making it. I thought if we were going to celebrate tonight, we ought to have something special. It should be done in a little while. Why don't we go into the living room until then?"

"Sure." He had the feeling he was failing some sort of test. If he had some idea what it was Brittany wanted, he might have been able to figure out his role. But the least he could do was try to drum up a little enthusiasm.

"Beef Wellington sounds terrific," he said too heartily.

He sat on the sofa while Brittany sat in the chair across from him. he looked at her and she looked at him. It occurred to him that someone should say something, preferably her. But she seemed to have run out of cheerful remarks, and he couldn't seem to think of anything intelligent to offer. The silence stretched. Seeking inspiration, his gaze fell on the fireplace.

"Why don't I light a fire?" He didn't wait for a response. At this point, any action he took had to be better than sitting there like a wax dummy.

Unfortunately, lighting a fire only took a few moments. Once the flames started licking at the kindling, there was really no excuse to continue kneeling on the hearth, unless he wanted to take up fire worship.

Returning to the sofa, he reached for his wineglass and took a healthy swallow before looking at Brittany again. As she stared at the tiny flames, he had the awful impression that she was fighting the urge to cry.

"The weather sure is cooling off," he said loudly. "I guess winter will be here before too long."

Great. You sound like the weatherman. Couldn't you think of something intelligent to say? Like the fact that she's never looked more beautiful? Or is her hair as soft as it looks?

"It is getting cold, isn't it?" She didn't take her eyes off the fire. "It's hard to believe how quickly time passes."

Michael swirled the wine in his glass, watching the lights in the cabernet. She was thinking about Dan. The name hovered unspoken between them. Did she think about him often, wonder how her life might have been if he hadn't died?

Of course she thinks about him, you idiot. She was in love with him—she's carrying his child.

The thought was unpalatable, and he tossed down most of the wine without tasting it.

"Dinner smells terrific." His tone was too forceful, almost challenging her to disagree, but it snapped her out of the melancholy he sensed creeping over her.

"I'd better go check it," she said.

He followed her into the kitchen a couple of minutes later, for the first time really noticing the beautifully set table in the dining room. She really had gone to a lot of trouble in an attempt to make this a special evening. He'd started off on the wrong foot, but he would do the best he could to try to recapture the mood she'd been trying to set.

That didn't seem likely, however, considering what awaited him in the kitchen. When he walked in, Brittany was staring at the stove, her shoulders slumped, her whole posture indicative of defeat. Sitting in a roasting pan on top of the stove was dinner.

Michael had eaten beef Wellington once or twice, and he was sure it wasn't supposed to look quite the way this one looked. The crust was not the golden brown he recalled.

Rather, it was quite dark. Some people might have called it burned, but he wasn't quite so tactless.

"It looks...done."

"It's burned.

"Not really. It's just a little...darker than usual. It looks great."

"Do you really think so?" Once she brightened a little, Michael was determined to eat every centimeter of blackened crust.

"I think it looks wonderful. Why don't I carve it while you serve whatever else it is you've made."

He lifted the roast onto a cutting board and got out the butcher knife, feeling his spirits lift. There was something very domestic about the scene. Here he was about to carve the roast, and Brittany was putting broccoli into a bowl. It was right out of a Norman Rockwell.

He sliced the end off the roast and the good cheer faded. The meat inside the blackened wrapper was raw. Not rare but raw.

"How does it look?"

He quickly scooped the end slice back into place, holding it there with the knife as Brittany came over to inspect it.

"It's...well..." He groped for something to say. This dinner seemed very important to her. He didn't want to be the one to tell her that it looked as if it needed another hour or so in the oven. "Actually, it may need just a minute or two more in the oven," he said carefully.

"It's not done? Let me see."

Reluctantly, Michael lowered the knife, letting the end slice fall to the cutting board. Brittany stared at the meat in dead silence.

"It's raw."

"Well, not raw, exactly. Just a little too rare."

"It's raw. The crust is burned and the meat is raw." She set the bowl of broccoli on the counter with a crack. "All I wanted to do was cook a decent meal."

"It would only take a little more time in the oven, and I'm sure it would be fine."

"Don't patronize me, Michael."

"I'm not patronizing you. If we just put the roast back in the oven and cook it awhile longer, it will be fine."

"Right. We cook it until the crust actually turns to charcoal instead of just coming close."

"So, we peel the crust off."

"I don't want to peel the damned crust off," she snapped furiously. "All I wanted was to cook a simple meal, sit down and enjoy it."

"Beef Wellington is hardly a simple meal." He'd intended to offer consolation, but it wasn't taken that way.

"Right! I should have tackled a nice simple frozen lasagna. Is that what you're trying to say?"

"No. I just meant—"

"I don't care what you meant. I know you think I'm a helpless idiot." She shoved past him, snatching up the roast and throwing it into the sink, jabbing it with a fork in a vain attempt to make the entire piece of meat disappear down the garbage disposal.

Michael looked on in confusion. He'd obviously done something to upset her but, for the life of him, he couldn't figure out what. Maybe this was one of those mood swings pregnant women were supposed to experience. He watched her furious attack on the roast for a moment before venturing a comment.

"I don't think that will go down the disposal that way."

Brittany spun away from the sink, the fork held like a weapon in her hand. "I'm perfectly capable of running a garbage disposal."

"Okay. Sorry." He lifted his hands, palm out. His acquiescence only seemed to make her madder.

"Don't you ever get mad?" She didn't give him a chance to answer, turning back to continue her attack on the roast. "Why should you bother to get mad at me? You probably don't think I'm worth it."

"You're not making any sense, Brittany."

"Of course I'm not. Poor, stupid Brittany. She can't manage anything on her own."

"Would you stop this?"

If she hadn't been so engrossed in her own emotional turmoil, she might have heard the edge in Michael's voice. But all the frustration and helplessness of the past few months had finally come to a boil. There was no stopping the torrent now that she'd started.

"You think I can't manage anything. After all, I was stupid enough to get pregnant. You can hardly blame me for Dan's death, but I undoubtedly didn't manage things too well after that, did I? I bet you pat yourself on the back every night for coming to my rescue. You're so damned noble. So bloody self-sufficient." She jabbed furiously at the uncooperative roast, oblivious to the taut silence behind her.

"Well, maybe I'm not as good at taking care of myself as you are. But I'm damned if I'll stay here, damned if I'll let you make me feel like a helpless child. You can take your charity and stuff it— Oh!"

She broke off on a gasp as Michael's hand closed over her upper arm, spinning her away from the sink. At first glance he looked no different than he usually did... until she saw his eyes. Anger darkened them to almost black, and the hand that held her arm was not hurtful, but it was far from gentle.

"I think you've said just about enough," he suggested. The quiet tone restored the voice that surprise had stolen from her.

"Let go of me."

"Shut up." He used his grip on her arm to pull her closer. "You've been babbling on for the past five minutes, making very little sense."

"It all makes perfect sense," she muttered mutinously.

"Do you really think that I pat myself on the back for helping you? That I think you're helpless?"

"Well, you act that way."

"How do I act that way? Explain to me what I'm doing to give you the notion that I think so little of you."

"You treat me like I can't reason for myself. You're always telling me to take care of myself, questioning whether or not I should be drinking wine or vacuuming the floor or dressing myself."

"Did it occur to you that I might be concerned?"

"Of course you're concerned. After you've made all these noble sacrifices for me, I'm sure you're concerned."

He drew her even closer, leaning down until only inches separated their faces, his eyes blazing directly into hers. "If you say one more word about my 'noble sacrifice,' I swear I'm not going to be responsible for my actions."

He paused but Brittany had run out of words. She'd wondered if he had a temper, although now that she was seeing it up close, she decided that she'd rather not push him any further. Not that she thought he'd do her any physical injury. Still, he looked more than a little intimidating.

"I didn't make any noble sacrifices when I married you. I married you because I wanted to. I wanted to help you, and I felt like I owed it to Dan."

"You thought I was a helpless nitwit," she muttered to his shirtfront.

"No, I didn't. Even though you'd gone through some rough times, I thought you'd come out pretty damned good. Just because you need a little help doesn't mean you're a nitwit."

"Then why do you act like you think I'm helpless?" She lifted her eyes to his, her anger gone but not the hurt she felt. "You're all the time telling me not to lift things or move anything. I feel like I can hardly breathe."

"I just don't want you to hurt yourself." His fingers dropped from her arm.

"You make me feel like I'm too stupid to take care of myself, like if you're not there to watch over me every minute, I'm going to do something dumb."

"I don't mean to do that." Michael looked away, thrusting his fingers through his hair.

"Then why do you? Do you think I'm helpless?"

"No, of course not," he said impatiently.

"Then why?"

The silence stretched out until Brittany wondered if he was going to answer. When he spoke at last, his voice was husky. "About a month before Dan...before Dan was killed, my mother had a miscarriage."

"Oh, Michael, I didn't know."

"They really wanted that baby. It hurt her terribly. Dad finally took her on a cruise to try and get her mind off it. She took good care of herself, but she lost the baby anyway." He shrugged. "I guess if I'm a little overprotective of you, maybe that's why."

"Oh, Michael." Brittany wondered if it were possible to simply slither into a corner somewhere and melt away. She'd been so sure that his attitude toward her had nothing to do with anyone but her. It hadn't even occurred to her that it might have a basis in something totally unrelated. All these weeks she'd been so angry and frustrated.

"It must have been very difficult for your mother."

"It was rough." The simple statement told her as much as any lengthy explanation of what Beth had suffered.

"I'm sorry I acted like a shrew."

"I'm sorry if I was smothering you."

Silence settled awkwardly between them. The kitchen seemed suddenly much too quiet. Brittany laughed uneasily. "I guess we just had our first fight."

"I guess we did."

"I guess maybe we're really married now."

Michael half smiled, his eyes shadowed. "More or less. Do I really make you feel stupid?"

Brittany shrugged. "Not really. You just seem so self-sufficient. I guess I feel a little useless around here."

"I didn't marry you so you could be useful."

"I know, but I'd feel better if there was something I could do."

"Like what?"

"I don't know," she admitted. "But something. I can't just sit around for the next five months twiddling my thumbs."

"Aren't there things you need to do to prepare for the baby?" he questioned with some vague image of her knitting booties.

"Nothing that's going to take up all my time."

"Well, there must be things around here. What about cooking?" His eyes fell on the mangled roast that lay pathetically in the sink. "Maybe not."

Brittany laughed, feeling as if a weight had lifted. They were talking. Really talking. The quarrel seemed to have used up the tension that had been building between them.

"Don't you trust my culinary expertise?"

"Well, I wouldn't put it that way, exactly. Let's just say that I wouldn't want to depend on you to keep us from starving to death."

"Coward."

"You didn't see how dangerous you looked with that fork in your hand," he teased.

"Speaking of food..." She looked at the roast, suddenly aware that she was hungry.

"I'm starving. A friend of my parents' has opened a new Mexican restaurant."

"I love Mexican food."

That evening marked a turning point in their marriage. It was as if, by surviving their first quarrel, they'd established a relationship separate from the events that had brought them together. Brittany and Michael had formed a rapport that was not dependent on the relationships they'd had with Dan.

It was, as Beth had told her, impossible to live with someone and not become involved with them. A marriage license tied them together, but it was more than that. There was a bond there, and with each day that passed, it grew stronger.

"Brittany, I'm so glad you could join me for lunch." Beth's smile was welcoming as Brittany settled into the chair across from her and took a menu from the waiter.

"It isn't like my schedule is heavily booked these days. Most of my friends are in school."

"It gets lonely, doesn't it? I felt as if I'd fallen into some kind of black hole where no one knew I existed anymore."

There was such feeling in the words that Brittany looked over the top of her menu, her eyes curious.

"You sound like you know what it's like."

"I do. I was younger than you are, only sixteen, when I quit school."

"You quit because you were pregnant?" The menu was forgotten.

"I was pregnant with Michael. In those days, there was no question of my staying in high school. Heaven knows, I might have contaminated the other girls." She laughed, her eyes sparkling with amusement, but it didn't take psychic ability to know that it must have been painful at the time.

Brittany hesitated, her eyes dropping to the table. In the two months since she and Michael had been married, Beth and Donovan had never by word or look made her feel less than a member of the family. At Thanksgiving, she'd been welcomed as if she and Michael had a real marriage, as if the child she carried were his.

Still, she sensed a slight barrier between her and her in-laws. She knew Beth feared that Michael was going to end up hurt. Perhaps they also feared growing too close to her or to the child she carried. After all, she wasn't going to be part of their lives forever, as they might expect a real daughter-in-law to be.

She stirred in her seat, uncomfortable with the thought of a *real* daughter-in-law, a real wife for Michael. She'd grown accustomed to thinking that he belonged to her, even if it was only for a few months.

"Brittany?" Beth's voice snapped her out of her thoughts, and she looked up to see the waiter standing next to the table. Flustered, she asked for a chef's salad, hoping there was such a thing on the menu. Since he didn't question the order, she assumed she hadn't revealed her total unfamiliarity with the menu.

"You looked like you were miles away," Beth commented when the waiter was gone.

"Not really. I was thinking that it must have been very hard for you, being so young and all."

"It wasn't easy but I had Donovan." The way she said it made it impossible to doubt that that had been enough. "And you have Michael."

"I don't know where I'd have been without him," Brittany admitted.

"The two of you seem to be settling in quite well." If there was a touch of maternal anxiety in the words, Brittany could hardly blame her.

"It took a little bit of adjusting, but we're doing all right. You know, I've thought a lot about what you said—about the fact that a marriage has a certain life of its own."

"Goodness, did I say that? How pompous of me." Beth leaned back as the waiter brought their salads.

Brittany waited until he was gone again before continuing. "It wasn't pompous. It was very true. I mean, even though Michael and I don't have a real marriage, there's a definite bond between us. Maybe it's because we were sort of friends before this, but we've made some adjustments and learned to talk to each other more openly. We've even had a quarrel or two. We've learned to compromise."

"What do you think a real marriage is, Brittany?" Beth asked gently. "A real marriage is all about compromise, about each of you giving a little and taking a little. There are so many ties that come with living together day to day. Don't make the mistake of thinking that either of you is going to be able to walk away from this without hurt."

Beth's words lingered in Brittany's mind long after the lunch was over. Walking along the street, past shop windows full of Christmas displays, she thought about it. Ties. She hadn't expected to feel tied to Michael. Gratitude, affection maybe, but not this feeling that their lives were bound together.

She stopped in front of a toy store window, looking in at the displays. Next year at this time, she'd be shopping for her son or daughter. And she'd be shopping alone. The thought slipped in unbidden, causing a surprising ache in her chest.

It was getting harder and harder to think of the time when Michael would no longer be a daily part of her life. But that had been the plan from the start. He'd only married her because she was carrying Dan's child. Once that child was born and she'd had a chance to get on her feet again, the time would come to break those ties.

Dan. She closed her eyes, trying to picture his face, but the image was fuzzy around the edges. The eyes showed a tendency to darken from Dan's icy blue to Michael's sky blue. She couldn't make the hair stay sun-streaked brown. It was darker, richer. And the face... Why couldn't she call the face more sharply to mind?

Hands shaking, she dug in her purse for her wallet, snapping it open to the picture of Dan. Yes. That was it. He was laughing into the camera. How could she have forgotten the way his eyes laughed? She stroked her thumb over the photograph, feeling tears fill her eyes.

Things would have been so different if he'd lived.

But would they have been better?

She hushed the tiny voice, closing the wallet and tucking it back into her purse. She'd loved Dan. Nothing was going to change that. Nothing. And no one.

Chapter 7

Christmas arrived with a snowfall worthy of a postcard. Remembrance became an enchanted town, full of beautiful drifts of white.

Michael drove the Mustang slowly along the icy streets. Brittany watched the houses along the way, unaware of the quick look he shot her from time to time.

"Something wrong?" he finally asked.

"No." She turned her head, conjuring up a smile. "Should there be?"

"You look…sad." He braked carefully at a stop sign before turning to look at her, his eyes searching. "You don't like Christmas?"

"I love Christmas." She smoothed her hand over the soft wool of her coat. "I was just thinking about my parents. Wondering if they think about me."

Michael felt a familiar surge of anger at the thought of her parents. Brittany rarely mentioned them, but he knew their absence in her life was a source of hurt. Personally, he thought they were no loss. Remembering the woman who'd so coolly told him that she had no idea where her daughter was, all he felt was a strong desire to go back and give her a piece of his mind. But he supposed Brittany might feel differently.

"You could call them," he suggested evenly, keeping his own feelings out of his voice. "Tell them you're married."

"No." She shook her head. "I miss them but if they can't put me ahead of the opinions of other people, then I won't go crawling to them."

"You wouldn't have to crawl. A phone call would probably do." He thought she was well rid of them. Why was he arguing in their favor? Because he hated seeing the sadness in her eyes.

"No. They made their choice. Besides, I don't think they're the kind of people I want influencing my child. I don't want my son or daughter growing up thinking that other people's opinions are more important than love and loyalty."

Since he wholeheartedly agreed with her, there was really nothing Michael could say in argument. They finished the rest of the drive in silence.

The gathering at Beth and Donovan's was small. Just the family and Carol Montgomery, who Brittany had learned was as close to family as it was possible to get. She and Beth had been friends since childhood. Brittany liked Carol, with her slightly acerbic wit and dry practicality. She didn't know if Carol knew the truth about her marriage. If she did, she'd never shown it.

Presents were unwrapped before the late afternoon meal. Brittany had spent a considerable amount of time trying to decide what to get her in-laws. It had to be something personal but not too personal, hovering somewhere between a gift a real daughter-in-law might give and a gift a near stranger might give. In the end she'd settled on a delicate silk scarf for Beth, the floral print swirling across a peacock-blue background.

Donovan had been much more difficult. He was more reserved, harder to know. At first she'd thought it was only with her that he showed that unapproachable air, but she'd realized that it was a natural part of his makeup. Desperation had finally driven her to pick up her knitting needles three weeks before Christmas. The sweater was a simple pullover, but she'd chosen the yarn with great care, trying to find something that matched his green-gold eyes.

She'd been pleased with the results until she saw him opening the box. Now that the moment was at hand, she was sure that the gift had been much too personal. Besides, he probably hated sweaters. Donovan reached into the box, drawing the sweater out, studying it silently while Brittany held her breath.

"She made it," Michael told him, ignoring Brittany's squeak of protest.

Donovan's eyes left the sweater to settle on her. "You made this yourself?"

She nodded, sure that he was going to hate it even more than he already did now that he knew she'd made it.

"If you don't like it..." she began weakly.

"It's beautiful, Brittany." The quiet words seemed utterly sincere. He stripped off the sweater he'd been wearing and pulled the one she'd made him on over his shirt. The fit was perfect and Brittany felt a small glow of pride. She'd judged his size by Michael's. Donovan tugged the sweater into place and then looked at her again.

"Thank you." He smiled at her, the first time he'd really smiled at her, and Brittany felt her heart bump. It wasn't hard to see why Beth looked at him as if the sun rose and set on him. When he smiled like that, it was hard to imagine *not* falling in love with him.

"You're welcome," she murmured, her eyes dropping to the package she held.

"Well, it's a sure bet this is the first handmade sweater you've ever gotten, Donovan." That was Carol, her tone lightly acerbic. "The last time Beth picked up a pair of knitting needles, it looked like she was knitting a hat for Godzilla." She paused, her expression considering. "Come to think of it, Godzilla is a better dresser than that."

Beth threw a wad of wrapping paper at her friend, and everyone laughed, the small moment of tension forgotten. But Donovan left the sweater on, and every time she saw it, Brittany felt as if she were truly a part of the family.

While Beth and Carol squabbled over Beth's skills of the needle or lack thereof, Michael unearthed a small box from under a mound of wrapping paper.

Brittany's eyes met his, as he handed it to her and she wondered if it was her imagination that read uncertainty in his gaze. Was it possible that he was as nervous as she?

"I wasn't sure what to get you, but when I saw this, I thought of you."

She took the package from him, aware of the subtle tingle when her fingers touched his. Slipping the bright red wrapping paper from the box, she held a plain blue jeweler's case, the firm's name discreetly embossed on the lid in gold.

She glanced up at Michael but could read little from his expression. Taking a deep breath, she snapped open the case and felt the air leave her when she saw the delicate band of sparkling jewels lying on the dark velvet background.

"Oh!" The only word she could get out.

"If you don't like it, we can exchange it," Michael offered when the silence stretched.

"Not like it!" Brittany's fingers tightened over the case. "I'd have to be crazy not to like it. It's absolutely gorgeous. But it's too much."

"You can't have it both ways. Either it's gorgeous or it's too much."

Glancing up, she caught the teasing light in his eyes, and she smiled reluctantly.

"It's perfect but it's much too expensive. You shouldn't have spent so much money."

"Did I ever tell you that I hate people telling me what I should or shouldn't do?" he asked conversationally. He reached out to take the box from her hand, lifting the bracelet from its bed of velvet. "Hold out your hand."

Staring at the bracelet, Brittany reminded herself of all the reasons she couldn't possibly accept a gift like this from Michael. It wouldn't be right. She'd insist that he return it.

Her hand lifted and she watched as Michael clasped the bracelet around her wrist. It felt cool against her skin, yet it seemed afire with light. The contrast was oddly seductive. Michael held her hand as he studied the sparkling diamonds.

"It suits you. I knew it would when I saw it."

That was all he said, but there was something in the tone of his voice that brought a flush to Brittany's cheeks.

Twisting the bracelet around and around on her wrist, she watched, as Donovan lifted an enormous box from under the tree, then set it in front of Michael. It had seemed like such a good idea when she saw the ad. Now, she wasn't so sure. Just because he'd admired an antique train set in a store didn't mean he actually wanted one. It had cost her virtually every cent she had left of her own money.

The man she'd bought the set from had inherited it from his uncle who'd once worked on the railroads. Every car was in the box it had come in.

Michael didn't say a word when he saw what the box held. Brittany was acutely aware that everyone was watching. They probably couldn't believe she'd actually done something so stupid. Who bought train sets for a grown man? She finally couldn't stand the silence another moment.

"There's more track. I couldn't get it all in the box. As it was, your father had to carry it in for me." She watched nervously as he lifted one of the cars out, sliding it from its box and studying the construction. "I wasn't sure... You liked one you saw in a toy store. I thought you might like one of your own..." She trailed off, feeling like a total idiot. How could she have been so dumb?

Michael slipped the car carefully back into its box before looking at her. It wasn't annoyance or disappointment she saw in his eyes.

"It's wonderful, Brittany." The quiet sincerity in his words brought a foolish flood of tears to her eyes, and she looked down to conceal them. "I don't think I've ever gotten a gift I liked more. Thank you."

"You're welcome." She couldn't think of anything more to say, though it seemed as though there should be something.

The silence might have grown awkward, but Beth broke it by standing up. "I don't know about anybody else, but all this greed has made me hungry."

Dinner was a Christmas celebration like Brittany had always thought they should be. Her own parents had tended toward a formal meal with a few close friends from their church. The main focus had always been the importance of being grateful for the good things that had happened in the past year.

At the Sinclair home, the main requirement seemed to be that there was plenty of laughter and plenty of food. They gave thanks by showing their joy in their lives and each other. It seemed a more fitting celebration.

Brittany couldn't put her finger on quite what it was, but there seemed to have been some subtle shift in her relationship with Beth and Donovan. Maybe it was the holiday spirit. Maybe it was the fact that her gift to Michael had clearly meant a great deal to him. Whatever it was, that subtle barrier seemed to have come down. She no longer felt like a visitor in their lives; she felt a part of the family.

If she'd had any lingering doubts about Michael's pleasure in her gift, they were dissolved when he and Donovan began setting up the track immediately after supper. They squabbled good-naturedly over how it should be done, ignoring Beth's mild protest when they decided that the only suitable place was the middle of the living room floor. Donovan gave his wife an absent kiss, telling her that they'd be careful not to make a mess. Brittany couldn't help but giggle at the way Beth rolled her eyes.

The two men crawled around on the floor, hooking track together, mumbling about transformers and currents. The women sat near the fire, talking in a desultory fashion, watching the antics of the supposed adults on the floor.

When the track was at last pronounced ready, everything else came to a halt while the switch was thrown, promptly plunging the room into darkness. There was a moment of stunned silence, and then Beth giggled. Even in the firelight it was possible to see the disgruntled look Donovan threw her, and Brittany bit her cheek, trying not to laugh out loud.

"Good thing you guys aren't running a major railroad," Carol said.

Muttering about transformers and fuses and overloaded circuits, Michael and Donovan trooped down to the basement. Light was restored a few minutes later, and a short time after that, the train was ready for another test run.

"Shall I get some candles?" Beth asked politely when informed that it was time to throw the switch. The look Donovan shot her promised retribution, but she didn't look worried. Everyone held their breath while the switch was thrown, but the lights remained on and the train began to move.

From the look on Michael's face, it could have been the first transcontinental train. He glanced up at Brittany with a bright boyish grin, sharing the moment with her. She smiled at him, unaware of the fact that Beth was watching the two of them, a faint frown in the back of her eyes.

Carol left not long after the triumph with the train. More snow was predicted, and she wanted to get home before the storm. After she was gone, Beth announced that Donovan could help her with the dishes. Brittany offered to help, but Beth waved her back into her seat.

"You stay there. Let the mighty engineer do something useful, for a change."

"That's right, make fun of me. My ego can take it." Donovan's long-suffering tone didn't match the laughter in his eyes. He slid his arm around Beth's waist, leaning down to murmur something in her ear. Whatever it was, she blushed and laughed as he led her from the room.

Brittany leaned her head against the back of the sofa, watching as Michael sent the train circling around and around the track. The motion was hypnotic, and she closed her eyes, letting herself drift contentedly in a state somewhere between waking and sleeping.

She opened her eyes slowly when she felt the cushion next to her dip. The train still circled lazily around the track, but Michael was sitting beside her, his eyes on the slow movement.

"Are you tired?" he asked.

"A little. It was a nice day. Probably the nicest Christmas I've ever had."

"I'm glad." He looked at her, wondering if she had any idea of how utterly beautiful she was. She'd left her hair down, clipping it back from her face with a pair of bright red combs that matched the softer wool of her dress. Her eyes were soft in the firelight. She looked drowsy and contented. And so desirable.

He wanted to take her in his arms and kiss her, feel her mouth soften under his, her arms steal around his neck. He looked away, surprised by the intensity of the urge.

A startled gasp brought his gaze back to her. She was looking at him, her eyes wide, one hand pressed to the mound of her stomach. His heart bumped with panic.

"What is it? What's wrong?"

"Nothing." She laughed unsteadily. "Nothing's wrong. The baby just moved."

"Moved?" His eyes dropped to her stomach.

"Here. Feel it." She reached for his hand, pressing it against her rounded tummy. Michael started to draw back, uneasy. He froze when he felt a sudden quick pressure against his hand. His eyes lifted to Brittany's, sharing the wonder.

"He's kicking," she said quietly.

"It could be a girl," he reminded her, a slow smile breaking when he felt the movement again. "Does it hurt?"

"No, it feels…funny. It makes it real, somehow. There's a person in there, someone totally new."

Michael's eyes dropped to where his hand rested against her belly. Until now, he'd rarely thought of the child she carried, and when he did, it hadn't been as a real, living being. Her pregnancy had been the catalyst for their marriage, the reason for all the upheaval in both their lives. Beyond that, he'd given it little thought.

Suddenly, the child she carried was real. It was something more than merely the instrument that had brought them together. It was a person, a human being in its own right.

When the child kicked again, he looked up at Brittany, grinning. "Feels like he's going to be a football player."

"Or she." Her smile matched his.

Without realizing, in that moment, Michael became as much a father to the child Brittany carried as Dan could have been. The conception hadn't been his, but the child suddenly was.

So absorbed were they in the miracle of the moment that neither of them noticed that Beth and Donovan had come into the room. When Beth turned away, Donovan followed her, catching up with her in the dining room.

She was standing at the window, staring out at the snow that was just starting to drift down, her hands clasping her elbows. When he stopped behind her, she leaned back, her head resting on his shoulder. In the light reflected off the snow, he could see the gleam of a solitary tear on her cheek.

"Does it still hurt so much?" he asked, wrapping his arms around her, wishing he could take away her pain.

"Not always. Most of the time I don't think about it. It's just that it's Christmas. Our baby was due about now. This might have been her first Christmas." Her voice broke on the words, and she turned, burying her face against his shoulder.

"Don't cry, sweetheart. You know the doctor said we could try again." He stroked his hand over her hair.

"I'm too old."

"No, you're not. Lots of women older than you are have babies."

"But what if I can't?" She lifted her face from his shoulder, looking up at him searchingly.

"Beth, having another child with you would be wonderful, but I don't need that to make me happy." A touch of anger flared in the back of his eyes. "You shouldn't have to ask that."

"I know. But sometimes I wonder."

They were quiet for a few moments, Beth held safe in Donovan's arms, his gaze on the snowy world outside.

"Does it bother you, watching Brittany?" he asked at last.

"Once in a while." She stirred, turning in his arms so that his hands were linked in front of her and she could look out the window. "They remind me so much of us when we first got married. They're so young and so sure that they can make life do what they want it to. I'm afraid they're going to end up hurt."

"There's not much we can do about it."

"I know but I can't help but worry." She tilted her head back until their eyes met. "I love you, Donovan. I love you so much."

He looked down at her with so much love in his eyes she didn't need the words he gave her.

"I love you, Beth. I always will."

Christmas had marked another subtle turning point in Brittany's marriage. She and Michael had drawn closer together. In some way she didn't quite understand, they were becoming a couple, just as Beth had predicted. There was a new ease between them, a casual intimacy that she found unnerving when she thought about it.

It was sometimes hard to remember the reasons behind this marriage, hard to remember that it wasn't a real marriage. Every night, when she climbed into her solitary bed, she was reminded of those reasons. But when she was with Michael, they became distant, foggy things that didn't seem quite real.

It wasn't that she was falling in love with him. Dan was certainly the only man she would ever love—there could be no doubt about that. With Michael, it was more a case of falling in like. How could you not like a man who thought Laurel and Hardy were the funniest comedians of all time, who considered a banana split the height of culinary achievement and who never once made her feel as if marrying her had caused him the slightest moment's doubt?

No, she'd never love again, but with Michael she was discovering that life could be full again, that she could be happy.

"I want some popcorn." Brittany's announcement came just as John Wayne was dismounting, preparatory to stalking through the milling cattle in search of Montgomery Clift.

"You can't leave now," Michael protested. "This is the big finale."

"I've seen *Red River* at least five times. I think I can remember the finale. Besides, we can always run the tape back."

Michael rolled his eyes. "It's not the same. If you want to wait a minute, I'll make the popcorn."

"That's okay. If I don't move soon, I'm going to sink into the sofa permanently."

Michael might have argued further, but John Ireland had just called John Wayne's name. Brittany shook her head as she stood up and went into the kitchen. She smoothed a hand over her belly beneath one of Michael's old shirts. At six and a half months there was no longer any way to conceal her condition.

Reaching for the popcorn, she smiled. In the living room, she could hear the sound of fighting. There'd be no peeling Michael away from the set until the last of the credits had rolled. John Wayne movies were a not-so-secret vice of his.

She poured a thin layer of oil in the bottom of the pan, waiting for it to heat before adding the popcorn. It was only after she'd added the golden kernels that she realized she didn't have a lid handy. Muttering at her lack of planning, she lowered herself to search through the bottom cabinets.

The lid proved more elusive than she'd hoped. She was halfway into a cabinet when she realized that if she didn't turn the popcorn off, it was going to end up all over the kitchen. She backed awkwardly out of the cabinet, but she lifted her head too soon, banging it solidly against the frame, startling a cry of pain out of her as she collapsed on the floor.

She'd barely had a chance to lift a hand to her throbbing head when Michael showed up, drawn by her cry.

"What happened? Are you all right?" He was on his knees beside her, concern darkening his eyes.

"I hit my head."

"Did you fall? Do you feel dizzy? Sick?"

"No, no and no. I was looking for a lid, and I tried to stand up before I was out of the cabinet. Help me up, please."

"Are you sure you should stand up? Maybe you should just stay where you are for a few minutes."

"Michael, I'm not going to stay sprawled on the kitchen floor like some obese kitchen witch. I just bumped my head." Her tone was mildly exasperated. She'd come to accept that he couldn't control his overprotective streak.

He stood up reluctantly, taking her hands and lifting her to her feet. Brittany was grateful for the help. Standing up these days wasn't as simple as it had been. Michael released her hands but didn't move away, and she knew at the slightest sign of dizziness, he'd have her wrapped safe in his arms. She had to admit that there was a certain comfort in that knowledge.

She reached up to try to judge the extent of the damage to her head, but Michael's hand was there first.

"Let me see." His fingers were gentle at the back of her head, but when he touched the place she'd hit, she sucked in a quick breath.

"Sorry."

"That's okay. It's just a little tender." She lifted her eyes to his face, half smiling. "What do you think, Doc? Will I live?"

"I don't think the skin is broken, but you're going to have a bit of a lump. Are you sure you feel okay?"

"I feel fine. You want to check to see if my pupils are dilated and reactive? That's what they do on all the best hospital shows."

"I'm not sure I'd know what a dilated pupil looked like." He looked at her eyes, his hand lingering in her hair. "You really should be more careful." But he wasn't thinking about the bump on her head. He was wondering how it was possible that she could be so beautiful.

Maybe it was true that pregnant women took on a special glow. Brittany seemed lighted from within. He lifted a hand to her cheek, stroking the impossibly soft skin. Her eyes widened in surprise.

For months he'd forced himself to pretend that he felt nothing but friendship for her, that the fact that she was his wife meant nothing. Now, with his hand tangled in her hair, that suddenly seemed such a foolish waste.

His head lowered, his mouth catching Brittany's surprised little gasp. It was the first time he'd kissed her since that stilted little moment at the wedding. Her mouth was softer than he remembered, opening beneath his like a flower drinking in the sun.

There was none of the hesitation that went with a first kiss. They were married; they'd lived together for months. There were bonds of intimacy between them that flared to life the moment he kissed her.

Brittany's hands came to rest on his chest, hesitating there a moment before sliding up to his shoulders. Desire flared in the pit of his stomach, and his arm dropped to her back, drawing her closer.

He felt as if he could absorb her into his skin, make her a part of himself. His mouth slanted across hers, and Brittany's arms tightened around his neck. The need he felt was so immediate, so basic that it left no room for thought. He'd wanted this for so long, from the moment he'd first met her.

There was a sudden small pressure where her rounded belly was pressed against his hip. He ignored it, his arms pulling her still closer, his mouth hungry on hers. The pressure came again, tugging at the fog he wanted to draw between them and reality. It felt as if someone was kicking him. He felt the movement again and dragged his mouth from Brittany's, suddenly aware of what he was doing.

The baby. The baby was moving within her, as if in protest of what was happening. His arms dropped away from her, and he took a step back. Brittany swayed as if the abrupt end to the embrace had thrown her off balance. Michael reached out, steadying her with a hand at her elbow, drawing back from even that small contact the moment he was sure she didn't need the support.

"I'm sorry." He couldn't meet her eyes, focusing his gaze on the floor between them, one hand shoved into his pocket, the other clenching and unclenching at his side.

Brittany stared at him, still dazed by the unexpected flare of passion.

"I'm sorry. I didn't mean—I had no right—" He broke off, his jaw tight.

What was he talking about? She lifted a hand to push her hair back, trying to corral her scattered thoughts into order. Why was he apologizing?

"Michael." The husky sound of her voice surprised her, and she cleared her throat before she continued. "Michael, there's nothing to apologize for. You didn't attack me." She waited but he didn't smile, didn't look at her. He just stood there, a muscle ticking in his jaw and that hand clenching and unclenching. She tried again.

"We *are* married." That got a reaction, but not the one she'd expected.

"That's not why I married you," he said fiercely. "This was never supposed to be anything more than a marriage in name only. That's what we agreed to. It was never supposed to be a real marriage."

Brittany drew in a sharp breath, hurt flowering inside her at his sharp words. *Never supposed to be a real marriage.* Funny, she almost never thought of that anymore. Somewhere along the line, it had begun to seem pretty real to her. But apparently she was alone in that feeling.

Michael might want her—she knew that much—but he had no intention of getting any more involved with her. Did he think she might try to hang on to him if they made this a *real* marriage?

Hurt filled her throat, making it impossible to speak. Without a word, she walked by him and out of the room. A moment later, Michael heard the door of her room shut. His shoulders slumped.

How could he have been such a fool? He'd spent months walking a carefully balanced line. They'd established a relationship that was close but not too close, friendly but not too friendly. If he'd occasionally wanted more than that, he'd squashed the thought.

All it had taken was the feel of Brittany's hair against his fingers to show just how fragile that balance was. The feel of her mouth under his, the way she'd responded to him... He groaned and shoved his fingers through his hair, trying to shut the memory away.

She'd responded. But that didn't mean that she'd felt the same things he'd felt. She felt grateful to him. He knew that. How was it possible to separate that gratitude from whatever else she might feel? He didn't want her to come to him because she felt she owed it to him—to repay a debt.

He groaned again, rubbing at the ache that had started to throb in his temples. Why wasn't anything simple anymore?

As if in response to his silent inquiry, loud popping sounds broke the quiet, and fluffy white kernels of popcorn began exploding out of the uncovered pan on the stove.

Cursing, Michael turned the burner off, but the residual heat kept the process going, and in a matter of seconds, puffy spots of white were dotting the counters and floor.

He set the pan in the sink, then he just stared at the mess, wondering if this was a silent commentary on the current state of his life.

Chapter 8

Michael came awake suddenly, startled from sleep by some sound he couldn't quite remember. He sat up, swinging his legs out of bed, his first thought—as it so often was—of Brittany. She'd been so uncomfortable this past couple of weeks.

And she'd been particularly uncomfortable tonight. Not that she'd said anything, but he'd seen it in the way she'd shifted restlessly in her seat, trying to find some position that relieved the ache in her back.

The baby was due in two weeks, but he sometimes wondered how she could bear the discomfort for much longer. The bloom that had marked the earlier months of her pregnancy had faded. She looked pale and worn. When he'd pressed, she'd admitted that she wasn't sleeping well, but she'd insisted that this was a normal phase of pregnancy. She just had a hard time getting comfortable.

He was halfway into the hallway when he heard the sound again. This time he knew what it was, and his heart started to beat faster. He covered the distance to Brittany's door in three quick strides, pushing it open without bothering to knock. She was half in and half out of bed, her head bent forward, her hands pressed to her stomach as she took quick, shallow breaths. Despite her efforts, a tiny whimper of pain escaped—the sound that had awakened him.

The pain eased as he knelt beside her, and she lifted her head to look at him, her eyes wide in her pale face. She'd turned on the lamp next to the bed, making it easy to read the fear in her eyes.

"Michael?" His name was all she could manage.

"I'm here." Was that his voice? He sounded so calm. "How far apart are the pains?"

"I'm not sure." She looked at the clock as if she could read the answer there. "Ten minutes, maybe."

"Why didn't you call me?" He reached around her, plumping up the pillows before taking her hands and easing her back against them.

"I didn't want to bother you."

"Don't be silly. Isn't this what I spent all those weeks in training for?" He didn't wait for an answer, disappearing into the bathroom and coming back out with a damp washcloth. Brittany sighed with pleasure as the cool cloth stroked her forehead.

"That feels nice."

"Of course it does." He pushed her hair back from her face. "This is what I learned in boot camp."

"Boot camp?"

"All those classes we took. Did you think I spent all that time practicing with pillows and breathing like a fish just to be robbed of the chance to use it when the time came? Ms. Olafson would be sorely disappointed in me if I failed after all the hours she spent barking orders at us."

"She didn't bark," Brittany protested drowsily. "She was very nice."

"To those among us with large stomachs, maybe." Michael put down the washcloth and stretched out an arm to grab the hairbrush that lay on the dresser. "You don't know how brutal she was on the husbands."

He began to pull the brush through her hair, easing her forward with a hand behind her back so that he could brush the hair up off the nape of her neck.

"Somehow I doubt that."

"You didn't see the way she looked at me," he insisted. "I was shaking in my boots."

She leaned against him, letting the rhythmic stroking of the brush lull her. The nonsensical conversation helped distract her.

"I don't think you've ever been afraid of anyone in your life."

"Only Ms. Olafson," he assured her. "She was—"

He broke off as Brittany's fingers suddenly clutched at his arm, another contraction rippling through her. Michael dropped the brush, catching her hands in his.

"Look at me and breathe. Remember your breathing. Concentrate."

Her eyes clinging to his, Brittany inhaled and panted, following his instructions. She lay back when the contraction eased, but she didn't release his hands.

"I'm scared, Michael," she admitted shakily. "What if something goes wrong?"

"Nothing is going to go wrong," he promised her. "In a few hours, we're going to have a beautiful son or daughter."

She didn't even notice his automatic use of "we're." Now that the time was here, she was suddenly filled with doubts and fears.

"But—" His finger across her lips stopped her before she could even get the words out.

"No 'buts' about it. Everything is going to be fine, Brittany."

"You won't leave me?" She was beyond caring that her tone was openly pleading. In the past few months, Michael had been the one steady thing in her life.

"I won't leave you. Breathe."

A few minutes later, he slanted a quick look at the clock as another contraction took her. When it had eased, he lifted her gently.

"The contractions are about five minutes apart," he said in answer to her protesting moan. "I think we should get you to the hospital."

"Oh!" The exclamation made him freeze.

"What is it? Another contraction?"

"No. I think my water just broke." She looked up at him, her expression a mixture of fear and embarrassment. "I'm sorry. I've been so much trouble. Since the very beginning, I've done nothing but cause you trouble. I'm sorry." Tears welled up in her eyes and trickled down her pale cheeks. "I'm so sorry."

"Stop it. If you apologize again, I won't be responsible for my actions." There was a kind of gentle anger underlying the words.

Brittany gasped, gripping his arm, her nails digging into his skin. Michael coached her through it, casting a worried glance at the clock. The pains seemed to be getting closer together faster than they should be. When the contraction eased, she lay back, too exhausted to protest when he stripped her soaked nightgown over her head and moved to the dresser to get a dry one.

When she'd hesitantly asked if he wanted to be her labor coach, she hadn't really thought ahead to the intimacy that was going to result from the request. First there'd been the classes, where it had been assumed that they were a typical couple—how else would she have gotten in the condition she was in?

She'd gradually grown accustomed to the feel of his hands on her stomach as he followed the teacher's instructions. Only occasionally did she think of the kiss they'd shared in the kitchen, never to be repeated, never to be spoken of, never to be forgotten.

It was only now that she was realizing the extreme intimacy of the task she'd given him. He eased the fresh gown over her swollen body, making it seem the most natural thing in the world.

She lay back, drifting, hazily aware that Michael was calling her doctor, warning him that she was on her way. She roused when he brushed the hair back from her face, opening her eyes. Somehow, it wasn't possible to believe that anything could go wrong when she looked into the calm blue of his gaze.

"Come on, let's get you to the hospital." She held his arm as he lifted her gently to her feet, guiding her into her slippers and then through the living room to the front door. He dragged her coat out of the closet, directing her arms through the sleeves as if she were a child.

The next contraction hit before he could get her out the door. Michael held her, coaching her through it. He glanced at his bare wrist, wishing he'd thought to pick up his watch. He didn't know exactly how far apart the pains were, but he knew they were coming faster than he'd been told to expect. When the pain eased, he bent and scooped her into his arms, carrying her outside and down the steps.

The frosty ground crunched beneath his feet. Spring might be only a few weeks away, but winter was in no hurry to release it's chilly grip. Brittany looped her arms around his neck, totally confident that he held her safe and sound.

The Mustang started with a roar, and Michael cranked the heater on high, though looking at Brittany, he didn't think the chilly air was high on her list of discomforts. She looked so pale and so young. For an instant, he felt a blinding flash of rage that she was going through this. How could Dan have been so bloody irresponsible?

He wasn't sure what made him madder, the fact that Dan had gotten himself killed or the fact that he'd left Brittany alone and pregnant.

He backed the Mustang out of the driveway, shifting it into gear as gently as possible, as if afraid that the smallest jolt might cause her pain. Glancing at her, he felt a stab of fear. She was lying back in the low seat, her eyes closed. She was so small. What if this delivery didn't go smoothly?

The thought haunted him all the way to the hospital. Twice on the short drive he pulled off to the side of the road, coaching Brittany through contractions. The streets were empty. At 3:00 a.m., Remembrance slept.

The doctor arrived at the hospital only minutes after Michael carried Brittany in. His calm assumption that they'd have plenty of time before the baby arrived disappeared when he examined Brittany. Contrary to medical tradition, this was one first baby who was in a hurry to make an appearance.

Michael never left Brittany's side. With each contraction that wrenched at her, new lines etched themselves beside his mouth. He felt so helpless in the face of her pain. The breathing exercises seemed a frivolous contribution as the contractions became almost continuous.

For Brittany, Michael was the only reality in a world that had become alien and full of pain. She held his forearms, feeling the strength of the muscles there. Her eyes clung to his through a haze of pain, drawing on the strength she saw there as surely as she drew on the physical strength of his arms.

Sweat dripped from Michael's forehead as he struggled to maintain the calm facade that was all he could offer. In the final, wrenching moments, Brittany dug her nails into Michael's arms drawing blood. He welcomed the pain, wanting nothing more than to be able to draw her agony into himself.

"Push, Brittany." The doctor's voice was calm, coming to her through a fog.

"I can't," she gasped. But suddenly she had to push, as if a force outside her control demanded it. Her neck arched with the effort, Michael's soothing touch the only reality. There was a moment of tremendous pressure and then a sudden relief. She sagged, panting.

"You have a beautiful little girl."

Brittany blinked, trying to clear her vision. "Is she all right?" she got out raggedly.

"She's just fine." As if to punctuate the doctor's words, a thin cry pierced the air. The doctor turned to Michael. "Would you like to introduce your wife and daughter?"

Michael held out his arms automatically, unable to drag his gaze from the squirming red bundle the doctor was handing him.

"Let me see her." Brittany struggled up, unaware of the nurse who propped pillows behind her, giving her exhausted body support.

Michael bent, laying the tiny infant in her waiting arms. Brittany laughed tearfully as she tugged aside the soft blanket, carefully counting tiny fingers and toes.

"Look at her. She's perfect," Brittany's tone was soft in deference to the miracle she held.

Michael reached out to touch one of the little fists that waved aimlessly. His heart bumped as tiny fingers closed over his finger.

"She likes her daddy already." The nurse's comfortable comment brought Michael's eyes to Brittany's. Need lodged in his throat. Her eyes never left his as she answered the nurse.

"She does seem to know him, doesn't she?"

Michael's eyes fell to the infant she held. The baby still held his finger, but, in that instant, his heart dropped into her tiny fists.

Danielle Elizabeth Sinclair was his by right of ties much stronger than shared genes.

Brittany turned her head when she heard the door of her room open, smiling at her visitor.

"Beth."

"How are you feeling?" Beth crossed the room, setting a small arrangement of baby's breath and pink rosebuds on the table next to the bed before bending to kiss Brittany's cheek.

"I'm fine. Have you seen her?"

"I stopped by the nursery on the way up. She's beautiful."

"Thank you." Brittany leaned back against the pillows, filled with a mixture of elation and lingering exhaustion.

"Donovan will be up in a minute. I left him parking the car. I think Michael has plans to collar him in the lobby and take him to see Danielle before he gets up here."

Brittany laughed. "Michael thinks she's more of a miracle than I do, I believe. He was wonderful during the delivery. I don't know how I'd have gotten through it without him."

"He called us at five-thirty this morning to give us the news. He sounded almost drunk."

"It was quite an experience," Brittany said softly.

"I know." Beth's eyes dropped but not before Brittany caught the flare of heartache in them.

"Oh Beth, I'm sorry." She reached out to touch the other woman's arm. "We never talked about it, but Michael told me about—" She stopped, wondering if she was stepping over a boundary she wasn't welcome to cross.

"About me losing the baby?" Beth finished for her.

"Yes. I wondered... I mean, I hope it wasn't too painful for you, my being pregnant and now this."

"It wasn't painful for me. Or, at least, it wasn't very often. Besides..." She hesitated as if debating whether or not to continue. Her eyes lifted to Brittany's, and she finished in a rush. "I think, maybe, I'm pregnant again."

"Oh, Beth, congratulations."

"Well, it's too soon for congratulations. I haven't even mentioned it to Donovan. I don't want him to worry. I haven't had it confirmed yet, but I'm sure."

"Everything will be fine this time. I just know it will."

"I hope so."

The conversation lagged briefly, and then Beth shook her head, forcing a wide smile. "Why are we talking about me when you've just produced a small miracle? What a selfish idiot I am."

Brittany protested that she was nothing of the kind, but she was not adverse to changing the subject. Beth sat on the edge of the bed and listened to her talk, concern clouding her eyes. She wondered if Brittany realized how often Michael's name came up. Remembering his call this morning and the look of dazed pride in his eyes when she'd seen him at the nursery, she couldn't help but worry.

The two of them had gone into this marriage with such clear-cut plans. She didn't think either of them had given much thought to the way emotions could shift, making all their plans irrelevant. Whatever it was they felt for each other, she knew that Michael loved that baby as if it were his own. What would it do to him if Brittany was to take her and leave?

"Beth?" Brittany's questioning tone snapped her out of her thoughts.

"What? I'm sorry. I didn't mean to drift off on you."

"You looked so distant, as if you were a million miles away."

"Did I? I guess I am a little."

"Why?"

Beth smoothed a hand over her skirt, telling herself to keep out of it. It was really none of her business. Michael wouldn't welcome her interference. Still, she couldn't just stand by and see him get hurt without trying to do something to prevent it.

"Actually, I'm worried about Michael."

"About Michael?" Brittany's brow furrowed, her eyes darkening with apprehension. "He seemed fine when I saw him a little while ago. What's wrong?"

"Nothing," Beth assured her hastily, already doubting the wisdom of this conversation. Donovan would have told her to keep her nose out of it. "There's nothing wrong with him."

"Then why are you worried?" Brittany asked.

"Well . . ." Why had she started this? Michael would be furious. "It's just that Michael seems to feel very close ties with Danielle." She spoke slowly, trying to pick her words with care. "I'm concerned about what's going to happen when you . . . when you and he . . . I'm sorry. This is none of my business. God, I'm getting to be a busybody in my old age. Forget I said anything."

Brittany reached out, catching Beth's hand when she went to stand up. "Wait. Please. I don't think you're a busybody."

"Well, I'm sure you'd be alone in that opinion," Beth said ruefully. "Michael would disown me if he knew I'd said anything, and Donovan would think I was crazy to interfere. Really, forget I said anything at all."

"Beth, I don't mind. Really, I don't. I think—I hope that we've become friends over the past few months," she said shyly. "I know I think of you as a friend."

"And I think of you as a friend." Beth's handclasp was warm. "I just don't want to see Michael hurt, that's all."

"I understand." She looked down, plucking at the bed cover, her eyes on the aimless movement. "I hadn't thought about it much. In fact, I'm realizing that there were a lot of things I didn't think about," she added ruefully. "But when Danielle was born and the doctor handed her to Michael and he gave her to me..." She shook her head, lacking the words to describe the moment. "It felt...right, as if it couldn't have been any other way, as if he really was her father. I don't know, maybe it sounds silly."

"I think it sounds beautiful."

"It was an incredible moment. I wouldn't ever want him to feel any less of a father to her. If we go our separate ways, I would still consider—like for him to—I don't want her to grow up without a father, and I can't imagine anyone who'd make a better one."

"I think that's probably the nicest compliment you could give him," Beth said, and she wondered if Brittany was aware of what her words revealed. *If* they went their separate ways?

"There she is." Michael said it as if he were presenting something so miraculous that his audience was likely to be struck down. Donovan peered through the window of the nursery, studying the sleeping child. It was clear some comment was necessary.

"She's very...small."

"Seven pounds," Michael informed him proudly, as if her weight were a significant accomplishment.

"That's great. How is Brittany?"

"Fine. The doctor said it was an easy delivery. It didn't seem like it at the time, but I guess everything did go pretty fast."

Donovan slanted a glance at his son, noticing that he hadn't taken his eyes off the sleeping child. He felt a twinge of concern at the look of adoration on his face.

"I'm glad everything went smoothly."

"It was quite an experience." Michael's smile was reminiscent. "You know, you hear so much about the miracle of birth, but it isn't really real until you actually see it happen. When they put her in my hands—" He broke off, laughing self-consciously. "I probably sound like an idiot, like I'm the first father in the world."

Donovan winced. "It is an incredible experience." He stopped, wondering if he should say anything more. But someone had to say something. "Look, Michael, it's none of my business and I know this is probably a stupid thing to say, but don't get so caught up in this that you lose sight of reality."

Michael didn't take his eyes from the baby, but his mouth tightened. "You mean the fact that she's not my child?"

Seeing the pleasure fade from Michael's face, Donovan half regretted saying anything, but it had to be said. "When you went into this marriage, it was only supposed to be temporary," he reminded. "Just until Brittany had the baby and got back on her feet. Well, she's had the baby. How are you going to feel if she takes that child and leaves?"

Michael's hand, resting on the ledge in front of the window, clenched, giving Donovan the answer even before he spoke.

"When they put her into my arms this morning, it was an experience I can't describe. It was like she filled something in me, an empty place I hadn't even known existed. I know that Dan was her father, but I was the one who was there. I was the one who felt her move for the first time and I was the first one to hold her, even before Brittany."

He shook his head, finally turning to meet his father's eyes. "She's not mine by blood, but she's mine by every other right."

"Does Brittany feel the same way?" Donovan asked quietly.

"I think so."

Donovan shook his head, looking back at the baby. "I hope you're right."

The first few weeks after Danielle's birth, Michael and Brittany were so busy concentrating on the baby that it was easy to ignore the changes occurring in their relationship. Neither mentioned the plans they'd made when they'd agreed to marry.

When Michael thought about it, he told himself that the idea had been to wait until Brittany had a chance to get on her feet again, which she certainly couldn't do while caring for a newborn. It would take time to find a job, a place to live and someone to care for Danielle while she worked.

The thought held little appeal. He didn't like the idea of someone else raising Danielle. She deserved to have her mother with her full-time. Besides, he was coming to realize just how empty the house was going to seem without the baby—without Brittany.

It was a thought he wasn't sure he wanted to examine. But he knew he didn't want to lose either of them.

Brittany smoothed her hands over her stomach, turning sideways in the mirror to check her silhouette. Not quite what it had been before she got pregnant, but not bad. It was important that she look good tonight. Michael was attending this dinner as a representative of his father's company.

The bright blue silk dress had been a present from Beth, who'd given it to her to celebrate getting her figure back.

They'd grown closer these past few weeks since the baby's birth. Beth's pregnancy had been confirmed and, as she laughingly complained, Donovan had practically chained her to the house.

It seemed odd to think that, when Beth's baby was born, Danielle would have an uncle or aunt who was a year younger than she was. An uncle or an aunt. Brittany's hands shook as she smoothed the dress again, no longer seeing her reflection.

It was so easy to think of Michael as Danielle's real father. He *was* her real father in every sense but blood. He changed diapers and mixed formula as easily as she did. And Danielle responded to the sound of his voice as readily as she did to her mother's.

Sometimes it frightened her that she so rarely thought of Dan. She'd thought that the birth of the baby might bring him closer, make his memory more vivid. But it hadn't. When she looked at Danielle, she didn't think of Dan.

Was it possible that she hadn't loved him as much as she'd thought she did? Or was she just so incredibly shallow that she could let the memories go so quickly?

She reached up to touch the heart-shaped pendant Dan had given her. It seemed like decades ago now. She'd been so much younger then, so naive. So sure that life was going to work out exactly as she wanted it to.

Nothing had worked out as she'd planned. Dan had died, her parents had proved more interested in the opinions of others than they were in their daughter's welfare. She'd married a man she barely knew in order to provide a life for a child who had become the center of her life.

No, it wasn't exactly what she'd planned. But thinking about it, she realized that the only thing she regretted was Dan's death. He'd been much too young, too alive to die.

But her marriage, her daughter, even the break with her parents—those things she couldn't be sorry for. She had a ealthy, beautiful child, a home. In Beth and Donovan, he'd found something of the family she'd never really had. And she had Michael.

Her fingers tightened over the pendant for a moment before dropping away.

Michael. There was the big question in her life. He was her friend, her husband in name, the person she knew she could count on. But what else?

Since Danielle's birth, they'd avoided discussing the future. But sooner or later, the future had to be faced. Their bargain had been until after the baby was born and Brittany was on her feet again. Danielle was almost two months old, and there'd been no mention of leaving.

Brittany reached for her earrings, slipping them into place with fingers that weren't quite steady. The future had to be dealt with soon, but not tonight. Tonight she was going to enjoy herself, enjoy a night out. Enjoy being Michael's wife.

Chapter 9

"And so, in conclusion, I'd like to say..."

Michael shifted restlessly in his seat. This was at least th
third time old Harry Labell had said "in conclusion," an
yet, he'd shown no signs of concluding his speech. Glan
ing sideways at Brittany, he saw her straighten her shou
ders and open her eyes wide as if trying to stay awake. Sh
looked as bored as he felt.

Half the room was dozing, and the other half looked a
though they wished they were, too. The dinner had bee
even worse than the usual run of business dinners. The foo
had been served late and cold, but he didn't think it woul
have helped if it had been on time and hot. It might hav
been edible in a former life, but that life had probably bee
three or four days ago.

He'd pushed the mystery meat that had been smothere
in secret sauce around his plate, while Brittany had take
two or three polite bites and then tried to look as if she we

ust too full to finish. An hour and three speeches later, his tomach was beginning to wonder if his throat had been cut.

On an impulse, he leaned forward and spoke in Brittany's ear.

"Are you hungry?"

"Starved," she whispered back. "But I think there're two nore awards to be given."

"Are you getting one of them?"

She cast him a startled look. "Of course not. I'm not an rchitect."

"Well, I am and I'm not getting one, either. Let's get out of here."

"We can't. I thought this was important."

"We've made an appearance. I think that's enough. Come on, the door is just behind us. We can slip out discreetly and go get a hamburger somewhere."

"Do you think we should?"

"If we don't get out of here soon, I'm going to create a cene by eating the centerpiece," he promised her.

Brittany put a hand over her mouth to stifle the giggle that hreatened to escape. "I think it's plastic."

"I don't care. It looks better than the meal did. Let's go."

He pushed back his chair, reaching for the shawl she'd draped over the back of hers. Brittany stood up, aware of eyes turning in their direction. Was it her imagination or was here real envy in some of the glances they were receiving? She followed Michael to the door, walking on tiptoes to avoid the click of heels on the hard floor.

"I'd just like to add..."

The door shut before they could hear what it was Harry planned on adding.

"They should erect a statue to that man," Michael said, "and they can put him in it."

Brittany laughed. "He is a little dull, isn't he?"

"Duller that dishwater. He's even worse face-to-face. Michael gave an exaggerated shudder. "If Dad had told m that Harry was going to be speaking, I'd have flat refuse to cover for him at this thing. No wonder he stayed hom It has nothing to do with making sure Mom doesn't strai herself. He just didn't want her bored to death. And po soned," he added with feeling.

"The food wasn't that bad."

"It was worse," he insisted. "It'll be a wonder if the aren't cases of ptomaine reported all over the state tomo row."

"So, where are we going to get some real food?"

"I don't know." He peered through the doors of the Civi Center. "It's raining a little. Why don't you wait here whil I bring the car around? Maybe by then one of us will thin of something."

When the Mustang pulled up in front of the doors, Bri tany hurried out and slid onto the seat.

"How about Joe's?" Michael asked the minute the doc was shut.

"Joe's?"

"You know, that place that opened about six months ag on the west side of town. It's supposed to be an authenti recreation of a fifties diner. One of the secretaries at the o fice said they serve great food."

"Aren't we a little overdressed for that?" She looke from his dinner jacket to her silk skirt, but Micha shrugged.

"So, let's slum it a little. Right now, an enormous ham burger with a side order of chili fries sounds incredible."

Brittany's stomach chose that moment to growl. Sh pressed a hand to it, giving Michael an embarrassed smil "I guess that's your answer."

Neither of them was old enough to say for certain whethe Joe's was authentic. But there was no denying the appeal c the red vinyl booths, black-and-white tile floor and waitresses dressed in poodle skirts and ankle socks.

The jukebox was just a shade too loud, blasting out Elvis and Buddy Holly, but it only added to the atmosphere. Since they'd lingered at the Civic Center until after the normal dinner hour, they got a table right away, though from what Michael had been told, there was frequently a wait to get a booth.

Sliding onto the vinyl seat across from Michael, Brittany suddenly felt young and carefree in a way she hadn't felt in a long time. Chuck Berry was complaining about Nadine, the waitress looked like something out of *American Graffiti*, and the food smelled wonderful.

Michael ordered for them. Since Danielle's birth, Brittany had been watching her diet religiously, but she didn't protest when he asked for hamburgers, chili fries and Joe's special onion rings, as well as a milk shake for each of them. Tonight, she wasn't going to bother about things like calories.

Danielle was safely tucked away at Donovan and Beth's. Brittany was out on the town for the first time in months. She felt foolishly happy.

She waited until the waitress was gone before leaning across the Formica-topped table toward Michael. "Do you realize that this is the first time we've been out together on something remotely resembling a date?"

Michael stared at her, a slow smile lighting his eyes. "So it is. And both of us married, too. How very decadent of us."

"You won't tell my husband, will you?" Brittany widened her eyes at him, and his smile deepened.

"Does he have a very bad temper?"

"Just awful. He got extremely upset because I didn't cook the roast long enough one night."

"What a beast," he commiserated. "I won't tell him i you promise not to tell my wife."

"Is she a shrew?"

"Terrible." He nodded solemnly. "I quiver in my boot every night when it comes time to go home."

"Well, I certainly won't tell her."

Their milk shakes arrived just then, and Brittany picke hers up, lifting it to bump against Michael's in a toast.

"To guilty secrets," she said.

"To Harry Labell," Michael offered. "If he hadn't bee so boring, we might still be at that dinner."

The food was as good as it smelled, and they devoure every scrap of it, though afterward, Brittany swore sh couldn't possibly move, she was so full. The meal finished they were both reluctant to see the evening end. It had bee a pleasant interval, like taking a break from reality.

They lingered over the rapidly melting milk shakes as i they were glasses of fine wine, talking of everything an nothing in particular. It was almost eleven o'clock whe Michael looked at his watch and reluctantly suggested tha they should go pick up Danielle before his folks sent out search party.

The rain was falling harder now, and the quiet whoosh o the windshield wipers was the only sound breaking the si lence in the car. Odd, how they'd had so much to say only few minutes ago, and now they were suddenly out of words

Brittany was vividly aware of Michael's hand on th gearshift, so close to her leg. If he moved it just a few inche to the right... She cut the thought off, drawing her wra closer around her shoulders.

"Are you cold?" Noticing the movement, Micha reached to turn up the heater.

"Thank you." She could have explained that it wasn't th temperature that had made her feel the need to draw som protection around her. Her eyes were drawn to his hands o he wheel. She'd always loved his hands. They were so trong. An artist's hands but with the strength of a builder.

What would they feel like on her skin? She flushed at her ausings. What had gotten into her tonight? Why was she uddenly thinking things like this? Or was it really all that udden? Hadn't she been aware of Michael for a long time ow?

Well, yes, but there was aware and then there was *aware*. t was one thing to notice that he was attractive, to notice hat his eyes were the same blue as a summer sky, to be ware that his hair had just the faintest touch of red woven nto its darkness. It was something else altogether to start vondering what his hands would feel like on her skin, how is hair would feel threading through her fingers, what he ooked like naked.

"Brittany?" Startled, she realized that the car was topped. In front of them, a train made its leisurely way cross the road.

"I'm sorry. Did you say something?" She had to clear her hroat to get the words out, and her voice still held a husky ote.

"Nothing important. You looked like you were a million niles away."

"Did I?"

"Yeah." But his tone was absent and, stealing a look at im, she saw that his eyes held an odd expression.

"Do I have smut on my nose or something?" she asked ervously.

"No." But he didn't look away.

"Then why are you looking at me like that?"

"I was just thinking how beautiful you are." Her eyes napped to his, her breath catching in her chest. It was hard o see his expression in the shadowy darkness of the car, but he didn't need light to read what was in his eyes.

She didn't move, didn't blink when his hand lifted. H fingertips caressed her cheek. She couldn't take her ey from his, couldn't breathe, couldn't think.

Her lashes drifted shut as he leaned toward her. At th first touch of his mouth on hers, she felt a deep upwellin of feeling. He'd kissed her before, but it hadn't been lik this. The last time, she'd been confused, uncertain, tor between guilt and desire. Not even sure what it was she wa feeling.

This time, she knew exactly what she was feeling. Desir plain and simple.

Michael's fingers lingered against her cheek, and Bri tany's hand came up to grasp his wrist as his tongue trace the line of her lips, coaxing her to open her mouth for hin Her lips parted, her fingers tightening around his wrist as h tongue explored the soft invitation of her.

He tasted of hunger. There was a promise of somethin warm and exciting in the feel of his mouth, the feel of h hand on her cheek. Passion.

She moaned softly, her head tilting back in a surrender a old as time. Michael's mouth hardened over hers, deepen ing the kiss, letting her taste his desire.

Brittany forgot where they were, forgot the tangled his tory that lay between them, forgot everything but the feel o Michael's kiss.

The raucous blast of a horn behind them shattered th fragile web of the moment. Still, it wasn't possible to brea away too quickly. Brittany opened her eyes, feeling as if he lashes were much too heavy. Michael's eyes were locked o hers, their expression unreadable. For a moment, she felt a if he were about to say something.

The horn sounded impatiently behind them, and Mi chael turned away, reaching for the gearshift. The train wa gone, the barriers lifted. Brittany shifted in her seat, star ing through the windshield at the rainy night as the ca bumped over the tracks. Except for the slap-slap of the wipers and the low growl of the engine, there wasn't a sound in the car.

Surely one of them should say something. Hadn't everything just changed? They'd just tossed all the rules out the window. This wasn't like the other kisses. This time, there was no baby to remind them of their reasons for marrying. This time, if there'd been no interruption, if they'd been at home instead of where they were, she wasn't sure it would have stopped with a kiss.

Brittany shivered. She'd wanted Michael. If they'd been somewhere private, if Michael had taken it a step further, would she have gone along? Would she have slept with him, made love with him? She closed her eyes on the realization that the answer was yes.

She didn't love him, at least not the way she'd loved Dan, but she would have made love with him. Her skin tingled at the thought of him touching her intimately, holding her, making love to her. She flushed, her eyes snapping open. Sleeping with Dan had gone against everything she'd been taught, but she'd loved him.

How could she feel this way about Michael when she'd buried her heart with Dan? How could she forget him so easily? Seeking comfort, she reached up to grasp the pendant Dan had given her.

Michael glanced at her, noticing the gesture, and his hands tightened on the wheel until the knuckles showed white, his jaw hardening. He had to restrain the urge to reach over and rip that damned necklace off her throat. He was coming to hate everything it represented.

Dan was your best friend.

But he was dead. He was dead and nothing in the world could change that. Brittany was *his* wife, not Dan's.

In name only.

The reminder didn't improve his mood. Tonight, that could have changed. If circumstances had been different...

If wishes were horses, beggars would ride. What makes you think she'd have you?

She'd wanted him. He hadn't dreamed the way her mouth had softened under his. She'd practically melted. And she hadn't been thinking about Dan then. For those few minutes, she'd been all his.

He wanted her that way again. Wanted it so badly it was an ache in his gut. He should have been appalled at the jealousy he felt toward Dan, his best friend—his *dead* friend.

Not another word was spoken between them as they picked the baby up and drove home. They exchanged polite good-nights in the living room, then retired to their separate bedrooms.

Michael watched Brittany disappear into her room, Danielle in her arms. Restless, he poured himself a short Scotch. He no longer had any doubts about what he wanted. He wanted Brittany. He wanted her and the baby as a permanent part of his life.

He stared into the empty fireplace, his expression brooding. All he had to do now was convince Brittany that she wanted the same thing.

Summer arrived in a blast of heat. Spring was rushed aside to allow sweltering sunshine to bake the Indiana cornfields. Farmers watched the endless blue skies and muttered of drought. Public swimming pools were jammed with people seeking a momentary respite from the heat.

Michael and Brittany skimmed over the surface of their lives, avoiding any conflict, any discussion of the future. Those few moments of shared passion had thrown a new element into their relationship.

Brittany kept telling herself that the time had come for her to start looking for a job, looking for day care for Danielle. She should be pulling her life together so that she could leave Michael to get on with the life he'd put on hold to help her.

But each day she put it off. It was too hot to drag the baby around looking at apartments and jobs. As soon as the weather broke, then she'd really knuckle down.

But the weather didn't break. It ground on, shortening tempers as it baked the cornfields. Brittany would have liked to blame her own irritability on the weather, but honesty demanded that she admit, at least to herself, that the heat had nothing to do with it.

Danielle was unusually fussy, protesting the extreme temperatures in the only way she could, but that wasn't what had her mother's temper on edge. Brittany didn't have to look far for the cause of her moodiness. It could be summed up in one word.

Michael.

He was so...there. He wasn't home any more than he had been. It was just that when he was home, he seemed to take on more of a presence, somehow.

She stirred restlessly against the sheets. Danielle slept peacefully in her crib, carefully placed to catch just the edge of the breeze from the window air conditioner Michael had installed last week when he'd realized how miserable the heat was making the infant.

The cool air was enough to soothe Danielle, but her mother needed something more. A rumble of thunder sounded in the distance, and Brittany swung her legs out of bed. A look at the clock told her that it was after midnight. Danielle would be awake by six. She should go to sleep. But sleep didn't seem likely.

She moved to stand in the middle of the room, directly in the flow of air from the air conditioner. It felt wonderful and she opened her arms wide as if embracing the breeze. It stirred her nightie, molding it to her figure like a lover's touch. Her nipples puckered in response, and she closed her eyes, letting her thoughts drift.

What if Michael was to open the door and see her standing here? Would he want her? Would his eyes darken to that stormy blue? Would he want to touch her breasts, kiss them?

She groaned, her eyes flying open. Ever since the night he'd kissed her in the car, her thoughts had shown a tendency to drift in this vein. It was as if he'd lighted a fire inside her that wouldn't go out.

It wasn't right to want a man like this. It was one thing to love a man, and a natural outgrowth of that love was physical desire. But she didn't love Michael. She cared about him, cared a great deal. And maybe in a way she loved him. But she didn't *love* him. Not the way she'd loved Dan. She had loved Dan. Hadn't she?

Shocked that she could even ask that question, she turned, catching a glimpse of herself in the mirror. A ghostly figure in white, with no more substance than a spirit. That was how she felt, as if she'd been drifting through her life, letting events push her here and there, never really taking control.

She turned away from the reflection, suddenly feeling as if she were suffocating. The room was too small. She fled, aware that she was running away from her own thoughts more than anything else.

Despite the hour, the heat lingered in the rest of the house. Michael had left the windows open, and a breeze drifted through, giving at least the illusion of cooler temperatures. Was it her imagination, or was there a hint of dampness in that breeze? Thunder rumbled again as she moved to a window, looking out over the broad sweep of flat land behind the house. Far off, into the distance, she could see a flash that might have been lightning, but it was impossible to be sure.

Lifting her hair with her hands, she closed her eyes, turning her face to the breeze. Restlessness gnawed at her. She wanted. She couldn't define what it was, but there was an aching hunger inside that had to be assuaged.

"Looks like we might get some rain."

The quiet comment made her spin around, and she put a hand against the window frame to catch her balance. Michael stood there, his face in shadow. Brittany's eyes caught the muscles of his bare chest, the dark hair that dusted across it before narrowing into a fine line that ran over his taut stomach and disappeared into the waistband of his unsnapped jeans.

Sheer force of will dragged her eyes upward to his face. Michael lifted the glass he held, ice tinkling as he sipped the Scotch.

"What do you think?"

"'Think'?" Her voice came out too high, and she cleared her throat, trying again in a more normal tone. "Think about what?"

"Do you think we're going to get some rain?" He took a step closer to look out the window, and Brittany closed her eyes for an instant, feeling almost dizzy. He was so close. Too close. Not close enough.

"I...don't know. Maybe. This heat wave has got to break sooner or later."

"So the weather bureau keeps saying." He let his eyes settle on her again, but his expression was hooded, impossible to read. "Is your room cool enough?"

"Yes. Danielle is sleeping like a baby." She giggled, putting her hand to her throat. "I suppose she would have to sleep like a baby, wouldn't she?"

She was babbling like an idiot. Why was she so nervous all of a sudden? This was Michael. Steady, dependable Michael. So he'd kissed her once or twice; so she'd sometimes caught him watching her with an expression she didn't understand. That was no reason to be nervous.

"I'm surprised you aren't in there, where it's comfortable," he commented, lifting the glass again.

"I couldn't sleep." She shrugged, trying not to notice the width of his chest. "I felt restless."

"So did I."

"Really? Well, this heat is enough to make anybody restless." She cleared her throat, aware that he hadn't taken his eyes off her face. "I guess I ought to get back to bed."

"Are you hot, Brittany?"

Had he moved closer or did it just seem that way? And why did that question seem to have a double meaning?

"I . . . it is rather warm in here, isn't it?"

"You look cool in that nightgown," he told her.

"Do I? Well, I guess it's about as cool as you can get. Except maybe being naked."

She bit her tongue, wishing she could take the last word back. Now was not the time to be mentioning things like being naked. Not even when all she could think about was what it might feel like to be naked with Michael.

Thunder rumbled again, sounding closer this time. She should move, should go back to her room and shut the door, lock out the madness she could feel stirring inside. She'd be safe there, safe from what she was feeling, what she wanted to feel.

She gasped when Michael reached out, gently pressing the icy glass just above the scooped neckline of her nightie, the shock against her skin creating a white-hot sensation.

"I could help you cool off," he whispered, his voice husky.

"I don't think cooling off is what would happen—" She broke off, biting her lip against a moan as he let the glass slide lower until it pressed against her nipple through the fine batiste.

"Do you want to cool off?" He moved the glass back and forth in tiny stroking movements, dampening the fabric with the condensation on the glass.

Brittany reached behind her, her fingers clenching over the windowsill. This wasn't what she'd planned.

Wasn't it? Then why did you come out here half-dressed?

"Do you really want to cool off?" He moved closer, subtly trapping her. The glass moved to the other nipple, and this time she couldn't bite back the tiny moan. "You don't sound like you're ready to cool off," he murmured. "You sound hot. As hot as I feel."

Her back to the window, she couldn't move when he stepped closer, his free hand settling on her hip, drawing her forward until their thighs were touching. She could feel him through the fabric of his jeans, pressing against her.

"Tell me what you want, Brittany."

Odd, how the cold glass could start a fire in the pit of her stomach.

"Tell me." He pressed closer, letting her feel how much he wanted her.

A breeze swirled through the window, catching the fabric of her nightie and blowing it forward so that it wrapped around Michael's hips, binding them together.

"Please." The one word was all she could get out. It was enough. The heavy glass thudded to the floor. One hand flattened against her back, jerking her forward until she lay on the warm skin of his chest. The other wrapped itself in her hair, anchoring her for his kiss.

At the first touch of his body, Brittany felt as if something had broken loose inside. Months of pent-up passion were in that kiss. How long had she wanted him? Since that kiss in the car? Since the wedding? Since the first moment she'd met him? How could she not want him?

Her hands were shaking as she ran them over his chest, feeling the hard muscles there. His tongue thrust deep, engaging hers in erotic love play. His hand slid down her back to her thighs, finding the hem of her nightie and inching it upward. Cupping her buttock, he drew her up so that she could feel his aching need against the very heart of her.

She moaned, her head falling back, hair streaming down her spine. Michael began to explore the length of her throat, leaving soft, moist kisses at every interval. She shared his frustration when the neckline of her gown blocked his path. His hand left her hair, and she laughed shakily at the sharp sound of ripping cotton.

He cupped her breast, the callused surface of his palm abrading the delicate skin. She sighed, her fingers coming up to lock in his hair when his mouth closed over her at last. The feel of his tongue and teeth on her nipple was something she'd dreamed of. Dark, secret dreams she hadn't admitted to—not even to herself.

She felt the tugging at her breast and felt it deep inside, a visceral drawing that she wouldn't—couldn't—deny. She drew him closer, arching her back to offer herself to him.

Outside, lightning flashed, unmistakable now as the storm swept across the prairies. The boom of thunder was barely heard over the pounding of two hearts, the soft moans of pleasure.

Michael moved his attentions to her other breast. Brittany lowered her hands, suddenly impatient with the remaining barriers between them. The zipper of his jeans rasped in the still air, and then her hand slid inside, cupping him. He shuddered and she felt a surge of purely feminine power that this man trembled at her touch.

He dragged away from her breast, catching her mouth with his. His hand moved between her thighs, finding her damp invitation. Brittany trembled, her moan lost in his mouth. If she hadn't been pinned between Michael's broad frame and the window, she would surely have sunk to the floor, her knees unable to support her.

Michael pulled his mouth from hers, his chest heaving with the effort he was making. "I don't think I can wait. I want you so much."

"I don't want to wait. I want you now." Later, she'd wonder if that wanton invitation could really have come from her.

Michael groaned, reaching to rid himself of his jeans and stripping the ruined nightie from her willing body before he lowered them both to the floor. The carpet was soft against her back, but she wouldn't have noticed if it had been rock-covered ground. All that mattered was the man poised above her.

Lightning flashed, illuminating him in silhouette as he nudged her knees apart, settling against her. Thunder cracked, drowning her cry of pleasure as he thrust deep.

It was everything she'd ever fantasized and more. He filled her, surrounded her, made her whole. Nothing had ever felt like this; nothing could ever feel like this again.

There was a rush of sound as the storm reached them. The clouds opened, pouring rain onto the thirsty earth. Moisture blew through the open window, dampening the taught muscles of Michael's back. Brittany's fingers slipped on his tanned skin, as she sought something to cling to in a world that spun crazily around her.

The emptiness was filled. Not just the physical emptiness, but a deeper, aching hollow she refused to acknowledge. It was as if a part of her had been missing and was now found in Michael's arms.

Thunder cracked, the sound so close it rocked the house. But the storm outside paled in comparison to the storm that was raging inside. Every movement, every touch sent the tension inside her spiraling higher until Brittany thought she would surely explode. But it was the world around her that dissolved into a million pieces, leaving her floating on a sea of pleasure so intense, she could hardly breathe.

Michael's mouth caught her cry of fulfillment, his body arching heavily against hers as he followed her into the wildly spinning glory.

It was a long time before Brittany returned to earth. The thunder and lightning had moved on, leaving the rain behind. She was aware of the cool dampness that blew in through the window, vaguely aware that the carpet was probably getting ruined. But the only important thing was Michael's solid weight over her. She murmured a protest when he lifted himself.

"I'm not going anywhere," he told her, his voice husky. She caught the gleam of his teeth as he flashed a smile. "How dumb do you think I am?"

He sank down beside her, stroking his hand along her side. She stretched, feeling like a particularly well-fed cat. Michael's palm covered her breast, surprising a whimper of pleasure from her. Her eyes flashed wide as his fingers caught a tender nipple, tugging it gently. She'd never have believed that passion could be roused so quickly after what they'd just shared. But his touch brought a familiar tightness to her lower stomach.

His knee wedged between her thighs as his head bent, his teeth catching one taut bud.

"You aren't tired, are you?"

"No," she managed breathlessly, feeling every nerve come to quivering life. "I'm not tired."

"Good. Because neither am I."

He twisted, drawing her over him, and Brittany gave herself up to the pleasure he sent pulsing through her.

Chapter 10

It was still dark when Michael woke, though the darkness was faintly gray around the edges, as if to show that dawn wasn't far away. The rain that had started with a bang now fell gently on the parched fields. Somewhere in the distance, he could hear the muffled rumble of thunder.

Brittany slept beside him, her body curled confidingly close. Her hair spilled across his chest like a silky black web. Even though the scent of their lovemaking lingered in the air, he tried desperately to ignore his body's response to the musky smell.

He eased his arm out from under her head. She stirred but didn't wake, cuddling up to the pillow in a way that made him want to kiss her awake. But he needed to think.

He picked up his jeans on the way out of the room, thrusting his legs into them in the hallway. He eased open Brittany's door and padded quietly over to the crib. Danielle was awake, and she stared up at him solemnly, as if asking why it had taken him so long to get here.

"Hello, sweetie. Have you been awake long? You were certainly very good to keep quiet. Mommy's still asleep, so you'll just have to muddle through with Daddy for now."

He kept up the silly patter as he changed her diaper, then he carried her into the kitchen. He held her on one hip while he got a bottle out of the refrigerator and set it to warm in the microwave. Carrying her into the living room, he settled her in a corner of the sofa with the bottle propped on a pillow while he shut the window. His toes squished in the carpet underneath, but he had other things to think about besides the possibility of a ruined carpet.

Sitting on the sofa, he lifted Danielle into his arms, holding the bottle. She watched him with wide eyes as she nursed, eyes that were changing from baby blue to a more distinct blue. Her hair was darkening, too, showing promise of being the same rich black as her mother's someday.

"You know, life's easy for you now. Enjoy it while you can, angel. It certainly does get complicated when you grow up."

He leaned his head back against the sofa, staring up at the ceiling. Outside, the rain fell steadily. The back of the heat wave had been broken, and the air felt pleasantly cool.

Everything had seemed so simple last night. When he'd seen Brittany in that sweetly sexy gown, felt the restlessness in her—a restlessness he more than understood… He shook his head, looking back down at the baby he held.

Dan's child.

That was harder and harder to remember. From the moment of her birth, she'd been his. Just as he'd come to look on Brittany as his. His wife.

Somewhere along the way, like some great cosmic joke, he'd ended up living the life Dan should have had. His wife, his baby. It all should have been Dan's. And what did that make him? Instead, he'd stolen that life and made it his own.

"Michael?" He lifted his head at Brittany's soft call. She stepped into the swath of light that spilled from the kitchen. Despite his confused state of mind, his body tightened in familiar reaction. She'd pulled on one of his shirts, and the blue cambric draped her figure in a way that revealed nothing but hinted at everything. Her hair lay in a thick black cloud on her shoulders, tousled with sleep and loving.

His hand tightened around the bottle he still held, though Danielle had long since drained it and was drifting off to sleep. How was it possible for one woman to be every fantasy he'd ever had?

"Did Danielle cry?" Brittany moved closer, a slight frown creasing her forehead, disturbed by the thought that the baby might have cried and she hadn't heard her.

"No. I went in to check on her and she was awake, so I changed her and fed her. Looks like she's just about asleep again."

"Why don't I put her to bed," Brittany suggested.

"Sure." Michael stood up, letting her take the drowsy infant from his arms. This close, he could smell the warm, womanly scent of her, and his jaw tightened against the urge to take her in his arms, bury his face in her hair.

Her eyes met his and he read the uncertainty she was feeling. His hand half lifted and then dropped. If he touched her, he was going to take her back to bed. She looked away.

"I'll make a pot of coffee," he said, stalling for time. There was no need to discuss the fact that they had to talk. The events of the night before had rearranged all their neat plans, changed everything.

When Brittany came into the kitchen, she'd changed into a pair of jeans and a loose top, and she'd brushed her hair. But there was still a touch of color in her cheeks, a certain look in her eyes that spoke of a woman who'd been thoroughly loved. Despite his own doubts about where they went from here, Michael took a purely masculine satisfaction in that look.

"Here. I thought you might want to put this on." Brittany's eyes settled on his bare chest and then skittered away as she held out the shirt she'd been wearing earlier.

Michael half smiled as he took the shirt from her. It was obvious that she found his naked chest a distraction. The knowledge was not unpleasant. He shrugged into the shirt, buttoning it halfway before he turned and lifted a pair of coffee cups from the counter.

"The dining room?" he questioned.

"Sounds fine."

Neither of them said a word as he carried the cups into the dining room and set them on the table. The rain fell in a gentle gray curtain outside the window, muffling the dawn that struggled to sneak through the clouds.

Brittany sat down and picked up her cup, sipping at the steaming black liquid. Not that she particularly wanted coffee, but she did want something to do with her hands. Michael sat across the table from her. If she lifted her eyes from her cup, she could see a wedge of tanned flesh between the edges of his shirt.

Since their marriage, she'd seen Michael without a shirt dozens of times but never before when she had quite such an intimate knowledge of exactly what those muscles felt like beneath her fingers.

She still wasn't sure what had happened last night. The heat, the storm, Michael. Everything sort of blended together in her mind.

"We sort of skipped a few steps," Michael offered when the silence threatened to stretch too long.

"I guess we did." She knew what he meant. There should have been stages that came before last night's explosion of passion. Somehow, they'd jumped over all the hand holding and kissing and working up to sleeping together.

He twisted the coffee cup between his hands, staring down at the aimless movement.

"Look, Brittany, I feel like I should—"

"If you're going to apologize, I'm going to dump this coffee in your lap." The guilty way his eyes swept to hers told her that that was exactly what he'd been about to do. "Michael, I wasn't a victim last night."

"I didn't think you were," he protested.

"Didn't you? Then why do I have the impression that you were about to apologize?"

"I just felt that—maybe—you might have felt that you... Well, that you owed me something."

"I do owe you. I owe you a lot more than I can ever repay, but I didn't sleep with you because I owe you."

"I don't think the sleeping part of it is the problem," he murmured drily.

Brittany felt her cheeks warm. "No, I guess it isn't."

"This changes things," he said after a long pause.

"Weren't things changing before this?"

"Yes. But this changes them with a vengeance."

"In what way?"

"I can't go back to the way things have been. After last night, making love with you, I can't pretend that we're just friends who happen to be sharing a house and a marriage license. I want you too much to even try," he said bluntly.

This time the flush started at her throat and worked its way over her face. She felt a foolish flutter in her chest. It wasn't as if his words were news. Heaven knows, he'd proved how much he wanted her last night. It was just that having it laid out as he'd done was startling.

"Okay," she managed at last, trying to sound calm and collected. "I'd agree with that. There's obviously an... attraction between us."

Michael's mouth twisted as if in silent commentary at the careful way she stated things. "I think that's pretty obvious."

There was another long silence while Brittany stared at the table. The rain continued to fall, but the sun had accomplished a partial victory, and it was at least light outside.

"So, where do we go from here?" she asked when she couldn't stand the silence another second.

"Where do you want to go from here?"

"I asked you first." She gave him a quick, nervous smile that held more panic than amusement.

"Fair enough." He nodded. "It seems to me that we only have a couple of choices. Either we stay together and make this a real marriage—" He stopped, as if weighing his next words.

"Or..." Brittany prompted at last.

"Or we break the whole thing off right now."

He said it quietly, but it still struck a blow. What he meant was that she would take Danielle and move out, just as they'd planned from the beginning. Only nothing was the way it had been in the beginning. She'd come to think of this house as her home, of Donovan and Beth as part of her family, of Michael as Danielle's father. As her husband.

She looked away quickly before he could see the impact of his words. "Is that what you want? To break it off? That's what we planned, isn't it?"

"It's what we planned," he agreed slowly.

"Is it what you want?"

The seconds ticked by as she waited for his answer. If he said yes, her whole life was going to come tumbling down around her ears. And if he said no? If he said no, then she was committing herself to something she wasn't sure she was ready for.

"No, it isn't what I want."

The simple answer set off turmoil in the pit of her stomach. She wanted to take the question back, pretend last night had never happened. She wasn't ready to make this decision, to make a commitment like this.

"What do you think?"

She opened her mouth, but no sound came out. She was at a loss for words to try to express her thoughts. She didn't even know what she was thinking, what she was feeling. How could she possibly give him an answer?

"Is it that difficult to answer?" The question brought her eyes to his face. He was looking at her, one brow raised slightly quizzically. The lightness of his tone eased some of her tension. He made everything seem a little less earth-shattering, a little less frightening.

"Yes. I mean, no." She raised her hands. "I don't know."

"That's what I've always appreciated in you—your absolute decisiveness. Your ability to make snap decisions without a moment's hesitation."

Brittany shook her head, laughing softly at his blatant teasing, but the fingers she wrapped around her coffee cup were shaky.

"I know I sound like an idiot, but I wasn't really prepared for this. I mean, until last night, everything was so simple."

"Not really." Michael leaned back in his chair. "We couldn't have gone on like that forever. I think you knew it as well as I. Something had to give, sooner or later."

"I suppose," she said.

"Look, I'm not going to pressure you. This decision is important to our future—yours, mine and Danielle's. But I'd just like to point out that we've muddled along pretty well together so far. In a couple of months, we'll have been married a year. I don't think we've done too badly."

"No, we haven't."

"Would it be so difficult to start thinking of this as a permanent arrangement?"

If she was honest, she'd admit that it wouldn't be difficult at all. Hadn't that been in her mind for the past few weeks? Why was she so nervous? They'd already built a life together.

"No." The word came out a whisper, and she cleared her throat. "No, it wouldn't be hard to start thinking of this as a permanent arrangement." She lifted her eyes to his face and brought the next words out in a rush. "Michael, are you sure you're doing this because you want to? You're not doing it because you think I can't take care of myself? Or because you don't want to lose Danielle?

"Because you've got to know that, no matter what happens between the two of us, I would never try to keep you away from her. You are her father in the truest sense of the word. I mean that.

"But I wouldn't want to try to make this a real marriage if we weren't doing it for the right reasons. We should do it because we care for each other. And because we think we could be happy together..." Brittany trailed off, aware that she'd been on the verge of babbling hysterically.

"I agree. I don't think you're helpless. And I know you wouldn't try to keep me away from Danielle, for which I thank you." He reached across the table, catching her hand in his. "Brittany, the only reason I want you to stay is because I think we could make a good marriage. I think we could be happy. I...care about you. I want to be with you."

"I care about you, too." She looked at their linked hands, and suddenly the answer seemed so simple. Why was she so panicky? This was Michael, who'd been there for her from the start. They already *had* a marriage, in all the most important senses. What difference would it make if she verbalized the commitment she already felt?

"Yes. Yes, I think I'd like to make this a real marriage."

Michael's hand tightened convulsively over hers and then relaxed. "Good." He stopped and cleared his throat. "Good."

He was nervous, she thought. The realization made her relax. He always seemed so sure, so self-confident, as if he knew exactly where he was going and never doubted that he was going to get there. But he hadn't been sure of her answer. And it had been important to him.

"Well," she said, feeling as nervous and giddy as a teenager.

"Well." Michael didn't seem to have anything to add, but his smile was wide.

"I feel like we should do something to mark the occasion."

"We've already got a marriage license. Maybe we should seal this with a kiss." The look in his eyes made her flush, but she didn't resist when his hand tugged hers, urging her out of her seat. She came around the table slowly, her fingers still in his. After last night, it was a little foolish to feel shy with him. But then, last night they hadn't just made commitments to each other.

She stopped in front of him, not quite meeting his eyes, feeling like a new bride, which, in a sense, she was. She gasped when his free arm came up to catch her around the waist, tumbling her down into his lap. Tossing her hair out of her eyes, she looked at him, meeting the teasing laughter in his look.

"I just thought we should start this marriage off on the right foot."

"You mean on the right lap?"

"I mean in the right way," he said softly, reaching up to stroke the hair back from her face. "We can make this work, Brittany. I know we can."

As she melted into his kiss, she hoped they weren't making a big mistake.

* * *

Brittany adjusted a ruffle on Danielle's lemon-yellow romper with a nervous twitch.

"Okay, when Daddy comes in, I want you to give him a big smile. Tonight is special."

Danielle stared at her, greeting this announcement with the same solemn attention she gave most comments. Looking at her, Brittany felt a surge of love. It seemed incredible that this tiny, perfect human being was really here, really hers.

At the sound of the Mustang pulling into the driveway, she straightened quickly, smoothing a hand over her hips to make sure the slim skirt of her dress was lying properly. It was silly to be so nervous, but in a sense, this was a new beginning. From now on, her marriage was much more than a piece of paper.

She'd spent the day moving her things into Michael's room. One minute she'd been sure that she was making a terrible mistake, the next sure that this was the best decision she'd ever make. By late afternoon, the seesaw of emotions had left her almost dizzy.

A long, hot bath had served to relax some of the nervous tension. She'd taken time with her makeup and pulled her hair up in a soft Gibson girl pouf, leaving a few tendrils free to caress the nape of her neck. The dress was one she'd bought more than a year ago, hoping for a special occasion that justified wearing it.

At the time she'd assumed that special occasion would include Dan. Her hand had lingered on the dress uncertainly. Things had changed so much. The dress had languished in the back of her closet, serving as a reminder of dreams unfulfilled. Tonight it could serve to celebrate the beginning of new dreams.

After she'd pulled the slim turquoise silk over her head, she'd smoothed it into place, turning sideways to make sure there were no odd bulges. All her hard work in the gym after Danielle's birth had paid off, and the silk revealed nothing she had to be ashamed of. The square-cut bodice and tiny sleeves showed just enough skin to be intriguing. Maybe it was a little fancy for dinner at home, but she wanted to show Michael that this new beginning was important to her.

Now she twisted the slim diamond bracelet on her wrist, suddenly sure that she had overdone things. Especially since, with all the time she'd spent preparing herself, she'd had very little time to worry about dinner.

Hearing Michael's footsteps on the porch, Brittany put her hand to her throat, panic all but choking her. It wasn't as if she didn't know him. After last night, they were certainly intimately acquainted. And it wasn't that she was doubting the decision to turn their marriage into something real and lasting. It was just that she was standing on the brink of a major change.

The door opened and Michael stepped into the hallway. Brittany was standing at the end of the breakfast bar that divided kitchen and dining room, one hand resting casually on the maple surface of the bar, the other clenched at her side. Michael saw her as the door shut behind him, and the smile he gave her drained most of the tension.

This was Michael. Michael, who'd become her best friend. There was nothing to be afraid of. He wasn't suddenly going to change just because they'd decided to change the terms of their bargain.

Her smile was bright with relief. She lifted her face as he crossed the distance between them. His kiss was brief but thorough, and she rested her forehead against his chest for a moment before he drew back. It seemed incredible that they'd lived together all these months, and she was just now discovering that he could melt her knees with one kiss.

He took her hands as he stepped back, holding her arms out so that he could study her.

"You look fantastic."

"Thank you." Brittany flushed at the look of blatant male appreciation he was giving her. That look set off little tingles in the pit of her stomach.

"Are we celebrating?" He glanced over her head at the steaks sitting on the counter.

"Kind of. Well, not exactly."

"There you go again, being decisive. What are we 'kind of, not exactly' celebrating?"

She laughed at his teasing, feeling the last of the nervous tension drain away.

"I thought it might be nice to mark the beginning of our marriage, the real beginning, this time. I mean, if we're going to do this, we should do it properly. Don't you think?"

"Sure. Sounds like a great idea. I wish I'd thought of it myself. How's my best girl?" He bent over Danielle, lifting her into his arms. She smiled, showing her delight in his presence as he cooed over her, telling her how beautiful she was.

Brittany watched, trying to ignore the tiny twinge of irritation she felt. She hadn't expected Michael to look at this quite the same way she did. After all, he was a man and men were notoriously insensitive when it came to things like anniversaries and celebrating new beginnings. Still, it did seem as though this were something significant enough that even a man might have taken note of it.

He glanced up from the baby, catching the annoyance on her face. Something unreadable, amusement perhaps, flashed in his eyes. Surely that was amusement.

"You know, you're right. This really is a new beginning. I think we should go out to celebrate, unless you're particularly crazy to have dinner here? You look much too pretty to be spending time in the kitchen."

"It's Friday night. We probably won't be able to get in anywhere." She was not in a cooperative mood. Saying she looked pretty wasn't enough. She wanted him to share her feelings about the significance of the step they'd taken.

"We can give it a try," Michael suggested. "We can always come home and eat steak if we can't find a restaurant. Why don't you give me a few minutes to shower and change, and then we'll see what we can do."

He didn't give her a chance to argue, thrusting Danielle into her arms and loping off to the bedroom. Brittany stared after him, aware that her lower lip was poked out in something perilously close to a pout.

"Insensitive clod," she muttered. Danielle waved her fists and made an unintelligible comment of her own.

Michael stepped out of the shower and toweled off, trying to school the grin from his face. Brittany had looked so annoyed. He probably shouldn't tease her, but he found it hard to resist.

Stepping into the bedroom, he opened the closet and reached for a shirt, only to come up with a handful of silk. She'd moved her clothes into his room. He stared at the slightly overcrowded closet, feeling an odd tightness in his chest. Strange, how something as small as seeing her dresses hanging next to his shirts should seem so significant.

He pulled a shirt and a pair of slacks from the closet and shut the door, his expression thoughtful. He dressed and combed his hair, shrugging into a linen sport jacket before reaching for the small box he'd tucked into his back pocket before coming into the house.

He didn't open the box. He knew what it contained. Maybe this hadn't been such a good idea. Maybe he should wait awhile before giving it to her. His jaw set stubbornly. If they were going to make a new start, they might as well make a clean sweep. He thrust the box into the pocket of his jacket before leaving the bedroom.

Brittany said very little as they got in the car, settling Danielle into her car seat. She was still a trifle disgruntled that Michael seemed to be taking this whole thing so casually. Though, glancing at his profile, she wondered if that was really the case. He looked rather stern, as if he had something on his mind.

Her first clue that things weren't quite what she'd thought was when Michael took the turn to his parents' home.

Catching her questioning glance, he shrugged.

"I thought we'd drop Danielle off with my folks so we could have the evening to ourselves."

"Don't you think we should have called first, to make sure your mother is up to it?"

"I'm sure she won't mind. She and Dad both love having Danielle around." He stopped in front of the house and reached for the buckle on the baby's car seat. "I'll take her up," he said hastily when Brittany moved to get out of the car. "There's no sense in you getting your feet wet."

Since the sun had been out since early afternoon, and there was a walkway all the way to the front door, Brittany couldn't see how she was going to get her feet wet by getting out of the car. But something in Michael's tone made her acquiesce, and she settled back into her seat, watching as he carried the baby up to the door, diaper bag slung over one shoulder. The door opened and he handed Danielle over to Donovan, who held her comfortably in the crook of one arm. The transfer was so prompt and smooth, it was almost as if it had been arranged ahead of time. But Michael had suggested going out on the spur of the moment. Hadn't he?

She studied his face surreptitiously as he got back in the car. There was something there she couldn't quite define.... Excitement? As though maybe he knew something she didn't know? As though maybe this dinner out hadn't been quite so spontaneous as it had seemed?

She snuggled back into her seat, feeling suddenly much better.

Brittany was hardly surprised when he pulled the car to a halt in front of Chez Coeur, Remembrance's one and only French restaurant. It also happened to be the fanciest restaurant in town, with a reputation for fine food, superb service and prices that compensated for both. High prices or no, she knew they pulled their clientele from as far away as Indianapolis.

A bubble of excitement threatened to explode in a smile. Michael would never have brought her here unless he had reservations. And, if he had reservations, then he'd planned this long before he'd gotten home and found her dressed up. Which meant that this new beginning was just as important to him as it was to her.

But she kept her expression still, allowing just a hint of pout to show. If he wanted to spring this on her as if it had just occurred to him, then she wasn't going to spoil his fun.

She didn't have to maintain the facade of indifference for long. The moment they walked in the door, it was obvious that they were expected. The maître d' greeted Michael by name, his smile ingratiating enough to indicate that he'd been very well tipped ahead of time. They were shown to a table in a dimly lighted corner and seated with a flourish.

Once alone, Brittany looked across the table, raising her eyebrows at Michael. "Why don't we just see if we can get in someplace?" she questioned.

"I wanted it to be a surprise. And I managed to pull it off, didn't I?" He grinned at her, looking pleased with himself.

"I actually called you an insensitive clod in front of Danielle. I could have marked her for life."

"Well, I'm sure when you explain to her that I'm really a rather wonderful guy, she'll understand."

The evening seemed blessed. The atmosphere was quietly elegant. The service was prompt and nearly invisible, a perfect combination. And the food was superb. Brittany knew it was superb because it couldn't have been anything less but she couldn't have said just what it was she ate.

The conversation was intermittent, but the occasional silences were comfortable. For the first time, they spoke of the future, because for the first time, they had a future together.

Michael told her of his plans for his career, his hopes, his aspirations. And Brittany told him that she'd always dreamed of being a writer, how she'd wanted to major in journalism but her parents had insisted on a more practical degree.

It wasn't until the meal was over and they were lingering over coffee so smooth it practically evaporated on the tongue, that Michael sprang his final surprise.

"I bought you something to celebrate our marriage."

Brittany glanced up from her cup, her eyes showing her surprise as he set a small flat box on the table.

"You didn't have to do that."

"I know I didn't *have* to. I wanted to." He fiddled with the box, sliding it back and forth on the thick linen tablecloth. "I wasn't sure what you'd like."

"I'm sure I'll love it." There was a pause, but he made no move to hand her the box. She had the odd impression that he was uncertain now that the moment had come, and her curiosity inched up a notch.

After a long moment where he continued to toy with the box, he suddenly pushed it across the table to her.

"Maybe I should have gotten something else," he muttered as much to himself as to her.

Brittany took the box, trying to imagine what on earth he could have gotten her that would inspire such doubts. She peeled the wrapping away to reveal a small jeweler's box bearing the same name as the one that had held her bracelet. Snapping open the lid, she was stunned to see an exqui site diamond pendant lying on the dark velvet background. The stone caught the light, refracting it back in a hundred rainbow patterns.

"Michael, it's beautiful." She tore her gaze away from the pendant and looked at him, her eyes shining with excitement. The look of brooding uncertainty didn't leave his eyes when he smiled.

"I wanted you to have something really special to remember this night by. The night that we are truly starting our marriage."

"I certainly won't be able to forget it with something like this to remind me. I can't belive you thought I might not like this. Would you help me put it on?"

He moved around the table to the chair next to hers, but he didn't immediately reach for the necklace she was holding out.

"You'll have to take off the one you're wearing," he said quietly, his eyes searching hers.

It was suddenly clear why he'd had his doubts about the gift. Brittany's smile faded, the hand holding the diamond sinking to the table while the other reached up to grasp the simple gold heart she'd worn almost constantly since Dan gave it to her more than a year ago.

Michael saw the realization come into her eyes, and he felt a hard knot settle in his chest. He hadn't gone into the jewelry store planning on buying her something to replace the locket. He'd simply wanted something to commemorate the occasion, just as he'd told her.

But when he'd seen the necklaces, he'd suddenly flashed back to the night before. Brittany boldly straddling his thighs, her head thrown back with the pleasure of their joining, her hair streaming down her back until it almost touched his thighs. In a flash of light, she'd been revealed—woman personified. She'd been every fantasy, every dream he'd ever had. His. His wife, his lover.

And there was the dull gleam of the golden heart hanging between her breasts.

In that instant, he'd felt a flash of rage like nothing he'd ever known before. That she was wearing something given to her by another man was a reminder that she hadn't always been his, might never belong to him completely. He'd wanted to snap the chain and throw the necklace to the ends of the earth.

Instead, he'd grasped her hips, holding her still for the rhythm he set, not satisfied until she was crying out *his name* in her pleasure. Until he was sure that, at that moment, *he* was the only man on her mind.

It had all come back to him when he saw the necklaces. Before he could think about it and decide whether or not it was really a wise move, he'd picked out the diamond Brittany now held, paying far more than was wise, determined that she wouldn't spend another night in his bed wearing the locket.

It was only later that he'd begun to wonder if he had the right to feel as he did. It wasn't as if they were going into this with stars in their eyes. Did he have the right to ask her to set aside something that linked her to Dan? But some stubborn core of him insisted that she was *his* wife, sharing *his* bed.

Now, in Brittany's eyes, he saw that she understood exactly what he was asking. This was not a gift without strings. Her fingers clung to the locket as if to a safety line.

Fool, he castigated himself. *She isn't ready for this. You had no right. You've blown everything with your stupid, macho pride.*

"Look, it was a stupid idea. I shouldn't have bought it. We can return the necklace, and you can pick something else out."

He reached for the necklace, hoping that they could just pretend this never happened. But Brittany didn't release the delicate chain, and Michael's hand dropped away. She stared at it for a long moment, as if studying the way it caught the light, but he didn't think she was even seeing the beautiful stone.

"No. No, I don't want to return it," she said slowly, as if reaching a decision as she spoke. "It's a beautiful necklace."

"We could get something else," he insisted. "A ring would probably be more appropriate, anyway."

"I don't want a ring. I'd like to keep this." The words came more strongly, and she lifted her eyes to his face. "I'd like to keep this," she repeated.

Michael felt the knot in his chest dissolve. Just as she'd known what he was doing when he gave her the necklace, he understood what she meant now. She was willing to let the past stay in the past. She was looking ahead to the future—a future spent with him.

"Are you sure?" His eyes searched hers.

"I'm sure." There was no doubt in her voice, and her hands were steady as she reached up to unlatch the locket. She set it in one hand, coiling the chain into her palm, staring down at it. "I've worn this long enough, I think." Drawing a deep breath, she closed her fingers over the locket and looked up at him. "Would you help me put your necklace on, please?"

Michael took the pendant from her, aware that his fingers weren't quite steady. Brittany turned so that her back was to him, and he reached over her shoulder to set the necklace in place. The tiny clasp balked at first but then slipped neatly together.

When she turned back to him, the diamond winked against the turquoise silk. Rainbow fires shot from it, like delicate promises. Which was just what it represented. Promises he hoped would never be broken. Promises he was going to do his damnedest to fulfill.

He bent to kiss Brittany, feeling her mouth soften under his. This was their true wedding ceremony. This was the real beginning of their lives together.

Chapter 11

It was Christmas Eve, a year and a half later and Remem-rance bustled with good cheer and people trying to get ome to spend the holiday with their families. The snowfall ad been light so far this winter, little more than a dusting f white covered the fields nearby and nestled in sheltered ockets in the town itself. But snowfall was promised be-ore morning, so there was a good chance of waking up to white Christmas, after all.

Hardly anyone noticed the lone man who walked down Main Street, coming from the bus station. If anyone had oticed him, they might have thought that he needed a eavier coat. The thin jacket he wore over his jeans was ardly protection against the chill in the air. They might also ave noticed the limp that dragged at his step, and, if they appened to look real close, they might have realized that he vasn't as old as he looked at first glance.

But everyone was absorbed in the need to finish last-ninute shopping at the one or two stores that remained open and get home to start celebrating. So the man walked down the sidewalk alone, his eyes hungry as he stared in every shop window. Occasionally, he reached out to touch a window or a winter-dormant tree, as if to assure himself that they were real.

He paused outside a café, drinking in the scent of coffee that drifted out as patrons entered or left. The Scout Café would be open until midnight, even tonight, he knew. And they'd have a few customers until then—those who had nowhere else to go, no one to be with.

But he wasn't one of those. In this place, he did have somewhere to go. So he turned away from the inviting smells, hunching his shoulders inside the jacket and turning the collar up to give some protection against the biting wind that skidded around the corner of the building and sought out every worn spot in his clothes.

He barely noticed the cold. His eyes were set on a goal as he limped away from the center of town. He could have called a taxi, gotten out of the biting cold, but he wanted to savor every icy step of the path he was on. Home. He was almost home.

The Sinclair house was brightly lit, light spilling from every window to create gleaming patterns on the patchy snow outside. Inside, the holiday was being celebrated in style. Family and friends filled the big house to the rafters. An enormous Christmas tree dominated one corner of the living room. Underneath it, an antique train circled. Earlier the train had been a source of great fascination for the gathering's youngest members.

But Danielle Sinclair and young Colin Sinclair had been dispatched to beds in the nursery upstairs as befitted their extreme youth. How the babies could sleep through the friendly noise below was hard to imagine, but when either

Beth or Brittany checked on them, they were sleeping the sleep of the innocent.

Just now, Brittany wasn't thinking about her daughter. She wasn't thinking about anything beyond the warm promise of her husband's hands at her waist and the wicked gleam in his eyes.

She and Michael had been sent to the kitchen to get ice, but Michael didn't seem to have any intention of opening the refrigerator. He'd trapped her in a corner by the cupboard, claiming that there was mistletoe above her and she couldn't break tradition by denying him a kiss.

Laughing, Brittany pointed out that she didn't see any mistletoe, but he just told her to use her imagination and proceeded to kiss her quite thoroughly. She wound her arms around his neck, melting into the kiss, just as she always did. Two years of marriage hadn't dulled the response she felt each time he kissed her.

"I told you not to send the two of them for ice." Beth glanced up at her husband's muttered comment. Her eyes laughed into his, seeing the amusement he wasn't trying very hard to hide.

"It's Christmas Eve, Donovan. You can't expect people to be quite as efficient as they usually are."

"By the time they get out here with the ice, it very well may be New Year's Eve.

"Then we'll have a head start on that party."

Donovan grinned at her, slipping an arm around her waist and pulling her against his side. "You know, we could slip away from this shebang. Go upstairs and inspect the linen closet."

Beth smiled but whatever she'd planned to say died unspoken as she looked past him, her eyes falling on the new guest one of their friends had just opened the door to.

"Oh my God." The words were more a prayer than an exclamation.

"What is it?" Donovan turned, staring at the newcomer.

He didn't look much like a party goer. His jeans were too worn for fashion, his boots were frankly worn down at the heels. His shaggy blond hair looked as if it hadn't been cut in months, and there was a stubble of beard on his lean cheeks. But it wasn't his lack of sartorial splendor that made Donovan curse and start forward.

The move came too late. The kitchen door swung open, and Brittany stepped into the hallway, her cheeks flushed, her eyes bright. She was carrying a tray of glasses, her head half turned to see if Michael was bringing the ice. She caught Donovan's quick movement out of the corner of her eye and turned to see what had caused it. Her gaze settled on the scruffy stranger. As if sensing her look, he turned, too, his eyes meeting hers.

The tray dropped from her suddenly nerveless fingers. The resultant crash brought instant silence in its wake as people looked to see the cause. Brittany stared at the stranger, her hands coming up to cover the sudden pallor in her cheeks, her wide eyes disbelieving.

"Dan." The name was a whisper.

"Hello, Brit." He half smiled, his eyes uncertain. "Merry Christmas."

"Oh my God. Dan. It's really you."

The paralysis left her, and she flew across the hall, throwing herself into the arms he held out to her.

"I can't believe it! You're here. You're alive." She was half laughing, half crying, oblivious to the people watching their reunion, to the murmurs starting up as the guests realized who the shaggy stranger must be. Oblivious to Michael standing in the kitchen doorway, his face white as he watched her embracing Dan.

After a stunned pause, Donovan and Beth acted together. As if they'd planned for just this eventuality, each moved forward, Donovan toward Dan and Brittany, Beth toward her son.

"I think a little privacy might be in order here," Donovan said. Dan drew his eyes from Brittany's face, a grin breaking through the worn lines that bracketed his mouth.

"Donovan! Sorry to cause a scene."

"Don't worry about it." Donovan put his hand on the younger man's shoulder, squeezing roughly. "But in a minute, you're going to be mobbed. Why don't we move into the den?"

"Sure, sure. Where's Michael? Is he here?" Dan's eyes skimmed the crowd, looking for his friend.

"I think he's probably waiting for you in the den." Donovan gently shepherded the two of them across the hall. No one approached, though it was obvious that they were all aware of the drama going on in their midst as they watched the three of them disappear into the den.

Michael turned as the study door opened. He noticed that Dan still held Brittany's hand. She was looking up at him as if she couldn't believe the miracle of his presence. But all of that he noticed peripherally.

"Michael! My God, you haven't changed a bit!"

"It hasn't been that long." The two men clasped hands, their grips too tight, each searching the other's face as if to reconfirm the familiar features.

"You look great! God, everybody looks great."

"Well, you look like hell," Michael told him with a grin.

"Thanks." If Dan's grin had gotten any wider, it would surely have split his face in two. "Good to see you, too."

There was an awkward little pause, and then Michael pulled Dan forward, throwing his arms around him in a rough hug.

"You'd better have a good explanation, you SOB."

Dan laughed, returning the hug before stepping back. "Don't I always have a good explanation? Remember the time I convinced the music teacher that your dog had run off with my trumpet?"

"Yeah, and she believed it until she found out I didn't have a dog."

"Well, I had her going for a while there." Dan reached for Brittany's hand.

"I think we'll leave the three of you alone. You can fill us in on the details later." Donovan took Beth's hand and pulled her out of the room, shutting the door behind them.

"Do you think that's wise?" Beth asked him, her worried eyes on the door.

"I think they've got a lot to work out, and I don't think we can help them do it."

"I suppose." But she didn't sound sure.

In the den, Dan sat down on the sofa, pulling Brittany with him, reluctant to lose contact with her for even an instant. Michael sank into a chair across from them. He still found it hard to believe that Dan was sitting here, just like old times.

"So come on, out with it. Where have you been for the past two and a half years? And I hope this is a better explanation than 'the dog stole my trumpet.'"

"It's better, I guess. More complex, anyway."

"The search party found the plane. They said there were no survivors," Brittany told him gently.

"I know. At least, I know there were no survivors except me. I left the site of the crash before the search party arrived." He looked down, his face shadowed, and Michael was suddenly aware of the lines that creased his face. Dan looked older than his years. Older and worn.

"What happened?" Michael leaned forward, resting his elbows on his knees. "We thought you were in the plane. If I'd known you were alive..."

"I know, buddy. You'd have come looking. I knew that."

There was a moment's silence while each of them considered how different their lives would have been if Dan had been found by the search party. Michael avoided looking at Brittany, his emotions in a turmoil.

"What happened to you?" It was Brittany who broke the silence, her eyes tracing the lines in his face.

"I was in a prison, actually." Dan tried to speak lightly, but there was nothing light about the expression in his eyes. "In a stinking hellhole of a prison."

"Why?" The single question was all Brittany could manage.

"Mistaken identity?" He laughed bitterly, robbing the answer of any humor. He sighed, leaning back on the sofa, his eyes on things only he could see.

"I suppose it will be easier if I start at the beginning.... The project started out great. Everybody gathered in L.A., and we all had our equipment. Dad—" He broke off, swallowing. "Dad was like a little kid. I don't think I ever saw him more excited. He was convinced we were going to discover some new civilization. More likely we'd have all ended up with sunburn and dysentery, but he was still excited.

"We took off on time, and the whole team was in good spirits. It was a good group. Nice people."

He stopped again and Michael knew he was thinking about the fact that those people were all dead.

"Anyway, everything was going great until we developed engine trouble. Right over miles of jungle. The pilot tried to set down in a clearing, but there wasn't really enough room. We hit hard, sort of like belly flopping into a pool. I was right next to an exit door, and the impact popped the door open. It wouldn't have done me any good except that my seat belt snapped, and I was thrown out. The plane skidded across the clearing and slammed into the side of a hill we hadn't even been able to see from the air. It blew like the biggest firecracker you've ever seen."

No one spoke for the space of several slow heartbeats. Brittany's hand tightened over Dan's, trying to imagine what it must have felt like to watch the plane explode, knowing that your father was inside. To know that everyone in it was instantly dead.

"Were you hurt?"

"A broken leg."

Dan shrugged, dismissing the injury as minor, which she supposed it must have seemed then, compared to what he'd just seen.

"Why didn't the search party find you?" Michael asked.

"That was my fault. I wasn't thinking too clearly at that point. Shock, I guess. For some reason, I decided that the only logical thing to do was to try and walk to civilization. I had this knife Dad had bought me, one of those with every tool known to man in the haft, and there was a compass in there, so I figured I could find the coast and there was bound to be a town on the coast."

He shrugged. "Like I said, I wasn't thinking too clearly. Anyway, I found a branch I could use as a crutch, and I started walking. If I'd had an ounce of sense, I'd have stayed with the wreckage. But I didn't.

"Anyway, to make a long story short, before I found the coast, I stumbled into this little village. Turned out that they were guerrilla fighters trying to overthrow the government. I don't know why the hell they didn't shoot me on the spot, but I probably looked close enough to death that they figured I wasn't worth wasting a bullet on.

"They even patched me up, more or less. They didn't have a doctor, but they had a guy who was pretty skilled in basic medicine. He set my leg and kept me from dying of infection. By the time I was ready to travel, we'd developed a pretty friendly relationship.

"The only problem we had was that they wouldn't let me leave. They were afraid that, if I went to the capital, I might reveal their position to the government. But they were going to be moving camp soon, and they'd let me go then. Since I wouldn't know the position of their new camp, I couldn't do them any harm."

"Couldn't they have gotten a message out? Something to let us know you were alive?"

He shook his head at Brittany's question. "We were miles away from a phone, and there was no other way to communicate with the outside world. Besides, these people were considered criminals. They didn't dare risk being seen."

"You must have loved kicking your heels." Michael remembered Dan's impatience with delays of any sort. Once he'd made up his mind to do something, he wanted to do it now, not five minutes from now.

"Well, I was damned grateful to be alive. Besides, by then weeks had gone by. I knew I must have been given up for dead. I figured another couple of weeks wouldn't make much difference to me or the people back home. And they'd been good to me. They didn't have much, but they shared what little they did have."

"So what happened? Why didn't you come home?" Brittany asked.

"Well, it was really a matter of bad timing. They were going to be breaking camp in a couple of days, and they'd already provided me with a map to the capital. My leg wasn't very strong, but I knew I could make it that far.

"Only, the government got there first. They hit the village hard. It was like the Fourth of July, with rockets screaming everywhere. Except people were dying all over the place." He rubbed his hand over his face as if to wipe away the memories.

"I was one of the lucky ones. Or at least that's what I thought. I wasn't even hurt. When the troops rounded up the few survivors, I started trying to explain who I was. That I was an American and not part of their little war."

"They didn't believe you?" Michael asked.

"Well, they believed the part about me being an American. But they didn't believe the part about me being a noncombatant. I had a map to the capital in my pocket, and they were convinced that I was part of some subversive plot."

"Didn't you demand to talk to the American ambassador or consul or whatever?" Brittany questioned.

"Sure. I asked, I coaxed, I shouted. I tried reason, I tried the Bill of Rights, I tried everything I could think of. It didn't do much good. Although maybe that's what kept them from killing me outright, which is what they did with most of the prisoners they took.

"They threw me into this tiny cell and told me that my case was being reviewed. I kept telling them to call whatever representation our government had in the capital, and they kept saying it was being reviewed. They *reviewed* my case for two bloody years.

"I'd probably still be there if it hadn't been for this nun who came to visit the prisoners. I told her who I was. It turned out that she was the sister of the guy in charge of the jail. She believed me and convinced her brother to let me go. She probably threatened him with the wrath of God. For a nun, she was one feisty lady.

"That was a few weeks ago. I went to the American consul, and he got the paperwork moving." He shrugged. "Here I am."

"If you got out of prison a few weeks ago, what took you so long to get home?" Brittany asked. "Why didn't you call or write, let us know that you were alive?"

"I wasn't much to look at, honey. A year and a half in a Central American prison don't exactly leave you in prime physical condition. If I'd have come home then, I'd have scared everybody half to death."

Michael tensed at the casual way he'd called Brittany "honey" and then forced himself to relax. Dan didn't know how much things had changed.

"Speaking of everyone—" Dan glanced at Michael, one brow raised in inquiry "—where's my mother? I went home tonight first, but the people who were living there seemed to think I might be a dangerous killer, and they wouldn't tell me anything. Did Mom sell the place?"

"About a year ago," Michael told him. He thrust his fingers through his hair, wishing there was some way to delay this conversation. His best friend had just come back from the dead, expecting to pick up the pieces of his life. How did he go about telling him that the pieces were so fragmented he was going to have to start over again?

"Where is she living now? An apartment? Somehow, I can't see Mom in an apartment."

Michael glanced at Brittany, but she hadn't taken her eyes off Dan since they'd sat down. Apparently, explanations were his department.

"Your mom is living in Europe. France, I think."

"Europe? Mom?" It was clear that didn't fit with the woman he remembered, and Michael knew his next piece of news wasn't going to make it easier.

"She's remarried."

Dead silence followed his words. Dan stared at him, his eyes startled. "Remarried? I don't believe it. When? To who?"

"About a year ago and to nobody that anybody knows. After your...the crash, she started traveling a lot. Maybe it hurt too much to stay here. Most people lost touch with her, and then we heard the house was on the market. Apparently she met someone in Europe and married him."

Michael shrugged, wishing he had a more detailed explanation.

"Married." Dan shook his head slowly. "I can't believe it. I thought about a lot of things that might have changed while I was away, but I never thought of her remarrying. Do you have an address?"

"No. But I'd guess you could get it from the real estate agent. I know who sold the house."

"Sure. I hadn't thought of that. I'll have to call them. I guess things have changed even more than I'd expected."

Was that ever an understatement. Michael rubbed at the ache that was building in his forehead. How could he even begin to explain the changes that had taken place? There Dan sat, holding Brittany's hand. Michael wanted to pull her away from him and announce that she was his wife. But he couldn't do that. At least not quite so abruptly.

After what Dan had been through, how was he going to take the news that the woman he'd loved had married his best friend, that she'd had a child who now called that same best friend Daddy?

"Fill me in on the news." Dan's smile might have been forced, but it was clear that he didn't want to dwell on the melancholy. "I feel as if I've been gone centuries instead of just a couple of years. The town has really grown. Is anybody we used to know still around?"

"A few," Michael said, feeling the ache intensify.

"I was surprised to see you here." Dan turned to Brittany, his eyes studying her as if he still couldn't believe she were there. "This was the first place I thought of when I drew a blank at home. I figured I'd have to spend some time tracking you down."

"I've . . . become rather close to the Sinclairs," Brittany murmured weakly, careful to avoid Michael's eyes.

"You couldn't get close to a greater bunch of people. This place was pretty much a second home to me."

Under other circumstances, Dan might have noticed the awkward silence that followed his remark. But he was still absorbing the fact that he was home at last.

"So, fill me in on what's been happening," he asked again. Michael drew a deep breath and began to talk, telling him what had happened to old friends—who'd married, who'd divorced, who had children. Dan listened, absorbing the small details like a man dying of thirst who'd finally been given water.

During his time in prison, there'd been little enough to fill his time, and he'd spent a lot of it thinking about the people back home, wondering what they were doing, trying to imagine what paths their lives might have taken. Foolish speculations but they'd helped to take his mind off his own situation.

Brittany listened to Michael's words with half an ear. She felt as if she had fallen into a dream and couldn't wake up. It just didn't seem possible that Dan was sitting next to her, holding her hand. How many times had she dreamed of just this, fantasized about it? In those first few months after the crash, she'd thought of little else.

But things had slowly changed. Her grief had been muted by time, her life filled with other things. Michael. Danielle. How were they going to explain things to him? He'd just come back from the dead. It seemed cruel to simply dump it all in his lap. And yet, her marriage to Michael, her child—Dan's child—those weren't the kind of things you could hide for long.

Brittany didn't know how long it had been since Michael had stopped speaking when the silence penetrated her absorption. Dan was staring at her, his thumb moving back and forth over her wedding ring. Her wedding ring. Her eyes met his, wondering if he'd realized the significance of the plain gold band. It was clear from his eyes that he had.

He looked more regretful than surprised, and Brittany felt a tremendous surge of guilt. He'd been through so much, lost so much. It didn't seem fair that he had to deal with yet more changes so soon after returning home.

"You're married," he said quietly, a statement, not a question.

Brittany opened her mouth, fumbling for an appropriate answer. She was vividly aware of Michael watching the awkward little exchange.

"It's not important," she blurted finally, thinking that this conversation could surely be postponed.

Dan's mouth twisted in a half smile, his eyes still sad. "I doubt if your husband would agree. Who is he? Anyone I know? Is he here tonight?"

Brittany stared at him, her mouth half-open as she sought the proper answers to his questions. He had a right to the truth, but she couldn't bring herself to hurt him.

Unconsciously, her eyes sought Michael's. More than two years of marriage had taught her that he could always be depended on. But for once, he couldn't help her. He seemed just as tongue-tied as she was. The silence stretched.

Dan looked from one to the other, suspicion flaring in the ice-blue depths of his eyes. His gaze dropped to Michael's left hand, which lay clenched against his knee.

"You bastard." The quiet words held a wealth of bitterness.

Michael felt the pain of betrayal as sharply as if it had been his and not Dan's. "It's not what you think," he said quietly.

"You and Brittany aren't married?"

"We're married."

"Then it's exactly what I think." He dropped Brittany's hand as if it had suddenly become contaminated, and he stood up.

Michael rose to his feet, his eyes meeting his friend's. "We need to talk about this," he began.

Hot rage flashed in Dan's eyes. Remembering the volatility of his temper, Michael braced himself, aware that Dan was just as likely to lash out with a fist as he was with words. But perhaps spending two years in a prison cell had taught him control.

"I don't think we have anything to say to each other."

"Dan, please. Listen to him." Brittany stood and set her hand on his arm, but he shook it off, the contempt in his eyes as searing as a hot brand.

"Save it. You're Michael's wife. That's all I want to know."

He spun on his heel and strode from the room without another word. Brittany took a step as if to follow him, but Michael caught her arm, stopping her.

"Let him go. He's not going to listen to either of us right now. Give him some time to cool off."

"He was so hurt," she whispered. The eyes she turned to him swam with tears. "Did you see the look in his eyes?"

"I saw it," he said grimly.

"I feel like we've just stabbed him in the back."

"We didn't." He released her arm. "Dan always had a hot temper. He'll get over this and start thinking a little more rationally."

"I hope so."

Michael watched her, wondering if that was all she hoped. Did she hope that Dan would come back and open his arms and his heart to her again? It was clear that Dan had had no thought of anything else until he'd realized that she was married.

And she'd gone into his arms as if it were the only place in the world she wanted to be.

Don't be a fool. Of course she was happy to see him. You felt the same. That doesn't mean she's still in love with him.

You've had a lot of time with her. You've got a strong marriage. She's not going to walk out on that just because Dan has returned from the dead.

But she loved him. She had his child.

That was a long time ago. Danielle is your daughter in all the important ways. And Brittany is your wife.

He wanted to let the little voice convince him, but doubt roiled in his gut. He kept hearing Dan ask about her marriage and Brittany saying that it wasn't important. Had she only been trying to avoid hurting Dan, or had she been speaking what was in her heart? Now that Dan was back, just how important was their marriage to her?

The answer to that question could have stilled the uneasiness, but he didn't ask. He was too afraid of the answer.

Chapter 12

Christmas was a rather subdued holiday in the aftermath of Dan's appearance. This year, the Christmas feast was to be at Michael and Brittany's house, and Brittany had been looking forward to hosting the small family gathering.

But the joy had gone out of it. She kept looking at the snow outside, wondering where Dan was, wondering if he was warm enough, if he had enough to eat.

Michael entered the kitchen after she'd started the dinner preparations. His parents and Colin were due to arrive any minute. Danielle was perched on his hip, chewing on a cookie, more of the cookie getting on her face than into her mouth.

"How's everything going?"

"Fine."

They'd spoken very little since last night, each wrapped in thought. Last night, for the first time since they'd made their marriage a real one, they'd slept on opposite sides of the bed, carefully not touching.

"Is there anything I can do to help?" Michael asked politely.

"No thanks. I think everything is under control."

"So you wanted to put brown sugar on the turkey and vinegar on the ham?"

It took a moment for his words to penetrate. Brittany stared down at the box of brown sugar in her hand. She'd been carefully pressing the sweet substance to the turkey, while the ham sat looking forlorn under it's coating of vinegar. The two should have been mixed and used to coat the ham.

Muttering under her breath, she began dusting the sugar off the turkey. Luckily, it didn't seem inclined to stick to the snowy skin anyway. In a matter of minutes, the small turkey was in the oven, properly basted with butter this time. The ham received its coating and was set aside to wait its turn in the oven.

Brittany glanced over her shoulder at the window, frowning. Was the snow coming down harder than it had been?

"You keep looking out the window." Michael folded the top of the brown sugar box over with one hand, sealing it tight. "Are you looking for something?"

"No." But the guilty flush betrayed her.

"Thinking about Dan?" His tone was casual, but there was a hint of frost in his eyes. Unfortunately, Brittany wasn't looking at his eyes. She was once again looking out the window. It was definitely snowing harder now.

"I'm worried about him," she admitted.

"I told you, give him some time to cool off, and he'll be ready to listen to reason."

"I don't mean that," she said with a touch of impatience.

"What are you worried about, then?"

"I'm worried that he might not have a place to stay. Or enough money. Did you see his clothes? They were old and worn. What if he's out in this cold somewhere?"

Michael reined in his impatience, reaching for another cookie as Danielle polished off the one she had and held out a grubby hand for more. Right now, he didn't care if it did ruin her appetite. It was more important to keep her quiet and occupied.

After a sleepless night spent wondering if Brittany was regretting her marriage to him, the last thing he felt like doing was discussing Dan. There was nothing more to be said at this point. The look of worry in her eyes as she glanced at the window did nothing to soothe his ruffled feathers.

"I'm sure he's okay."

"How can you be sure? He just spent two years in some awful prison, and now he's come back to find that nothing is the way he left it. We shouldn't have let him go without making sure he was all right. We don't even know if he has any money."

"Brittany, one thing I know about Dan Remington and I'm willing to bet hasn't changed is that he's more than capable of taking care of himself. If he can survive a plane crash and prison, then I'm sure he can survive a winter day in Indiana."

He'd meant his words to be reassuring, but that wasn't how she took them.

"How can you be so callous." She slammed the refrigerator door shut, turning to look at him with a bunch of celery clenched in one fist as if it were a weapon. "He's supposed to be your best friend, but you don't seem to give a damn about him."

"I give more than a damn about him," Michael said tightly, his temper snapping. "But that doesn't mean I want him shoved down my damn throat along with the damn Christmas dinner. Dan is a survivor. He'll be fine. Do you think we could just forget about him for the rest of the day and try to enjoy the holiday?"

"I don't see how I can just forget about him, but I won't mention him again. I wouldn't want to spoil your damn dinner," she snapped.

"Damn." Danielle smiled at both of them as their eyes jerked to her angelic little face. "Damn." She seemed pleased with this new word and repeated it again with emphasis. "Damn."

"Now see what you've done." Brittany reached for the toddler as if to remove her from contaminating influences.

"Look what *I've* done? As I recall, I wasn't the only one slinging the word around."

Brittany flushed but refused to back down. "You're the one who started it."

"Actually, I think you were the first one to use the word in question."

"Damn." Danielle studied her cookie, clearly pleased with herself. Her parents stared at her, wondering how you explained to an almost two-year-old who was rapidly discovering the joys of language that some words weren't for repeating. Especially when they'd greeted every other word with lavish encouragement.

"Damn."

Their eyes met over her head. Michael was the first one to break. His mouth quivered and then widened in a smile that rapidly became a chuckle. Brittany looked as if she might hold on to her annoyance, but the obvious humor in the situation couldn't be denied. She laughed, hugging Danielle close. How was it that a child could always put something into perspective, even when she didn't know she was doing it?

"I guess we're going to have to watch our language from now on," Michael said, laughter still tinting his voice.

"I guess so."

He reached out to ruffle Danielle's silky, dark hair and was rewarded with a cookie-encrusted smile. "Let's hope she loses interest in it after a while."

"How are we going to explain this one to your parents?"

"Let's just keep her mouth full," Michael suggested.

"A coward's way out, but I like it."

The small quarrel broke the tension between them, but it didn't really solve anything.

During the past two years, they'd built a marriage based on friendship and mutual respect. It took something like this to show how shaky that foundation could be.

The days between Christmas and New Year's were tense. The one cardinal rule in their marriage had been that they didn't discuss their feelings for each other. It was enough that they were married and working toward the same goals. Not even in the darkness of their bedroom had either of them said anything about love.

It had worked well enough until now. Now, it was clear that they'd been existing as if they were acrobats working without a safety net. When something happened to shake the foundations of their marriage, they had nothing to fall back on.

Michael, uncertain of Brittany's feelings, withdrew emotionally and physically. He knew they should talk about Dan's return and what it might mean, if anything. But he was afraid to probe too deeply, afraid he might not like the answers he came up with.

Brittany didn't encourage a discussion. How could she discuss her feelings about Dan's return when she didn't know what they were?

Brittany leaned back in her chair, staring out the window at the snow that was drifting down. It had turned out to be an exceptionally cold winter, with more snow than usual.

Despite Michael's assurances that Dan was a survivor, she couldn't help but wonder where he was, if he was all right.

It was almost three weeks into the new year, and as far as she knew, no one had heard from him since he walked out of Donovan and Beth's house on Christmas Eve. What if he never came back? There were so many unanswered questions, things she wanted to say to him, to ask him.

She picked up her pen, doodling on the edge of the grocery list she was supposed to be making. Danielle was sleeping in her room, and the house was quiet, that special kind of quiet that seemed to descend with the snow.

How *did* she feel about Dan?

It was a straightforward question. She should have been able to come up with a straightforward answer. She was happy that he was alive, that he was back. His death had been so senseless, such a waste of life. Seeing him alive and well was like seeing a miracle—something you wanted so badly, even though you knew it could never happen.

She'd loved him once. In fact, she'd been sure that she'd love him always. She'd had his child. Wasn't that an indication of how deeply she'd cherished him and his memory?

Did she still love Dan? She knew the question was in Michael's eyes when he looked at her. It was a complicated question that couldn't simply be answered with a yes or no. She frowned, trying to define her feelings to herself. He'd been her first love. And he had, albeit unwittingly, given her Danielle. How could she not love someone who'd given her something so precious?

But it had been Michael who'd enabled her to have Danielle, to care for her. Michael who'd been there through mood swings and swollen ankles and childbirth. Michael who'd changed diapers, warmed bottles and walked the floor with a colicky infant. Dan might have been present at Danielle's conception, but he wasn't her father, not in the deepest sense of the word. That wasn't his fault, but it didn't change the facts.

But what about her own feelings? Her time with Dan seemed so long ago. She'd been a different person then. The Brittany who'd loved him didn't exist anymore.

And there was Michael. Always her thoughts circled around to him. They'd never said they loved each other. But that didn't mean that the emotions weren't there. *Did* Michael love her?

It was a relief when the doorbell rang. Anything was better than sitting here thinking and rethinking and getting nowhere. The snow had almost stopped. Maybe it was Beth.

But it wasn't Beth. Brittany's heart gave a bump when she saw who was standing outside the door.

"Dan."

"Hi. Maybe we should talk." He didn't smile and it was impossible to read anything in the ice blue of his eyes.

"Yes." She swallowed, summoning up a smile. "I think you're right. Come in."

He wiped his feet on the mat before stepping into the hall and shrugging out of his coat—not the thin jacket he'd been wearing Christmas Eve but a heavy sheepskin-lined one, more in keeping with the weather.

"I had a chance to do a little shopping." He must have noticed her looking at the coat.

"I'm glad. You didn't really look prepared for winter," she said, taking the coat and hanging it in the closet.

"I wasn't. I'd forgotten what bone-deep cold felt like."

"I suppose it was pretty warm . . . where you were." Brittany led the way into the living room, aware that she sounded very hostessy.

"Hot might be a better description," Dan said easily.

"I can imagine."

"No, I don't think you can." But there was no anger in the contradiction.

"You're probably right. I'm sorry. I didn't mean to sound like a handbook on how to make polite conversation."

"That's okay." He half smiled but it didn't reach his eyes. "The situation is a little awkward, I suppose."

"Yes."

Brittany sat on the sofa, and Dan chose a chair opposite her. Once seated, there was a momentary silence. She racked her brain for something to say. She'd once been in love with this man. Surely they couldn't be completely without words.

"I wanted to apologize for reacting the way I did the other night," Dan said, breaking the silence. "I had no right to act as if you'd committed some crime by marrying Michael."

"That's all right. I know it must have been a shock to you. So much has changed."

"That it has. You know I used to dream about you while I was in prison."

"Did you?" Brittany wasn't sure what she should feel at his admission. Flattered? Touched? Moved? She felt a little of all those emotions. But most of all, she felt a deep sadness for the time he'd lost. Time he could never regain.

"Yeah." He hunched his shoulders and looked around the living room, obviously sensing her discomfort. "So, what do you do these days?"

The change of subject was obvious, but Brittany was too grateful to mind.

"I stay home with—" She broke off, coughing. For a moment, she'd almost forgotten that he didn't know about Danielle. It seemed incredible that he had a daughter and didn't know it. "I...ah...stay home most of the time. I've been doing some writing. I've sold a couple of articles. Nothing major yet, but I keep working at it."

"That's great. I know you wanted to go into journalism. Did you switch majors?"

"I...ah...didn't get my degree, actually."

"You didn't?" He was surprised. "You only had another year to go. What happened?"

"It's rather a long story."

"I've got time. I'd like to know what's been happening in your life. It's obvious it didn't follow the scenarios I was building."

His mouth twisted in a quirky smile that made her heart ache. He looked so alienated. What must it feel like to come back to find everything you'd known had changed almost beyond recognition?

She looked at him helplessly. He had a right to know about Danielle. After all, it hadn't been by his choice that he'd been denied knowledge of his child. She wasn't ready to tell him now, but then, maybe there was no such thing as being ready to tell a man he had a year-and-a-half-old daughter.

"Why don't I make a pot of coffee?" She'd tell him but she needed a few minutes to gather her thoughts, put them in a coherent order.

"Sure. Coffee was something I missed while I was... away."

"Well, I don't promise that it will be good. Michael usually makes the coffee around here..." She trailed off, aware that the reminder that she shared this home with Michael had, perhaps, been illtimed. Dan said nothing, the half smile frozen in place. "I'll go make the coffee," Brittany murmured.

In the kitchen, she reached for the filters and coffee automatically, her thoughts whirling. It seemed so strange to have Dan here. After the crash, memories of him had lingered in so many places—places they'd been to together. But this house had been associated with Michael only—there'd been nothing of Dan here. Now here he was, in one of the few places she'd never pictured him.

Her hand was shaky as she poured water into the coffee maker. She had to tell him about Danielle. He deserved to know, and she wanted him to hear it from her. The questions was *how* to tell him. Did she just blurt it out, or did she lead up to it carefully?

As it turned out, she didn't have to worry about how to tell him.

When she walked into the living room with the coffee, at first glance she thought he'd gone. A feeling of relief swept over her. If he'd gone, she'd been spared the ordeal of having to tell him anything. But then a movement caught the corner of her eye, and she turned to see Dan standing near the baby grand piano in the corner.

The piano had been a gift from Donovan and Beth on their first wedding anniversary. She dabbled on it a bit, but Michael was the one with the real talent. They'd spent a lot of wonderful evenings, especially in the winter, with Michael playing the piano and family and friends singing off-key and occasionally off-color songs.

"That's Michael's toy," she said casually, setting the cups down before approaching the piano. "He's quite good," she added with unconscious pride.

She had almost reached him when she noticed the rigidity of his back, the hand clenched into a fist at his side. It was only then that she realized what had caught his attention. It wasn't the piano he was looking at; instead, he'd been drawn to the photos that lined one corner of the grand. Photos of her and Michael and Danielle.

"Oh." The small exclamation escaped her as she lifted a hand to her throat.

"Yes, 'oh,'" he snarled. He spun away from the photos, and Brittany took a step backward when she saw the fury that glazed in his eyes.

"Dan, I was going to tell you. I didn't want you to find out this way."

"I just bet you didn't. Just how did you expect to tell me about this?"

"I thought we'd sit down over some coffee, and I could explain it to you."

"Explain it to me?" he asked incredulously. "Explain how you jumped into bed with my best friend the minute you heard I'd been killed?"

Brittany blinked at him, uncertain of his meaning. "That isn't how it was."

"No?" He turned and pointed at the photographs. "I'm no expert on babies, but that's not a newborn in those pictures. What did you do? Go straight from the funeral into his arms?

"My God, Brittany, I know it may have been a little naive of me to think you'd be waiting for me if and when I got home. But I sure as hell thought you'd grieve more than a day or two."

He spun away as if the sight of her made him physically ill. Brittany stared at his rigid back, trying to sort his words into some sensible pattern. Her eyes widened when she realized what was in his mind. He thought Danielle was Michael's child, that she had slept with Michael soon after he had been supposedly killed.

"No. Dan, it wasn't like that."

"Don't give me that. What was it like, Brittany?" He turned toward her, his eyes narrowed. He looked as if he hated her. "Are you going to try and tell me that you were so overcome with grief, you didn't know what you were doing? Or did you just see Michael as a way out?"

"What are you talking about?"

"You were pushing me to get married before I left. When I wouldn't bite and then was so inconsiderate as to turn up dead, did you turn to Michael? Play on his sympathies? Or did you just tumble into bed with him and then tell him you were pregnant? A strong sense of responsibility—that's Michael. He'd have married you in a minute."

The crack of her hand on his cheek was loud in the quiet house. His head jerked with the force of the blow which left a red welt across his face.

"You don't know what you're talking about."

"Then why don't you explain it to me." But the contempt in his eyes told her that he'd already made up his mind.

"I don't owe you an explanation," she said steadily. Their eyes locked in silent battle, neither giving an inch. A plaintive wail broke the tense standoff as Danielle announced that she was awake and not happy at being left alone.

Dan's jaw tightened. Brittany put up her chin. She was damned if she'd explain anything to him. How could she have forgotten that arrogant streak in him?

"I'd like you to leave now," she said quietly.

"With pleasure."

She didn't move as he turned and stalked to the door, snatching his coat out of the closet. He opened the door and then seemed to hesitate. He turned.

"You were all that kept me alive, you know." The anger seemed to have drained from him, leaving a soul-deep weariness that tore at her. "Thinking about you kept me sane. All those months, I kept fantasizing about what it would be like when I finally got home."

Danielle began to cry louder, unaccustomed to being ignored. Dan glanced in the direction of the sound.

"This sure as hell wasn't part of my fantasies."

He was gone before Brittany could say anything. The picture of him standing in the doorway, the snow drifting behind him, lingered in her mind a long time. He'd looked so alone.

* * *

Michael cursed as he bobbled a line, creating a new and rather exotic wall in the house he was supposed to be drafting. With a sigh, he threw down the pencil. It hadn't been going well, anyway. The preliminary stages of a design were usually fun because almost anything was still possible. This project wasn't working out that way.

But then, nothing had been much fun lately. Not since Christmas. Dan's return had been like a live stick of dynamite landing in the middle of his life. He hadn't realized just how fragile the foundations of his marriage were until now.

If asked, he would have said that he and Brittany had a strong relationship. They didn't need mushy declarations of affection. But now he was beginning to think that a few mushy declarations might make him feel a whole lot better.

Just how did Brittany feel about him? Affection? Passion? She cared about him. He'd have to be blind not to see that. But did it go deeper than that? Their sex life was good, more than good—it was downright terrific.

But there had to be more to it than that. Affection. Sex. Those things weren't enough to build a marriage on. He ran his hand through his hair, staring at the drafting board without seeing it. A marriage took... love.

And that was exactly what he felt for Brittany—what he'd felt for a long time. It was hard to remember a time when he hadn't loved her. Even when he'd first met her, he'd been drawn to her. But she'd been his best friend's girl, and he'd buried that awareness so deep he hadn't even been able to admit to himself why he was marrying her, why he'd wanted to stay married to her.

And during the past couple of years, he hadn't had to contemplate his feelings. After all, he'd had Brittany and Danielle. Why would he need to analyze what he felt about them?

It was only when something happened that threatened the even keel of his life that he took the time to really look at what she meant to him, at what it would mean to lose her.

A knock on the door broke into his thoughts and he turned, running a hand over his hair, trying to put on a professional face.

"Come in."

He felt the professional face stiffen into a mask when Dan walked into the room, closing the door behind him.

"Dan. What a . . . surprise." The words held a flat note, but he was helpless to project more enthusiasm into them. This man had been his best friend, almost a brother, yet now he was first and foremost a potential rival. And Michael was discovering a possessive streak he hadn't known he had.

"Michael." Dan stood just inside the door, his hands in the pockets of his jeans, his eyes skimming over the room without really seeing it. "Great office."

"Thanks. It's adequate."

"I've run into some of our old friends, and they tell me you're doing well." The words did not sound very complimentary.

"I do all right," Michael admitted cautiously. He could feel the tension in the other man. There was some purpose behind this visit.

"Looks like you're doing better than all right." Dan smiled thinly, his eyes cool. "Great job, great house, great wife. Great kid."

There was a beat pause before he added the last, and Michael tensed. So Dan knew about Danielle.

"You've been to see Brittany."

"Yeah, I've been to see Brittany. You lousy son of a bitch!"

The punch came too quickly for Michael to do more than duck back so that it caught him on the edge of the chin instead of breaking his jaw as it might have if it had connected as intended.

He blocked the next one, catching Dan's wrist, using the hold to spin the other man around and slam him face first into the wall.

"What the hell was that for?" he panted, pinning Dan against the wall with his superior weight.

"You know what it's for." Dan heaved backward but he couldn't dislodge Michael. Two years in prison had taken their toll.

The door crashed open and Donovan strode into the room, taking in the situation at a glance.

"Let him up, Michael."

"Why? So he can try and tear my head off again?" But he stepped back, eyeing Dan cautiously as he felt the tender spot on his chin. Dan spun, his eyes burning hatred as he leaned against the wall, out of breath.

"What's the problem here?"

"I don't know. He came into my office and took a swing at me."

"Dan?"

Dan shrugged his jacket back into place, throwing Donovan a quick glance. "This is something between Michael and I. Nobody else."

"When you start a fight in the offices of my company, that makes it my business." Donovan paused, looking from one to the other. "If this is about what I think it's about, I'd suggest that the two of you sit down and talk before you start throwing punches again." He turned to leave but stopped in the doorway. "You might try remembering that you were friends once."

The door shut behind him, and each man was silent, trying to anticipate the other's next move. Dan smoothed a hand over his hair.

"He's right, you know," Michael said, leaning back against the desk. "We need to talk. We should have done it before this."

"I don't know what there is to talk about." Dan seemed more weary than angry.

"Brittany, for one. And Danielle."

"Danielle? You named your kid after me? My God, Michael, that's rich." He laughed bitterly. "You actually named her after me. God, don't you have any shame at all?"

"Shame?" Michael's brows rose. "What have I got to be ashamed about?"

Dan stared at him as if he couldn't believe the question. "You don't think there's something wrong with having married the woman *I* loved?"

"We thought you were dead. Besides, it didn't seem like there was much choice at the time."

"Not much choice? You mean I was right? She actually got pregnant and that's why you married her?"

"I thought you said you talked to Brittany." Michael frowned, feeling as if he were missing some vital piece of the conversation.

"I did talk to her."

"What did she tell you?"

Dan shrugged. "She said you make the coffee. She's working on her writing. And you play piano."

"What did she say about our marriage? The baby?"

"She didn't have to say anything," Dan told him, anger flaring in his eyes again. "I saw the pictures. You and her and the baby. My God, did you even wait till I was cold in my supposed grave?"

Michael leaned back, enlightenment dawning. "You saw the pictures and jumped to a bunch of conclusions, and you either walked out without talking to Brittany or you said awful things to her and she threw you out."

"More the latter than the former." Dan reached up to touch his cheek.

"You jackass. You haven't changed a bit. You're still always going off half-cocked without waiting for an explanation."

"The cozy little family portraits didn't seem to need much explanation," Dan snapped, annoyed with Michael's half-amused tone.

"Things aren't always what they seem, if you don't mind me being a little trite."

"As a matter of fact, I *do* mind. If there's some *explanation* for the fact that you jumped right into bed with Brittany as soon as I was out of the way, then I'd like to hear it."

"I don't know why I should bother to tell you, but I will because I think you have a right to know." Michael stood up, moving to the window to stare out at the snowy landscape. His voice was quiet when he began speaking.

"I did marry Brittany because she was pregnant. We got married a couple of months after the crash."

"A couple of months? That's all the time you waited?"

"That's all we waited." Michael turned from the window, his eyes on Dan. "Brittany was carrying your child."

He saw the impact of the words. Dan actually took a step back, his eyes disbelieving.

"My child?" he choked out. "She was pregnant when I left?" He read the answer in Michael's eyes and turned away, running a shaking hand through his hair. "My God, I had no idea. She didn't tell me. Why didn't she tell me? I'd never have left her alone if I'd known."

"She didn't want you to marry her because she was pregnant. She wanted to be sure you loved her."

"'Loved her'? I adored her. We quarreled before I left," he said slowly, remembering. "I hated that. I tried to call her from L.A., but I got hold of her parents, and they told me she was out. I was going to call her again when we got to the site, as soon as I could find a phone. Only we never reached the site."

He sank into a chair, his expression dazed. "A baby. I have a child."

Michael turned away, feeling a stab of pain in his chest. It hurt to hear Dan refer to Danielle as *his* child. He wanted to protest that she'd belonged to him since the moment the doctor put her in his hands. But he said nothing.

It took Dan a few minutes to absorb the shock. "I can't believe it. I have a daughter and I don't even know how old she is."

"She'll be two in March."

"Two. Two years old." Dan rubbed his hands over his face, grief flashing through his eyes.

Michael felt a twinge of pity. He'd been there for the first two years of Danielle's life. He knew just how terrible Dan's loss was.

"I...how did you end up marrying Brittany?" Dan asked at last, still struggling to comprehend the way his whole life seemed to have been turned upside down in a matter of minutes.

"She was alone." Michael shrugged. "She needed help."

"What about her parents?"

"They felt that she'd shamed them by getting pregnant. They wanted her to go off and have the baby and then give it up. She left. When I found her, she was living in a shabby apartment in a neighborhood I wouldn't send my worst enemy to. She had no insurance. She was running out of money. I talked her into marrying me, at least until the baby was born."

"Why?" Dan stared at him, trying to imagine what had happened.

Michael shrugged again. "I told myself I was doing it for you."

"For me?"

"You were my best friend. Brittany was carrying your child. I thought you were dead, and it seemed like the only thing left that I could do for you was to make sure Brittany and your baby were all right."

"You said you 'told' yourself you were doing it for me?"

Michael hesitated and then looked up, his eyes meeting Dan's. "I don't think that was the whole reason."

"I don't think so, either. I mean, we were friends, but that's going a little bit above and beyond the call of duty." There was no rancor in Dan's voice. "I suppose I should thank you for taking care of them."

"That's not necessary."

"You love her, don't you?"

"I love her."

The flat statement hung in the air between them. Michael had staked a claim, making it clear that whatever had happened in the past, he now regarded Brittany as his. Friendship, past or present, didn't have the strength of his ties to her. He wasn't going to give her up easily.

If Dan wanted her, he was going to have to fight for her.

Chapter 13

Dinner that night was a silent affair. Michael was waiting for Brittany to tell him about Dan's visit. Brittany was still wrestling with the realization that she hadn't been as hurt as she should have been by Dan's harshness.

There was a time when having Dan think badly of her would have broken her heart. Now, it was upsetting but hardly the end of the world. She didn't love him anymore. And that hurt more than the cruel accusations he'd made. In the beginning she'd been so sure that she'd love him forever, that if only he'd return, her life would be complete.

But he hadn't returned, and her life had been pretty fulfilling without him. She looked across the table at Michael, who was eating his dinner with a dogged determination that made it clear he had only the vaguest idea of what was on his plate.

Michael had completed her life. Brittany stared at him, feeling a shock of awareness. Without Michael, her life would be so empty.

He looked up, catching her eyes on him. He arched one brow in inquiry, but Brittany shook her head and looked down at her plate. What a time to suddenly realize that you were in love with your husband. There should have been candlelight and flowers and soft music.

How long had she loved him? It seemed like forever. The feeling had been inside of her for so long. How could she not have known it? He was good and kind but never boring. He made her laugh, he believed in her, encouraged her to be happy. As a lover, he was wildly exciting, teaching her things about herself she'd never known.

"I think it's about time Danielle went to bed. She's about to fall asleep in her peas."

Brittany's head snapped up, her thoughts so far removed from toddlers and strained peas that it took her a second to register what he was saying.

"Oh. Right." She pushed back her chair, reaching for the tray on Danielle's high chair. "It is pretty late for her to be up." She lifted the baby out of the chair, soothing her when she began to fuss irritably.

Michael watched Brittany leave the room before pushing back his own chair and reaching for their plates. From the looks of Brittany's dinner, she hadn't had much appetite. He carried the plates into the kitchen and began stacking them in the dishwasher, his movements made jerky by irritation.

Didn't she plan to tell him about Dan's visit at all? Did she think he wouldn't find out? And why would she want to hide it from him? From what Dan had said, it hadn't been a terribly pleasant encounter. Unless it had hurt her so badly she couldn't talk about it. And for it to hurt that much, she'd have to care about Dan very deeply.

He slammed a glass into the dishwasher with enough force to break it. Muttering under his breath, he fished the broken chunks out of the silverware tray and dropped them into the trash.

"What happened?"

He turned quickly at the sound of Brittany's voice. Seeing her, he wanted to take her in his arms, tell her he loved her, tell her he'd never let her go.

"Michael?" Her tone made it clear that she found his behaviour odd, and he shook his head, turning back to flip on the dishwasher.

"I broke a glass."

"You didn't cut yourself, did you?"

"No." *God, you're pretty far gone when you find yourself wishing you had cut yourself just so she could fuss over it.*

He leaned against the counter, looking at her. "Dan came to see me today."

Brittany's head jerked up, her eyes startled. "He did?"

"He said he'd already seen you."

"Yes, he did. I was going to tell you, but it wasn't a very pleasant visit." She pushed her hands into the pockets of her jeans, looking away from him. "He found out about Danielle, more or less."

"So I gathered. He seemed to have the wrong impression, though."

Her eyes flickered to his and then away. "Did you tell him the truth?"

"That he was Danielle's father? I told him."

"Everything?"

"Everything. Why we married, the whole thing."

"How did he react?"

"Just about the way you'd expect. He was stunned, a little hurt, maybe."

She sighed, pulling one hand out of her pocket to run it through her hair. "We made such a mistake," she said, thinking that they should have told Dan the whole truth that first night.

What Michael heard was that their marriage had been a mistake.

"No." He moved so quickly that Brittany didn't have a chance to react. She gasped as he caught her upper arms, pulling her against his body. Startled, she looked up into eyes that blazed a fiery blue. "Don't ever say that."

"Say wh—" His mouth smothered her confused question, his arms sweeping around her to crush her so close she could hardly draw a breath.

He didn't ask for her surrender. He demanded it. His tongue plunged into her mouth, sweeping across the tender surfaces as if to conquer them, make them his own.

Brittany's hands pressed against his chest in automatic protest before slowly relaxing and sliding upward to circle his neck. Her fingers burrowed into the silky, dark hair at the nape of his neck as her mouth opened to him, her tongue coming up to fence with his.

He dragged his mouth from hers, but only to find the warm skin of her neck. Brittany's head fell back, her fingers clinging to his shoulders as his tongue found the pulse that pounded raggedly at the base of her throat.

Her head spun with the quick rise of passion. He wasn't giving her time to think, and there was something she needed to think about. But the knowledge was a foggy, far-off thing, without urgency.

He pushed her away just long enough to strip the sweatshirt over her head, and then his hands were cupping her breasts, the nipples growing taut beneath his fingers. She was vaguely aware that he was shifting her backward, but it didn't really register until his hands closed over her waist and he lifted her onto the dining room table.

"Michael!" She'd meant it to be a protest, but it came out as more of a whimper as his mouth closed over one swollen nipple, teasing it with lips and tongue until it throbbed.

Satisfied, he switched his attentions to the other breast, drawing a sob of pleasure from her throat.

Not until he'd reduced her to quivering awareness did he lift his head, catching her mouth in a long, drugging kiss.

"Tell me you want me," he whispered against her lips.

"I want you." How could he think she didn't? Couldn't he feel how she burned for him?

He unsnapped her jeans, lifting her as he slid them and her panties off her legs, tossing them both aside. The table was cool against her bare skin, a vivid contrast to the heat of him. When had he taken off his clothes? she wondered distractedly.

His hand slid up her thigh as he eased her back on the table, and she trembled when his fingers found her. He stroked the moist flesh of her, drawing a ragged whimper of pleasure as he slipped a finger inside, feeling the heat of her.

"Tell me again," he said against her breast.

"I want you," she gasped. His tongue swirled lazily across her belly. "I want you." His hand probed deeper, taking possession of her. "I want you. Ah, Michael."

She arched, her hands clenching in his hair as his mouth found her, his tongue tasting her passion. Brittany kept her eyes closed, sparks of red fire darting across her vision as her body responded helplessly to his ministrations.

He drove her relentlessly, rushing her toward the peak so that when it came, she fell breathlessly into it, hardly aware of herself anymore.

The last pulsating sensation had not yet died when she felt him over her. She opened dazed eyes as he wrapped his hands in her hair, holding her still as he looked down at her, watching every flicker of expression as he slowly filled her with his strength.

"Michael." Something flared in his eyes when she spoke his name. Where before, he'd rushed her toward a climax, now he seemed intent on taking his time. Now it was Brittany who quivered with impatience, her hands on his hips urging him to pick up the pace. He smiled, his eyes still holding that watchful look, and slowed until he was barely moving, seeming to take pleasure in the fact that she so blatantly wanted more than he was giving.

"What's the hurry, sweetheart?"

"Please." The breathless little moan was all she could manage, her head tossing back and forth, scattering thick black hair across the pale wood.

His laughter held pure masculine triumph, but he gave her what she wanted. Brittany's hands sought purchase on his damp back, needing something to cling to as the world exploded into a million sparkling pieces all around her.

His voice came to her through a fog, low and husky, holding a note of promise. "We've got all night, and this is only the beginning."

It was a promise he kept, and it was a night neither of them was likely to forget. Brittany lost count of the number of times he made love to her. He carried her into the bedroom, laying her across the bed and bringing her to sweet ecstasy again and again until she begged for mercy. And then he carried her into the shower, supporting her trembling body with his as the warm water sluiced over them and he proved to her that she wasn't as tired as she thought.

When she finally fell asleep, it was almost dawn. She slept deeply, dreamlessly, not waking until Danielle's plaintive cry dragged her from the arms of Morpheus. She staggered out of bed, fumbling for a robe as she went down the hall to the baby's room. She changed Danielle, lifting her onto her hip to carry her into the living room, then setting her on the floor.

Michael was gone. That much was clear. She wasn't sure if she was glad or sorry. Still rubbing sleep from her eyes, she began to warm a bottle for Danielle and make a pot of coffee for herself.

Every muscle in her body ached, every nerve ending tingled from the night before. She felt achingly tired and startlingly alive at the same time. Still, there was something odd about the whole thing. It was as if he'd been trying to prove something to her.

Brittany poured a cup of coffee and sipped it, feeling the caffeine enter her system, banishing some of the fog from her brain. What had set him off? She frowned at the coffee maker. It wasn't as though she'd been wearing anything particularly sexy or had said anything provocative. In fact, they'd been talking about Dan right before Michael had jumped her bones.

She'd just said something about them having made a mistake. And he'd said no. No what? No, it wasn't a mistake. But what wasn't a mistake? She'd meant that they should have told Dan the truth right away. Was it possible that Michael thought she'd meant something else altogether? Their marriage?

"He couldn't think that," she muttered out loud, reaching for the bottle and testing it against her wrist.

But if he *had* thought that... Would that explain last night? Maybe he'd been trying to prove something to her, to make her see that they were compatible? She flushed, remembering the abandoned response she'd given him. Well, there was no doubt he'd proved that.

She carried the bottle into Danielle, who took it eagerly. Brittany was halfway to the bedroom to get some clothes on when the doorbell rang. Glancing at the clock and then at the rather scruffy terry robe she'd thrown on, she went to answer it. If it was a salesman, he was going to get short shrift from her.

She pulled open the door, the words of polite dismissal dying on her lips. "Dan."

"Hi." There was a short silence while they stared at each other. "I've come to apologize," Dan said at last, his uneasiness obvious.

"Come in."

"Thanks. I wouldn't blame you if you booted me out."

Brittany shut the door, reaching up to push her hair back from her face, wishing she'd had a chance to comb it or brush her teeth or get properly dressed. After last night, she could have used a little time to pull herself together before having to deal with apologies from anyone.

"You've been under a lot of strain." She shrugged. "I don't blame you for jumping to conclusions."

"It was stupid of me," he said as he pulled off his coat and draped it over a chair.

"A little." She smiled, taking the sting out of the words. "I've made some coffee. Would you like some?"

Dan's eyes went past her, his face suddenly whitening. Brittany turned, comprehension dawning when she saw Danielle toddling toward her, bottle clutched in one hand.

"Hi, sweetie. Did you come to see who Mama was talking to?" She bent to scoop the little girl up, turning with her in her arms. "Danielle, this is Dan. He's a . . . friend."

Dan stared at the child, his face pale. Danielle looked at him for a minute and then turned away, more interested in the collar of her mother's bathrobe than she was in this stranger.

"She's beautiful," Dan said softly. Brittany glanced at him and then looked away. There was too much vulnerability in his eyes. No one should see another person that naked.

"Thank you."

"May I hold her?" There was so much hunger in the question, so much pain that Brittany felt her eyes sting.

"Of course. Why don't you take her into the living room while I change and get us some coffee?"

She pretended not to notice that his hands were not quite steady as he took Danielle from her. Danielle stared at him, trying to decide whether or not she approved of this person holding her. He appeared to pass some test, because she stuck her bottle in her mouth, watching him over it with wide blue eyes.

Satisfied that they were going to be all right, Brittany made a quick trip to the bathroom, splashing water on her face and running a comb through her hair before tugging on a pair of jeans and a sweater. There was a faint bruise on her shoulder, and she flushed, remembering Michael's hands on her. She'd be willing to bet that his back bore the marks of her nails.

Shaking her head, she forced her mind back to the present. Last night required some thinking, and she couldn't do it with Dan waiting in the living room.

When she came back out, he was sitting on the floor with Danielle, carefully stacking blocks so that she could knock them over with one blow. It was one of her favorite games. Brittany brought cups of coffee into the living room, sitting one on a table near Dan, holding the other close to her chest.

He looked up at her as she sat on the sofa, drawing one leg under her.

"She's truly beautiful. You and Michael have done a wonderful job." The compliment was given freely, and Brittany accepted it in the manner given.

"Thank you. We think she's a pretty terrific kid ourselves."

It was funny how she could look at him and feel nothing more than a nostalgic fondness. There was no more doubt, no more wondering what might have been. He was silent for a long moment, watching the child.

"I'd never have left if I'd known you were pregnant," he said at last.

"I know. I always knew that."

"If I'd known—We would have married. I wonder if we'd have been happy?" He seemed to be speaking more to himself than to her, trying to look at a path not taken.

"I don't know. I used to think about it a lot. Wonder what it would have been like."

"You don't think about it much anymore, do you?" He glanced up, his eyes catching hers. Brittany wasn't sure what answer he hoped for, but she couldn't give him anything but the truth.

"Not much," she said gently.

He nodded, looking back at Danielle, who was stacking blocks into an extremely shaky tower.

"She has my eyes." The comment might have been random, but Brittany thought she understood. He'd come back to find that everything he'd left behind was gone, never to be regained. He needed some connection, however small, to the life he might have had, the person he'd once been.

"She has your eyes," Brittany agreed.

The answer seemed to satisfy him. He reached out to steady the blocks.

"I suppose I really came to say goodbye," he said at last, without looking at her.

"You're leaving?" She was surprised. "You just got home."

"There's really not much here for me. I got my mother's address from the agent who sold the house. I thought I'd take a trip to Europe, see how she's doing. We spoke on the phone and she was going to fly home, but I told her I'd rather come to her. After two years in the tropics, the winter doesn't suit my bones." He gave an exaggerated shiver, his mouth twisting in a half smile.

Brittany didn't think his leaving had anything to do with the weather, but she didn't argue. Maybe he was right. There didn't seem to be much left for him here.

"We'll miss you, Michael and I. We're just now getting used to knowing you're alive."

"I don't think Michael will miss me all that much," Dan said ruefully. "I think he'll be relieved to see me gone. Not that he isn't glad I'm all right," he added. "But there's a real possessive streak in him. One I never suspected."

Brittany flushed, well aware that he was referring to her. The idea that Michael was possessive of her was not displeasing.

Dan hadn't taken his eyes off Danielle, as if he were trying to store up memories of her for when he was gone.

"You'll always be welcome here, Dan. When she's old enough to understand, we plan to tell her about you. I know she'll want to know you."

He was quiet so long, she wondered if he'd even heard her, but his hand was clenched over a block, the knuckles turning white.

"Thanks," he said finally, his voice husky. "I'd like a chance to know her."

He stood up not long after that, announcing that he ought to be on his way. Brittany didn't try to persuade him to stay. She was not entirely at ease around him. There was a lingering feeling that she should feel something more for him, some deeper tie than she did.

They stood in the hallway for a moment without speaking. He reached out to take her hands, and Brittany didn't protest. His touch aroused nothing in her but a warm feeling for someone she cared about. His eyes searched hers, a rueful smile twisting his mouth at what he saw there.

"I'll always think that we could have had something good together. But I'm glad you're happy. Truly glad. And I'm glad you're happy with Michael. He's a hell of a guy."

"I know you'll find someone, Dan. And whoever she is, she'll be a lucky woman."

"Thanks. I may come to you for a reference."

His smile faded as his hands tightened over hers, and he bent to kiss her. It was a light kiss, a farewell, a fleeting gesture to what might have been, and Brittany accepted it as such.

A wave of cold air swept into the hallway, and Dan stepped back from Brittany, turning to look at Michael, who'd stopped dead in the doorway. A muscle ticked in Michael's jaw when he saw their linked hands. It was obvious that he'd seen the last of the kiss and, despite the perfect innocence of the situation, Brittany felt a twinge of uneasiness at the look in his eyes.

"You always did have a rotten sense of timing, Michael," Dan said calmly, dropping Brittany's hands and reaching for his coat.

"Should I remember to knock before entering my own home?" Michael's eyes followed Dan's every movement as if looking for an excuse to pounce.

"Don't be an idiot, Michael." Brittany stepped forward, setting her hand on his arm, feeling the tautness of the muscles beneath her fingers. "Dan is leaving."

"Good," he said bluntly.

Her fingers tightened chidingly. "I mean he's leaving Remembrance."

"Why?" Michael addressed the question to Dan. The other man shrugged into his coat before answering.

"There's really not much for me here."

Brittany felt the arm beneath her fingers relax as his meaning sank in.

"Where are you going?"

"I thought I'd head for Europe. I guess I've got a stepfather now. I probably ought to meet him."

"I hope you have a safe trip," Michael said quietly.

"Thanks."

Michael held out his hand. Dan looked at it for a moment before taking it. The handclasp was tight, their eyes meeting over it, saying things neither of them could say out loud. They'd been friends most of their lives, closer than most brothers. Saying goodbye wasn't easy.

"Well." Dan cleared his throat as his hand left Michael's. "I guess I'd better be on my way." He looked from Brittany to Michael. "Take care of that little girl in there. She's special."

"We will," Brittany told him, slipping her hand through Michael's arm. "You take care of yourself."

"Hell, I've come back from the dead once. I don't intend to tempt fate again." He lifted his hand and then was gone, the door shutting behind him.

Brittany reached up to wipe a tear from her cheek, her eyes bright. Looking down at her, Michael swallowed hard.

"If you want to go with him, I won't stop you," he said huskily, the words dragged from him.

Her eyes met his and she felt her heart swell at what she read there. "Why would I want to go with him when I have everything I want right here?"

"I just thought—" He broke off, his eyes dropping to where her hand rested on his arm. "You loved him."

"Yes, I did. But I loved him the way a girl loves. I love you the way a woman loves. And it's so much stronger."

She saw the impact of her words in the way his eyes jerked to hers, the color seeping up in his face and then receding, leaving him pale.

"You love me?"

"More than anything in the whole world," she said, her voice shaky.

"Oh God." His arms swept around her, crushing her to him, and she gasped. "I love you so much. I didn't even realize how much until Dan came back and I thought I might lose you."

"Never. You'll never lose me," she promised. His kiss smothered anything she might have added, but there was really no need to say more. The kiss said it all.

A cranky wail from the living room brought them slowly apart. Brittany stared up at him with eyes shining with love, seeing the same emotion reflected back at her.

"I love you."

"I love you, Brittany. I don't know what I'd do without you."

"You won't have to find out," she assured him.

The wail grew in volume, demanding attention. She linked her arm with his, leaning her head on his shoulder. "I think Danielle is having trouble with some of the finer points of constructing a high rise. Maybe her Daddy could give her some pointers."

* * * * *

A Note from Linda Turner

When I was working up the idea for "Wild Texas Rose," I wanted a story that was set in Texas, one that would hopefully capture the essence of the cowboys, who work under the blazing sun of summer and the north winds of winter and wouldn't dream of doing anything else. The hill country was a favorite stomping ground of my uncle's, and I only had to think of him to come up with characters like Sullivan and Pop, men who are tough and weathered but wouldn't dream of passing a woman in trouble without stopping to help.

And Rose, of course, was the woman in trouble. The best kind of trouble—a baby. My twin sister was pregnant with twins, and it just seemed natural to add a baby to the story. I wanted Rose—and Sullivan—to experience the special anticipation that only the imminent birth of a new baby can bring to life. I hope you enjoy reading their story as much as I enjoyed writing it.

Linda Turner

WILD TEXAS ROSE

Linda Turner

To my agent, Lettie Lee, for
always being in my corner.

Prologue

The wind swirled through the granite tombstones of the old cemetery, scattering dead leaves among the graves. His shoulders hunched under his worn blue jean jacket, Sullivan Jones stared blindly down at the simple tin marker that indicated his father's grave. Bitter memories slashed at him, carving hard lines in his already chiseled face and pulling him back five years to the last time he'd seen his father alive.

As usual, they'd been arguing over the way the old man's drinking was driving the ranch right into the ground. They'd had the same argument countless times before, and it had always consisted of nothing more than hot words and curses. That particular day, however, Travis Jones had been mean drunk and spoiling for a fight. The only weak link in a long line of strong men, something had just seemed to snap. When Sullivan had unwisely told him that his grandfather would turn over in his grave if he could see what he was doing to the ranch, he'd snarled, "To hell with you and your grandpa! For as long as I can remember, I've had to listen to one or the other of you tell me every damn little thing I do wrong. I'm tired of it, you hear? Get out!" Marching over to the front door, he'd thrown it open and ordered Sullivan off the premises as if he was a bill collector instead of his only son. "You get out of here and don't come back till I'm dead. Then you can run things any damn way you want."

His hands balling into fists in the pockets of his jacket, Sullivan's mouth set in a flat line as he remembered the way he'd stormed out. Twenty-six and hot-headed, his pride demanding that he take his father at his word, his one thought had been to get away. Before the day had ended, he'd left Kerrville without a backward glance and gone to San Antonio to join the marines.

It was a stupid thing to do in the heat of anger, but he'd signed on the dotted line and there was no backing out. Eating crow, he'd called his father to tell him where he was and make peace. But his father hadn't been interested in healing the breach then, or two years later, when Sullivan got out of the service.

You aren't welcome at the Lazy J.

Even now, Sullivan could hear the cold, bitter words whispering in the wind. Even now, he could feel the hurt and anger that had driven him out west, where he had moved from one ranch to another, working as a hired hand, all the while longing for Texas and home.

After three years he'd had enough of working other people's cattle, enough of long, brutal winters and short summers that were never as hot as he wanted them to be. He was through with the emptiness, the loneliness he could never seem to shake. His father could raise bloody hell for all he cared, but nothing was stopping him from going home.

But he'd waited too long. He had arrived in town just this afternoon only to discover that Travis Jones had been dead for over a year and the ranch was gone.

Pain burned like a branding iron in Sullivan's chest, each breath searing him. His stinging eyes as dry as an empty water hole, he lifted his gaze to the horizon and saw everything he had lost. His father, the chance to make amends, the land that five generations of Joneses had worked and sweated and died over. All gone.

He should have been here! he wanted to cry. He could have found a way to stop the old man's mismanagement of the ranch. And he damn well could have stopped him from going to Frank MacDonald for a loan when things got so bad even the bank wouldn't loan him money.

Dammit, how could he have gone to Frank for anything? he wondered furiously. The Joneses and MacDonalds had ranched side by side for decades, sharing a common boundary line, but they'd never been friends, never even been neighborly. Everyone in Kerr County knew the MacDonalds had always resented the fact that it was they who had the much smaller spread and seemed to stand in the shadow of the Lazy J. And Frank was the worst of the lot.

For as long as Sullivan could remember, Frank had coveted everything Sullivan had—toys when they were younger, then horses, cars, women. And always the ranch. How he must have laughed with glee when Travis Jones showed up on his doorstep with his hand out. He'd only had to wait for the first missed loan payment to snatch the ranch right out from under his nose.

A month later his father died a lonely, broken man, his old drinking buddies the only people at his funeral because no one had had any idea where his only son was. For no other reason than that, he would have given anything to have five minutes alone with Frank MacDonald.

But that, too, was to be denied him. Frank was dead, killed six months ago by a fall from his horse. There was no one left to get revenge from. No one except Rose, Frank's widow. The girl Sullivan had left behind when he'd joined the marines. The girl who'd married his worst enemy before he had even finished boot camp. The woman who now, at the tender age of twenty-three, had inherited not only Frank's ranch, but his, as well.

Somehow he was going to make her pay.

One

Rose MacDonald cast a quick, anxious look over her shoulder at the dark, bruised clouds hovering on the horizon, silently gathering strength. By nightfall the full force of the late winter cold front was expected to sweep unrestricted across the Texas Hill Country, bringing freezing rain and sleet with it. The temperature, already in the mid-thirties, would drop to near zero.

Hurry. Urgency tingled on the cold wind that whipped around her, threatening to tear her blue knit cap from her head. Tugging it back in place over her dark curls, she knew she was running out of time. She had food and supplies to get in town, extra feed to pull out for the cattle, supper to cook. The only three ranch hands she had were scattered over her vast spread, battening down the hatches for the icy weather, and somewhere in the east pasture a fence was down. Sometime between now and darkness she'd have to find time to fix it herself.

She groaned at the thought. The weight of the responsibility on her shoulders seemed to grow heavier with each passing day. Ever since she'd been forced to fire Buck Hastings, her foreman, she'd known she couldn't handle the ranch alone. She should have hired someone to replace him immediately, but too many of the cowboys who had approached her about the job had looked her over as if they were more interested in taking her over rather than her ranch if she made the mistake of trusting them.

But trust didn't come easy to her. Not now. Not after years of being manipulated by the men in her life without her even realizing it. Wincing at the memories that slapped her in the face, she wondered how she could have been so blind, so naive. Her mother died when she was seven, and she was so terrified of being alone that she childishly thought the safety and security of her world depended solely on her ability to please her father. It never entered her head that he might use her fears and her need to please to control her. For years he subtly influenced what she thought, how she dressed, who she made friends with. He even went so far as to pick out a rich husband for her—Frank MacDonald—and she never thought to buck him. Then she met Sullivan Jones.

And fell in love.

Lawrence Kelly detested him on sight. He wanted her to marry money, and although the Jones name was synonymous with ranching in Texas, the family fortunes were on the decline. To add insult to injury, Sullivan was a man her father knew he would never be able to control. By nothing more than his silence, he made his disapproval clear.

But for Sullivan she would have been willing to defy the world and her father. She never got the chance. He took her from innocence to passion, then left town without a word of explanation or goodbye.

After that, nothing seemed to matter. Her father stepped up his efforts to push her into Frank's arms, and she couldn't find the energy to fight him. A month after Sullivan disappeared from her life forever, her father had a heart attack and died hours later. On his deathbed he pleaded with her to accept Frank's proposal, claiming he could die happy knowing she wasn't alone. Her world caving in on her, she buckled under the weight of the guilt trip and gave in.

Young and trusting and sick at heart, she never thought to question Frank's reasons for wanting to marry her. Although he had never said the words, she'd assumed he loved her. It wasn't until five years later and a week after Frank's funeral, on the day she fired Buck Hastings, that she learned the truth. Just before he walked out with most of her ranch hands, Buck viciously told her that she'd never been anything but a means to an end for Frank, the weapon he was going to use against the only man in the world he hated... Sullivan Jones. For years he'd dreamed of building a dynasty that would one day equal, then surpass that of the Joneses. What better way to do it than with Sullivan's woman and his ranch?

She winced, trying once again to convince herself that Buck was lying. But his words had carried a ring of truth to them and the bitter sting of betrayal. All lies, she thought numbly. She'd been taken in by lies, used by opportunists, her self-worth stomped on until it was in shambles. But that was all in the past. At the moment there was only one male in her life she cared about.

Shivering, her cheeks already chapped, she buried her gloved hands deep in the pockets of Frank's old plaid coat and struggled to find her patience as she surveyed Bubba, her prize-winning Brahman bull. He was a beautiful animal, his dark gray hide sleek and shiny, his huge body built along powerful lines. For the second time in a week he'd knocked down a stretch of fence so he could go courting the neighbor "ladies." Now he stood on the side of the road, a mile from home, all but ignoring her as he stared wistfully at the cows on the other side of the electric fence that marked the boundary of Joe Pearson's ranch.

"This is not a good day to play Casanova," she scolded. "The storm's coming and I've got to get to the store to get supplies before the roads ice up. Now why don't you be a good boy and get in the trailer so I can take you home? I've got a nice big bale of hay waiting for you in the barn."

Bubba only lowed longingly for the cows that had turned their backs on him and headed for their own barn.

Swearing under her breath, Rose pulled her coat closer and tried to ignore her freezing feet, the ache in her lower back that never seemed to go away, the tiredness that pulled at her like an undertow. If she could just sit down for a moment... But one look at the stubborn animal beside her told her that wasn't going to be possible.

"All right," she sighed. "Time for a change in strategy. How about a snack, hmm?" Pulling out one of the molasses-flavored treats she always kept in her pocket, she waved it under Bubba's nose temptingly. She almost laughed when he hesitated, clearly torn between the treat and the cows that were just out of reach.

"I know it's a tough choice," she chuckled, "but trust me, you don't want to go through a hot fence to get to those cows."

Bubba, obviously deciding the same thing, turned to follow her as she backed away from him toward where she'd parked her truck and trailer on the other side of the road.

Grinning, she held the treat just out of reach. "You're so easy, sweetheart. C'mon, just a little further. Once you get in the trailer, it's all—"

Suddenly, without warning, a battered pickup thundered around a blind curve in the road and raced toward her and Bubba like a bat out of hell. The treat she held fell unnoticed to the ground. Time froze. She had only an instant to scream, to move, and found to her horror that she could do neither. Paralyzed with shock, every drop of blood drained from her face.

Brakes screamed. In what seemed like slow motion, the truck swerved to a stop at cross angles to the road. Before it shuddered to a stop, the driver was kicking his door open, the heated curses he spit out hanging in the air like blue icicles. Then, while Rose's dazed brain was still registering the fact that she hadn't been hit, the driver stepped out of the truck and her past came marching toward her with long, angry strides.

Sullivan Jones.

Shaking her head in denial, she tried to back up, to run, but a sudden darkness pressed down upon her. She lifted a trembling hand to ward it off, but there was no stopping it. In the next instant everything went black.

"What the hell!" Sullivan jumped toward her, lightning quick as he caught her only seconds before she could hit the cold pavement. Speak of the devil, he thought, tightening his grip on her sagging body. He'd been on his way out to see her, his thoughts on the revenge he had planned for her, when fate had thrown her right in his path. If he hadn't been holding her, he might have enjoyed the irony of the situation. But she was too close, her body too boneless, the memories dredged up by her half-forgotten scent too vivid—the smoothness of her skin under his hands, the heat of her mouth destroying his control, the innocence of her eyes driving him mad.

Suddenly realizing where his thoughts had wandered, he almost snorted in contempt. *Innocence!* Rose Kelly Mac-

Donald hadn't been innocent the day she was born. His father had claimed she was nothing but a little gold digger after the richest bachelor in the county, and the day she had married Frank MacDonald, she'd proved him right. If she could marry to get a ranch, why couldn't he? It was the ultimate revenge.

Ignoring the feel of her in his arms, he hoisted her closer to his chest and started toward his truck. But he'd only taken two steps when the huge Brahman bull that had been following her across the road like a puppy only moments before snorted warningly. Sullivan stiffened, his eyes trained unwaveringly on the bull, who stood only five feet away. He'd seen bulls as protective as a watchdog and twice as mean. His heart thudding, he backed cautiously away from the animal. "Easy, fella," he crooned soothingly. "I'm just going to put her in my truck and make sure she's okay. There's no need for you to get all bent out of shape. I'm not going to hurt her."

Bubba, unconvinced and wary of strangers, followed him slowly across the road.

Making his way to the truck step by deliberate step, beads of sweat dampening his forehead despite the steadily dropping temperature, Sullivan turned to carefully ease Rose through the open door of his pickup and lay her on the bench seat. Behind him, he sensed rather than saw the bull come to a stop, but Sullivan never took his eyes from Rose's unconscious body.

His green eyes as cold as the approaching storm, he noted dispassionately that she'd changed in the last five years. The pretty, gangly teenager he'd taught to kiss was now a beautiful woman. Oh, she'd never have the kind of face that would stop traffic, but there was something about her that was far more dangerous than high cheekbones and bedroom eyes. She had a delicacy, a vulnerability that called out to a man's protective instincts before he even knew what hit him. Everything about her was soft—her small but tempting mouth, her rosy cheeks and pert nose, her slightly rounded chin, the sooty lashes that hid large, wide-set sapphire eyes a man could drown in.

And beneath all that daintiness, she had a cash register for a heart, he reminded himself bitterly as he reached for the flapping edges of the shapeless man's coat she wore. But before he could pull it closed, the wind caught it and dragged it open. He sucked in a sharp breath. Beneath the coat she wore a loose-fitting, red flannel shirt that did nothing to disguise her very rounded stomach. Dear God, she was pregnant!

He stumbled back, conflicting emotions hitting him from all sides—horror that he'd nearly run her down, relief that she was okay, blind rage as his plans for revenge fizzled into smoke. Damn her, he hadn't counted on this, hadn't even considered it. A baby ruined everything! Rose was the one he had a grudge against, the one who had betrayed him, the one he intended to make pay. But he wanted no part of hurting an innocent child.

So what the hell was he supposed to do now?

Scowling down at her, he captured her wrist. Her pulse was strong and sure beneath his fingers, but her bones were impossibly fragile. His eyes flew to her face, his dark brows knit in a single fierce line above his narrowed eyes. She was too still, too pale, her skin as white as death but for the twin spots of color the cold wind had whipped into her cheeks. Leaning over her, his broad shoulders partially blocking the biting wind that raced in through the open door, he molded his hand to her cheek, patting her gently to nudge her into consciousness. "Come on, Rose, wake up," he growled. But her eyes remained stubbornly closed, her thick lashes dark smudges of color against her pale skin.

Helplessness stole through Sullivan, infuriating him. It wasn't often that he found himself out of his depth, but what he didn't know about pregnant women could fill books. Was it possible to scare a woman into labor? His blood iced with panic at the thought. If she didn't wake up in the next thirty seconds, he was rushing her into town to the hospital!

Weighted down by darkness, Rose returned to consciousness in fits and snatches. The wind keened mournfully, a low, eerie sound that sent goose bumps racing across her skin. When had she found time to lie down? she wondered groggily. It felt so good. On the heels of that thought, she heard a muttered curse. Frowning, she slowly forced her eyes open.

Oh, God, it was really him! He hovered over her like a fierce, avenging warrior, a beat-up black cowboy hat shadowing the well-remembered rugged features of his face. His jade-green eyes were hard enough to cut glass, hot enough to burn, his jaw a wedge of immovable granite. In another lifetime his tender lovemaking had brought tears to her eyes, but there was no softness to him now, no gentleness. His face tight with displeasure, he glared at her just as he had the last time she'd seen him, when he had demanded that she quit seeing Frank. Without giving her a clue as to his own feelings or any mention of the future, he'd arrogantly insisted that she risk her father's wrath for him. She'd tried to reason with him, explaining that there was nothing between her and Frank but a friendship encouraged by her father, but he'd been in no mood to listen. He had stormed out, then left town the next day. With another woman.

Deep inside the chambers of her heart, an old familiar pain throbbed, and suddenly she was aware of how close he was, how intimately his legs pressed against hers as he leaned into the truck. Instinctively she shrank back against the seat, avoiding the unwanted memories his touch stirred. "What are you doing here?"

Her voice was as weak as a kitten's, but his razor-sharp eyes watched her as if he expected her to lash at him like an angry rattler. "I came home to see my father."

She paled at his accusing tone. So he knew. Everything. Guilt washed over her even though she knew in her heart she'd done everything humanly possibly to convince Frank not to take the Lazy J from Travis Jones. She'd known Sullivan would come back one day demanding answers, and now here he was. And from the looks of him, he was fighting mad. How could she blame him? His family had once had the largest land holdings in the county. Now he had nothing.

Her throat as dry as a west Texas dust storm, she swallowed, searching for words that could never make up for the loss that he had suffered. "I'm sorry about your father," she finally managed quietly, pushing herself upright on the seat. "And the ranch. Frank made the loan before I knew anything about it—"

"Why don't you just save the pretty apology?" he jeered. "You got what you wanted. Don't start making excuses at this late date."

She frowned in confusion. "Got what I wanted? What are you talking about?"

Irritation skimmed across his brow at her innocence. Did she actually think he'd fall for the act a second time? he thought furiously. "Isn't it obvious? You went after Frank and landed in clover. Two ranches for the price of one. Not bad."

Like a well-trained parrot, Rose heard herself repeating, "Two ranches for the price of—" before she realized what he was accusing her of. Outrage flashed in her blue eyes like summer lightning. "I didn't *go after* anyone!" she cried.

"Don't you dare come back after five years and start throwing accusations at me. You weren't here. You don't know what I went through." *The nights I cried for you. The fear of having no one. The loneliness. The way Frank was always there, playing on my emotions, my fear.*

Suddenly cold, she pulled the folds of her coat close against the mound of her stomach and slammed the door shut on a time in her life she would rather forget. "If you want to blame someone, blame yourself. None of this would have happened if you hadn't run off. Now if you'll excuse me, I've got a loose bull who's going to try busting through Joe Pearson's electric fence if I don't hurry up and get him in the trailer."

With a defiant lift of her chin, she scooted off the seat and pushed past him, leaving Sullivan staring after her incredulously. She was kidding. Wasn't she? "Wait! You can't handle that monster by yourself. You're pregnant, for God's sake!"

"Don't worry, it's not contagious," she retorted, never checking her pace as she headed for Bubba, who was once again standing at the fence.

Gritting his teeth on an oath, Sullivan started after her. Confound the woman, didn't she have any sense? he wondered irritably just as a horn blared right behind him. Coming to an abrupt halt, he scowled at the driver of a white sedan that had just come around the curve and was impatiently waiting for him to move his truck from the middle of the road. "All right, all right," he muttered. "Hold your horses."

It only took him a minute to move his truck out of the way, but that was all the time Rose needed to get Bubba into the trailer. Intending to do the chore himself, Sullivan stepped out of his truck just as she lured the bull to the front of the stock trailer. He swore his heart stopped when she began to ease alongside the huge animal so she could get out the back.

In the next heartbeat he was crossing the road in five long strides and furiously telling himself that he was making a mistake getting tangled up with her again. Her pregnancy had caught him flat-footed. She might look like she was the kind of woman who could make a man wish he was a knight in shining armor, but the truth of the matter was, she was nothing but a soft-spoken barracuda in lace.

He reached her side just as she stepped down from the trailer, a concern he didn't want to feel irritating the hell out of him. "Hellfire and damnation!" he thundered. "Don't you have any better sense than to get into a trailer with an animal that size in your condition? He could have crushed you like a grape!"

Unperturbed, Rose leaned down to pick up the trailer's tailgate, which had served as a ramp for the bull. "Oh, Bubba would never hurt me. He's as harmless as a puppy."

"That *puppy* seriously considered charging me when you fainted. Dammit, stop that!" he snapped, jerking the heavy tailgate out of her hands. With an ease that she could only envy, he slammed it into place, glaring at her all the while. "What are you doing out in this kind of weather, anyway? Where are your ranch hands? They should be shot for letting you do this alone!"

Rose stiffened. His concern was a little late. Five years, to be exact. "My hands don't *let* me do anything. They answer to me, not the other way around." She stepped past him and headed for her truck. "And right now they're spread out over the ranch getting ready for the storm. I've got to get to town before it hits."

If she hadn't dismissed him as if he were a cowboy with smelly boots, he would have let her go and forgotten his revenge. But before he had time to think, before he could stop himself, he was striding after her, catching her just as she climbed into the cab of her truck. The minute she started to swing the door shut, he grabbed it. "I heard in town you need a foreman."

Startled, Rose's eyes flew to his. He stood right at her side, his lean, imposing figure crowding yet not touching her, his green eyes boring into hers. Her heart jerked in her breast at his closeness, her pulse pumping as if she'd been running uphill. Suddenly the anger she wanted to cloak herself in had a breathlessness to it that terrified her. Fighting panic, she squared her shoulders and stared him down. "It's common knowledge that all but three of my hands walked out on me. Is that why you tracked me down? You've come to gloat?"

He didn't bat an eye at the contempt in her voice. "No, I want a hell of a lot more than that," he retorted grimly. "I want the job."

Two

Rose's jaw dropped. What kind of game was he playing? She couldn't work with him; she didn't want him anywhere near her! She was just putting the past behind her and learning to take control of her life. She'd thought she was making progress, but she only had to look into his eyes to catch a haunting reflection of the naive, tractable girl she'd been at eighteen. She was still there, lingering somewhere in the shadows of her subconscious, terrified of being alone.

Frank and her father, however, had taught her there were worse things than being alone.

Sullivan saw the denial before she even opened her mouth. He had expected no less. Every time she looked at him she'd be reminded of how she betrayed him and married a man she couldn't have possibly loved just to get her greedy little hands on Frank's money. "Your husband took advantage of a sick old man," he said silkily. "Because of him, I lost my father, my home, *everything*. Don't you think the least you owe me is a job?"

Just that easily, he sent guilt coursing through her.

Don't listen, her heart cried. Think of all the times your father pushed your buttons. And Frank, for God's sake! Remember when you wanted to wait to start a family because you felt your marriage wasn't as strong as it should be? You needed reassurance, but all Frank did was accuse you of being the one with the problem if you didn't even want to have his baby. You foolishly let him convince you a baby would bring you closer together, when all he really wanted was a son to start his dynasty.

Mind games. She wasn't up to them anymore, wanted no part of them. And Sullivan thrived on them. If she had any sense, she would ignore the guilt trip and tell him no.

But she was seven and a half months pregnant. There was no avoiding the fact that soon she wouldn't be able to run the ranch at all, and the three ranch hands who had stuck by her side were hardly management material. Tommy, at nineteen, lacked the experience and maturity for the job, and Slim had a weakness for whiskey. That only left Pop, who should have retired ten years ago. Like it or not, she had to find someone else. Soon.

Which brought her back to Sullivan. Galling though it was, she had to admit that he knew ranching better than most people knew the lines in their hands. It was in his blood, as instinctive as breathing. But could he accept working as a hired hand on the River Bend Ranch, which now included land his family had owned for almost a century?

Answers. She needed dozens of them, some to questions she knew she wouldn't dare to ask. But the side of the road was no place to hold an interview. Casting a quick, measuring glance to the north, she judged the storm was still an hour or so away before turning her attention back to Sullivan. "Let's go back to the house. We need to talk."

But when they returned to the sprawling old ranch house she'd shared with Frank, the questions she needed to ask flew right out of her head at the sight of Sullivan in her living room. She'd never liked the room's grim colors, the heavy, old-fashioned furniture, the pine paneling that had darkened with age. But it had been six months since Frank's death, and she hadn't changed so much as a lamp shade. The house was and always would be Frank's. Yet Sullivan walked into it and seemed to make it his.

"Well?"

With nothing more than the single word and the lift of a dark eyebrow, he took charge of the interview. Temper flared in the depths of her eyes. If she expected to have even a ghost of a chance of holding her own with him, she would have to let him know right here, right now, that she was the boss.

Struggling for a coolness she was far from feeling, she motioned to the brown plaid Colonial sofa against the wall. Only when he was seated did she ease down to the adjacent wing chair that matched the couch. "I know you left Kerrville to join the marines," she said in an emotionless voice that never hinted at the pain his actions had caused her, "but not much more than that. Did you spend all of the last five years in the service?"

"No, I got out after two years," he said flatly, studying her through half-shuttered eyes, searching for signs of the young girl he'd known in the past. But that Rose had never been as sure of herself as this self-contained woman. Endearingly nervous whenever she'd had to take charge, she'd only had to look up at him with her big blue eyes to make him want to slay dragons for her. And all the time she'd been about as helpless as a piranha.

"Since then I've been working different ranches in Montana," he continued, his expression now as unrevealing as hers as he named several of the most famous ranches in the West. "If you want references, you can contact Leander Dawson at the Broken Spoke outside of Butte."

The subtle dig struck home, but she never even batted an eye. It wasn't his expertise with cattle she was worried about. Cursing the heat that climbed in her cheeks, she deliberately brought up the subject of her ex-foreman. "I suppose you heard why I fired Buck Hastings."

What he'd heard was that when Buck had tried to kiss her, he'd wound up face-to-face with the wrong end of a shotgun. It was no more than the old reprobate deserved, and folks in town were still laughing about it. So why was she bringing this up now? Did she actually think he gave a tinker's damn who she kissed?

He shrugged carelessly. "He made a pass. You objected. What has that got to do with me?"

"Nothing," she snapped, stung by his unconcern. "I only brought it up to make a point. Buck made the mistake of thinking I was a lonely widow in need of a man." In spite of the tight rein she kept on her emotions, she couldn't stop the shiver of revulsion that slithered down her spine at the memory of his hands on her. Agitated, she rose abruptly to her feet. "I wasn't then and I'm not now. If that's the kind of benefit you're looking for in a job, you're wasting your time. I'm not part of the deal."

Any last lingering traces of doubt he had about his plans for her vanished at her words. She thought she'd won the game hands down. He was going to show her it hadn't even begun. "Don't worry, I'm not going to jump you in the middle of the night," he retorted. "All I want is a job." For now. "Do I have it or not?"

She would have given anything to say no, but she had quit running from the realities of life the same day she'd discovered she was pregnant, the same day she'd discovered Frank's real reason for marrying her. Dragging in a bracing breath, she prayed she was doing the right thing. "You have it. You can start immediately."

An hour later the storm pushed through the Hill Country just as Rose headed home from town, her pickup loaded with enough supplies to feed an army for a month. The road was deserted, her truck headlights cutting a path through the gloom as an early darkness settled over the countryside. In the silence of the cab the windshield wipers beat out a steady, reassuring cadence, but she hardly noticed. All her attention was focused on the tinny sound of sleet tap dancing on the hood. The slushy mess had been falling for nearly fifteen minutes and showed no sign of letting up. How long did she have before the bridges iced up?

Her fingers tightened on the wheel at the thought, sweat beading her upper lip as she crawled along at fifteen miles per hour. "Smart, Rose," she jeered out loud, breaking the tense silence. "Nothing like a little negativism to top off a day that's been nothing but one surprise after another. If you want something to worry about, worry about Sullivan and that glint in his eyes when you hired him. If that wasn't satisfaction, then I don't know what is."

She scowled, fighting the uncomfortable feeling that she had been set up. But how? He hadn't made a single move toward her. In fact, once they had agreed on salary, he'd been all business as she'd told him what needed to be done before the storm hit. Even someone who knew him well would have never suspected that he'd been her first lover.

So what was the problem? Before she could come up with an acceptable answer, she started across the first of three bridges she would have to cross before she reached the turnoff to the ranch. Her breath lodged in her throat at the sight of ice already building up on the side of the pavement. Don't panic, she told herself sternly, but it was too late. Her insides were churning like a steam engine. Clamping her fingers on the steering wheel, she tried to bring her thoughts back to the safer topic of Sullivan, reminding herself that he'd done nothing to warrant her suspicions.

Yet.

And that was what worried her.

His cowboy hat pulled down low over his eyes and the collar of his jacket turned up to his chin, Sullivan headed for the house the minute he saw Rose drive into the ranch compound. She'd been gone almost two hours. Two hours, for God's sake! While he was repairing the fence Bubba had knocked down, he'd tried to tell himself that he didn't care if she stayed gone all night, then was incensed when he found himself watching the road for her. Damn her, what did he care if she got caught out in the storm? She was a big girl and it sure as hell wasn't his job to watch over her. Then it started to sleet. That was when he started thinking about murdering her. The woman had no right to make him worry about her!

Reaching the truck only moments after she parked at the rear of the house, he jerked open the vehicle's door, intending to give her a piece of his mind. But even in the near darkness he could see she was hunched over, her forehead resting on the steering wheel, her fingers biting into the wheel until her knuckles were white.

Alarmed, Sullivan stepped between the open door and the cab. "What's wrong? Are you all right?"

Her neck knotted with tension, Rose could only manage to nod as she waited for her galloping heart to slow. For the last half hour the truck had skated over the icing road like a drunken sailor. Even with her eyes closed, she could still see herself sliding toward the guardrail of the third bridge, unable to do anything to help herself. Swallowing the coppery taste of fear, she whispered, "The last two miles were a real bitch. Give me a minute."

An image of the twisting turns and climbing grades that led to the ranch flashed before his eyes. The road would be coated with ice by now, treacherous. A string of curses fell from his lips. Sending her a hard stare that dared her to argue with him, he growled, "You sit there until you stop shaking. I'll take in the groceries."

Rose couldn't have offered a word of protest if her life had depended on it. He made two trips to the house before she was even able to convince her fingers to let go of the wheel. By that time his hat and coat were damp from the now heavily falling sleet. Guilt hit her. He was getting soaked while she sat there and tried to pull herself together.

"Let me help," she said, and stepped down from the cab. Turning toward the back of the truck, she never saw the nearly invisible ice covering the sidewalk that led to the house. Her foot slipped, and suddenly she was falling. Horrified, she grabbed at the air as she started to go down. Oh, God, the baby!

"Dammit to hell!" The curse exploded from Sullivan the second he saw her start to wobble. Within seconds his hands closed around her, jerking her off her feet and into his arms.

In the next instant Rose found herself cradled against his chest, his mouth only inches away from hers as he bent over her to protect her from the sleet. Green eyes locked with blue, and the rest of the world faded to black. In the sudden silence, awareness throbbed.

Even through his coat, Sullivan felt the jolt, the burning sensation that seemed to leap between them. Stunned, he told himself that what he felt was nothing more than the aftershock of the scare she'd given him when she'd started to fall. His racing pulse didn't mean he wanted her. He couldn't! All he wanted was what was his.

Dazed, Rose could only stare at him, her heart beating madly. It had been so long since he'd held her. Another lifetime, when first love was sweet and innocent and...

Fleeting, a voice in her head bluntly reminded her. Wake up, Rose! This is the same man who broke your heart, the same turkey who walked out of town and your life without a word.

She stiffened at the thought. What was she doing? "You can put me down now," she said tightly, drawing back as far as his arms would allow. "I can walk."

His green eyes mocking, he continued toward the house without even checking his step. "Oh, really? I hadn't noticed. It seems like every time I turn around, I'm grabbing you before you can hit the ground."

Temper flared in her eyes. "Are you accusing me of deliberately throwing myself into your arms?"

"Considering the fact that I've had to catch you twice in the last three hours, I'd say, yeah, I guess I am." At her gasp of outrage, he grinned and shouldered his way through the back door. "The truth hurts, doesn't it?"

"Your ego is incredible!" she seethed, pushing out of his arms the second he set her on her feet in the kitchen. "You actually think I wanted you to hold me?"

As quick as a hawk snaring its prey, his narrowed eyes trapped hers. She couldn't fool him. Those first few seconds when he'd caught her close against him, she'd felt the pull of attraction, the warmth of memories, as strongly as he had. A blind man couldn't have missed the surprise in her eyes, the flash of hunger as sharp as lightning. "Why not?" he taunted softly. "You did once. Why not again?"

"Because I'm not that stupid now," she threw back. "I'm a big girl. I've learned how to take care of myself." Hearing the pain and bitterness in her voice, she cringed and hurried on, hoping he hadn't noticed. "I don't want a man—*any* man," she stressed. "You were hired to handle the cattle and the ranch, not me. So just keep your hands to yourself and we'll get along fine. Okay?"

Frowning, he studied her in silence, the knowledge that something wasn't quite right plaguing him like a bothersome gnat. There was disillusionment in her eyes and a hurt he didn't want to see. He told himself that whatever problems she'd had during her marriage to Frank were none of his business, but ignoring them wasn't as easy as he'd have liked as he forced a shrug. "Whatever you say, boss lady," he drawled, unconcerned. It was only a matter of time before he proved her wrong, and time was the only thing he had plenty of.

An hour later the other hands came in just as Rose was putting huge bowls of food on the round clawfoot table that dominated one end of the large kitchen. Tommy Lawson, always the first one to arrive, came bounding in like a puppy, tall and gangly and stumbling over his own feet. His dark blond hair wind-whipped and his baby smooth cheeks as red as strawberry ice pops, he sniffed the air and grinned boyishly. "I knew it! Chili! I could smell it all the way over at the Jones place. Just what a man needs when it's colder than hell outside."

Pop Kincaid followed him inside and cuffed him on the ear. "That's colder than *H* to you, *boy,*" he teased sternly. Barely five foot six, the iron-gray hair on his head nearly as short as the whiskers that grizzled his sharp jaw, he had a good fifty years or more on Tommy and didn't mind letting him know it. "Watch your mouth or you won't be putting nothing in it but your foot."

Returning to the stove for a large pan of corn bread, Rose laughed. "You're going to have a fight on your hands, Pop, if you think you can keep Tommy away from the chili. Where's Slim?"

"Right here." The tall, thin man who stepped through the doorway had the bloodshot eyes and florid complexion of a habitual drinker. Quiet and soft-spoken, with a drawn, angular face, he did his work without complaint and never touched a drop of liquor until after quitting time. Even then, he bothered no one. Rose had never known anyone to call him anything but Slim. "Something sure smells good."

"Chili," she said with a smile. "I thought you might need something to warm you up."

They started to agree, only to suddenly turn their attention to the doorway of her office, which opened directly off the kitchen. She didn't have to glance over her shoulder to know that Sullivan stood there, quietly waiting for an introduction. While she'd cooked supper, he'd closeted himself in the office and started going over the books.

Turning to face him, she said, "Guys, this is Sullivan Jones. The new foreman." She couldn't have surprised them more if she'd announced dinner was going to explode in their faces.

"Foreman?"

"Jones? Did you say Jones?"

"Well, I'll be damned."

Pop scowled at Tommy's comment and growled, "You probably will be if you don't learn to quit cussin' around a lady." Turning back to Sullivan, he studied him shrewdly, then nodded, liking what he saw. "You've got the look of your grandpa, son," he said, offering his hand. "He was a tough old bas—" suddenly realizing that Rose was watching him with a grin, he choked "—buzzard, but no one knew cattle better. I'm Pop Kincaid. These other two outlaws are Tommy Lawson and Slim."

Shaking hands with each of them, Sullivan said, "I don't know how the three of you kept a ranch this size going without more help."

"We worked our...tails off," Tommy said, editing his choice of words in midsentence. "But it was worth it to get rid of Buck Hastings."

"The son of a bitch," Pop added flatly, this time making no attempt to call a spade anything but a spade. "You should have shot him, Rose, when you had the chance."

"The worm wasn't worth it," she retorted. "Come on, let's eat before the chili gets cold."

The minute they all took their seats and a hasty blessing was said, conversation practically ceased as they dug into the food as if they hadn't eaten in a week. Oversized bowls of chili and Spanish rice were passed around the table, along with corn bread and hot flour tortillas. The only sound was that of forks scraping plates clean. Then they started on seconds.

Only after the first pangs of hunger had been appeased did the talk among the men resume. Horses and cattle were discussed, of course, and then the ranches in Montana when the men learned Sullivan had spent the last three years there. But even as he carried on a detailed discussion with them, he couldn't tear his attention from Rose. She spent more time on her feet going back and forth between the table and stove than she did sitting and eating. She'd only take a few bites at a time before she'd jump up like a jack-in-the-box to pull more corn bread from the oven or refill iced-tea glasses.

Watching her move around the table with an army-size pitcher of tea, Sullivan frowned, disturbed by the sight of her waiting hand and foot on grown men when she was as big as a house with the baby she carried. She'd obviously worked all day, gone grocery shopping, then come home and cooked a huge meal. She had to be dead tired. Why didn't she sit down and let everyone get their own damn tea?

Why the hell do you care, Jones? his conscience taunted him. She's not your wife and it's not your baby she's pregnant with.

Rose, reaching his side, poured him half a glass of tea before she noted his scowl of disapproval. "What's the matter?" she asked in surprise. "You don't want any more tea?"

He blinked, jerking back to attention. What was the matter with him? "No. The tea's fine."

"Then why the frown? It can't be the chili," she added quickly, a smile tugging at one corner of her mouth. "Tommy will tell you I make the best chili in the state."

"That's right," the younger man said between mouthfuls. "The best!"

Sullivan laughed in spite of himself. You couldn't help but like the kid, but dammit, that's all he was—a kid. How had Rose managed to hold the place together for so long with nothing but a kid, an old man and a drunk to help her? He knew the stories going around town—that no one would work for her after the way she fired Hastings—but suddenly he wanted to hear her version of the story. Slanting her a glance, he asked, "Why didn't you hire anyone to replace the hands who left with Hastings? You had to know you couldn't get by with just three men indefinitely."

She shrugged, her eyes on Tommy's glass as she refilled it. "Things have changed since you left. There aren't that many good cowboys in the area now that most of the big ranches are grazing exotic game instead of cattle. And the hands that are available aren't exactly beating a path to my door thanks to the tales Hastings has spread about me,'' she admitted ruefully.

"You pulled a gun on the man,'' Sullivan pointed out dryly. "That's hardly going to win you votes for employer of the month.''

"The jerk got no more than he deserved,'' she retorted. "Anyone else who tries the same thing is going to find himself looking down the barrel of my shotgun before he can pucker his lips.''

The warning was tossed down as carelessly as a gauntlet, and there wasn't a doubt in Sullivan's mind that it was meant for him. The others obviously knew it, too, because they were all grinning like Cheshire cats.

"You don't have to worry about me, Rose, honey,'' Pop said with a chuckle as he wiped his mouth and pushed back from the table. "These old lips are too old to pucker.''

His eyes dancing, Tommy, too, set down his napkin and pushed to his feet. "No offense, Rose, but my mama would skin me alive if I fell for an older woman. I promise I'll never lay a lip on you.''

Not missing a beat, Slim said, deadpan, "I save all my kisses for my horse.''

Her cheeks pink, Rose laughed along with the rest. "You don't know how much better I'll sleep tonight knowing I have nothing to fear from the three of you. Now get out of here and get some sleep,'' she ordered, shooing them toward the back door. "Tomorrow's going to be another rough day. And be careful on the way to the bunkhouse. I don't know what I'd do if something happened to one of you.''

With much good-natured grumbling and teasing, they straggled out the same way they had straggled in, their gruff good-nights trailing behind them as they hunched their shoulders against the cold wind and disappeared into the icy darkness. Smiling, Rose softly closed the door behind them and turned to find Sullivan still sitting at the table, watching her every move. Her smile faltered, the pounding of her heart setting the silence humming as she suddenly realized that Sullivan was the only one who hadn't claimed he had no intention of kissing her.

He wouldn't.

Even as she tried to deny it, there was something in his eyes—a hunger, a need—that made her palms damp, her throat dry. If her shotgun had been nearby she would have reached for it and tried to convince herself she really would use it. Instead all she could do was move to the table and begin to clear it as if his presence didn't offer the slightest threat to her composure.

The quiet shattered by the plates she stacked, she kept her eyes trained on her task. "You must be wondering where you're going to sleep," she began, then could have died when she glanced up to see him lift a dark brow in amusement. Sending him a withering glare, she said stiffly, "What I meant was that the foreman doesn't sleep in the bunkhouse with the others. One of the benefits of the job is a house of your own. You passed it on your way in today. It's near the ranch entrance."

He remembered the small brick house, but he had no intention of staying there, not when the house that he grew up in was less than a mile away. The only problem was that it was now hers, not his, and he could hardly just demand to move in. Swallowing his pride, he replied, "I'd rather stay in my old home. If you don't mind?"

Rose paled, nearly dropping the stack of plates. Oh, God, she should have seen this coming! Of course he would expect to go home since she obviously wasn't using the house. Bracing herself for an explosion, she reluctantly admitted, "You can't. I rented it out."

"You rented it."

She winced at his dangerously soft response. "I thought it would be better than having it stand empty and deteriorate. And it's not as if I rented it to the Manson gang, you know," she added, defending herself. "The Goodsons are a retired couple from San Antonio who always wanted to live in the Hill Country. They're taking very good care of it."

Sullivan wanted to tell her he didn't care if they were from Mars, they were still strangers living in his home. Only it wasn't his anymore, he reminded himself. It was hers now, just as everything else was that he had once taken for granted. For a while there, during the laughter and easy conversation he'd shared with her and her hands over supper, he'd allowed himself to forget what she was and why he was there. It wasn't a mistake he intended to make again.

His chair scraped the floor as he pushed it back abruptly. "Where's the key?" he demanded coldly, rising to his feet.

He was livid. Guilt-ridden, even though she knew she had no reason to be, Rose tried to explain. Hastily she set down the plates she still held and moved toward him. "Please, Sullivan, I know you're upset—"

"Where's the key?"

Every syllable dripped icicles, daring her to push him further. Without a word she wiped her hands on a dishcloth, then moved to the rack of keys that hung near the back door. Handing him the one to the foreman's house, she said quietly, "It's pretty bare. I've got some things in the attic that I was able to save from your home after Frank took it from your father. I'll get them out tomorrow and bring them down to the foreman's house. That should make it a little homier."

"Those things are yours now, not mine," he retorted. "I don't want them."

"But—"

She might as well have saved her breath. He was gone, slamming the back door behind him.

Stung, Rose watched him leave and told herself she didn't like the man he had become at all. But later as she lay in bed, the movements of the baby keeping her awake, she stared up at the dark ceiling and remembered the way he'd caught her when she'd slipped on the ice. In spite of all her best intentions, her heart hammered faster.

Three

Dawn was just a pale promise on the horizon when the clock on Rose's nightstand screamed like a banshee. Groaning, she slapped at it until she managed to hit the snooze button and silence fell like a shroud. Her body heavy, a dull ache throbbing in her head, she rolled to her back with a tired sigh. The night had seemed endless, the sleep she finally managed to find restless rather than restful. Two more hours, she thought longingly, refusing to open her eyes. If she could just have two more hours of sleep, she might be able to make it through the day. All she had to do was pull the covers over her head and forget the world. Sullivan could handle the ranch—that's what she'd hired him for—and she could rest as her doctor had been pleading for her to do for the last six months.

But outside she could hear the crack of tree limbs weighted with ice swaying in the wind that still whistled around the house. The storm had raged all night, the sleet continuing without letup until an hour ago. She didn't have to look out the window to know that the ice was at least an inch thick. It was going to be a long, arduous day of busted pipes and faucets, frozen gates and water tanks, and hungry cattle. Sullivan would need every available pair of hands to help get things back to normal. With a groan of defeat, she had to literally push her sluggish body out of bed.

When Sullivan stomped into the kitchen ten minutes later, she'd already traded her flannel nightgown for a pair of black maternity pants and a thick black and white sweater and was trying to work up the energy to start breakfast. Clinging to a steaming mug of coffee, she took one look at him and felt her heart jump into overdrive. How did he manage to look so sexy at the crack of dawn? she wondered resentfully. Dressed for the cold in old tan corduroys, a faded red sweatshirt over a black turtleneck, and a beat-up but obviously well-loved bomber jacket, he looked like he'd just walked out of a cigarette ad.

But no model in an ad ever scowled the way he was. Alarmed, she set her cup down. "What's wrong?"

Wrong? he wanted to snap. You're what's wrong! He'd spent the night chasing her in his dreams, all because he'd had to catch her when she'd slipped on that damn ice yesterday. Where was his self-control? He'd known from the beginning, when he'd first come up with the plan to make her fall in love with him again, that he'd never be able to do it without touching her. But he had to keep his own emotions on a tight leash. She was the one who was supposed to ache, not him!

Thoroughly disgusted with himself, he'd risen an hour ago with the realization that he was going to have to back off a little, at least until he was able to look at her without recalling the feel of her in his arms. He needed space—lots of it—to get his head on straight.

So much for his plans, he thought irritably, trying not to notice the violet circles under her eyes and the tiredness that seemed to weigh her shoulders down. Why wasn't she taking better care of herself? And why the hell did he care?

"Pop's arthritis is acting up," he finally answered, "so we're short-handed. Slim and Tommy are already putting out extra hay at—" *my old ranch.* Grinding his teeth on the three words before they could escape, he continued tightly, "the other ranch. Can you help me here? I need someone to drive the truck while I dump the bales from the back."

No. For a startling moment she was sure the word had just popped out, so strongly did it ring in her ears. No, she didn't want to work with him. She was already too aware of him and the memories she'd thought she had buried long ago. If she made the mistake of spending time with him, getting to know him again, it would only be a matter of time before he invaded her thoughts at will and heated her dreams. And that was the last thing in the world she wanted. Let him wait for the others to return.

But Slim and Tommy already had a full day ahead of them without taking on Pop's work, too, her conscience reminded her. Was it fair to ask that of them just because she didn't want to be alone with Sullivan? What was she afraid of, anyway? She was seven and a half months pregnant, and Sullivan had already hurt her once in this lifetime. She wasn't stupid enough to let that happen again, was she?

She almost cried out that she didn't care about being fair; the only thing she was interested in was protecting herself from Sullivan. Instead she was appalled when she heard herself say, "While you're loading the truck, I'll fill a thermos with coffee. We'll need it by the time we're finished."

At the sight of the truck slowly making its way over the uneven ground of the pasture, the cattle came running, their breath puffing from their nostrils like smoke from steam engines in the crisp, cold air. Bawling like calves, they hardly waited for Sullivan to clip the baling wire from the bales and dump the hay from the back of the pickup before they were tearing into it hungrily.

From her position in the cab, Rose kept one eye on the path ahead of her and the other on the rearview mirror, which gave her a clear view of Sullivan. Slowly driving from one pasture to the next, she watched him repeat the procedure over and over again, hardly straining as he lifted one bale after another. The wind was brutal, the weak sun that rose in the sky offering little heat. Despite the warm coat, ski mask and suede work gloves Sullivan wore, Rose knew he had to be nearly frozen. As soon as the last bale of hay was dropped in the last pasture, she quickly parked and turned the heater to high.

Seconds later an icy blast of air hit her as the passenger door was jerked open and he quickly jumped inside. "Damn!" he cursed, whipping off his ski mask and briskly rubbing his gloved hands over his stinging red cheeks. "If I didn't know better, I'd swear I was in Montana!"

Rose unscrewed the thermos top and poured him a large mug of coffee. "Here. This should help warm you up."

He took it gratefully, for a long moment just letting the steam warm his nearly frozen face. When he finally took a sip of the bracing brew, it almost scalded his tongue. Gasping, he choked, "That's strong enough to melt lead! Where did you learn to make coffee like this?"

Rose grinned. "Pop taught me. Actually he insisted. He said what I called coffee wasn't anything more than colored water and there wasn't any use drinking the stuff if it wasn't thick as tar. Want some more?"

His grin matching hers, he held out his mug. "I hope you brought more than that one thermos. It's going to take at least a gallon just to warm up my feet."

Without a word, she held up another thermos. "When the cook walked out with Buck Hastings and the rest of the hands, I learned real fast that if you're going to cook for cowboys, always make twice as much as you think you'll need and you might have enough. If we run out, we can always run back to the house for more."

Settling more comfortably on the truck's worn seat, they sipped cautiously, taking time to savor the brew now that the first chill had worn off. Silence drifted into the cab, the only sound the droning hum of the heater and their nearly soundless swallows. Outside the sun rose higher in the sky and set aglow the icicles that clung to the barbed-wire fence. Each lost in their own thoughts, neither noticed.

The combined warmth of the heater and coffee soon pulled Rose out of the reflective silence. Suddenly sweating, she tugged off her gloves and reached for the buttons of her coat. Before she could lift her hand to the stocking cap on her head, Sullivan's fingers were there first to ease it off. Startled, her eyes flew to his as her dark loose curls tumbled free.

He was close, though she'd never felt him move, so close she could see her face reflected in the depths of his green eyes. Her heart missed a beat, then picked up its pace, a half-forgotten memory escaping from the dark corner of her mind where she had tried to hide it long ago. Wrapping around her, it tugged her back in time.

Once before they had sat like this in the cold and steamed up the windows of a truck.

He'd nearly forgotten, too. Staring down at her, Sullivan could feel the chill in the air from another February day, the bite of the hunger that had gnawed at him, destroying common sense. He'd reached for her then because he hadn't been able to stop himself, because nothing could have stood in the way of his need for her—not her innocence, not his experience, not the warnings of his father that she was only using him to bait a bigger fish.

But he wasn't twenty-six anymore, and she no longer had the power to tie him in knots. He wanted, *needed,* to believe he'd moved to help her with her hat and coat because he was deliberately trying to make her aware of him, to see if he could set her heart pounding with nothing more than the touch of his fingers in her hair.

But the lie just wouldn't wash. His eyes locked with hers and there was no denying that his move had been an instinctive one. He wanted his hands on her, just as he had when she was eighteen and he should have known better. Telling himself he was giving into it only because it would further his own cause, he brought his fingers to her cheek and slowly traced the faint flush that bloomed there.

Liquid heat cascaded through Rose, pulling her under, stunning her with its strength. *Move.* The silent command drifted through her like smoke from a fire that was just starting to flare, warning her to get out of the truck before she was singed. But the flames were already licking at her, melting her bones until it took all her strength not to melt into his arms.

In growing desperation she clutched at the past and dragged it between them like a shield. "Why did you leave the way you did?" she whispered, shattering the expectant silence.

His hand fell from her face as if he was the one who had been burned, leaving her as cold as the chill that suddenly spilled into his eyes. He made no other attempt to move away from her, yet her question had managed to create a chasm between them.

For a moment she didn't think he was going to answer her. He stared out the windshield, his rugged face as expressionless as stone. "The old man was drinking," he finally stated unemotionally. "So what else was new? He didn't care about anything or anyone as long as he could drink himself into oblivion. Usually I ignored it, but that day he'd sold three of our best bulls to restock the wine cellar. I knew I should have waited until he sobered up to talk to him, but I was looking for a fight before I even found out about the damn bulls."

Glancing over at her, his accusing look reminded her that that was the same day he had argued with her about her friendship with Frank. "We lit into each other, and when it was over, I no longer had a home. There didn't seem to be any reason to stick around, so I went to San Antonio and joined the marines."

"Without even saying goodbye?" she asked, her words ringing with the hurt she'd sworn she wouldn't let him see. "How could you just walk away without even warning me you were leaving? Didn't you think I had a right to know?"

He shrugged, refusing to believe the pain he heard in her voice could have possibly been caused by him. If he'd hurt her, it had only been her pride. "You made your choice. What more was there to say?"

"Choice?" she echoed, confused. "What choice? Don't you remember? I refused to make a choice. That's why you were so mad."

"You made a choice when you refused to choose," he said coldly. "By not choosing me, you chose him."

Oh, she wanted to shake him! "I refused to make a choice because there wasn't any choice to make. At that time Frank and I were just friends."

"So when did you become lovers?" he tossed back. "The next day? You were married within six weeks of my leaving, so it had to be pretty damn fast." Before she could de fend herself with justifications that changed nothing, h effectively ended the discussion by saying, "We'd better ge back. The men will be coming in for breakfast soon. Whil you're cooking, I've got things to do in the barn."

Rose glared at him, wanting to argue, but one look at hi set face told her she'd have better luck talking to a bric wall. Without another word she put the truck in gear an headed for the house.

He wasn't being fair. All through the busy morning th injustice of his accusation gnawed at Rose, destroying th peace she usually found by working around the house. H blamed her for everything—the loss of his home, his fa ther's death, the end of their romance. Swiping angrily a the plate she was washing, she wondered if he actuall thought she could have stopped Frank from taking the ranc once his father reneged on the loan. He would have laughe in her face if she'd even tried. Last in a long line of chau vinists, he had never tolerated her interference in what h considered his business. Surely Sullivan knew that.

Working herself into a fine temper, she noisily finishe the last of the dishes, the banging of the pots and pans a childish display she couldn't resist. Oh, how she'd like to tel him a thing or two! She knew he was hurting, that the com bined loss of both his home and father was a blow no ma could take without staggering. But she would not let hin foist the blame onto her. She'd spent a lifetime trying t make up to her father for disappointments he himself ha caused, learning too late that she couldn't be responsible fo anyone's happiness but her own.

And if there was any one person who could be blamed fo what had happened, then maybe it was time Sullivan too a good long look at himself. He was the one who had left without a word, then waited too long to come home.

And she was going to tell him just that if he kept pushing her, she decided as she grabbed her coat and headed for the back door, intending to slip outside to check on the newborn calves in the nursing barn. But the minute she stepped through the door, she stopped in her tracks, her eyes on the flagstone walkway that led to the barn. Someone had thoroughly sanded it.

Sullivan.

Any one of the four men could have done it, but somehow she knew he was responsible. With so much work to do because of the storm, the others had grabbed a hurried bite to eat at breakfast, given Sullivan a report on the ice damage they had discovered so far, then rushed back to work. Only Sullivan had taken the time to realize that she intended to check on the calves after breakfast to make sure they'd weathered the storm safely.

And all the time she had been silently railing at him over the breakfast dishes, ready to give him a piece of her mind the next time she saw him, he'd been out in the cold sanding the walkway for her. Her hands clenching into fists in the pockets of her coat, she stared at the thick layer of sand, touched in a way she didn't want to be. Emotions churned in her like a tornado gathering strength, threatening to sweep her away if she didn't find something strong to hang onto. Scared, she told herself she didn't want his kindness, his concern. He couldn't act like he hated her one minute, then take time from all the work that needed to be done to see after her safety. In less than twenty-four hours he'd somehow managed to complicate her life in ways she'd never expected or wanted. It had to stop!

She would ignore him, treat him as impersonally as she would any new employee, she decided as she stomped toward the barn. And that, after all, was all he was—a new employee. She wouldn't let him wander through her mind, stirring up memories she wanted no part of. All she had to do was keep busy.

For a while she almost convinced herself it was working. She spent hours in the barn, fussing over each new calf, cleaning out the stalls, making sure there was plenty of feed and water. But the minute she stepped outside again, the sanded walkway was there to remind her of Sullivan's protective presence in her life.

Against her will, her eyes found the small foreman's house at the bottom of the hill. Almost sitting on top of the graveled ranch road that led to the highway, it seemed to huddle against the cold, without a single tree or bush near it to protect it from the wind. Rose didn't need to see through the bare windows to know that it was just as cold and stark inside as it was outside. The walls were bare of pictures, the floors naked and scarred from years of abuse from booted feet. What furniture there was, was limited to the absolute necessities—a simple iron bed that had withstood the test of time, a dresser with a cracked mirror, a sagging couch and chair in the living room and a small chrome table in the kitchen. The appliances—an old refrigerator, stove and a black and white TV—were serviceable, nothing more. Frank hadn't believed in spoiling his foreman.

An image of the house Sullivan had grown up in flashed before Rose, giving her a quick, poignant glimpse of the past. She'd only seen the Lazy J headquarters once, but she had never forgotten it. She'd expected a showplace, a large, richly furnished mansion that would reflect the wealth it had taken the family generations to achieve. Instead she'd found herself in a comfortably cluttered home decorated with family pictures and keepsakes that were more treasured than modern gadgets and opulence. By happenstance rather than design, sturdy antiques had blended in with more contemporary furnishings to create an easy, laid-back atmosphere where booted feet on a coffee table hadn't even raised an eyebrow. When Rose had compared it with the precise, everything-in-its-place house she had shared with her father, she had felt true envy.

Now, staring at the blank windows of the foreman's house, Rose tried to tell herself that Sullivan had no doubt lived in countless places just like it during the years he'd roamed the West working as a hired hand. No doubt by now he was used to barren rooms devoid of personality or life, and anything else would only get in his way. But she couldn't shake the image of him walking the bare floors, staring at the bare walls, calling a place home that didn't have a single memory to it. He had lost so much. The least she could do was give him what little of his past he had left.

Why? The question dodged her footsteps all the way back to the house despite her best attempt to ignore it. Why was it important to her that he not live in emptiness? His happiness, his well-being, had ceased to be her concern the day he'd left town with another woman. Where he laid his head at night was none of her business, and that was just the way she wanted it. Nothing had changed just because he had come home. She wouldn't let it! But still her feet led her to the attic and the things she had saved for him even when she'd thought she would never see him again.

The dull, nearly useless sun was hovering on the sharp edge of the horizon when Sullivan finally made his way back to the foreman's house. The wind had blown all day, never ceasing its whining moan as the temperature had gradually risen above freezing. Cursing the busted pipes and faucets that hadn't revealed themselves until the ice had begun to melt, he'd rushed from one disaster to another, working bare-handed in the cold for most of the afternoon. Half-frozen, his hands chapped and scraped, his face numb, he ached in every bone in his body. All he could think about was slipping into a hot tub of water and thawing out.

But the first thing he saw when he stepped through the front door was his grandmother's picture hanging on the wall across from him. At the sight of the old woman's familiar mischievous smile, he stood as if turned to stone. Slowly his sharp eyes took a deliberate inventory of the changes in the room, noting the sturdy oak coffee table stretched out in front of the ragged couch. Pain grabbed at his heart. It still bore his grandfather's spur marks. On a newly erected shelf on the wall sat the horse and carriage clock that his great-great-grandmother had brought to Texas in a covered wagon. As a child he'd been fascinated with the way the driver kept track of the seconds with his whip. It was motionless now, waiting.

His jaw clenched on an oath, he felt a slow burn crawl through his stomach, heating his blood. In all the years that he'd been gone, he hadn't allowed himself to think of any of the things he'd left behind him. Now they were here before him, reminding him of everything he had lost. Damn her, why hadn't she listened when he'd told her he wanted nothing from his past? Did she think he wanted her charity?

It was all going back, he thought on a red tide of fury, his long, angry strides quickly taking him to the door of the bedroom. Everything, right down to the nails she had used to erect the shelf for the clock. And if she didn't like it, she could damn well—

The rest of his thought fizzled and died at the sight of Rose at the room's only window, hanging the heavy blue drapes that had once kept the cold north wind out of the bedroom that had been his from the day of his birth.

Standing on a rickety chair that looked as if it would collapse beneath the weight of a kitten, she never noticed him as she pulled at the dragging weight of the drapes. The chair, protesting with a moan, swayed precariously.

In the next instant he was at her side. His heart slamming against his ribs, he grabbed her and dragged her down from the chair before she could do anything but gasp. His fingers bit into her arms, the image of her losing her balance and crashing through the window sickening him. "What the hell do you think you're doing?" he thundered, wanting to shake her when he heard the fear that thickened his voice. Dammit, what was she doing to him? "Answer me! What are you doing here?"

Stunned, her head spinning from the way he had swept down upon her like a hawk snatching its prey, she clutched at him. She'd expected his anger. Foolishly she had even thought she was prepared for it. But nothing could have prepared her for the rage that burned in his eyes, scalding her with its heat. Instinct warned her it would take only one wrong word from her to set it blazing out of control.

Her heart jumping in her breast, Rose told herself to put some space between them and try to reason with him. After all, she had a perfectly good reason for being there. But her feet refused to move and suddenly it was difficult to draw a full breath. Tension crackled in the air. "I was just hanging s-some drapes," she began, wincing when she stuttered like a schoolgirl. Lifting her chin, she struggled for a calmness that was just out of her reach. "I thought it would make the house warmer."

"Oh, you did, did you?" His fingers tightened their grip. "While you were at it, did you stop to think what would happen if you fell off that miserable excuse for a chair? You could have gone right through the window—"

"I wasn't going to fall. The chair's stronger than it looks."

It was the wrong thing to say. The last traces of softness in his face hardened into stone. "Oh, yeah?" he mocked. Releasing her as if he couldn't stand to touch her any longer, he turned to the wobbly piece of furniture and put his foot through it as easily as if he was shoving his fist through a paper bag. "You were saying?"

She stared at it aghast, her eyes wide in her pale face when she finally raised her gaze to his. "I didn't realize—"

"Then maybe it's time you did," he retorted. "A pregnant woman's got no business moving furniture or hanging drapes. There are three men on this ranch who would do cartwheels for you and you know it. If you need help, all you have to do is ask one of them for it."

The cold words lashed at her, slicing right through the wall she'd built around her heart the day he had walked out five years ago. If she'd wanted plain speaking, she'd gotten it. He wasn't a man to do cartwheels for any woman, especially her. Hugging herself, she said stiffly, "Everyone already has so much to do, I didn't want to bother them. And I thought I could do this myself."

"Well, you thought wrong." Snatching up the heavy drape she'd dropped when he'd grabbed her off the chair, he wadded it up and shoved it into her arms. "I told you last night that I didn't want your handouts and I meant it. So you can just pack all this stuff back up and cart it up the hill again. I don't want it in my sight."

He turned toward the living room without another word, arrogantly assuming the matter was settled. Rose stood her ground and glared at his retreating back. "No."

The single word stopped him in his tracks. Pivoting on his heel, his glittering green eyes silently dared her to repeat the denial. "I beg your pardon?"

She never even flinched. The young girl who would have once done anything to please him was long gone. "You heard me. *No!* I've kept these things for you for years, but now that you're back, they're your responsibility. If you don't want them, then you can throw them out. But I'm not taking them back." Stepping toward him, she shoved the drape she held at him. "Here. I believe this is yours. I'm going home."

He had to take it; she gave him no other choice. But the minute his fingers closed around the thick material, he tossed it aside and reached for her again as she started around him, the tight rein he held on his temper stretched to the limit. "You're not going anywhere until I reload your truck."

"Oh, no? Watch me!" Jerking free of his touch, she marched around him and headed for the door.

Sullivan told himself he never would have touched her if she hadn't given him the smug, superior look of a queen who was too far above him to be bothered by his anger. But at the sight of her small half smile, something in him just seemed to snap. Muttering a curse, he hauled her against him, frustration eating at him from the inside out. Without another thought, he lowered his mouth to hers.

Four

Sullivan tried to convince himself that if he hadn't kissed her, he'd have shaken her until her teeth rattled. For half a heartbeat, he actually believed it. Then he tasted her. Expecting her mouth to be flavored with the spice of anger, he savored instead the hot, wet, subtle sweetness of a need that seemed to surprise her as much as it did him. Like a silently invading fog, it drifted between them, around them, seeping into the senses, destroying thought, dulling memories, seducing.

Alarm bells clanged a warning. *Let her go.* Somewhere in the back of his mind he knew it was a command he'd do well to obey. He'd forgotten how drugging, how maddeningly addictive, kissing her could be. One taste and a man could lose his head completely and fall into his own trap. He had to let her go. Now!

The silent demand, like a shooting star, faded and died as his fingers tunneled into her hair, urging her closer. At the feel of her soft, swollen breasts crushed against his chest, the past faded into oblivion, the future into the shadows. Driven to the edge of reason, he took the kiss deeper with the slow, languid sweep of his tongue.

Dazed, her head spinning, Rose clutched at him as he swept her into the eye of a hurricane. His hands, sure and knowing and oh, so gentle, stroked her back, stealing her breath, turning her bones to water, claiming her. She should have protested—should have, at the very least, tried to push out of his arms. But she couldn't move, couldn't think, couldn't do anything but drown in a pleasure that she had never found with anyone but him.

Lightning in a bottle, that was what he'd stirred up inside her...heat that crackled with electricity, fire that streaked through the darkness of her soul, setting her aglow. She wanted to melt around him, draw him inside her, and forget the world. It had been too long since he'd held her like this, too long since he'd kissed her as if he would never get enough of her. She'd almost forgotten the taste of him, the feel of him. How had she survived the last five years without him?

You had no choice. He was the one who left.

No! She tried to block the thought, to push it out of her head before it could take root like a weed, but it was too late. Sanity returned in a cold rush that left her stiff in his arms, overwhelmed with the horrifying need to cry. Oh, God, she couldn't! With a muffled cry, she wrenched her mouth free of his and pushed out of his arms, hastily turning away before he could see the suspicious moisture already gathering in her eyes. The headache that had been plaguing her all day intensified, picking up the throbbing cadence of her heart.

One second she was coming alive in his arms and the next she was halfway across the room, her back turned to him as if he didn't exist. His blood raging, his breath tearing through his lungs, Sullivan slammed back to earth with a jolt that had curses backing up in his throat. Without thinking, he reached for her.

"Don't touch me!"

She never looked at him, never raised her voice above a whisper. But something in her tone warned him he had pushed her to the edge. Frowning, he let his hand fall to his side and watched in concern as she just seemed to fold in upon herself and wrap her arms tight across her breasts. "Are you all right?"

All right? She would have laughed at the very idea if she hadn't been afraid it would sound more like a sob. Blinking back hot tears, she choked, "Oh, I'm just peachy keen! Why shouldn't I be? Five years ago you left town with another woman without even bothering to warn me, and now you think you can just waltz back into my life like it never happened." The very idea of his arrogance infuriated her. Turning to face him, she sent him an ice-chipped glare that would have frozen a lesser man. "Well, I've got news for you, bub. I'm not the gullible, trusting girl I was back then. You touch me again, I'll fire you on the spot."

There was no doubting her sincerity, but Sullivan hardly heard the threat. His brow knit in confusion, he stared at her as if she had lost her mind. "What woman?"

His innocence almost severed the last threads of Rose's control. How dare he act as if he were lily white when he'd set the whole town talking and broken her heart at one and the same time! "Have you run away with so many women that you've forgotten all their names?" she demanded angrily. "Surely you remember Norma Jean Perkins."

Whatever reaction Rose had been expecting, it wasn't the puzzlement that still clouded his eyes. "Well, of course I remember her," he retorted in growing exasperation. "Her mother was our housekeeper and Norma Jean and I were buddies from the time we were both old enough to walk. Her old man used to beat her." His expression turned hard. "The day I left, I passed her on the outskirts of town. She had a split lip and a black eye, and she was madder than hell. She'd taken all she was going to take. She had a brother in San Antonio who had been begging her to come live with him. I gave her a ride." Looking up from his memories, he frowned. "Don't you remember? I wrote you all about it."

Stunned, she went utterly still. "You wrote me? When?"

So she didn't even remember. His mouth twisted bitterly. "A week after I left. I'm not surprised you don't remember. In the note your father returned with the letter, he said you were going to marry Frank. A man can't expect a woman to remember an old lover when she's planning to wed a new one, can he?"

Stricken, Rose could feel herself coming undone, shattering on the inside like old glass. No! Her father wouldn't have done that to her. He couldn't have. But even as she sank to the side of the bed, struggling for a composure that was beyond her, she knew that he had. "I don't suppose you still have the letter, do you?" she whispered. "I—I'd like to read it again."

He laughed shortly, a hard, cynical bark of disillusionment. "No, I didn't exactly consider it a keepsake. I burned it."

She gasped as if he'd slapped her. "Why?"

"Because six weeks after I asked you to wait for me, you married Frank," he retorted icily. "Do you think I wanted to be reminded of that?"

Pain squeezed her heart. Oh, God, he'd asked her to wait! And her dear, sweet, *loving* father had known. Yet he'd never said a word. How could he? That would have destroyed all his plans. She would have never let herself think of Frank as anything but a friend if she'd known Sullivan planned to return to her.

A silent cry of agony echoed through her, the taste of regret bitter on her tongue. Nothing would be as it was now if she'd gotten his letter. Nothing! And he blamed her. One look at his set face told her explanations would do her little good at this late date. Even if he believed her about the letter, even if he accepted the fact that they were both victims, it changed nothing. He'd lost everything that had ever mattered to him. To her. And for that, he would never forgive her.

Despair fell on her shoulders like the weight of the world. She had learned to deal with her own hurt and loss, but his was more than she could bear. Fighting tears, she struggled to her feet, her gaze avoiding his as she headed for the door. "I... have to g-go fix supper." She gestured blindly at the drape that was still on the floor where he had dropped it. "If you don't want your things, then throw them out. I won't take them back."

Sullivan made no attempt to stop her—they both needed some time to cool off. It wasn't until he heard the slam of her truck door that he saw her jacket lying on the bed. Swearing, he grabbed it and started after her, but he reached the front door just as she headed up the hill to her house, her pickup tires spitting out a trail of gravel behind her. There was no reason to be worried about her just because she was upset and had rushed off without her coat, he told himself. She was a grown woman. She could take care of herself. But he still didn't move from the doorway until he saw her park at the side of her house and hurry inside.

The hands rushed in for supper just as they did every night, nearly knocking each other over to get to the table. Usually Rose laughed at their antics, but tonight they couldn't even drag a whisper of a smile out of her. Pale and drawn, her head throbbing, she answered their cheerful greetings in monosyllables and turned to the stove to dish up the food.

Taking his usual seat at the table, Pop shot her a worried look. "You feeling all right?"

She'd never felt worse, but she only nodded, her eyes on the green beans she was pouring into a large bowl. "Fine."

He snorted, unconvinced. "Any unexpected problems crop up today?"

Tears stung her eyes at that, but she hastily blinked them away. "No," she said huskily. "Nothing."

Shrugging in defeat, he gave Tommy a look that clearly said, *your turn.* But before the younger man could work up the nerve to ask her if all the calves in the nursing barn made it through the night, the back door swung open and Sullivan walked in carrying Rose's jacket. Silence, like a dead weight, dropped into the room.

Rose kept her gaze stubbornly trained on the green beans. She'd known it was him the minute he stepped through the door. She could feel the touch of his eyes as strongly as she felt the sudden skip of her heart. Without a word she began carrying the food to the table.

The tension thickened. Every male eye in the room, dark with sudden suspicion, immediately turned to Sullivan. Ignoring them, he told Rose, "I brought your jacket. You forgot it."

She had no choice but to take it, her whispered "Thanks" little more than a murmur. Avoiding his gaze, she moved to the coatrack while he took the seat directly across from hers at the table. When she turned to find all four men waiting for her, watching her, she knew she couldn't sit there and pretend that nothing had changed. Moving to the stove for the last bowl of vegetables, she carried it to the table. "That should be all you need," she said quietly. "I'm not hungry so I think I'll go to bed. It's been a long day. Good night."

"Bed?"

"But it's not even seven o'clock!"

"Don't you even want your share of dessert?"

She only shook her head and turned down the hall to her room, leaving a stunned silence in her wake. Seconds later her bedroom door whispered shut.

Sullivan stared at the empty hallway, his green eyes brittle with resentment. She'd looked right through him as if the kiss they'd shared had never happened. He wished to God it had been that forgettable, but he knew better. He'd held her in his arms, tasted the surprise on her tongue, the unexpected yearning she'd tried so desperately to conceal. Whether she wanted to admit it or not, she'd wanted him.

And he had ached for her. Still ached for her.

He wanted to deny it; he wanted to throw something. But the frustration burning deep in his gut called for a different kind of release. With deliberate care he dredged up every grudge he had against her, every wrong she'd done him. She had a hell of a nerve accusing him of running away with Norma Jean when all the while she'd been planning to marry Frank. Talk about a selective memory! Over the years she'd made him out to be the bad guy in this, the one who had left her high and dry, conveniently forgetting that he'd poured his heart out to her in a letter she hadn't even bothered to answer herself. He'd all but proposed to her, and she'd left it to her father to tell him no.

How the old man must have relished that! He'd always hated his guts. He'd have done anything to keep him away from his precious daughter.

Including intercepting her mail?

The thought stopped him cold. Was it possible she hadn't even gotten his letter? That Lawrence Kelly had seen his hance to finally come between them permanently and had one it without even batting an eye? Could he have treated is own daughter that cruelly?

Yes. His greed would have found a way for him to justify is every move.

Sick with realization, Sullivan didn't even notice that the thers were just as silent as he until Pop shifted in his chair nd grumbled, "I don't like it."

Slim lifted a brow in surprise, his gaze shifting to the ta-le full of food. "I thought you liked meat loaf."

"Not that," the older man retorted, jerking his head to-vard Rose's closed bedroom door. "Something ain't right. t ain't like Rose to miss a meal. You know how careful she to eat all her vegetables and drink plenty of milk."

"Maybe she's just tired," Tommy suggested. "Don't regnant women get tired real easy?"

"She's been tired before but that didn't keep her from ating," Pop reminded him. "Somebody should check on er and see if she's okay. It wouldn't hurt to take her a tray, either. She's not doing her or the baby any good by not ating."

Sullivan didn't know how they all voted without saying a vord, but suddenly all eyes were on him. "Looks like you're lected," Pop drawled. "Don't forget the ketchup. She eats t on everything."

For what seemed like an eternity, Rose leaned against her edroom door without moving a muscle, her eyes closed gainst the too bright light that shone from the lamp on her ightstand. Exhaustion pulled at her, the kind that dulled he senses and weighted the limbs and made every move an ffort. Releasing her breath in a tired sigh, she wished she ould just stand there for a while, propping up the door, her nind a complete blank. But behind her closed lids the events f the afternoon played like a rerun on TV, the images hauntingly clear and painful. Sullivan kissing her, touchin emotions in her that she'd have given anything to believ were long dead. A letter she had never received, a betray by her father she'd never suspected. With that one simple ac of interference, he had destroyed forever what might hav been.

Pain clawed at her, ripping what was left of her heart int shreds. Forcing back the sob that threatened to strangle he she gathered her strength and pushed herself away from th door. She couldn't do this to herself. She couldn't tortur herself with the past and all its mistakes. Yesterday wa gone, and she had to think of tomorrow. Of the baby Nothing else mattered.

Sniffing back tears, she pulled her nightgown from he dresser and turned toward the bed, her body trembling wit fatigue. Sleep, she thought numbly, dropping down to th side of the bed to pull off her boots. She just needed sleep Everything would look better in the morning.

But when she leaned over to work the scuffed leather boo off her left foot, her protruding stomach severely restricte her reach. Her fingers closed around the heel, but sh couldn't get any leverage. Frowning, she tugged again. The again. But she was already tired, her strength nonexisten Time after time her fingers slipped harmlessly off the worn down heel, not even budging the snug-fitting boot. Trem bling with exhaustion, she was finally forced to face facts She was too fat to get her boots off.

On a day that had been nothing but one disaster after an other, that was the last straw. Her shoulders slumped in de feat, her misery complete. Hot tears filled her eyes an spilled over her dark lashes to flow unchecked down her pal cheeks.

She never knew how long she sat there in silence, he control shattered, hugging herself and feeling nothing

There must have been a tap at her door, but she never heard it until it was repeated and Sullivan called out in concern, "Rose, are you okay? I brought you something to eat."

She stiffened, her eyes swiveling to the door in horror. She wasn't surprised that someone had come to check on her—ever since she'd discovered she was pregnant, Pop and the others had fussed over her like concerned uncles—but why had they sent Sullivan to look in on her? He was the last person she wanted to see now. She was too vulnerable, too hurt, her emotions all topsy-turvy. Maybe later, when she had come to grips with the events of the afternoon, she would be able to deal with him. But not now.

Quickly rising to her feet, she hastily wiped her cheeks and smoothed her hair as if he could see through the closed door. Irritated, she forced back the tears still clogging her throat and choked, "I'm not hungry. Please, just go away and let me get some sleep."

Out in the hall, Sullivan scowled at her door and seriously considered taking her at her word. He was still reeling from his suspicions about Lawrence Kelly, and he had some serious thinking to do before he found himself alone with her again. But something in her voice wouldn't let him walk away. He hesitated, listening, and heard only a silence that should have satisfied him. It didn't. With a muttered curse, he held the tray he'd brought her with one hand and reached for the doorknob with the other. He knew he was acting like a mother hen, but he had to see for himself that she was okay.

He expected to find her standing right on the other side of the door, ready to slam it in his face the minute he pushed it open. Instead she was halfway across the room near her bed, poised there like a deer caught in the beam of headlights, longing to run. Still dressed in the black maternity pants and bulky black and white sweater she'd worn all day, she glared defiantly back at him, her blue eyes drowning in tears.

Stunned, Sullivan felt something he wouldn't put a name to clutch his heart. Her emotions had always been close to the surface, anger and joy, disappointment and laughter, chasing themselves across her face as her moods changed. He'd seen her so mad her eyes had sparked fire, so anxious to please her father he'd wanted to shake her. But he'd never seen her in tears. Whatever crying she'd done in the past, she'd done alone.

He knew he should give her that privacy now, leave her alone with her pain and forget he'd ever seen a helpless side of her. But her tears drew him to her in a way he couldn't fathom and damn sure didn't like. Before he could stop himself, he stepped inside her bedroom and nudged the door shut with his foot. "What's wrong?"

Everything. The word hovered on her tongue and almost escaped before she snatched it back. "Nothing," she said quickly, too quickly. Her nerves suddenly strung tight, she jerkily lifted her hand to her cheek to wipe back an errant tear. "I'm just tired, okay? It goes with the territory. All I need is a good night's sleep and I'll be good as new. So if you don't mind—"

Without a word he crossed to her nightstand and set down the tray of fruit and cheese he'd brought her. When he turned to face her, he was only two steps away. Up close her eyes were shadowed with secret hurts, the strength with which she usually faced him brittle and fragile. Only sheer, unyielding stubbornness kept her on her feet before him.

His fingers curled into fists to keep from reaching for her. "Are you going to tell me what's wrong or do I have to guess?" he growled softly.

"I told you—"

"You told me nothing."

"It's none of your business. *I'm* none of your business."

"So I'm making you my business," he countered. Holding her captive with his eyes, he stepped closer. "Tell me, Rosie."

The nickname, half-forgotten and never used by anyone but Sullivan, whispered over her like the softest of caresses, touching her heart. Sweet memories flooded her, weakening her, freeing the tears that had all but dried up. Blinking them back, she tried to protest, but the words just wouldn't come. Helplessly she gazed up at him and could only murmur thickly, "That isn't fair."

"I never promised to play fair." His eyes piercing hers, he slowly traced a loose ebony curl that twirled around her ear. At the first catch of her breath, his fingers stilled, cupping her cheek. "Tell me what's wrong."

She could have resisted the quiet command in his voice, the urging in his watchful eyes. But she'd never been able to summon much resistance to his touch. With his fingers alone he could draw her very heart from her. "It's stupid," she whispered, heat spreading from his hand to her cheeks. "I... I can't get my boots off. I'm t-too f-fat."

Sullivan *almost* laughed. She couldn't be serious! Of course she was fat, but she was supposed to be. She was nearly eight months pregnant! But one look at her anxious blue eyes turned trustingly up to his told him not only was she serious, she was waiting for him to reassure her that her weight was perfect.

Just that quickly the laughter died in him. He couldn't hurt her. The realization hit him from out of the blue, surprising him, but he had no time to question it. Silently he stepped back from her and deliberately ran his gaze over her.

He'd never taken the time to study a pregnant woman before, never had the opportunity of watching a woman's body change and adapt to the baby she carried inside. Fascinated in spite of himself, he compared the Rose before him with the one he'd known in the past. She had gained about twenty-five pounds, and most of it was right out front, adding curves to her figure that had never been there before. Even then, the slender waist that he'd once circled with his hands was only slightly thicker at the sides. Where she had once been as slender as a willow, she was now gently rounded, her breasts enticingly fuller. Staring at them, watching the way her sweater lovingly clung to her, his hands itched to hold her, to feel the weight of her in his palms.

Heat streaked through him, pooling in his loins, hardening him. Stiffening, he lifted his eyes abruptly and found hers waiting for him. "Of course you're not fat. You're just a little... plump."

It was clearly the wrong thing to say. Her blue eyes filled like a cresting river. "I'm as fat as a beached whale and you know it!" she wailed. "I can't even see my feet anymore!"

Flustered, Sullivan stared at her helplessly. What had he said? "Honey, you're not as fat as a beached whale—"

Too upset to even hear the endearment, she cried, "But I'm fat, right? You said I was fat!"

"I did not! I said..." he floundered, clearly out of his depth. Hell, what had he said? He'd only been trying to reassure her and she was acting as if he had insulted her! Were all women this touchy when they were pregnant? "I said *plump*," he stressed. "Plump as a chicken, okay?" he pleaded. "Pleasingly plump. *Beautifully* plump. The kind of soft, rounded plump that makes a man ache to hold you. Okay?"

She went stock-still, her eyes wide, the silence that surrounded them suddenly hushed, waiting. "Do I make you ache?"

It was the sort of question a pregnant wife asked her husband, a cry for reassurance that a husband answered with love and tenderness and caring, not words. When Sullivan realized he was only a heartbeat from taking her in his arms and doing just that, he knew he was in trouble. It wasn't supposed to be like this! Touching her, consoling her, making her want him, were supposed to be deliberate acts on his part, not involuntary urges that continually surprised him. Like a man with weights on his feet, he could feel himself sinking fast into an intimacy he wanted no part of. If he had any brains, he'd run like mad while he still could.

But she was still in tears, waiting for an answer he didn't want to give. How could he walk away and leave her like that, knowing it would devastate her? Sighing in defeat, he growled, "Yeah, you make me ache." He'd be damned if he'd tell her how much, but the rasp of his voice told her everything she wanted to know. Fighting the urge to run, he placed his hands on her shoulders, turned her back to the bed, and gently pushed down. "Sit down so I can take your boots off. Unless you're planning to sleep in them tonight."

His less than subtle teasing attempt to destroy the tension pulsing between them fell flat. Her heart galloping, Rose sank down to the edge of the bed and leaned back on her elbows. Never taking her drenched eyes from his, she stuck out her left foot.

His mouth cottony dry, Sullivan knew he had to get on with it, then get out of there while he still could. But it was a long moment before he swung his leg over hers and turned his back to her, straddling her leg. Cupping the heel of her boot, he glared at his unsteady fingers and said tightly, "Gimme a push."

Rose hesitated, her eyes on the slim lines of his jeans-clad backside. "Can't you just pull them off?"

"No, they're too tight." Glancing over his shoulder, he glowered at her impatiently. "Come on, Rose, I haven't got all night. Just put your other foot against my butt and push."

The last of her tears dried up at his tone. If she hadn't known better, she would have sworn that he'd never admitted to aching for her only moments before. Placing her foot firmly against his butt, she pushed. Seconds later her left foot slid free of her boot.

When Sullivan immediately turned his attention to the right boot, she sent up a silent prayer of thanksgiving for his brusqueness. She was, she realized, too vulnerable to handle anything else from him tonight. She needed to be held in the dark, her fears soothed, but giving in to those needs could be nothing but a mistake. He may have admitted to aching for her, but she couldn't allow herself to forget that he had every reason to hate her and probably did. And sooner or later that hate would destroy whatever desire he still had for her.

Seconds later her right foot slid free of both the boot and his touch. She felt the loss immediately. Cursing the heat that climbed into her cheeks, she struggled to sit upright, but made no attempt to stand. He was still too close, his green eyes too knowing. Grabbing the nightgown she'd draped over the end of the bed, she hugged it and prayed he wouldn't know she needed to fill her arms with something.

"Thanks," she said gruffly. "From now on, I'll wear my loafers."

So she didn't want him to have another excuse to touch her. He scowled, wondering what she would say if he told her he no longer seemed to need an excuse where she was concerned. His hands had a will of their own when she came within touching distance. And there didn't seem to be a damn thing he could do about it, except avoid situations like this until he had a better handle on his control.

"Then you won't need my help anymore," he retorted. "Good." Turning on his heel, he headed for the door without another word, obviously anxious to leave.

Could she have stopped him with a single word? The thought worried her long after he had walked out, not because of the answer, but because of her need to ask the question in the first place. What was happening to her? What had happened to the Rose who had sworn after Frank's death that she would never again let herself be put in a position where she could be hurt by a man?

Five

Her sleep that night was troubled, filled with shadowy images that prodded and poked and picked at her until she was thoroughly miserable. Her head tossing fitfully on her hot pillow, she knew she had only to wake up to escape the demons tormenting her, but she couldn't manage to open her eyes. Hours passed, the covers tangled around her, strangling her. Moaning, she pushed and kicked at them, but her arms and legs felt as if they were weighted down with lead. Then the alarm shrilled promptly at five.

You have to get up and make breakfast. The guys will be hungry. They're counting on you to have a hot meal ready for them.

The softly whispered words drummed in her head like a tom-tom, nudging her to wake up, nagging her, pricking her conscience with guilt until she finally rolled out of bed with a weary groan. Every muscle in her body cried out in protest. Moving stiffly, she struggled into her pink chenille robe, a frown quilting her brow as the tie belt kept slipping from her clumsy fingers. Silly thing, she thought hazily. What was wrong with it? Concentrating fiercely, she tried to tie it again, but the thick material just wouldn't cooperate. Exhausted, she let it fall from the belt loops. It was too hot to wrap it shut anyway, she decided blearily, and trudged through the darkened house to the kitchen.

Her mind on automatic pilot, she flipped the light on over the sink and carried potatoes and a knife to the table. Plopping down into a chair, she stared down blankly at the five-pound bag of potatoes in front of her and tried to remember what she was supposed to be doing. But suddenly the heat that surrounded her seemed to be coming from inside, making her dizzy. Swaying, she slammed her eyes shut when the room began to whirl, but it didn't help. With a weak groan, she pushed the potatoes out of the way and let her spinning head drop to the table.

She wasn't taking care of herself. His razor lifted halfway to his jaw, Sullivan stared at his lathered face in the mirror and almost snarled a curse at the worry that had been aggravating him all night, destroying any chance he'd had of sleeping. She had no right to walk through his thoughts as if she owned them, he fumed, dragging the razor down his cheek. If she'd gone to bed without touching the food he'd brought her, that was her business. She was and always would be another man's woman, carrying another man's child. How the hell had he allowed himself to forget that? She didn't need him to watch over her; she never had. Under all that softness that stirred a man's protective instincts was a woman who knew how to get what she wanted. He'd be damned if he was going to let her keep getting in his head this way!

Satisfied, he finished shaving and dressing, then headed up to the main house for breakfast, determined to keep her out of his thoughts for the rest of the day. With all the work he had to do, it shouldn't be too difficult, he decided. There was still damage from the ice storm to be repaired, breeding records to update, paperwork that had been neglected when Rose had been forced to manage the ranch alone. He could barricade himself in her office and fill his head with numbers and not think of her for hours.

But the minute he stepped through the back door all thoughts of avoiding her vanished. The kitchen was in darkness but for the light that burned over the sink, while an unnatural silence hung in the air. Sullivan froze, suddenly chilled. By this time of the morning Rose should have been at the stove cooking, the scent of frying bacon and brewing coffee drawing the men in for breakfast. Something was wrong.

He tried to tell himself she was probably just running a little late and still dressing. But the silence that grated on his nerves was too still. Uneasiness raising the hairs at the nape of his neck, he started across the kitchen toward the hall that led to her bedroom. Two steps later, he saw her. She sat in the shadows that engulfed the table, her head resting on its bare, smooth surface, her nightgown and robe draping her motionless figure. One hand lay on the table in front of her eyes, blocking out the light, the other near the sharp blade of a knife.

Sullivan paled, his heart shocked into stillness for one awful moment before jumping back into a jerky rhythm. Her name a hoarse cry on his lips, he rushed to her side. "Rose! Honey, what is it? What's wrong?"

She never gave any sign that she heard the endearment that fell so easily from his tongue. Her breathing a muffled rasp in the tense silence, she lay unmoving, her complexion a sickly white that was relieved only by the unnaturally bright flags of color that burned in her cheeks. Dropping to his knees, Sullivan carefully laid his hand against her face only to swear at the heat that radiated from her in waves. "My God, you're burning up!"

Panic surged through him. Jumping to his feet, he leaned down to carefully lift her in his arms and cradle her against his chest. Her head lolled against his shoulder, scaring the hell out of him. Was she unconscious or was she just too weak to open her eyes? "Rose? Wake up, sweetheart," he urged huskily. "Look at me!"

In the dark clouds of fevered sleep that engulfed her, Rose could just barely hear his frantic voice calling her. Swimming up through the blackness, she raised her head a fraction and tried to answer, but she was so tired. "Sul-van?" In her mind she called out loudly to him, but his name came out only as a weak whisper. Suddenly scared, she forced open eyelids that seemed heavy with lead to find him worriedly staring down at her. "Whazwrong?" she slurred. "Can't... keep eyes... open."

"You've got a fever, baby," he said roughly. "Just relax. I'm putting you to bed."

Her brow wrinkled. There was... something... she had to do. "Breakfast—"

"Will take care of itself," he growled, striding toward the hall. "You couldn't lift an egg if your life depended on it. You should have called me and told me you were sick."

The gentle reprimand fell on deaf ears. When she didn't answer, he looked down and saw that she had slipped back into a hot, restless sleep. His heart twisted in his chest. Tightening his arms around her as if she would somehow slip free, he tried to tell himself that she probably just had a touch of the flu. But her breathing was ragged, her face as pale as death, and he'd never felt so helpless in his life.

The back door opened suddenly. Slim, Tommy and Pop spilled into the dimly lit kitchen just as Sullivan reached the entrance to the hall. At another time he might have been amused at the shock that spread from one face to another, but all his attention was focused on the unconscious woman in his arms. She was so still! "Rose is sick," he threw over his shoulder as he turned back toward her bedroom. "Somebody call a doctor."

The minute he reached her bedroom, he gently set her in the middle of the bed and supported her with one hand while he used the other to tug off her robe. Flinging it out of the way, he eased her down to the pillow and pulled the quilt up to her chin. But within minutes she had kicked it off.

"Hot," she mumbled in her sleep. "It's so hot."

Retrieving the cover, Sullivan dragged it back over her, then sat on the side of the bed so she couldn't toss it aside. "Easy, baby," he soothed as he gently pushed her dark hair back from her stark white face. "You have to stay covered so you won't get chilled." But she never heard him. Locked in a world of heat and pain, she pushed weakly at the heavy comforter.

"How is she?"

He glanced up to find Pop standing in the doorway, his weathered face looking decidedly gray in the weak dawn light creeping through the blinds. "Burning up," he said flatly. "Did you get hold of the doctor?"

He nodded. "Dr. Walker. He's Rose's obstetrician and the only one I could think of who might make a house call. He'll come, but it's going to be awhile. There's a new strand of flu spreading like wildfire through the county, and every doctor in town's snowed under."

Sullivan swore, a short, pithy curse that didn't begin to express the fear rising in his throat. "That's great. Just great!"

"He said to try to bring her fever down and get some fluids in her," the older man continued. "Just tell me what you need and I'll get it."

Sullivan stared down at her white face, the dark, vulnerable circles under her eyes, the swollen belly that protected her baby, and felt his heart constrict painfully. "Orange juice," he croaked without taking his eyes from Rose. "And some cool water and a washcloth. I'm going to sponge her down."

During the next few hours he lost track of the number of times he ran a damp washcloth over her face, down her neck, under the dark curls that feathered her nape, then around to the damp patch of skin he'd revealed by unbuttoning her flannel gown to the middle of her chest. As soon as the cloth began to absorb the heat from her body, he cooled it in the bowl of water Pop had brought him and began the process over again.

If she was aware of his ministrations, she didn't show it by so much as a flicker of an eyelash. But her breathing grew smoother, her muscles less tense, her sleep less troubled. With agonizing slowness, she melted into the bedclothes as she finally began to relax.

The fever left her so suddenly Sullivan was caught off guard. One moment he was running the wet cloth over her chest and giving serious consideration to stripping her of her gown to cool the rest of her body, and the next she was shaking like a leaf, a soft moan squeezing from her throat. Alarmed, he snatched the washcloth from her brow, but the chills continued, racing over her shivering body like a cold north wind.

"Pop!" Thundering for the old man, he yanked the quilt up to her neck and quickly tucked it in around her. Her teeth chattered in the tense silence. Leaning over her, his hip brushing hers, Sullivan used his chest and arms to hold the covers close and wrap her in a cocoon of warmth. But her shivering only seemed to increase rather than decrease. Sweat popped out on his own brow at the violence of her chills, the worry he could no longer keep at bay sickening him. If the fever could do this to her, what was it doing to the baby?

"Where the hell is that doctor?" he yelled angrily when the door behind him opened. "Get on the phone again and tell him to get his butt out here—"

"His butt is here," an unfamiliar male voice drawled from the doorway.

Stepping into the room with Pop right behind him, Dr. Andrew Walker moved to the opposite side of the bed with deceptively lazy grace, his eyes meeting Sullivan's for only a second before dropping to Rose. He wasn't a tall man, and with his boyish features he could have passed for a college student. But any doubts Sullivan had about his abilities evaporated as the other man hardly waited for Pop to introduce him before he was taking charge of the sick room. Snapping his bag open, he pulled out his stethoscope and had it at Rose's breast before Sullivan had even shifted out of the way. His face inscrutable, he listened to her heart, then her lungs, then the baby's heartbeat.

His own heart slamming against his ribs, Sullivan watched the stethoscope hover over the mound of Rose's stomach, lingering as if something wasn't quite right. His palms damp, he waited with growing dread for the doctor to tell him the baby was in trouble. Instead the other man glanced up sharply and pinned him with his suddenly hawklike eyes.

"How long has she been like this?" he asked, snapping questions at him. "Did she take anything? Any medication? Has she complained of any pain or discomfort besides the fever and chills?"

"No, only the fever. As for taking anything, she hasn't even swallowed a sip of juice since I got here."

"What about before you found her? Is there any chance she may have taken a cold medication or even aspirin?"

"She wouldn't have done that," Pop said from the doorway before Sullivan could answer. "She's been real careful not to take anything that might injure the baby."

His eyes on his watch as he took Rose's pulse, the doctor nodded. "Let's just hope that in her fevered state, she knew what she was doing."

Sullivan felt his heart stop at the other man's grim tone. "The baby?" he asked huskily. "Is everything all right with the baby?"

"For now," Dr. Walker replied. Slipping his stethoscope from his ears, he pulled the covers back up over Rose's shivering form and stood, making no attempt to hide his concern as he faced Sullivan and Pop. "I don't want to give her anything unless I absolutely have to, so we're going to try to let this thing run its course. The fever's gone for now, but it'll be back and worse than before."

Letting the warning sink in, he shot them both a hard look as he closed his black bag. "You can't let it rage out of control, or she's going to be in trouble. The next twenty-four to thirty-six hours are going to be rough. You'll have to cool her down and get some liquids in her when she's hot, then warm her up when she's cold. So tell me now if you think you can't handle it. The hospital's already full to the rafters, but I'll find a bed for her even if I have to put a cot in the hall. I'm not taking any chances on her losing the baby."

Just the thought of that happening was enough to turn Sullivan's chiseled face gray. "I can handle it," he said flatly. "I won't leave her side."

For a long, silent moment the doctor just studied him, as if weighing the strength of his mettle, then finally nodded. "Good. Then I'll leave her in your hands." Pulling out a prescription pad, he wrote down his phone number and handed it to Sullivan. "That's my home phone. Have someone call my office every two hours today to update me on her condition, then again in the morning. If there's any change in her breathing, any sign that she or the baby may be in trouble, I want to know immediately. Don't hesitate to call me at home. Okay?"

"Don't worry," Sullivan assured him. "If she even looks like she's in trouble, you'll hear about it."

There were times over the course of the long day and evening that followed that Sullivan was only a fraction of a second away from reaching for the phone. When the fever held her in its fierce grip, she couldn't seem to stand the touch of anything against her hot skin. She tossed and turned, kicking away even a light sheet while her fingers worried at the flannel gown that covered her. Caught up in her misery, Sullivan reached for the hem, intending to strip it from her body and give her the relief she so desperately craved. But every time he started to ease it up, her hands were there to catch his, her murmured protests, disjointed and frantic, stopping him as nothing else could. For reasons she couldn't explain and he couldn't understand, he could run the damp cloth under her gown and over every square inch of her, but she wouldn't let him see her naked.

Touched by her modesty in ways he never expected, he couldn't bring himself to force the issue when she was as weak as a kitten. Defeated, he left the gown covering her thighs and gently rolled her to her side. Once again he dipped the washcloth in the cool water and wrung it out, then slipped it under her gown. With sure, steady strokes, he swept it over her back and hips, murmuring to her, calming her, before sliding his hand around to her rounded stomach and breasts.

Those were the moments that were most difficult. He tried to keep his touch impersonal, his thoughts trained strictly on the job at hand—cooling her down. But *he* was the one who burned at the feel of her soft, silken skin under his fingers. *He* was the one who found his thoughts clouded with a fever that had nothing to do with the flu.

Lunch and supper came and went with no change in her condition. Pop took over the cooking duties, supplying Sullivan with fresh water and washcloths, as well as every conceivable juice he could think of to tempt Rose. Sullivan didn't have the heart to tell him that the effort was wasted on her—if he was able to get two swallows down her at a time, he considered it a victory. And victories were few and far between. Chills chased after the fever, and in those moments all he could do was pile the covers on her and stretch out next to her on the bed so he could hold her and try to warm her.

When she finally fell into an exhausted sleep around midnight, he almost laid his head next to hers on the pillow and gave in to fatigue. He'd have given a hundred bucks for fifteen uninterrupted minutes of sleep, but he couldn't take the chance. He was so tired he might not hear her if she called for him.

Groaning, he rolled away from her and forced himself into an uncomfortable chair next to the bed. Pop and the others had reluctantly retired to the bunkhouse an hour ago, and the house was silent and deserted. Dragging his eyes from Rose's dark curls spread across the pillow, Sullivan's gaze landed on the book lying on the nightstand. He'd noticed it earlier but had hardly had time to even look at it, let alone read it. Casting a quick glance at Rose to make sure she still slept peacefully, he reached for it and flipped it open.

The first trimester of pregnancy is most critical—

Growling a curse, he almost slammed the book shut then and there. Dammit, he didn't need to know how babies developed in the womb from one month to the next or how pregnancy affected a woman's body. That kind of information was needed by husbands and fathers-to-be, not ex-lovers. In spite of that, however, his fingers refused to put the book down. Calling himself a fool, he turned to the last trimester and started to read.

Two chapters later an image of the baby formed in his head, its sweet, innocent features a fascinating blend of both Rose's and his features. How would he feel if the child she carried was his? If *she* was his? Would he be any more worried about the two of them than he already was?

The thought stunned him, terrified him, infuriated him. Muttering an oath, he banged the book shut and dropped it as if he'd been slapped. Had he lost his mind? This wasn't a game, a fantasy. They weren't two children playing house, pretending they had a make-believe baby. The situation was all too real, and the child she carried was Frank's. He wasn't going to fall into the trap of thinking of it as his.

Trapped in the tide of heat that reclaimed her helpless body, Rose didn't hear him swear as he wrestled with his thoughts. He paced restlessly at the foot of her bed, talking to himself, but it was Frank's voice that echoed inside her head, Frank's voice that haunted her, taunted her.

A son. I want a son to start my dynasty. A son to own everything that was once Sullivan Jones's. You will give me a son!

"No!" Her cry little more than a hoarse whisper, she fought the sheet that covered her, hot tears spilling from her tightly squeezed eyes. "You can't use my baby. I won't let you."

"Easy, honey. It's all right. No one's going to use the baby, especially me. It's okay."

The softly spoken voice came to her through the darkness, accompanied by cool, soothing hands sweeping over her, calming her. But she wasn't fooled. Frank couldn't trick her by using Sullivan's voice and pretending nothing was wrong. He wanted her baby! Agitated, she shrank away from the hands on her, her temperature skyrocketing with every frantic beat of her heart. "No! That's a lie. It was always a lie," she sobbed. "You never wanted me, just me. All you could think of was a MacDonald dynasty. Well, I'm not having a dynasty, just a baby. A girl." She hugged the thought to her, her arms wrapping around her belly fiercely, protectively. Half to herself, she muttered, "I'm having a girl. You've got no use for a girl."

Sullivan felt like he'd been kicked in the gut. What the hell was this? he thought with a scowl, rage building in him at the sound of the hurt thickening her voice. Just what exactly had that bastard Frank done to her? Promising himself he would one day find out, he gently smoothed her hair back from her hot face. "It's all right, sweetheart," he soothed quietly. "Everything's going to be just fine. You have a little girl if that's what you want. No one's going to take her from you, I promise."

He never knew how long he sat there, murmuring assurances to her as his hands tenderly worked to draw the fever from her. But for nearly an hour his words fell on deaf ears. Struggling against his hands and calming words, she stubbornly insisted she was having a girl and he couldn't have her. He just let her talk and rewet the washcloth, promising over and over again that everything would be all right.

Gradually the tension drained out of her, taking with it the worry that churned in her. Her mumbled protests turned to sighs, her agitation to peace. Her breathing slowed and deepened until Sullivan was sure she had gone to sleep. With painstaking slowness, he started to ease from the side of the bed, trying not to wake her. But he'd hardly moved at all when her hand reached out to grab his.

Surprised, his gaze flew to hers. Her eyes were swimming in tears, yet lucid as they met his. "I—I never got . . . your letter," she whispered brokenly. "I thought I'd never see you again."

All his suspicions confirmed, Sullivan could only stare at her and tell himself that the loss of one letter changed nothing. Frank was the man her father had wanted her to marry, and God knows she would have walked on water to please her old man. Even if she'd known he was coming back for her, he doubted she would have ever found the strength to defy Lawrence Kelly. But now he would never know for sure.

Feeling the familiar anger that had simmered in him for five long years weakening, he gently wiped away the tears that spilled from her eyes. "I would have never done that to you," he told her with gruff sincerity. "But none of that matters now. Close your eyes and rest. I'll be right here if you need anything."

She nodded and gave in to the need to close her eyes. Her hand still holding his, she drifted into sleep, his closeness bringing a comfort to her that in her weakened state she never thought to question. He was there, at her side, for as long as she needed him. Nothing else mattered.

Her fever broke hours later. Exhausted, Sullivan just stared blankly at the moisture dotting her face and wearily wondered if he'd forgotten to wring out the washcloth. Too tired to think, he leaned over her in concern and placed his fingers across her damp brow, only to jerk back in surprise. She was cool!

Unable to believe it, he quickly moved his hand to the side of her neck, her arm, the silken smoothness of her back underneath her gown. At the feel of her skin, he almost laughed out loud. She was as cool as a cucumber to his touch, her body drenched in her own sweat!

The grin that started to stretch across his face fell away abruptly as he realized that the sheets and her nightgown were damp and heavy and clinging to her. He couldn't leave her like that, not without taking the chance that she might get even sicker. Somehow he had to find a way to change both her and the bed.

Frowning down at her still form, Sullivan swore at the idea of having to wake her, but there was no other way. Even in the grip of fever, she'd clung to her gown, refusing to let him see her naked. If she woke now and found him stripping her, the fat would be in the fire. And upsetting her now was something he wasn't willing to do.

The first step, however, was to change the sheets. After collecting the necessary linen from the closet in the bathroom, he leaned over her and carefully rolled her to her side. As limp as a rag doll that had lost half its stuffing, she let him place her where he would. Satisfied, he unhooked the corners behind her, then placed a dry, fresh sheet in position. Pulling it tight until it and the damp one were close behind her, he laid a towel on the clean sheet to protect it, then slowly rolled Rose back over. She sighed and settled herself more comfortably as he finished making the bed.

Next came the more difficult part. Sitting on the side of the bed nearest her, his hip only inches from her rounded stomach, he shook her shoulder gently and murmured, "Rose? Wake up, honey. You've got to change gowns."

A fleeting frown whispered across her brow, but she only snuggled deeper into the mattress. "Hmm?"

"Your fever broke, and your gown's damp," he explained, lifting his fingers to the dark curls clinging to the nape of her neck. "You need to change."

But she just shook her head and turned her face into his palm, unconsciously seeking his touch. "Too tired. Later," she promised faintly, drifting back into sleep. "Tonight."

Her sensuous movement went through Sullivan like a heat-seeking missile, shooting straight to his loins. And she didn't even know what she was doing. "Honey, tonight is already here," he said roughly. "And if you don't get out of that wet gown soon, you're going to chance getting pneumonia. C'mon, all you have to do is sit up and lean against me. I'll do the rest."

His coaxing tone tugged at her, penetrating the exhaustion that clouded her mind. Forcing open her weighted lids, she squinted up at him, frowning when his face wavered in and out of focus. "Sullivan?"

"That's right, baby." He flashed her a reassuring grin and slipped his arms around her shoulder. His face only inches from hers, he saw the start of surprise flare in her eyes. "It's okay," he said easily. "I'm just going to sit you up so I can get this gown off of you."

Before she could even think to protest, she was leaning against him and his hands were edging up her gown. "No!"

He stopped cold at her strangled cry and fought to ignore the feel of her in his arms. She was sick, he reminded himself furiously. And another man's woman. Why was he having such a difficult time remembering that?

"C'mon, Rosie, be reasonable," he pleaded gruffly. "The gown's wet and you're sick enough as it is. Let me help you into something warm and dry. I won't take two minutes, I promise."

Her mind foggy, she knew she couldn't afford to get any sicker, not without risking the baby. She had to think of the baby. "The light," she choked. "Turn out the light."

If that was all it took for her to trust him, he would have gladly turned off every light in the county. Without a word, he switched off the bedside lamp. Darkness enveloped them, warm and private and secretive. Somehow it only made the situation worse.

Feeling his senses start to hum, his imagination kick into overdrive, Sullivan croaked, "Okay, lean up a little and lift your arms." Blindly searching for the bottom of the long gown, his fingers encountered the warm bare skin of her thigh instead. He jumped like a virtuous teenager and muttered a terse curse. He'd had dreams of dragging her clothes from her, but not like this! Jerking his hand higher, he grabbed the gown and sighed in relief. In the next instant he whisked it over her head and tossed it aside.

In the darkness she was all but hidden from him, save for the nearly invisible paleness of her skin. The shadows that concealed her also intensified his senses, making him all too aware of her closeness, the heat of her, the shallowness of her breathing. His fingers unsteady, he fumbled for the clean gown he had draped over his shoulder. "Here," he said thickly. "Lift your arms again."

Silently she complied, tension crackling between them like firecrackers on the Fourth of July. Feeling his way, he guided her hands into the arms of the gown and let it drop, quickly dragging the warm folds down over her head and shoulders. It should have been a simple procedure, but the backs of his hands and fingers brushed against her naked breasts and belly as he pulled the gown down the rest of the way, her softness burning him alive. His body hard with need, he jumped off the bed and sent up a silent prayer of thanksgiving for the darkness.

Not that she would have noticed if he'd turned on the light, he thought in rueful irritation. His touch hadn't disturbed her in the least. Before he'd even sunk onto the chair next to the bed, she'd slipped back down under the covers and drifted into sleep.

Six

The dream began as a full-blown nightmare. Trapped in a burning forest with no way out, she choked on smoke and panic, and tried to run. But the heat was too intense, her body too tired. Her legs gave way, the crawling flames singeing her nightgown. She started to scream, but suddenly Sullivan was there, calming her fears, holding the fire at bay with nothing more than the stroke of his hands. She could almost hear his voice coming to her through the shadows, reaching out to her, gentling her as he pulled her into a hidden pool of clear, cool water. The heat that racked her body vanished, the heaviness that had seemed to push down upon her chest lifted. The vague, unnamed terrors that haunted her left as quickly as they'd come, and only Sullivan's hands remained, tugging at her gown. She felt his breath at her cheek, his powerful chest as he held her close while he tenderly pulled her damp garment from her and replaced it with a dry one. Touched by his thoughtfulness, she tried to hang on to the moment, to him, but the darkness encroached again and he disappeared into the night.

A dream, she thought sleepily. Sullivan would never show her such loving care anywhere but in a dream. From the moment he'd nearly run her down, he'd made no secret of the fact that he felt nothing but contempt for her. Even when he had kissed her, she'd felt his resentment, his anger, she reminded herself as she slowly stretched and opened her eyes.

Her tired body protested the abrupt movement at the same time her room snapped into focus. Stunned, she stared at the chaos that surrounded her. The nightstand was loaded down with bottles of juices, towels, glasses, even a bowl of water, and washcloths were everywhere—the carpet, the nightstand, even carelessly tossed across the footboard of her antique bed. But how—

Images suddenly played before her mind's eye—her head pounding, her body aching so that she had to literally drag herself out of bed to cook breakfast. The knife she hadn't had the strength to hold. Sullivan's voice coming to her through the haze of pain, telling her she was sick, her fever had broken, her gown was damp and he was going to help her change into a dry one.

The baby! Her hands flew to her stomach, a sob of fear ripping through her, tears filling her eyes. Beneath her palms the baby kicked strongly, as if she were protesting her mother's sudden clench of terror. A watery laugh bubbled up inside Rose. She was okay. Thank God!

She was still lying that way, her arms protectively wrapped around her stomach, when Sullivan soundlessly opened the door and stepped into her bedroom. His hat pulled low and the collar of his coat turned up to his chin, he stopped short at the sight of her tear-streaked cheeks. When he'd left her to check on the calves in need of attention in the nursing barn, she'd been sound asleep, lost to everything but the rest she so desperately needed. He'd expected her to sleep at least until noon and here it was barely seven and she was already crying.

Last night he would have taken her in his arms and consoled her. Today he stood firmly where he was, a frown darkening his face and concern making his voice husky. "What's wrong? Why are you crying?"

Startled, her heart jumped in her throat at the sight of him standing just inside the doorway. From the shadows cast by his hat, his bloodshot green eyes sharpened on her, pinning her to the bed. Rose felt her pulse scatter and couldn't stop her gaze from roaming over him. Unshaven, his granite jaw darkened with stubble, tiredness carving deep lines in his face, he had the rough, rakish look of a man who had weathered a hard night. There was no softness in his unyielding expression, no glint of tenderness in the flat line of his mouth. Was this really the same man who had touched her in her dreams, whose voice even now she could hear in the distance murmuring reassurances?

But then her eyes met his and held. Intimacy. It was there between them, an invisible force, a subtle knowledge that once achieved could no longer be ignored. It tugged at her like the moon pulls at the tide, crumbling her defenses, coaxing her to forget the past and all the pain he'd once caused her.

"Rose? Did you hear me? What's wrong?"

She glanced up to discover that he had stepped closer. "N-nothing," she stuttered, grimacing as muscles sore from fever tightened as she pushed herself erect. When he made a move to help her, her hands flew out, stopping him. If he touched her just once like he had last night, she'd be lost.

"I'm fine," she lied, avoiding his eyes to take in the disaster area that had once been her room. "This place looks like it was hit by a tornado."

Sullivan's hand fell to his side. "You were a pretty sick puppy—fever, chills, delirium, the whole nine yards."

"Delirium!" she echoed, horrified. "Did I say something I shouldn't have?"

He just shrugged noncommittally. "Not as far as I was concerned. Don't worry about it."

How could she not worry when she didn't even know what she'd said? She eyed him suspiciously. "What did I talk about?"

"Frank. The baby. Me."

Oh, God! "I see," she said carefully. "Anything else?"

He grinned. "Nope, that pretty much covers it."

Rose gritted her teeth, just barely resisting the urge to throw a pillow at him. Oh, how he was enjoying this! "Would you care to elaborate? My memory's pretty fuzzy."

"You want a girl," he said, holding up his fingers and ticking off the important points one by one. "Frank wanted a dynasty. You never got the letter I sent you five years ago. And you still like the feel of my hands on you."

A fiery blush spread across her cheeks like spilled wine on a white tablecloth. "I never said that!" How could she have told him such a thing when she was only just now coming to consciously realize it? "You made that up!"

He green eyes glinted wickedly. "Did I? I thought you didn't remember."

"I don't, but I know I would have never said something like that. Unless it was the fever talking."

He arched a dark, dangerous brow. Suddenly tired of her denials, he eliminated half the distance between them with a single step. "Shall I prove you wrong? It's going to take you a couple of days to get your strength back. A man can do a lot of touching when a woman needs his help just to sit up."

"No!" Her voice rose two octaves, but she didn't care. He wasn't touching her! "You just keep your hands to yourself, Sullivan Jones! The fever's gone so I don't need you hovering over me anymore. I'm not completely helpless, you know."

She didn't have the energy to walk three feet without needing to stop to catch her breath, and they both knew it. But he only mocked softly, "Whatever you say, boss lady. You're in charge. Just holler if you change your mind."

For two days he didn't come anywhere near her. She heard the low rumble of his voice in the kitchen when he came in for meals, but it was Pop who fixed trays for her and sat by her bed while she ate. It was Slim and Tommy who found excuses to drop in on her at odd times of the day and somehow managed to get a smile out of her. But it was Sullivan that she found herself watching the doorway for. It was Sullivan that she unconsciously listened for—his laughter, his footsteps in the hall, his truck driving into the yard.

Even then, she refused to admit that she missed him.

Then on the third day she felt strong enough to go to the table for breakfast. There were three pairs of male hands eager to help her to the table, three pairs of legs ready to jump to grant her slightest wish. But it was the fourth, distant, silent man who stood back from the protective crowd that she wanted at her side. The minute her eyes met his, she could no longer deny the truth. She was in big trouble.

And he knew it. She could see it in his eyes, an awareness, a complacency that came close to bordering on smugness. If he'd have pushed her just once, she would have told him exactly what she thought of him. But the man had the patience of the devil. He never crossed her; he didn't even speak to her unless it was about ranch business, but the message he sent her was clear nonetheless. *You can run but you can't hide.*

Over the next few weeks, as her strength gradually returned, she certainly tried.

Leaving the running of the ranch in his capable hands, she turned her attention to fixing up the nursery. There was wallpaper to choose and contrasting paint for the trim, a handyman to hire to do the actual work and baby furniture to buy. She already had a wonderful antique cradle that she'd bought the week after she'd discovered she was pregnant, but she'd never had time to refinish it until now. After clearing it with her doctor, she armed herself with paint remover, sandpaper and wood stain and retired to the back porch.

For three days she scraped and rubbed and sanded, hardly noticing the tediousness of the work, the ache in her lower back, the tiredness that stiffened her shoulders and knotted the back of her neck. Contentment stole through her like the first rays of the morning sun, warming her all the way to her bones as she pictured her baby lying in the cradle, her little rump in the air, a dreamy smile on her small mouth as she slept. One day the cradle would be handed down to *her* daughter, then to her daughter's daughter, on down the line through time, a symbol of love between mother and child. For that reason alone, it had to be perfect.

When it was finished and carried into the completed nursery by Slim and Tommy, everything was just as Rose had pictured it. Tiny, playful clowns tumbled over each other on the wallpaper, the bright primary colors, as well as the antics of the clowns, adding a festive touch that would catch the baby's eye as she began to acquaint herself with her world. Against one wall the cradle sat empty, waiting, the old mahogany as smooth as satin and as rich as the finɛst burgundy wine. Across from it stood a mahogany chest hat had belonged to Frank's mother, its drawers already ıalf filled with diapers, blankets and gowns that looked mpossibly small. By the time the baby arrived, she hoped o have it full.

The room only needed one thing to make it complete. A ocking chair. But not just any one would do. She planned o spend hours in that chair, nursing her baby, loving her, ɛuddling her close as she softly murmured her hopes and lreams to her. Together they would rock around the world n it, so, like the cradle, it had to be chosen with care.

The morning after she finished the cradle, she started a earch of every antique store in the Hill Country, convinced that the perfect rocking chair was just waiting to be ound in some little out-of-the-way hole-in-the-wall. The act that her search also took her away from Sullivan's watchful, infuriatingly patient gaze for long periods at a ime only made it all the better. He would never have to know that out of sight did not necessarily mean out of mind. Blast the man, when had he gotten into her head?

Sullivan plucked the note off the refrigerator and scowled at Rose's neat, flowing script.

Sullivan, there's a chicken casserole in the refrigerator for supper. Heat in the microwave at 70% power for 8 minutes or until hot in the middle. Enjoy!

Muttering an oath, he crushed the note in his fist and tossed it into the trash can. For the past three days she'd left early and come home late, always leaving a similar note on the refrigerator to taunt him. Did she think he didn't know what she was doing? She was avoiding him, and in the process, running herself ragged. All because he was getting to her.

He should have felt satisfaction. Revenge was sweet and he should have at least been able to anticipate the taste of it on his tongue. Instead he was worrying himself sick about her and it was all his own fault. He'd lost all his objectivity, all his anger, when he'd taken care of her while she was sick. And he damn sure shouldn't have read that baby book he'd discovered on her nightstand!

Talk about brilliant moves, he thought in disgust as he jerked open the refrigerator and took out the casserole she'd left for supper. There was a lot to be said for ignorance and bliss. A man who didn't know any better wouldn't worry about the effect of paint and varnish fumes on an unborn child. His gut wouldn't knot at the thought of a pregnant woman driving all over the state looking for a rocking chair when she needed to be home with her feet up. And that same unsuspecting fool wouldn't work himself into a state of agitation when his pregnant woman didn't eat enough to keep a baby sparrow alive. He wouldn't lose sleep over whether she was getting enough calcium, or a baby that wasn't even his.

Glaring at the casserole, he shoved it into the microwave and set the timer, but it was Rose he glowered at. Damn her, what was she doing to him? She had him acting like an expectant father! And he didn't like it one little bit. He wouldn't be suckered into acting like a substitute father for Frank MacDonald's kid! He didn't even want kids. He wouldn't do to an innocent child what his father had done to him. And when she got home, he was damn well going to tell her that!

But by the time she finally walked in the door it was after nine, black as coal outside, and he'd spent the last two hours pacing the floor, glancing out the window for her headghts, and swearing. When she strolled in as if she hadn't a are in the world, he wanted to throttle her for driving him razy with worry. Setting his jaw, he said stiffly, "I saved ou a plate. It's on the stove. I've got work to do."

She should have thanked him, then let him go. It was the ensible thing to do, considering the fact that she'd spent the ast two weeks avoiding him. But even though he hadn't said nything, she knew he'd been waiting for her, his hard face tched with lines that she could almost mistake for worry. 'Thanks for the food," she called after his retreating back. 'But I think I'll just wrap it up and put it in the refrigera-or for tomorrow. I've had this craving for Mexican food all lay—"

He stopped abruptly, his gaze razor sharp as he turned to ace her. "Where are you going to get Mexican food this ime of night? It's already after nine. All the restaurants in own are closed."

"Mi Tierra's isn't. It's open all night."

"You're going to drive to San Antonio? Tonight? Just for a taco?"

Rose grinned at his incredulous tone. "You don't have to nake it sound like I'm going to the moon. It's not that far. can be there before ten thirty."

Of all the harebrained ideas! "You've been on the road ll day. Don't you think it would be better to just eat some-hing here and get some rest instead of spending half the night on the interstate? You can have Mexican food tomor-ow."

"But I might not want it tomorrow," she replied simply. 'And I do tonight." Heading for her bedroom to change nto something more comfortable than the maternity jeans and white smock she'd worn all day, she patted his shoul-der in passing. "Don't worry, Sullivan, I know the highway ike the back of my hand. I'll be perfectly safe."

"I'm not worried!"

Rose bit back a grin. If he wasn't worried, then she was a bald-headed monkey's uncle! "Good. Then there's nothing more to discuss. As soon as I change into something that isn't covered in road dust, I'll be on my way." Shooting him a serene smile, she walked down the hall to her bedroom.

But Sullivan had no intention of giving up so easily. Ten minutes later, when she opened her door dressed in a free-flowing pink smock dress, her black curls neatly combed, her blue eyes sparkling, he was waiting for her. "You're not driving the highway alone in the middle of the night," he announced in a grim voice that dared her to argue. "I'm going with you."

Rose expected him to ruin the evening with his obvious disapproval. At the very least she'd have bet money that he would continue trying to make her see reason, as if what she was doing was totally *un*reasonable. She was all prepared to defend herself with a perfectly logical argument when he threw a curve by asking her how her day went. There was no hostility in his tone, none of the tension that had made all their conversations for the last two weeks stiff and uncomfortable. In fact he'd sounded almost friendly!

Surprised, she said, "All right."

"Any luck finding a rocking chair?"

"Not yet." Still not sure his interest was genuine, she told him about the type of chair she wanted, and before she knew it they were talking—really talking—for the first time since he'd returned, as if the past, with all its pain, had never happened.

The seventy-five miles between the ranch and San Antonio clicked off with amazing speed. The conversation shifted from the rocking chair to Bubba and his love for the cows on the neighboring ranch to politics and dream cars and

Montana winters as they arrived at the restaurant. For the first time in years they laughed together—there in a booth at Mi Tierra's, while mariachis played and the air was filled with music, friendly conversation and the tantalizing scent of fajitas sizzling on a hot plate. Time slipped away, forgotten.

It was after one in the morning when they headed back to the ranch. Silence, comfortable and easy, filled the cab. Relaxed, the warmth from the heater seeping into her feet, Rose sighed in contentment and tried to hang on to the wonder of the evening. But her eyes insisted on closing as they left the city lights far behind. Leaning her head against the passenger door, she promised herself she'd sit up straight in a few minutes and help Sullivan stay awake for the drive home. In the next instant she was asleep.

Taking his eyes from the dark road only long enough to take a quick glance at her, Sullivan frowned at the awkward angle of her head as she slumped against the door. Whipping his gaze back to the highway, instinct had him reaching for her before he even stopped to think. "Come here, honey," he murmured, urging her against him. "Lean against me before you get a crick in your neck."

Without protest, she settled against him, her head nuzzling into the hollow of his shoulder, her soft breath drifting across his neck in a sleepy sigh. Sullivan almost groaned, desire, hot and electric, charging through him until every nerve ending in his body seemed to spark fire.

This is a mistake, Jones, a voice in his head growled. *Let her go. She's too damn easy to hold.*

He heard the command, recognized the truth of it, and ignored it.

He held her all the way to the ranch, his senses throbbing with awareness. By the time he quietly parked in front of her darkened house, he was aching for the taste of her. Common sense warned him to wake her and get her out of the truck before he did something stupid, but it wasn't a night to play it safe. The moon was waning and hung low in a dark, cloudless sky, casting deep, hushed shadows where lovers could hide from the world. Giving in to the need, he gently shifted her in his arms and leaned down to kiss her awake.

Sleepily, Rose felt his breath trail across her lips once, then twice, nudging her toward consciousness. Still groggy, she resisted, her eyes closed in concentration as she waited for the caress to be repeated. She was dreaming, she thought drowsily, her heart slowly starting to pound. He was holding her, tempting her with a promise of a kiss. Sighing his name, she shifted closer, sinking deeper into the illusion.

Again and again his lips brushed hers, caressing, teasing, nibbling, never quite giving her what she wanted. In a dozen silent ways she tried to tell her dream lover that she wanted his mouth hard and hungry on hers, but he only gave her a taste of his tongue, a whisper of heat, the anticipation of passion yet to come. She moaned, need rushing through her veins, and reached for him.

Sullivan knew the exact instant she came fully awake. One minute she was whimpering in her sleep, and the next her searching hands ran into the solid wall of his chest. He felt her start of surprise, felt the soft, boneless weight of her body start to stiffen. Any minute she would be pushing out of his arms, demanding to know what the hell he thought he was doing. He'd been asking himself the same thing for the past five minutes.

But he couldn't let her go. Not yet. Not when his blood was roaring in his ears and his body was tight with desire. Not when he'd spent the last few moments nearly driving himself mad by denying himself a real kiss. With a groan, his mouth settled hotly, possessively over hers.

Startled, she sucked in a deep breath, ready to protest, but with a quick flick of his tongue, he stole the words from her. A shudder racked her, and suddenly it was difficult to breathe, let alone think. The heady, masculine scent of him surrounded her as surely as his arms did, drawing her into a world of white-hot heat and seduction. Passion, too long denied, heated to flash point in a heartbeat.

She could feel herself sinking into him, melting like hot fudge in a blast furnace, and could only gasp, clutching at him, her tongue wildly tangling with his. His hands flew over her, fighting her clothes, tearing at stubborn buttons, nearly ripping them free to reach her. She should have protested, was even gathering the words in her head when his fingers closed around her breast. Her *bare* breast. When had he found the clasp of her bra? She moaned, straining against him as his fingers began an exquisitely thorough exploration of her body, charting every sensitive inch of her breasts, her thickened waist, the spread of her hips, the heat locked between her thighs. And with each touch, each sliding caress, each bold rub of his thumb across her nipple, the need in her coiled tighter.

She had to stop him, stop herself. The thought danced to the frantic thundering of her heart the minute he lifted his mouth from hers, but then he buried his hands in her hair and ran quick, darting, desperate kisses over her face and throat and she was lost. Whimpering, she locked her hands around his wrists and held on for dear life.

Sullivan felt his control unraveling and made no effort to slow the pace. Not tonight. He couldn't stop now, not when he finally had her right where he wanted her. Sweet. How could he have forgotten what she was like when she was caught up in the sweet flames of desire? She could turn a man to cinders with just her kiss alone.

And she was his, all his. He could taste it in the red-hot heat of her response, feel it in the abandoned way she arched into him as he cupped a swollen breast in his hand, hear it in the cry that broke from her parted lips when his teasing fingers gently plucked at her nipple. He could have taken her then and there, in the cab of her truck, and she wouldn't have breathed a whisper of protest.

That thought alone was nearly enough to drive him over the edge. His mouth hungrily latched onto hers, while his hand slid under her dress to the tantalizing, silken smoothness of her inner thigh. Passion roared in his head, need screaming through him. He told himself she couldn't respond to him the way she did unless she felt something for him. He knew her too well—

Before his closed eyes, images from the past flickered hauntingly. A lifetime ago she'd melted in his arms, denied him nothing, made him think he was the only man in the world for her. But she'd walked down the aisle with someone else.

He jerked back abruptly, his breathing harsh and labored in the sudden tense silence. Glaring at her in the darkness, his emerald eyes spearing hers, he said hoarsely, "Why did you do it, dammit? Why did you marry Frank so fast?"

The swift, sudden descent from passion left her reeling. She shook her head in confusion, unable to believe he wanted to talk about Frank now. "What?"

His hands at her upper arms, he just barely resisted the urge to shake her. "Could he set you on fire with just a few kisses? Or did just knowing that you finally had what you'd always wanted make you melt in his arms like a prostitute?"

She gasped, stricken. How could he talk to her like that after what they had just shared? "Damn you, you keep talking about what I'd always wanted, but what I wanted was you!" she cried. Pushing out of his arms, she hastily scooted out of reach across the seat, her fingers trembling as she righted her clothing. "I thought you'd left town with another woman and Frank was the only friend I had. Do you hear me? We were just *friends.*"

Hugging herself, her eyes stared starkly into the past. "A month after you left, Dad had a heart attack," she said hollowly. "He was dying, and I was so afraid of being alone. If it hadn't been for Frank, I don't know what I would have done. He was there for me."

And you weren't.

The words were never spoken, but they hung in the air nevertheless. Sullivan wanted to snap back at her that they both knew why Frank had been there, but he held his tongue, a muscle ticking in his jaw. "So if you were just friends," he finally growled, "then how the hell did you end up married to him?"

"When I finally realized that Dad wasn't going to make it, Frank promised to protect me, to take care of me." She swallowed, forcing moisture into her dry throat. "I thought he loved me and he convinced me that I could love him if I just let myself." At Sullivan's snort of disdain, she snapped, "I was eighteen, just a kid, and I needed to believe him. And Dad had always wanted me to marry Frank. He said he could die happy knowing I was taken care of by a man like Frank."

Sullivan's mouth flattened into a hard line. She'd always been a sucker for the guilt trips her old man had laid on her. He could just imagine him putting her through a horrible deathbed scene just to push her into Frank's arms.

Suddenly realizing the direction his thoughts had turned, he brought them to a screeching stop. What the hell was he doing? Making excuses for her? Thinking of her as the innocent in all this? How could she be the innocent when she'd ended up with everything?

"Your dad would have pushed you off on Attila the Hun if he'd thought he had the bucks," he retorted contemptuously, clinging to his anger. "He didn't care about what kind of husband Frank would be, only how much money he had."

He didn't say anything she hadn't thought herself, but somehow knowing that he, too, knew how little value her father had placed on her was more than she could bear. Suddenly she'd had enough. Grabbing up her purse and coat, she searched for the door handle. "Believe what you like," she said coldly. "You will anyway. But if you came back after all these years just for revenge, you wasted your time. I didn't do anything to you, and I'm not going to let you hurt me. Not again. My days of being manipulated by men are over. Just stay away from me." Pushing open the door, she climbed out and slammed it shut, then walked into the dark house alone.

Seven

Ⱥfter that, a state of cold war settled over the ranch like a eat wave that showed no sign of breaking. Tension built ntil the air became so close and dense that even the hands oticed. Smiles faded, then disappeared altogether. Meals ecame something to be endured, the jokes that were usu-lly passed back and forth across the table turned into stilted onversations that swiftly faded into long, awkward si-ences. And with each passing day the threat of an explo-ion grew more imminent.

A black scowl on his face, Sullivan went about his duties rowling at anyone who got in his way. He knew the men vere cutting him a wide berth, but Rose didn't even bother) avoid him. She simply withdrew into herself. She didn't mile, she didn't talk except when it was absolutely neces-ary, and her appetite became nonexistent. Worry crept into he frustration eating at him, infuriating him all the more. Ie found himself wanting to shake her, to demand that she take care of herself, that she quit doing this to him. She was driving him crazy!

How could he carry out his plans when she continued to confound him the way she did? He'd been so sure his revenge was perfectly justified, so sure that nothing she could say would excuse what she had done. The facts had seemed cut and dried, damning. But nothing was turning out as he'd expected. He had underestimated Lawrence Kelly and forgotten what lengths the man would go to get what he wanted—a rich son-in-law. He wouldn't have hesitated to sacrifice his daughter's happiness to achieve his own blind ambition. Now that he'd had time to think about it, Sullivan could hear the pain thickening Rose's voice when she'd told him she wouldn't be manipulated again. A muscle ticked along his jaw. She wasn't supposed to be hurting!

Rose saw the way he watched her when he didn't think she was looking, his frown fierce, the concern darkening his eyes making her want to scream. How dare he act as if he cared about her! He was only out for revenge. That's all he had wanted from her since the day he'd returned. All his kisses, all his gentleness when he'd taken care of her when she was sick, all the worry he'd shown when she pushed herself too hard, was nothing but a ruse to hide his real intent. He was going to make her pay for what he'd lost with a piece of her heart. She had never been so miserable in her life.

Seven nights after their run to San Antonio, Rose stood in the kitchen and stared out at the dark, wet night, hugging herself against her own tortured thoughts and the dampness that seemed to slip beneath the window and crawl into her bones. The rain had started yesterday, sometime during the middle of the night, and was still coming down in buckets. Pop, Slim and Tommy had pulled on slickers after supper and gone out to move the cattle near the river to higher ground, their curses nearly drowned out by the umble of thunder directly overhead. Watching them disappear into the darkness, Rose silently agreed that it was a ousy night. But what other way could you expect to end a iorrible week?

She knew she was in a rotten mood, but there didn't seem o be anything she could do about it. There'd been a contant ache in her back ever since the rain had started; the aby's movements over the last three nights had robbed her of sleep, and every time she turned around, she found herelf wanting to cry. She was tired…tired of the waiting, tired of the rain, tired of the heartache that only seemed to deepen very time her eyes collided with Sullivan's.

"We need to discuss the buying trip I'm leaving on next veek."

She didn't have to glance over her shoulder to know that e was standing at the doorway to her office watching her vatch the rain. Stubbornly she stayed where she was, her iand absently kneading her lower back. "Can't it wait unil tomorrow?" She couldn't deal with him tonight, not vhen they were so cut off from the rest of the world and her ierves were skittish and shaky.

"Why not now?" he insisted. "I've already gone through he marketing tapes and picked out some good stock from everal ranches out west. I just need you to look them over ind okay what I've selected—"

Rose whirled, sparks flaring in her blue eyes. "What *ou've* selected?"

Her sharp tone, as well as her obvious objection, caught iim by surprise. Why, after nearly a week of hardly speakng to him, was she snapping his head off now? Feeling his vay carefully, he said, "Nothing's carved in stone. I've just oulled some tapes I thought you'd be interested in. I was inder the impression that was part of my job."

It was. Twin spots of color burned in her cheeks. How dare he be so reasonable! Of course buying new cattle to improve the herd was part of his job, but he didn't have to act as if it was *his* cattle, *his* ranch, he was improving. He was taking over with frightening ease, making it so easy for her to hand over all responsibility to him, to lean on him as if he would always be there for her. But how long would he stay after he got the revenge he thought he deserved?

"Which ranches do you plan to visit?" she demanded stonily.

His eyes narrowed, but all he said was, "The Broken Arrow in Montana, the Rolling R in Colorado and the Twisted Snake in New Mexico."

"Frank never did business with any of them."

It was the ultimate insult. He stiffened, so tempted to tell her that Frank wouldn't have known good bloodlines from a hole in the ground that he could taste it. But as he opened his mouth to do just that, he caught a glimpse of himself in his memory, sitting by her bed reading about how precarious a woman's emotional state was during pregnancy, especially as she neared her time. Helplessness stole through him, his irritation fizzling. How did any man live through his woman's pregnancy without going stark, staring mad?

Dragging in a steadying breath, he said with a calmness he was proud of, "Then give me a list of the ranchers Frank dealt with and I'll contact them. You're the boss."

She was, but she was beginning to hate having him remind her of it. "I'm not pulling rank—"

"I didn't say you were," he said patiently. "Just tell me what you want me to do, sweetheart, and I'll do it."

She wanted to ask him to hold her, to call her sweetheart again, to assure her that his kisses had had nothing to do with revenge. But she couldn't. Turning back to the window, she wrapped her arms around herself and gazed out at he wet night. "I'm sure the cattle you've chosen will be ine," she said huskily. "Just leave the tapes on the desk and 'll look them over tomorrow. I'm too tired tonight. I'm going to bed early."

It was a clear dismissal, but he hated leaving her when she eemed so upset. Yet if he stayed, he'd have to touch her, and in her present mood she might scratch his eyes out. Reuctantly moving to the coatrack next to the back door, he oulled on his bright yellow slicker, then tugged his cowboy hat down low over his eyes. "Then I'll get out of your way. See you in the morning."

Rose held herself stiffly, her quiet good-night cut off by he closing of the back door. Seconds later she caught the blurred flash of his headlights in the rain as he turned his ruck toward the foreman's house. Only then, when she was ure she was alone, did she allow herself the luxury of tears.

Flat on his back, Sullivan glared at the ceiling over his bed, listening to the rain that drummed against the tin roof. t was no use, he thought in disgust, giving up on the sleep hat wouldn't come. He couldn't get Rose out of his head. Every time he closed his eyes she came to him in the darkness, her blue eyes clouded and uncertain, dark with hurt, a trace of fear, a longing she wouldn't admit to. She'd given him just that same look earlier in the kitchen. He'd wanted o hold her then, to take her in his arms and keep her safe hrough the night, through all the nights to come until she had the baby. A woman in her condition, less than a month away from her time, had no business being alone. She needed a man at her side.

And he, like it or not, needed to be that man.

The truth, refusing to be ignored, shouted at him in the dark stillness that engulfed him. With a sigh of defeat, he dropped his arm over his eyes. What a mess.

* * *

When the phone rang an hour later he was just teetering on the edge of sleep. Cocking open one eye, he glowered at the clock on the nightstand. Two o'clock in the morning. Cursing under his breath, he fumbled for the phone and dragged the receiver to his ear. "Yeah?" he mumbled.

"Sullivan?"

At the sound of Rose's tremulous whisper, a sharp, inexplicable fear snaked into his stomach. He bolted upright, his bare feet hitting the floor with a thud. "What is it, honey? What's wrong?"

"It's..." She hesitated, as if her throat suddenly closed up and she couldn't get the words out. He heard her swallow what he thought was a sob. "I... th-think it's t-time."

Confused, he clutched the phone tighter. "Time for what, sweetheart? What's going on?"

"The baby," she choked. "I think the baby's coming."

"It can't be," he said stupidly. "It's not due for another month, is it?"

She almost laughed at that as her breath caught on a giggle. "I don't think she cares that she's early. She's com—"

A hiss of surprised pain cut through whatever she was going to say and leapt through the phone to stab Sullivan right in the heart. He paled. "Just sit tight," he ordered hoarsely. "I'll be right there."

He banged the receiver down without waiting for her to answer, then almost tripped over his own feet when he tried to tug on his jeans with fingers that were suddenly all thumbs. Panic, like a thief in the night, slid through his veins. She couldn't be having the baby now! It was too soon! Jamming his feet into his boots without bothering with socks, he snatched up the nearest shirt he could find—a torn T-shirt. He was pulling it over his head when he slammed out the back door into the driving rain.

Five minutes later he rushed into her kitchen like a wild man, his wet hair standing on end, his soaked T-shirt plastered to his chest, a wide hole exposing one hairy underarm. At the sight of Rose calmly pacing the kitchen in a red plaid flannel gown and matching robe, he stopped short, gasping for breath. "Are you okay?" he asked anxiously.

She nodded, her throat suddenly constricted with tears. The sick fear that had gripped her ever since she'd realized she was in labor vanished the minute Sullivan walked in the door, his wet face dark with stubble, his green eyes wide with worry. Peace settled over her. Everything would be okay now. He wouldn't let anything happen to her baby. Resuming her pacing, she shot him a relieved smile. "I'm fine. Just a little nervous. I haven't done this before."

Neither had he, but he sure as hell wasn't fine! Ignoring the water he dripped on the floor, he started toward her nervously. "Sweetheart, you should be in bed. C'mon, I'll help you, then I'll call the doctor."

She turned away. "No, I don't want to go to bed. I need to walk."

Oh, God, she was going to be stubborn, he thought with a groan. He could see it in the set of her jaw. Following behind her, he tried to reason with her. "You're only going to wear yourself out prowling the kitchen like a caged tiger, honey. Don't you want to lie down? You'll be a lot more comfortable in your own bed."

"No, I won't. The pressure starts to build—" Her words trailed off as she stopped suddenly and reached out to grab the back of a kitchen chair.

From half a room away Sullivan watched her breathing splinter, the soft lines of her face slowly tighten with the contraction that clawed at her with gradually sharpening talons. Her breathing changed, deepened. Inhale. Exhale. He could almost hear the rhythm of her thoughts, almost feel the concentration that helped to partially block out the pain.

Then, suddenly, it was over. She released a final gust of triumph and determinedly resumed her pacing, her heart-shaped face untroubled and free of pain. "I've got to walk."

Shaken, Sullivan couldn't manage a single word of protest. It was *his* gut that still clenched in a contraction, his heart that still wheezed with panic. Suddenly there was no avoiding the truth. In spite of all the times he'd warned himself not to get wrapped up in Frank's baby, he felt as if it was his baby she was having, his baby that was coming into the world a month too early.

He wasn't ready for this.

Panic skipped through him like a rock skipping water, the ripples spreading outward, threatening to swallow him whole. Galvanized into action, he jumped toward the bedroom. "To hell with calling the doctor now. I'll call him from the hospital. Where's your suitcase?"

"In the hall closet. But—"

He didn't wait to hear more. Striding into the hall, he jerked open the closet door and pulled out the overnight case sitting right in the front. The minute he felt its light weight, he glared at her accusingly. "You haven't packed."

"I didn't think I needed to for at least another couple of weeks," she defended herself. "How was I supposed to know the baby would come this early?"

"What do you need? Gowns? Underwear? Socks? Anything else?" Striding into her room, he yanked open drawers and pulled out the items she'd need, haphazardly throwing them into the small case. Seconds later he locked it and headed for the back door. "Let's go."

Rose stayed stubbornly where she was, fighting the urge to laugh. He was more nervous than she was! "Sullivan, there's plenty of time to get to the hospital. My contractions just started. The baby won't be here for hours."

He hesitated, then slowly turned back to face her, wishing he didn't have to worry her now, when she already had so much on her mind. But she had to know what they were up against. "The river's been rising for hours, honey. If we don't leave now, we might not be able to make it into town at all."

Her smile faltered as she reached out to steady herself, feeling as if her knees had just been knocked out from under her. "I never realized . . . I wasn't thinking . . ."

He was at her side instantly, gently swinging her up into his arms and carrying her to the back door. "Don't start panicking on me now, babe. I promise you everything's going to be fine. You just relax and let me take care of the details."

But everything wasn't fine. Ten minutes later Sullivan braked to a stop on a small rise, the steady beat of the windshield wipers loud in the sudden silence. Together they followed the beam of the headlights to the muddy, raging water rushing over the top of the first of the three bridges that stood between them and town. Without a word, he turned the truck around and headed back to the house.

Another contraction hit Rose the minute she stepped back into the kitchen. Worry clogging her throat, she started gritting her teeth as she fought the pain. She never saw Sullivan come in behind her, never felt him slip his arm around her and pull her against him. But suddenly he was there, his husky murmur in her ear calming her, soothing her, quieting her. "Easy, honey, don't tense up. Breathe through it. Take deep breaths and let them out through your mouth. Slow and easy. That's it. You're doing fine."

With agonizing slowness, the pain lessened, withdrawing like receding floodwaters until it disappeared altogether. Only then did Rose start to tremble. She wasn't going to make it to the hospital. "Sullivan..." She clutched at him, fear eroding her control. "The baby...it's too soon! I need a doctor. How can I have a premature baby without a doctor?"

Unnerved, Sullivan was wondering the same thing, but the last thing she needed now was his doubts. She was already unraveling in his arms. With a confidence that was nothing but pure bluff, he promised, "You'll have your doctor, honey. You said yourself that the baby won't be here for hours. That gives me plenty of time to find a way to get you to the hospital." Tightening his arm around her reassuringly, he led her to her bedroom. "While I'm doing that, I want you to stop panicking and get some rest. You're going to need your strength. Okay?"

She nodded. But as he helped her into bed, she couldn't let him go without voicing her biggest fear. Taking his hand, she held him at her bedside, her eyes searching his. "What do you know about delivering babies?"

"Honey, it's not going to come to that—"

"But what if it does?" she insisted. "I need to know from the outset if we're flying blind here."

He could have lied to her. She was looking for reassurance, not the truth, and at that moment he could have claimed to have delivered a half dozen kids and she never would have questioned him. But when her deep blue eyes gazed up at him so trustingly, he couldn't be anything but honest with her. "Not a heck of a lot," he replied grimly. "I read one of your baby books while you were sick, so I know pretty much what to expect. But if you're asking if I've ever helped deliver a baby, the answer is no."

She swallowed. She'd wanted the truth; she'd gotten it. "Then I guess this is a first time for both of us," she said with a forced lightness that fell miserably flat.

"Hey, don't give up on me so soon," he teased, brushing her hair back from her ashen face. "I may have to call in the National Guard, but I'll find a way to get you out of here in time." Easing his hand from hers, he backed toward the door. "While you're resting, I'm going to make some calls from the kitchen. I'll be back before the next contraction starts."

He was as good as his word. Her eyes closed, all her concentration focused on her breathing as the tension slowly started to tighten in her abdomen, she didn't realize he was there until his hand closed over her fingers where they gripped the sheet. Through the gradually darkening red haze of pain that shrouded her, she heard him whisper, "That a girl. You're doing great. Dr. Walker's going to have a helicopter here at dawn to take you to the hospital." His fingers squeezed hers. "You hear me, sweetheart? You just hang in there a couple more hours, and the baby will be born at Kerrville General just as you planned. Everything's going to be fine. Just fine."

Dawn, however, seemed a lifetime away. Caught in the never-ending cycle of pain, then rest, then pain again, Rose swore that time slowed to the speed of a snail on ice. Her world became her bedroom, the only sounds that of the never-ending rain pelting the roof, her labored breathing and Sullivan's hushed, gentle words of encouragement. He was her rock of strength. In constant contact with her doctor, he sweated through every contraction with her as they gradually increased in intensity, joked with her as she came down from the high of pain, then tenderly wiped the perspiration from her face.

Her defenses down, she stared at him, her eyes roaming over his rugged face, noting the lines of strain that bracketed his mouth when he thought she wasn't watching, the shadows in his green eyes that his lowered lids couldn't quite conceal. He looked tired, as worn out as she felt, but still he tried to tease a smile from her, to take her mind off the fact that her labor wasn't going quite as they had expected. Her contractions were already less than three minutes apart, and dawn wasn't even a promise on the horizon.

He was going to have to deliver her baby.

She let the knowledge curl through her like a breaking wave and braced herself for the fear that was sure to follow in its wake. Instead she realized that while she wanted a doctor with her during the birth of her baby, there was really only one man that she absolutely *needed* there. And that was Sullivan. Because she loved him.

"Rose? Honey?"

Stunned, she glanced up to find him watching her with a frown. Her heart started to thump. Surely he couldn't have read her mind! "What?"

Sullivan gritted his teeth on an oath, wondering how the hell he was going to tell her it didn't look like he was going to be able to keep his promise, after all. She'd probably never trust him again. "I'm sorry," he sighed roughly, tunneling his fingers through his hair for what seemed like the billionth time. "I don't think this baby of yours is going to wait for the helicopter. She seems awfully anxious to put in an appearance."

A smile as soft as morning sunshine flitted across her face and turned her eyes to sapphire. "I know. I'm ready. How about you?"

Just that easily, she gave him her trust. Just that easily, she pulled the rug right out from under him. Would he ever know this woman completely? he wondered, humbled. His throat suddenly thick with emotions, he could only manage a nod before he leaned down to brush a tender kiss across her mouth. When he finally lifted his head, his eyes stung and his smile was crooked. "Dr. Walker told me exactly what to do," he said huskily. "I'm ready when you are."

Twenty minutes later Caitlin Rose MacDonald came into the world kicking and screaming at the top of her lungs, her lusty cries shattering the expectant silence of the bedroom. Unknown tears streaming down his face, Sullivan held the tiny, slippery baby girl in his big hands and grinned broadly. God, she was beautiful!

"You got your wish, love," he rasped, his eyes lifting to Rose's as he gently placed the baby on her stomach. "Say hello to your daughter."

Her eyes filled. "Oh, God," she whispered, blinking back tears. She looked into the baby's tiny, wrinkled face and felt as if she'd been waiting for her all her life. Love, unrestricted and fierce, flowed through her like warm honey. Silently, reverently, with a touch as soft as thistledown, she ran her hands over every inch of her baby, committing her to memory. A laugh escaped her at the feel of her tiny toes, her perfect hands with her perfect nails, the dark, baby-fine hair that was so much like Rose's own. And her heartbeat, she thought in growing wonder as she moved her to the crook of her arm and cradled her against her breast. She could feel her heartbeat thundering beneath her fingers, strong and sure.

Impulsively Rose reached for Sullivan's hand and gently pressed it to the baby's chest. "Feel," she said softly, her eyes glowing as they met his. "Feel how strong and fast it beats. I was so afraid—"

He leaned over and stopped her with a kiss that was quick, sweet, and totally unlike any kiss he had ever given her before. Confused, her heart thundering as fast as the baby's, Rose could only blink, dazed, as he pulled back and said gruffly, "Forget what you were afraid of in the past. Let go of it. The baby's here now and she seems to be perfect, even if she is a little early. Enjoy her."

He would have withdrawn then to give her some time alone with Caitlin, but she held him tight, her blue eyes dark with a love she couldn't have hidden at that moment if her life depended on it. "I haven't thanked you. For everything—for being here for me and the baby. For taking care of both of us. I don't think we would have gotten through it without you—"

"You did all the work," he replied, uncomfortable with her gratitude. "I just gave you a little encouragement."

He'd done a lot more than that, but before Rose could argue the point the rhythmic pounding of helicopter blades seemed to beat the air directly over the house. "There's your ride to the hospital," Sullivan shouted over the noise. "Better late than never. Let's get you and Caitlin cleaned up and ready for company."

The paramedics rushed in with a stretcher less than ten minutes later and immediately took over. Throwing questions at Sullivan about the birth and any complications that may have arisen, the two men quickly, but efficiently, examined both Rose and the baby, pronounced them in excellent health, and made preparations to transport them to the hospital. With skilled, practiced movements, they wrapped mother and daughter in blankets, carefully shifted Rose to the stretcher, handed her the baby, and strapped them both in. Seconds later they wheeled them out to the waiting helicopter.

It took all of Sullivan's strength of will to let them go. Standing on the back porch, deep lines carving his face, he watched Rose and the baby disappear inside the helicopter. For a fleeting moment he thought he caught a glimpse of Rose's hand lifted in goodbye, but before he could be sure, the door slid shut. The rotating blades whined, picking up speed, and the copter rose into the wet gray sky.

Even before it disappeared from sight, Sullivan felt a sharp, painful tug on his heartstrings. *Go after them.* So strong was the urge, he started toward the porch steps and his pickup before he realized what he was doing. He stopped short, swearing at the empty sky, at the intensity of the emotions that had snuck up on him from out of nowhere. What was the matter with him? He had no right to feel this way about a woman and child who weren't his, a woman and child he tried desperately to convince himself he had no intention of ever making his. If he wasn't damn careful, he was going to get caught up in a wellspring of emotion that a man could happily drown in. And he didn't want that! He'd never wanted that. Somehow he had to find a way to put a stop to the wanting that kept Rose constantly in his mind, the wanting that had somehow become something more than sex, while he still could. Otherwise he was horribly afraid he'd never be able to walk away.

Rose waited expectantly for him to visit her in the hospital that evening. There was so much she had to tell him. The doctor had reported that Caitlin was perfectly formed, and he saw little danger of any complications. But as a precautionary measure, they would keep her in an incubator for a while. The last of her fears evaporating, Rose fed the baby and laughed over her hungry sucking; she'd bathed her and cried at her daintiness, at the clean, wonderful baby scent of her. For what seemed like hours she'd stood at the nursery window and just watched her sleep. And during all those precious moments, the only thing missing had been Sullivan. How many times had she found herself turning to look for him, reaching for the phone to talk to him, wanting to share everything with him? Just in time, she made herself wait. He'll come, she promised herself. Just wait.

But he didn't come that night or the next day when she was released to go home. Pop came instead and took her to a nearby hotel, where she would stay until the baby was allowed to come home the following week. When he'd explained that Sullivan had gotten tied up with a problem at the ranch, she told herself she couldn't expect him to drop everything just to see about her and the baby. She, of all people, knew the demands of running the ranch, and there were times when you just couldn't get away regardless of how badly you wanted to. She would see him tomorrow.

But six tomorrows came and went without any sign of him. Hurt, she couldn't believe that he was actually going to shut her out after the closeness they'd shared during the birth of the baby. There had to be some logical excuse for his behavior, some reason that he couldn't find any time at all to be with her. But then it was time to go home and she could no longer lie to herself. It was Tommy, Slim and Pop who oohed and ahhed over the baby and fussed over her the minute she walked in the door. Only Sullivan kept his distance. Polite as a stranger, he inquired about her health and somehow managed to never quite look at Caitlin even though she was right there in Rose's arms.

Bewildered, her heart throbbing with pain, Rose impatiently waited for supper to be over with her first night home so she could talk to him. But after Pop and the others did the dishes, then reluctantly left, Sullivan gave her no time to demand an explanation. Looking her right in the eye, he announced, "I'll be leaving at dawn on the buying trip we discussed the night before you had the baby. I'll be gone for several weeks."

Eight

He was leaving for the buying trip two weeks early.

Rose almost staggered from the unexpected blow to her heart. This couldn't be happening, she thought wildly, her arms unconsciously tightening around the baby. He couldn't leave her now, not after everything they'd shared. She loved him, for goodness' sake! She always had, though she was only just now coming to realize how much. He'd walked back into her life, back into her heart, as if he'd never left. Surely he knew that. Surely he felt the same way.

But the man who stood before her had the cold, empty eyes of a stranger. This was not the man who cared for her with such gentleness when she was sick. This was not the man who delivered her baby with shaking fingers and held her with his eyes when he laid her daughter in her arms for the first time. This was not a man who would ever want her love, let alone love her.

Suddenly realizing she was losing control, she knew she had to get out of there or she was going to make a complete fool of herself. "I have to put the baby to b-bed," she said shakily. "I'll be right back."

She flew from the room as if the devil himself was after her, her breathing tattered with pain by the time she reached the nursery and gently laid the baby in her cradle. "Get a grip on yourself," she whispered fiercely, blinking back hot, scalding tears. His leaving now could only mean one thing. He was trying to put an immediate stop to the growing intimacy between them.

She wouldn't let him do that to her! To them! Couldn't he see that what they shared was something you could never turn your back on, never leave behind you no matter how far you ran? Somehow she had to find a way to make him see that.

By letting him go.

Her fingers curled around the old, smooth wood of the cradle, instinct urging her to reject the idea without even considering it. As he was so fond of reminding her, she was the boss. She could simply refuse to let him change the original plans. But what would that accomplish in the long run? They didn't have a chance at a future together unless he couldn't stay away.

Later she never knew how she walked back into the kitchen without letting him see that she was taking the biggest chance of her life. She knew she surprised him, she could see it in his eyes. He was obviously waiting for her to demand an explanation, but he waited in vain. All business, she said, "Since we haven't had time to go over the tapes, why don't we do it now? You can also give me an itinerary so I'll know how to reach you just in case something comes up. Not that I'm expecting any problems," she added as she stepped into her office and took the chair behind her desk. "Now that I've had the baby, the boys and I should be able to handle anything unexpected that crops up."

Emotion flickered in his eyes before he could stop it. "The doctor said you shouldn't do anything for the next six weeks."

So he'd been talking to her doctor. Did he realize just how revealing that was? An indifferent man didn't concern himself with the health of a woman he wanted nothing to do with. Fighting to keep the hope out of her voice, she assured him, "I'm not planning to do anything more physical than picking up Caitlin. I just wanted you to know that you don't have to worry about anything here at the ranch while you're gone."

He frowned and jammed a tape into the VCR. "I'm not worried," he growled. "Can we get on with this? I've still got some packing to do."

Biting back a smile that she knew would infuriate him, Rose leaned back in her chair and silently motioned for him to begin.

During the next two weeks Sullivan almost convinced himself he'd done the right thing by leaving as soon as possible after the baby's birth. He had no intention of getting wrapped up in baby smiles and teddy bears the way the rest of the men were. And with a thousand miles or more between him and Rose, he would soon forget the silky smoothness of her skin, the deep blue of her eyes, the smile that could drive a man to drink. He had people to meet, cattle to inspect and buy, transportation to arrange before he moved on to the next big ranch. He wouldn't give Rose a second thought.

That was the way it should have been. But from the day he left her, she'd never been more firmly lodged in his thoughts. A bull grazing in a roadside pasture stirred images of Rose standing in the middle of a country road, nose to nose with Bubba as she tried to lure him to the stock trailer. Hours later he unthinkingly ordered chili at a truck stop outside El Paso and spent the entire meal comparing it to Rose's. It came up irritatingly short. And at his first stop, the Twisted Snake Ranch in New Mexico, wild roses climbed a trellis outside the guest bedroom, the first buds of spring just beginning to bloom. That night Rose came to him in a hot, aching dream that drove everything but the taste and feel of her from his mind. He woke up cursing, and if he could have gotten his hands on her at that moment he would have throttled her.

In the days to come it only got worse as two weeks stretched into three, each longer than the last. The long, lonely stretches of road gave him too much time to think, the long, empty nights too much time to dream of her. Thoughts of her followed him from New Mexico to Colorado to Montana, her constant, invisible presence at his side infuriating him. By the time he conducted the last of his business he was so obsessed with her that he almost started home that very day to demand that she stop tormenting him so. Then he came across a pregnant woman changing a flat all by herself twenty miles outside of Butte. Tall and raw-boned, with long blond hair and hazel eyes, she looked nothing like Rose. But when he stopped to help her, there was something about her uncomplaining willingness to do a man's job when there wasn't one around that reminded Sullivan of dark curly hair and sapphire eyes, of soft, womanly curves that fit so perfectly in his arms. He knew then he couldn't go home. Not without reaching for her the minute he saw her. He was missing her too much. He needed more time.

An hour later he called her from a pay phone at a service station. At the sound of her husky hello his fingers bit into the receiver. "I bought the last of the cattle yesterday," he told her. "They should be arriving in a week or so."

Rose sank down onto a kitchen chair, her legs suddenly unable to hold her. For three long, endless weeks she'd waited for a call that never came, terrified she was losing him. She'd only had to close her eyes to torture herself with images of countless women chasing him, catching him, seducing him. Those were the times she found herself reaching for the phone like a jealous teenager only to slam it back down again. It was his turn to make a move, she'd reminded herself. As time dragged on, she'd nearly given up hope that he would.

Her heart dancing to a wild beat, she struggled to adopt his businesslike tone as she asked, "Then you're on your way home?"

He hesitated, then finally admitted, "No."

Pain, unlike anything she had ever known, squeezed her chest until she could hardly breathe. So this was it. He was calling to tell her he wasn't coming back. Oh, God, why hadn't anyone warned her that the hurt was always worse the second time? Her voice thick with hurt, she whispered, "Why not?"

Because you're all I can think about. Because you scare the hell out of me. Because you're getting to me again and I can't let that happen, he wanted to shout. Instead he gave her the excuse he'd worked out before he called her. It was a legitimate one, but still an excuse nevertheless. "We're going to need more men once roundup starts. I didn't figure you'd want to hire the hands who walked out on you when you fired Hastings, so I thought I'd scout around up here and see who might be available. Montana roundups are later than ours, and I know quite a few good men who could use the work while they're waiting for their spring. That is, of course, if it's all right with you," he added stiffly. "It's your ranch."

Rose, reeling with disappointment and loneliness, hardly heard the curious desperation in the words he had once thrown at her like an accusation, as if he were trying with all his might to hang onto his resentment. "Of course it's all right," she replied. "You're the foreman. Hire whoever you want. I trust you."

He froze, guilt, unexpected and swift, nearly choking him. *Don't!* He wanted to caution her. *Five weeks ago the only thought in my head was doing whatever it took to get back what was mine. The last thing you should give me is your trust.*

"Sullivan? Did you hear me? When will you be home?"

He blinked, snapping back to attention. "I don't know—a couple of weeks, maybe. However long it takes me to round up some men."

A couple of weeks. Rose almost groaned. He might as well have said an eternity, but she couldn't complain. At least he was still planning to return.

In the weeks to come, loneliness took on a whole new meaning for Rose. When the baby was awake, all her energy was devoted to loving her, caring for her, building that special bond between a mother and child that lasts a lifetime. But Caitlin was a wonderful baby; she slept for hours at a time. During those quiet, endless moments Rose found herself starving for just the sight of Sullivan. Drawn like a magnet to the window that looked out on the foreman's house at the bottom of the hill, she stared at the empty, abandoned house and missed him in a way that terrified her. When had she come to need his presence in her life so much?

Then, suddenly, without warning, he was home. Arriving early one evening with the ten cowboys he'd brought with him, he strode into the kitchen just as Rose and the hands were sitting down for supper. Pandemonium broke out. Pop, Slim and Tommy greeted him as if he was a long lost brother, introductions were made, and amid all the laughter and catching up on news, more places were set at the table.

In the crowd of men, no one noticed that Rose didn't join in the conversation much as she whisked one of the casseroles she kept in the freezer for just such unexpected arrivals into the microwave. She shook hands with each of the newcomers and welcomed them to her home, but she had eyes for only one man. Hungrily, her gaze roamed over him, devouring him. Was he leaner? Harder? Dressed in snug-fitting jeans and a white cotton shirt open at the collar, there wasn't an ounce of fat on him anywhere. He laughed at something Pop said, the crooked smile that turned up one corner of his mouth unconsciously wicked, unbearably tempting. Tracing it with her eyes, Rose felt her heartbeat quicken, her blood thicken and heat. Six weeks, she thought, dazed. It had been six weeks since he had kissed her. It seemed like a lifetime.

He looked up abruptly, finding her unerringly in the roomful of tall men. Her heart lurched to a stop, the heat in his green eyes almost melting her knees. He didn't say a word, made no move to come to her, but she felt as if he touched her, stroked her, wrapped her close in his arms. Need. The urgency was there in his eyes, stark and bare, a silent testament of long days and even longer nights, of loneliness and desolation and too much time to think.

She wanted to run to him then, to throw herself into his arms and never let him go. But she couldn't. She wasn't the young, vulnerable girl she had been at eighteen, so insecure and starving for love that she'd misjudged first his, then Frank's feelings for her. She had given him her heart, only to have it trampled under his feet as he left town. She wouldn't make that mistake again. She loved him more than she'd ever thought possible, but if all he wanted from her was revenge, then she wouldn't let him use that love as a weapon to destroy her. Not this time.

At his side, Pop gave him a running account of everything he'd missed while he was gone, but Sullivan couldn't tear his gaze from Rose. She'd lost weight. He'd noticed it the minute he stepped through the back door and almost tripped over his own feet in surprise. She was as slim as a girl, her slender hips provokingly encased in jeans, her narrow waist hardly bigger than the span of his hands. With slow deliberateness he took his gaze higher to the full curve of her breasts concealed beneath her blue checked blouse. Did she know how he ached to feel the weight of her breasts in his palms? How he burned with the remembered feel of her hips melting into his? If he could just touch her...

He'd lose his head completely, he thought resentfully. After six weeks of torturous dreams, it would take nothing more than the brush of his skin against hers to destroy what little control he still had left where she was concerned. Infuriated by the very idea of it, he somehow found the strength to turn away.

Rose didn't doubt for a minute that he'd done it deliberately. After the way he had managed to put her out of his life for the last six weeks, she should have been prepared for it. They were back to being polite strangers.

She wasn't going to let him get away with it, she decided. Not after all they had shared. He could lie to himself all he wanted, but if he thought she was going to make it easy for him by going along with him, he was nuts. She loved him and it was high time she found out how he really felt about her.

But for the next two days he neatly sidestepped all her attempts to talk to him alone. Then roundup started, and suddenly there weren't enough hours in the day for everything that needed to get done.

When Frank had added the Lazy J to his own holdings, he'd used Jeeps and helicopters to gather the cows and new calves, reducing the operation to one of money-saving, practical efficiency. Sullivan, however, came from a long line of cowboys and wranglers who had clung to the ways of the past and the skills they had perfected only after long hours of practice in the saddle. There would be no Jeeps or helicopters at any roundup he was in charge of, no modern technology to ruin what was considered by most old hands as the highlight of the year.

Consequently the warm spring days were filled with hot, dusty work from sunup to sundown. There were horses to be broken, cows and calves to be rounded up then separated, branding and inoculations to be done. The old chuck wagon stored in the barn at the Lazy J was hauled out, cleaned up, and loaded down with enough supplies to feed an army. Pop hitched it up to an ornery mule named Trouble and followed the men around the huge ranch, taking over the duties of cook for Rose, since she could hardly cook on an open camp fire when she had a baby to tend to. Then at night the cowboys slept under the stars, just like in the old days, grumbling about rocks that didn't show themselves until after midnight and ground as hard as granite. But not one of them would have traded his sleeping bag for a bed in the bunkhouse.

Rose only saw the men when she was able to join them for meals. Even then, Sullivan kept his distance. She tried to tell herself it was probably for the best, but the hurt was still there—a constant pain in the region of her heart that only seemed to intensify rather than diminish with the passing of time. Still she didn't avoid the nightly gathering around the camp fire. She couldn't, so she simply ceased to try. Bundling up the baby against the cool night air, she usually arrived in time for supper, then stayed for just a little while to listen to the inevitable stories and tall tales that circled the fire as the men began to unwind.

The third night of the roundup, however, the laughter and easy conversation that followed the meal was slightly strained. Everything that could have gone wrong that day had, and the men were tired and sore. From across the camp Rose watched Sullivan through the dancing flames of the camp fire. His face shadowed, his thoughts well hidden behind his shuttered green eyes, he looked like a man who had stepped out of time, a man who knew little of civilization. His hair as dark as midnight, his jaw stubbled with whiskers, he could have been a rogue, a scoundrel, an outlaw lover.

Fascinated, entranced, Rose pictured herself going to him, easing the grim set of his sensuous mouth, kneading the tension from his stiff shoulders, touching the heat she knew lingered just under warm skin that had been bronzed by the firelight. When she grew hot just thinking about it, she knew it was time to leave.

Her heart pounding, she pushed to her feet and lifted the baby from the Portacrib Pop kept for her in the chuck wagon. Hugging Caitlin to her breast, she said, "I guess we'll call it a night. You guys look like you've had a rough day and need your sleep. We'll see you tomorrow."

There were a few halfhearted protests, and what had become routine good-night kisses for Caitlin, who had been adopted by just about every one of the men. But before Rose could move to her truck, Tommy called out, "Hey, Sullivan, you should go back to the house with Rose and let her look at your shoulder. That was a pretty nasty fall you took.''

"Fall?'' she echoed, her eyes wide in her suddenly pale face as she pivoted to search out Sullivan in the darkness. "What happened?''

He shot Tommy a look that could have coated the boy's vocal chords with ice. "Nothing. It was just a little accident.''

Tommy snorted at that, blindly ignoring Sullivan's efforts to shut him up. "He was breaking that mean-looking sorrel and got thrown into the fence. It ripped his shirt right off his back.''

Her gaze swiveled back to Sullivan's. "Were you cut?'' she asked in alarm. "Maybe you should come up to the house and let me take a look at it. You may need a tetanus shot.''

"It's just a scratch,'' he argued. "And I don't need another tetanus shot. I just had one six months ago.''

"You still shouldn't take any chances on it getting infected.'' Her jaw set as stubbornly as his, she headed for the truck. "It needs to be cleaned and bandaged. Come on.''

Caught in the gaze of thirteen interested pairs of eyes, Sullivan knew if he didn't go with her, someone was going to start wondering why he suddenly didn't want to be alone with her. Muttering a curse under his breath, he had no choice but to trail after her, promising himself with every step that he was going to keep this short and sweet.

But once they reached the house, she had to change Caitlin and put her to bed. Standing in he kitchen, Sullivan heard her soft murmurings to the baby, then the husky cadence of a whispered lullaby. He felt something deep inside him soften and give, the hard edge that always gave him the advantage blurring. He took a step toward the nursery, then another one, unable to resist the lure of her voice.

The minute he stepped into the open doorway, he knew he'd made a mistake. She stood at the window, her dark head bent to the baby's as she slowly swayed to the tune she hummed, the soft glow of the night-light wrapping both her and the baby in grainy, dreamlike shadows. Transfixed, drawn to her in spite of the alarm bells suddenly ringing wildly in his head, he couldn't turn away from an image he would carry with him to his grave.

Unaware of his presence, Rose gently laid the baby in her cradle and brushed a kiss across her petal-soft cheek. Whispering a soft good-night, she turned toward the door and stopped short at the sight of Sullivan watching her, his narrowed, intense gaze holding hers in the dark. Suddenly the night air was humming.

Silently she started toward him, easing past him as he stepped back only a fraction to grant her passage through the doorway. But instead of showing him to the back door as her common sense screamed for her to do, she wordlessly moved to the bathroom. The firm tread of his booted feet on the carpet assured her he was right behind her.

Her pulse quickened, scattering heat through her veins. But she was all business as she switched on the light and flipped down the toilet seat. "Take off your shirt and sit down." Not sparing him a glance, she pivoted toward the medicine cabinet for the antibiotic cream she kept there for minor scratches.

Tending his cuts should have been that simple. But when she turned back from the medicine cabinet, the tube of cream in her hand, she found herself confronting the naked expanse of his broad back. Her heart jerked to a surprised halt, then stumbled into a desperate, frantic beat that she was sure he could hear in the sudden, expectant silence. Say something, she told herself. Anything!

"Well? How is it?" he demanded in a gravelly voice when she made no move to touch the scratches the barbed wire had carved in his back.

How was it? Her throat as dry as a West Texas creekbed in the middle of summer, she couldn't have answered if her life had depended on it. How was she supposed to describe a strength, a power, that made her go weak at the knees? Her fingers, itching to explore, to caress, lifted to the angry red welts that marred his right shoulder.

The stroke of her fingers, as light and airy as a feather, sizzled through Sullivan like an unexpected charge of electricity. His spine snapped ramrod straight, his teeth clamping down on a moan of sheer frustration.

Alarmed, Rose snatched her hand back. "I'm sorry! I didn't mean to hurt you."

An ironic laugh nearly choked him. Didn't she know by now that just the sight of her made him hurt? "Just get on with it," he growled. "I'll live."

But would she? Being this close to him, having free rein to run her hands over his back, even if it was under the guise of cleaning his wounds, was almost more than she could bear. With infinite care she washed each scratch, each scrape, and applied the soothing cream, her hair brushing his shoulder, her breath warming his skin as she leaned close. Once she thought she heard him swear, but she couldn't be sure because he never took his eyes from the white ceramic toothbrush holder he broodingly stared at.

Then, all too soon, she was finished. She should have stepped back, should have wished him good-night and escaped to her room. Instead, as if of their own volition, her fingers lifted to the nape of his neck and slowly traced the dark edge of his hair.

Heat arrowed from her fingers straight to his loins. He froze, but only for an instant. Before she could guess his intentions, he swiveled around sharply and caught her in the act of moving closer, her fingers lifted to repeat the caress. Suddenly she was standing between his open thighs and neither could have said how she got there. "What the hell do you think you're doing?"

Answering without saying a word, a single finger skimmed over his shoulder with defiant tenderness, lingered at the curve of his collarbone, then trailed liquid fire to the pulse that hammered at the base of his throat.

His eyes closed on a groan. "I'm warning you, Rose. I'm in no mood to play games."

But this wasn't a game. She was deadly serious. She still didn't have any idea where she stood with him. He could use her, then walk away for good. But she couldn't think about the future when he was this close, couldn't worry about what revenge he might have planned when the only thing that mattered was the taste of his mouth on hers, the feel of his hard body pressed tightly against hers.

"Feel my heartbeat," she whispered, swaying toward him. "Then try to tell me I'm playing."

No! Later he never knew if he was trying to deny her or himself, but it ceased to matter the minute he clamped his hands on her hips, jerking her to him as he turned his head against her breast. Still standing, she arched against him with an inarticulate cry of surprise, her heart thundering wildly beneath his mouth.

"Tell me to stop," he groaned, his hot breath and the flick of his tongue sweetly puckering her nipple beneath the white cotton of her shirt. But she only melted into him with a whimper, her fingers tunneling into his hair to hold him closer. A shudder ran through him, hunger, hot and insatiable, making a mockery of his last-ditch efforts to hang onto reason. His hands, ignoring the dictates of his mind, were already moving, already relearning the intoxicating flare of her hips and reclaiming a waist that had no business being that small only six weeks after having a baby.

Impatiently, like a man starving for the feel of her, he tugged her shirt free of her jeans and spread his fingers over the smooth, flawless skin of her back. *Soft.* Damn, why did she have to be so soft? A man could sink right into her and lose himself before he ever thought to note the danger. He had to stop. Why wasn't she helping him stop?

Desperate, desire clawing at him, he pushed her back abruptly and surged to his feet. But even then he couldn't bring himself to let her go. Holding her in front of him, her breasts nearly brushing his chest, he struggled to think of a reason—any reason—why he shouldn't carry her into her bedroom and make love to her the way he was burning to. "The baby," he ground out, drawing her up on her toes until her mouth was just a promise away from his. "It's too soon after the baby. I don't want to hurt you."

She clutched at him, the only thought in her passion-clouded mind that of pleasing him. Hadn't Frank taught her that a man never drew back, never had any problems in bed, as long as his woman pleased him? She pressed her mouth to his, a quick, fleeting kiss that teased and tantalized for a second, two at the most, before she drew back scant inches, changed the angle and teased him all over again. "I'm fine," she huskily breathed into his mouth. "The doctor's already cleared me to resume all activities. Let me show you…."

She gave him no time to think, to argue, to even begin to withdraw. She forgot where they were, who they were, only that she couldn't let him stop. Not tonight. Every touch, every kiss, every teasing dart of her tongue was designed to drive him mad with pleasure, to pull his unresisting body into the hot, swirling eddies of desire. Murmuring his name over and over, she scattered kisses across his face and throat as her fingers blindly searched out the buttons to his shirt, then moved on to the snap of his jeans.

Something was wrong. Through the passion that dulled his brain, the thought nagged at him. She moved over him like a cat lapping up cream, but somehow he sensed it was *his* desires that drove her, *his* need that she sought to satisfy. She took nothing for herself.

Drowning in the taste of her, he wrenched his mouth from hers, his breathing ragged as he frowned down at her. "Honey—"

She rubbed her hips against his, her hands almost desperate as they slipped around his neck and tried to pull him back down to her. "Tell me what you want," she pleaded anxiously. "I can make it good for you. Just tell me—"

He silenced her by simply pressing his fingers to her lips, the suspicions that stirred in him unwanted, unacceptable. His frown darkened to a black scowl. "Sweetheart, why would you think it's your responsibility to make it good for me? I thought we were in this together."

She blinked, surprised that he even had to ask. "We are, but what kind of woman would I be if I couldn't please you?"

"What kind of wo—" he sputtered to a stop, suddenly wanting to kill a man who was already beyond his reach. Drawing back carefully, he said, "Tell me about Frank, honey. About your life with him."

"Now?"

"Right now. I've got a feeling this is something we should have discussed a long time ago."

She didn't want to tell him. Not now. Not ever. But she knew that look in Sullivan's eye. He wasn't budging until she told him what he wanted to know. Swallowing the pain that was already rising in her throat, she began.

She told him everything, leaving nothing out. Her voice wobbly with pain, she told him of her despair when her father died, the terrible loneliness and fear that had gripped her when it suddenly hit her that she was totally and completely alone in the world. If Frank hadn't been there, she would have been lost. She had thought she'd loved him then—he was always there for her, protecting her, promising he would always be there. When he had pressed for marriage, she'd thought they could find happiness together. But she hadn't known then why he'd wanted to marry her.

Sullivan's hands tightened on her arms as he listened to her tell him how Frank had used her to get back at him; how she'd tried to make her marriage work and blamed herself when it was never quite right; how Frank had not only let her carry the guilt for their less than satisfactory sex life, he'd encouraged her every step of the way.

A rage unlike anything he had ever known before filled him. Spitting out a curse, he leaned down and swept her up in his arms as if she were as fragile as spun glass. "Forget what Frank told you, sweetheart. The man never did know his ass from a hole in the ground. Making love isn't about one person making it good for the other. It's about sharing and giving and receiving. We make it good for each other. You got that?"

Her mouth so close he could feel the startled puff of her moist breath, she nodded. "Good," he said in satisfaction, heading for her bedroom. "Then let's go to bed."

Nine

He laid her on the bed with the utmost care, promising himself he would make this a night she would never forget. But the minute he came down to her, the minute his mouth covered hers and she wrapped her arms around him as if she would never let him go, the only thought in his head was Rose. Rose, with her petal-smooth skin that heated like honey under his hands. Rose, her legs moving restlessly, sensuously beneath his, her breath shattering on a moan of sheer frustration as she fought buttons and zippers and jeans that were suddenly too confining. Rose, somehow as naked as he, dissolving at the touch of his hand at her breast, her hip, the tender, sensitive skin of her inner thigh. Rose, who seemed so surprised that this first time, after all their years apart, was for her.

Drowning in a pleasure that was dark and intoxicating, she tried to stop him long enough to catch her breath, tried to remind him that he'd just told her that they were supposed to make it good for each other. But he wouldn't listen. The very second she opened her mouth, he gave her a slow, lazy, languid kiss, and rational thought skittered away.

Need. She had thought she'd known the boundaries of it even with him. But the last time she'd made love with him she had been little more than a girl, with a girl's dreams, a girl's needs. And what she'd shared with Frank had been nothing like this. This blurred the edges of reason, caressed the soul, pushed her toward a heat that seared, consumed, released. Her breath catching on a sob, she clung to him, his name on her lips a desperate, whispered call in the night.

"Easy, honey," he murmured against her throat. "We've got all night."

But she was hot now. Aching now. Dying for more now. She reached for him, her fingers sliding down the lean, muscled plane of his chest, past his trim waist to the hard, burning proof of his desire. "Please! I need . . ."

In a heartbeat she was flat on her back and he was between her thighs, pressing her into the sheets. In the darkness his green eyes met hers, his lungs gasping for the air she had stolen from him with her hand. He could take her now. With a deep thrust he could end the agony tearing at him and sheath himself in her sweet heat. But it was much too soon. He wanted her boneless, mindless with desire, the fire he knew raged in her belly burning her with a pleasure that destroyed all memories of any other man who had ever touched her.

Slowly, deliberately, he attacked her senses, playfully teasing her one moment, then dragging her down deeper into passion the next. Reality shifted and changed until it consisted of nothing more than the feel of his hands working their magic on her, the thunder of his heart beating in time with hers, his low, growling whisper as he murmured erotic words of praise in her ear. Tension gathered in her stomach, coiling tighter and tighter until she thought she would shatter into a million pieces if he didn't come to her soon.

"Sullivan!"

Her agonized cry destroyed him. There was no more time for teasing, no more time for drawing out a pleasure that had suddenly come too close to pain. Lifting her hips, he eased into her with maddening slowness, the groan that vibrated through him coming from his very soul. Just that easily, he rediscovered a completeness he'd never found with any other woman.

That would worry the hell out of him when he had time to think about it. But for now his body begged for release, demanded it. Tenderly, savagely, he stroked her again and again, stoking the wet heat inside her until it flamed out of control so quickly she gasped in surprise. Her nails raked his back. At the very core of her, he felt her splinter, the ecstasy that rippled through her like lightning destroying the last fine threads of his control. Impossibly his already thundering heart quickened, his muscles tightened, his hips surged powerfully against hers. Before he could catch his breath, pleasure exploded in him as wave after wave of ecstasy rolled over him.

"I love you."

A long while later the words were hardly more than a whisper in the darkness, a shy murmur half concealed in the shadows. But Sullivan stiffened as if she'd screamed them, as if she was making a demand of him he couldn't meet. Guilt pounded him, sickened him. This was what he thought he'd wanted, he told himself furiously, the revenge he'd planned from the beginning. Where was the elation? The triumph? He should have been doing handsprings, making plans to rush her into marriage so he could get his ranch back. Instead all he could think of was how much she'd hate him if she ever found out the truth.

His hand sliding over her back in a caress he couldn't deny himself, he warned roughly, "Don't love me, honey. You'll only get hurt because I can't love you back."

She stilled, her heart seeming to stop. *Don't,* she wanted to cry. *Don't do this to me, to us, a second time. I know you love me. I felt it pouring out of you only moments ago.* But the words wouldn't come. Instead she asked the one question she swore she wouldn't. "Why?"

"Because loving a woman like you means marriage, kids, the whole nine yards," he replied quietly. Bitterness crept into his voice along with something she hadn't heard before—acceptance. It terrified her. "I have nothing to offer you. Nothing except lust, and that's not enough."

"That's not true!" She clutched at him, wanting to shake him, wanting to cling to him. He hadn't moved, hadn't made any move to withdraw, but the panic rising in her told her she was losing him. "Why are you doing this?" she demanded. "Why are you trying to pretend you don't love me? I know you do—"

"Know this," he growled, his green eyes snaring hers in the darkness as he deliberately moved against her, letting her feel the extent of his arousal. "I want you more than I ever wanted anyone. Feel that? No one has ever made me want this bad, this hard, this long. It's all I have to give you. Let it be enough."

"But—"

He didn't want to argue. Not now, not when this was all he would ever have of her. Taking her mouth in a hot, carnal kiss, he swept her back into the hot, blinding flames of passion before she could summon another word of protest.

* * *

The next morning he was gone when she awoke, the tender ache between her thighs the only sign that the night had been more than a dream. Disappointed that he wasn't there to share the dawn with her, she pictured the night to come, when they could be together again, and smiled dreamily up at the ceiling. This time, she promised herself, there would be no talk of lust, no running from the truth. She would find a way to make him admit that what he felt for her was too strong, too binding, too complete, to be anything but love.

But when she saw him at lunch, he acted as if the night had never happened, as if they hadn't shared a passion that had nearly set the sheets on fire, as if she was nothing more to him than the woman who signed his paycheck. Stricken, she felt the pain hit her first, the force of it nearly staggering her. Then came the anger. Sharp and bracing, it brought her chin up and burned like a fire in the depths of her eyes. Did he think she didn't know what he was doing? He was cutting her out of his heart, denying them both any chance of happiness because of his stubborn pride.

Five years ago she'd accepted his abandonment of her because she'd thought she had no other choice. She had accepted whatever fate and the men in her life had decided to give her because she'd thought there could be nothing worse than being alone. Now she knew better. Now she knew that you could be married to the wrong man and still be alone. Now she knew that second chances were rare, a precious gift not to be squandered away because of self-doubts or fears. If she wanted Sullivan, she would have to fight for him. Because if she didn't, if she let him get away with ignoring her now, she knew he would never touch her again.

* * *

It didn't take Sullivan long to realize that war had been declared and *he* was under siege. During the next two weeks, as roundup ended and life returned to normal, Rose took advantage of every opportunity to touch him. With an innocent smile that did nothing to conceal the challenge sparkling in her blue eyes, she brushed up against him when he least expected it, her body softly tantalizing his for only an instant before she was gone, leaving him with nothing more than the seductive scent of her perfume and the pounding of his heart to assure him he hadn't dreamed the whole thing.

Irritated at the response he couldn't quite control, he found himself watching for her, waiting for her, bracing himself for her subtle torture. But she was clever, he had to give her that. Her attacks were always well-timed and geared for surprise, and she didn't give a hoot in hell who was watching. She walked up behind him when he was talking to Pop and scraped her nail teasingly along the sensitive skin above his collar, drawing a scowl from him and a speculative grin from the older man. One hot afternoon she and Caitlin showed up at the windmill he was helping Tommy and Slim repair and announced she was going into town for supplies. Bold as brass, she drew her fingers all the way down the buttons of his shirt to the snap of his jeans and asked him if he needed anything. Slim and Tommy nearly dropped their teeth, and he was reaching for her before he realized she'd slipped away with a soft laugh.

No, the woman didn't play fair. She knew she was wearing down his resistance, but did she show him any mercy? Hell, no! He was frustrated, his indifference in shambles, but she didn't give an inch. Then she brought in the big gun. Caitlin. How did she know he couldn't ignore that baby even though he tried his damnedest? He never touched her, never played with her like the other hands did, never allowed himself to hold her close as he longed to. But she didn't make a move in her crib that he didn't know about whenever he was in the house.

But that wasn't enough for Rose. She saw the longing in his eyes when he watched the baby from a safe distance, the love he wouldn't admit to, let alone allow himself to give. Taking matters into her own hands, she decided to do something about it one evening after supper when he stayed to catch up on paperwork.

Up to her elbows in the mountain of dirty baby clothes that piled up after just one day, she was transferring just-washed diapers from the washer to the dryer when she heard Caitlin start to fuss in her playpen. As usual her first reaction was to drop everything and run to her, but this time she forced herself to stay where she was. Sullivan was in her office and much closer to the baby than she was. "Sullivan, will you see about the baby for me?" she called out. "I've got my hands full."

For a moment her only answer was dead silence and the steadily increasing whispers of the baby. Disappointed, she was halfway across the laundry room when he asked in a voice raised in growing panic, "What do I do? How do I make her stop crying?"

Rose grinned. "Pick her up, but make sure you support her head. If she acts hungry, she has a bottle in the refrigerator."

Pick her up! Sullivan stared down at the red-faced baby in horror. He'd held her at birth, but that had been different. He hadn't had time to think about supporting her head or how small she was; he'd just acted on instinct. His heart beating jerkily in his chest, he leaned over and gingerly placed one hand beneath her small bottom and the other at the back of her curly head.

The minute he painstakingly lifted her to his chest, her crying ceased. Her deep blue eyes alight with what he would have sworn was recognition, she stared up at him silently, her tiny mouth forming an *O* of surprise. Emotion flooded Sullivan, a sweetness unlike anything he had known before, and in that instant he knew he was lost. He didn't give a damn who her father had been, whose name she carried. He delivered her and that made her part his.

"Well, hello, sweetheart," he sighed as he carefully transferred her to the crook of his arm and smiled down at her. God, she was tiny! "Your mama says you're hungry. What do you say?"

For an answer, she put her fist in her mouth.

A crooked smile tugged up one corner of his mouth. "Looks like she was right. Let's go get you a bottle."

From the laundry room Rose heard his soft whispers, the sound of his booted feet crossing the kitchen to the refrigerator, then returning to the nursery. After that there was only silence. Listening to the hushed quiet, Rose started the dryer and began to sort another load of clothes for the washer. By the time she'd added soap and fabric softener, her curiosity was killing her. On silent feet she slipped to the open door of the nursery.

Not sure what to expect, she stopped short at the sight of Sullivan holding Caitlin close, her sleeping face turned against his chest as he sat in the straight-back kitchen chair that was a poor substitute for the rocker she had yet to find. Blinking back sudden tears, her heart filled with love as her eyes met his. "She's asleep," she whispered. "You can lay her down now."

His voice as low as hers, he looked down helplessly at the baby and said, "I was afraid I'd wake her up."

Rose couldn't help but smile, understanding perfectly. There were times when just holding her was so sweet she couldn't put her down, even when she knew she would sleep more comfortably in her own bed. "Nothing short of an atomic bomb will wake her up once she's really asleep," she assured him quietly. "Go ahead. Just lay her on her tummy and pat her back and she'll never know a thing."

His heart pounding, he did as she said, half expecting Caitlin to let out a jarring yell of protest any moment. But she didn't blink a single tiny eyelash when he tenderly lowered her to the crib. With a touch so light it was little more than a whisper of movement, he gently patted her back.

Rose never knew how long they stood there side by side, watching the baby sleep. In the hushed stillness she could almost feel love pouring from Sullivan in an unconscious flow, warming both her and Caitlin, claiming them. She also felt the exact moment he realized it. He stiffened suddenly and stepped back jerkily, away from her, away from the baby, away from the emotions he was still so determined to deny.

"I have to go," he said tightly. "It's late." And before she could even open her mouth to tell him good-night, he was gone.

She didn't go after him. Not then or the next day, when she didn't see hide nor hair of him. He was running scared, and she had to believe that a man only ran that scared when he was fighting a losing battle. Hopefully, given enough time and space, he would see that.

Her patience, however, gave out by the middle of the second day. He filled her thoughts and destroyed her concentration by simply avoiding her for hours. And she wasn't going to let him get away with it. Leaving the baby with Tommy's sister, Maryann, who baby-sat for her one day a week while she ran errands, she went looking for him.

He was supposed to be at the Lazy J putting in a late alfalfa crop for feed for next winter. But the field he'd spent the last week preparing and plowing was deserted, the tractor abandoned midway down a long furrow. She frowned, wondering if she was going to have to search every inch of the old ranch to find him when she suddenly caught a glimpse of his pickup parked in the shade of the huge, towering cypress trees bordering the river at the far end of the pasture. Shifting her own truck into gear, she headed straight for it.

She expected to find him sitting on the bank by the slow-moving river, eating the sandwiches he now packed each morning for lunch so he could avoid coming back to the house—and her—every day at noon. But he wasn't by the river; he was *in* it.

Braking to an abrupt stop next to his truck, Rose cut the engine and stepped down to the grassy ground, her eyes lingering on the clothes and boots carelessly discarded on the bank. From there, she only had to look to the river to find Sullivan. He stood up to his bronzed chest in the dark green water, his black hair plastered to his head and water sluicing down his shoulders and arms as if he had just surfaced. He looked magnificent. He also looked irritated as hell that she had chanced upon him with his pants down.

Making no attempt to hide the slow grin that pulled at her mouth, she strolled toward him, wicked amusement spilling into her eyes. "Hi. How's the water?"

His eyes, as green as the river, narrowed. "Cool," he retorted curtly. "What are you doing here?"

"Looking for you. We need to talk."

The last thing they needed to do when he was naked as the day he was born was talk! "Save it for later. I'm busy."

"So I can see," she chuckled. Gracefully she sank down to the bank and slipped her arms around her up-drawn knees, as if she intended to stay awhile. "I'm serious, Sullivan. This is important."

Sullivan swore in frustration. The woman gave new meaning to the word stubborn. "If it's that important, go on back to the house and I'll meet you there in a few—"

"I want you to be Caitlin's godfather."

The simple request, hardly spoken above a whisper, took the wind right out of his sails. Rocked to the soles of his feet, he stared at her blankly. "What?"

She smiled, encouraged that he hadn't immediately given an out-and-out no. "I want you to be Caitlin's godfather," she repeated, looking him straight in the eye. "You brought her into the world. You were there when she drew her first breath. Maryann, Tommy's sister, is going to be her godmother but Caitlin needs a man in her life, someone she can depend on to be there for her if something happens to me. I want that man to be you."

Emotion—surprise, joy, fear, fury—whipped through him. She was asking too much, he tried to tell himself, grasping at weak straws of anger. He wouldn't let her play on the possessiveness that had gripped him from the moment the baby had slipped into his hands at birth. He wouldn't let her tie the three of them into a neat little family package when that was the last thing they could ever be.

"Nothing's going to happen to you," he replied stiffly.

"Probably not," she agreed. "But it's important to me that you'll always be a part of Caitlin's life. You don't have to decide now, but will you at least think about it?"

He hesitated, knowing he was making a mistake, but the words of refusal wouldn't come. "All right," he said grudgingly. "I'll think about it. But that's it. I'm not making any promises."

She flashed him a smile that was as bright as the sunlight that filtered through the leaves overhead and jumped to her feet. "Good. Now that that's settled—" Making a sudden decision, her fingers moved to the buttons of her yellow camp blouse.

Sullivan's heart shot up into his throat. "What the hell do you think you're doing?"

"Going swimming," she said innocently. "I'm hot."

Hot? He'd give her hot, he thought furiously. Hot was when you were standing up to your armpits in cold water and steam was starting to rise from certain body parts! "The hell you are," he grated. "Dammit, Rose, put that blouse back on! One of the men could come by and see you."

Grinning, she held the offending garment between her thumb and index finger and casually dropped it on top of his clothes. "The men have all gone to town," she retorted. "I gave them the rest of the afternoon off." Her blue eyes locked with his, she reached for the snap of her jeans and pushed it free. In the next instant the slow rasp of her zipper teased the sudden, tense silence.

Sullivan's jaw hardened as he refused to let his gaze drop to the path of her descending zipper. "I'm warning you," he snarled. "If you don't stop this instant—"

"You'll what?" she tossed back, softly goading him. "Come out of the water and stop me yourself?"

"Yes, dammit!"

Her zipper, grating loudly, called his bluff.

He was out of the water like a shot, moving so fast Rose didn't even have a chance to catch her breath before he was upon her, reaching for her, yanking her flush against his wet, aroused body the same instant his lips covered hers. She gasped, and that was the only advantage he needed. His tongue surged into the dark, moist recesses of her mouth, stealing her breath, her will, seducing her, telling her without words all the mad, passionate things he intended to do to her.

His hands rushed over her, wild and reckless, trembling with need. He fumbled with the clasp of her bra, only to swear against her mouth when he couldn't manage to release the hooks. "Help me!" he pleaded, wrenching his mouth from hers.

She moaned, his urgency catching her and sending the earth spinning away beneath her feet. Her fingers nudged his. A gasp, a sob, a muffled curse later, the clasp was nearly ripped from its binding and the bra went flying. Rose never saw, never cared, where it landed. Fiercely returning his kiss, she rubbed against him, loving the feel of him, the heat of him, the subtle friction of wet skin against dry. She heard his groan, felt his fingers flex at her waist as he dragged her closer still, and then he was reaching for her jeans.

He was going too fast. The thought registered dully somewhere in a dark corner of his brain, but he couldn't stop, couldn't even begin to curb the fever blazing out of control in his blood. Tearing his mouth from hers, he tugged down the zipper she had teased him with, his labored breath tearing through lungs that suddenly couldn't get enough air. With a rough jerk, he dragged her jeans over her hips and down her thighs. Before she'd kicked them free, he was reaching for her again, sweeping her panties from her, and lowering her to the sweet-smelling grass of the riverbank.

High overhead, the tops of the cypress trees swayed gently to a slight breeze, but flat on her back, Rose had eyes for no one but Sullivan. She loved him! She wanted to tell him, intended to keep telling him until he opened his heart to her and admitted that he loved her, too. But not now. Now she couldn't manage more than a groan of need when he ironed kisses along her jaw and down her throat to her breast. Latching onto her nipple with his mouth, his hand joined the attack on her senses, sliding up her thigh to the heart of her desire. He touched her and she whimpered, her thoughts clouding, her mind closing out everything but each gliding stroke of his fingers, each gentle, tender tug of his mouth.

A sob of pleasure escaping her parted lips, she arched up like a tightly strung bow, offering herself to him, opening to him. "Now," she panted brokenly, crying out. "Please—"

At that moment, caught in the loving heat of her gaze, Sullivan knew he never would be able to deny her anything she asked of him. Groaning her name thickly, he took her wildly, hotly, completely. And somewhere in the taking, in the satisfying of a desire that no woman but this one had ever been able to quench in him, he gave his heart and never felt the loss until it was too late.

Ten

Dawn broke on the horizon and washed the cloudless sky in muted shades of lavender and pink. Standing at his bedroom window, Sullivan never noticed the beginning of what promised to be a perfect spring day. Instead his eyes were trained on the house on the hill, his face set in grim lines. How had he let things get so far out of hand? he wondered in bewilderment. He was quickly sinking into what could only turn out to be a disaster, and everything he did to extricate himself only pulled him deeper and deeper into the quagmire.

How had she tricked him into agreeing to being Caitlin's godfather? He'd never actually said yes. But then again, he'd never actually said no, either, he reluctantly admitted. He'd been waiting for her to exert some sort of pressure on him, but in the week that had passed since they'd made love by the river, she had done nothing of the kind. She'd just assumed that he would accept. How had she known that his heart wouldn't let him do anything else? From the moment he'd held Caitlin Rose MacDonald at birth, he'd never had any choice but to love her.

Just as he'd never had any choice but to love her mother. Which was why, later this morning, he would stand at Rose's side and accept the responsibility of being Caitlin's godfather.

He turned from the window with a muttered curse, but there was nowhere he could run, nowhere he could hide from the truth. He loved her. Dear God, how had it happened? He'd been so sure he could never again feel anything but contempt for her, so sure that all he wanted from her was his ranch. He'd clung to his bitterness like it was an invincible shield, determined to guard his heart at all cost. But the woman he'd armed himself against was a money-hungry, manipulating little bitch, not a soft, vulnerable widow with wounds as deep as his. The minute he'd seen her pain, the second he'd realized that she was just as much a victim as he was, he'd lost not only the battle, but the whole stinking war. After five long years of trying to hate her, he loved her more than he'd ever thought possible.

And he didn't have a damn thing to offer her.

To some men that might not have been a problem, but the knowledge tore at him, ripping him apart. His pride was all he had left, and that was going to take a beating the moment he turned up at the church with Rose for the baby's christening. Some good-hearted soul would take one look at them together, remember their past, and wonder if he might be sniffing after her for the same reason gossips had claimed she'd married Frank so suddenly all those years ago—for the ranch.

Rose would hear the gossip, of course—she was supposed to. And there wasn't a doubt in his mind that she'd believe it. Hell, why shouldn't she? he thought bitterly.

When she'd accused him of coming back for revenge, he hadn't denied it. Then it had been true. She wouldn't care that he had changed his mind, that he'd backed off after she'd had Caitlin, that it was *she* who had pursued him then, and not the other way around. She would look him straight in the eye, see that he had intended to manipulate her just as badly as Frank and her father had, and hate his guts. And he had no one to blame but himself.

So run, a voice in his head urged. Leave before you have to see the love die in her eyes. All you have to do is get in your truck and drive until you can find a place where roses don't bloom. Maybe then you'll be able to forget her and the baby.

But he couldn't. Not yet. He had promised her he'd be there for Caitlin, and come hell or high water, he would be.

Dressed in a soft lavender crepe dress with a shawl neckline, Rose hitched Caitlin higher in her arms and anxiously paced the foyer of the church. Inside the organist softly played a hymn in preparation for the service, which would start in five minutes. Her heart starting to thud with panic, Rose pivoted toward the glass doors that led to the parking lot. Maryann had arrived ten minutes ago and was already seated in the first pew, but there was no sign of Sullivan. When he'd called earlier announcing that he had some errands to do before church, he'd promised he'd be there on time. So where the heck was he? Couldn't he see that time was running out?

Her stomach knotted with tension, she tried to ignore the fear that he wasn't going to show. He wouldn't do that to her or the baby, she told herself. But she couldn't quite shake the uneasy feeling that had been with her all week. He'd been like a horse trapped in a barn with the smell of fire, ready to bolt at the first opportunity. Every time he'd turned to her, every time his eyes had met hers, she'd half expected him to flatly announce that he couldn't be the baby's godfather, that he couldn't, wouldn't love her, that he had no desire to be a part of her life. The words had never come, but with each new day she'd waited for her hopes and dreams to blow up in her face.

Where was he?

"Are you ready?"

The softly spoken question came from directly behind her and nearly buckled her knees. She whirled, tears stinging the back of her eyes at the sight of him dressed in a dark blue Western-style suit, his cowboy hat in his hand. "Sullivan, thank God! The service starts in just a few minutes and I was so afraid—"

She broke off abruptly, refusing to acknowledge the fear, but it was still there in her wide blue eyes for him to see. "My errand took longer than I expected," he explained quietly. He wanted to slip his arm around her then, to apologize with a kiss, but that would really set the gossips talking. And he didn't intend to give them any more to speculate about than he had to. Drawing his gaze from Rose, he looked down at Caitlin in her pristine white christening dress, and the love he wouldn't risk showing Rose in public was there for the baby. "Hi, angel," he growled softly. "Ready for your big day?"

The baby's face lit up with an adoring grin. "We'll know soon enough," Rose chuckled. "This is her first church service. If we're lucky, she'll sleep through the whole thing. Let's find a seat."

His hand at the back of her waist, Sullivan guided her down the aisle to the front row, where Maryann anxiously waited for them. Quickly taking seats next to her, they had hardly sat down when the minister made his way to the podium and the service began.

The organ music swelled to the rafters and the first hymn was sung, but Sullivan could still feel the surprise that had rippled through the congregation as people caught sight of him with Rose and her baby. He could still hear the hushed murmurings that had marked their progress toward the front of the church. So it had begun, he thought in disgust. The speculations, the whisperings, the gossip that was taken more seriously than the evening news. He could hear it now. Five minutes after the christening, it would be all over town that Sullivan Jones and Rose MacDonald had unabashedly walked into church together to make him her baby's godfather, and poor Frank was probably turning over in his grave. Everyone knew how he'd always hated the Joneses.

No! Sullivan swore under his breath. Damn the old biddies who had nothing better to do with their lives than pass judgment on everyone else! He could only imagine the hell they'd put Rose through five years ago, when everything she had done had been grist for the gossip mill. Without even knowing her, they'd condemned her for being young and afraid and turning to the richest man in the county because she'd thought he was her only friend. How she must have hated being the subject of every wagging tongue, her most private decisions discussed over back fences by complete strangers who neither knew nor cared about the pain she was going through. And now she was right back in the same position she'd been before. Because of him.

This was a mistake, he realized too late. Why had it taken him so long to see that? She didn't need him at her side, stirring up the past. She'd had to defend her decision to marry Frank, and now she would be forced to defend her involvement with him. And she would hate him for that. He had to leave.

Her thigh and hip pressed to his, Rose felt his turmoil, the tension that had him strung as tight as a rubber band stretched to the limit. Cradling the baby close, she shot him a worried look, but his eyes were on the minister, the rough, angled lines of his face carved in granite. She moved closer, intending to ask in a low whisper what was wrong, but she never got the chance. The minister smilingly announced the birth of Caitlin to the congregation, then motioned for Rose, Sullivan and Maryann to rise and approach the altar for the baptism.

Moments later, it was over. Caitlin never even whimpered as water was sprinkled over her head, but smiled instead, drawing a wide grin from the minister. His blessing warmly falling over her, he kissed her, congratulated Rose on having a beautiful daughter, then turned to the congregation at Rose's request and invited everyone back to the ranch for a small celebration. A murmur of approval spread through the crowd as everyone spilled from the pews into the aisles. Ranchers that had done business with her father came swarming up to see both her and Caitlin, and before she knew it, Sullivan was pulled away by an old friend of his grandfather's.

She was losing him. It was a ridiculous thought to have when she was surrounded by well-wishers and separated from him by only ten feet, but instinct warned her something was terribly wrong. Plastering a smile on her face, she thanked one of the town's nosiest gossips who was gushing over Caitlin, but her gaze immediately strayed back to Sullivan the minute the woman moved on. Somehow he was farther away than ever, though she would have sworn he hadn't moved an inch.

He pointed to the parking lot. "I'll meet you back at the ranch," he mouthed, his words drowned out by the conversation swirling around them.

Rose wanted to protest that she'd rather ride back with him so she would have a chance to ask him what was wrong, but that meant someone would have to drive her back to town later to retrieve her truck. Reluctantly she nodded and began working her way through the crowd.

Rose never knew if the huge crowd that showed up for the small party she'd planned came out of a feeling of celebration or curiosity, but within moments of her arrival back at the ranch, a string of pickups and cars pulled in behind her. Stunned, she watched guests start toward the house and knew she didn't have nearly enough food prepared to feed them. Quickly unbuckling the baby from her infant car seat, she hurried inside, desperately trying to remember what she could pull out of the freezer and heat in the microwave.

But Pop was way ahead of her. The minute she stepped through the back door, he grinned at her harried look and said, "Calm down. I've got it all under control. While you were in church, I ran into town and got a ham, some of that deli potato salad that always needs half a bottle of mustard to give it some taste, and a couple of store-bought cakes. It ain't as good as what you'd make yourself, but nobody'll go away hungry."

"What about plates? Tea? Dear God, do we have enough ice?"

She started to turn toward the freezer, but he stopped her by simply stepping in her path. "We've got plenty of ice and everything else," he assured her. "You just leave it all to me and the boys and go greet your guests. Oh, and Sullivan got home a few minutes before you did. He's waiting for you in the nursery. Said to tell you he had something for you."

Surprised, the thought of food flew right out of her head. "Something for me? What?"

He chuckled and plucked Caitlin from her arms. "Go find out. I'll take care of the little one and introduce her around. You take your time."

Rose knew she shouldn't. She needed to see if someone had found the lawn chairs and make sure Pop had remembered to put on a pot of coffee. But all she could think of was Sullivan...waiting for her. Unable to resist the lure, she kissed Pop's grizzly cheek and Caitlin's silky soft one and murmured, "Thanks, Pop," before flying down the hall.

The nursery door was closed, shutting out the visitors milling about the house. Soundlessly opening it, Rose slipped inside only to gasp in delight. There, by the window, sat a beautiful white Victorian wicker rocking chair that was exactly like the one she'd dreamed about, exactly like the one she'd spent months searching the Hill Country for without success. Tears filled her eyes. He'd remembered just what she wanted.

Stepping from behind the door, Sullivan saw her tremulous smile, her suspiciously bright eyes, and just barely resisted the urge to reach for her. If he held her now, he'd never be able to let her go. And that was what he was doing—letting her go before she had the chance to despise him. Forcing a rueful smile that never reached his eyes, he said, "Does that mean you love it or hate it?"

Her chuckle was watery, her eyes brilliant with love as she whirled and flew into his arms. "I love it, of course! Where did you find it? How did you know—"

Fairly dancing with happiness, she never noticed how quickly he put her away from him or how rigid his jaw was as he urged her toward the chair. "I saw it yesterday sitting on the front porch of Carla's Antique Shop down on Main Street—she'd just gotten it in. The minute I saw it, it reminded me of you. Try it out."

Sinking down to the cushioned seat, she leaned back and set the chair in motion, the fingers of her right hand lacing with his. "It's perfect," she said softly. "Just perfect. I'll keep it always."

Keepsakes. That was all she would have of him; memories were all he had to give her. Cursing his stubborn pride, he said stiffly, "You'd better get back to your guests. They're probably wondering where you are."

She didn't want to go. Just a few more minutes, she promised herself. She still needed to talk to him, to find out what was bothering him, but that was something she knew would have to wait. She could hardly hole up in the nursery with him for a serious conversation when the house was full of people. Sighing in defeat, she pushed to her feet and turned toward the door.

But in the end he couldn't let her leave, not yet. Before she could take a step away from him, he grabbed her wrist and pulled her back into his arms, his mouth immediately lowering to hers in a hot, desperate kiss of longing and regret. He felt her surprise, her shudder of need, the instant heat that had her melting against him with a moan of surrender. He could have lost it then, just that quickly lost what little control he had left where she was concerned. Her tongue dueled with his in a frantic, hungry dance, and all he could think of was pulling her to the floor and losing himself in her. Now, before she had reason to suspect every kiss and touch they'd shared since his return. Now, before he got out of her life once and for all.

But that would only prolong the agony.

The kiss turned gentle, sweet, unbearably tender. Tears stinging her eyes, Rose reluctantly let him end the kiss and draw back until the only contact between them was the tips of her fingers grazing his hard jaw. "I'll see you after the party," she whispered huskily and slipped from the room without ever seeing the despair that burned in his eyes.

The party only lasted two hours, but to Rose it seemed to drag on half the afternoon. Forcing a smile, she circulated among the guests, kept a watchful eye on the food, and retreated for a short while to the nursery to put Caitlin down for a nap. And during all that time she only caught a glimpse of Sullivan once. He was in the kitchen on his way out the back door.

She tried to tell herself that he'd gone out to join the men smoking on the back porch. After all, he'd grown up with most of them, and this was the first time he'd had to socialize since he'd come back. But as the guests started to leave and she walked out with them to thank them for coming, there was no sign of Sullivan anywhere.

Alarmed without knowing why, her gaze flew to the foreman's house down the hill. His truck was parked out back, just as it always was when he was home. She should have been relieved, but the apprehension she couldn't explain never lessened its assault on the lining of her stomach.

Turning abruptly, she went in search of Pop and found him on the back porch enjoying a cup of coffee as the last of the guests departed. "They're leaving just in time," he said, nodding toward the cars and trucks dragging dust behind them as they headed for town. "The last of the ham disappeared five minutes ago." Suddenly noting her agitation, he frowned. "What's wrong?"

"I need to talk to Sullivan at his place," she said without preamble. "Will you watch Caitlin for me? I should be back before she wakes up, but if I'm not, just call me."

He didn't even hesitate. "Course I will. Go on."

"Thanks, Pop." Giving him a quick hug, she hurried inside and grabbed her purse, then raced outside to fire up her pickup, too anxious to take the time to walk the eight hundred yards between her house and Sullivan's.

She found him in his bedroom. Packing. Stopping in the doorway, she deliberately blocked it. "I'm not letting you walk out on me again."

Sullivan jerked around to find her glaring at him, hurt and betrayal darkening her eyes and sheer gut determination setting her jaw. She wasn't going to let him go without a confrontation, he realized, and suddenly, as quickly as it took a match to ignite a firecracker, he was blazingly mad. Did she think he wanted to leave, to put them both through hell again? Last time he'd been young and stupid and too damn ignorant, and like a fool, he'd turned his back on the best thing that had ever happened to him. But this time, he knew what he was losing. Couldn't she see that it was tearing him apart?

Throwing the last of his clothes in his suitcase, he slammed it shut and turned to face her. "I've got nothing to offer you," he said coldly. "*Nothing!* And don't you dare tell me it doesn't matter," he growled when she opened her mouth to answer him. "The minute we stepped in church this morning, the gossips had a field day. Every wagging tongue in Kerrville thinks I'm after you to get my ranch back."

"Then every wagging tongue is wrong," she snapped, her blue eyes blazing. "I won't let you destroy us because of a pack of lies started by a bunch of old women who don't know what they're talking about."

"How do you know they're lies?" he taunted softly, bitterly. "Think about it, honey. I was desperate, homeless, and you had what was once mine. Can you think of an easier way for me to solve my problems than to make you fall in love with me again, then convince you to marry me?"

If he expected her to be devastated, he was in for a rude awakening. "I knew what you were planning weeks ago," she confessed. "You were hurt and angry and bitter, and I might have considered the same thing if I'd been in your shoes. But you couldn't go through with it, could you?"

She stepped toward him, unable to bear the distance between them. "That's why you stayed gone six weeks after Caitlin was born. That's why *I* was the one who had to do the seducing. If you hadn't had a change of heart, you wouldn't be packing now—you'd be begging me to marry you."

"Considering that my only asset is a beat-up old pickup truck, what other way could I convince a woman to marry me than by begging?"

Rose winced at the bitterness of his tone, wishing with all her heart she could have spared him the humiliation of losing his ranch. Fumbling with the clasp of her purse, she drew out the papers she had been carrying around for weeks and held them out to him. "I believe this belongs to you."

He looked down blankly at the folded paper, then back up at her. Watching the emotions flickering across his face, Rose held her breath as he gingerly took the legal document and opened it. An instant later his narrowed gaze snapped up to hers. "This is the deed to the Lazy J."

"Yes. I had it put in your name while you were on the cattle-buying trip after the baby was born. I was waiting for a chance to give it to you when you wouldn't throw it back in my face."

His mind reeling, Sullivan could only stare at her. "Why?"

"Because it's yours," she said simply. "The Lazy J has always belonged to the Joneses. Frank was wrong to take it, to set your father up the way he did. When I found out about it, I tried to stop him, but he was determined to have it. If your father had let you come home when you wanted to, none of this would have ever happened."

His fingers curled around the paper, gripping it as if he were afraid it would disappear. "Why now?" he asked hoarsely. "Why are you giving this to me now?"

It was a question he had every right to ask. She could see by the look in his eye, that he, too, realized what a risk she was taking. He had what he'd come for, what he'd practically sold his soul for to get back. He could leave without a backward glance and there wouldn't be a thing she could do to stop him.

But the future she knew they could have together was worth any gamble. "Because I love you," she said quietly. "Once before I lost you because of misunderstandings and other people's interference. This time there can be no doubts. No misunderstandings. If you walk away from me, it can be for no other reason than you don't love me. That's the only excuse you have left, the only excuse I'll accept."

"And if I stay?" he growled softly.

"It can be for no other reason than you love me," she replied, repeating herself but for one crucial word. "That's the only excuse you have left, the only excuse I'll accept."

So this was it, do or die, the choice totally and completely his. But it was a choice he had made years ago, a choice that he had, during endless winter nights, often bitterly regretted and tried his damnedest to deny, a choice he was finally forced to admit he couldn't run away from. From the moment he'd first laid eyes on her when she was seventeen, he'd loved her.

His eyes locked with hers, he took a step *toward,* not away from, her. "Do you really think I could walk away from you a second time?"

Her knees would have totally given way in relief then if he hadn't reached for her and hauled her into his arms. "Say it," she whispered, aching. "I need to hear you say it."

He groaned, pulling her closer. "Oh, sweetheart, don't you know that I say it every time I kiss you? Every time I touch you?" Tenderly capturing her face in his hands, he tilted her chin up until he could gaze down into the deep sapphire pools of her eyes. “Let me translate,” he mumbled. “This—” he pressed a feather-soft kiss to each eye “—means I love you. This—” his voice deepened to a low sexy growl as his lips covered hers for a long, precious, heart-stealing moment filled with promises “—means adore you. Always. And this—” he reached for her lef hand and gently ran his thumb over her bare ring finger “—means I don’t ever want to face another day without you or Caitlin at my side. Marry me,” he urged thickly. “Take my name and my heart and promise me nothing will ever come between us again.”

She crowded closer. “Oh, yes.”

Just that simply, she gave herself into his keeping. Sullivan felt his throat fill with emotion, choking him. Wrapping his arms around her, binding her to him as if he would never let her go, he said huskily, “I want to adopt Caitlin.”

Her eyes blurred, a brilliant smile lighting her face. She would have never asked that of him—to claim as his own the child of a man who tried to destroy his family—but it was the one thing she hadn’t dared to let herself hope for that would make everything perfect. Rising on tiptoe, she kissed him with a tenderness that sent the tears welling in her eyes spilling over, telling him without a single word of the happiness she couldn’t express. “That will make it perfect,” she said softly. “In every way that counts, she’s been yours from the moment she was born. You’re going to be a wonderful father.”

He wanted to believe it, but every time he thought of being a father, he thought of his own. “My own wasn’t exactly a prime candidate for father of the year,” he reminded her quietly.

She drew back to look at him in surprise. “No, but your grandfather was. I remember you telling me stories of how he taught you to ride and hunt, and how you’d spend hours together down at that old cypress tree at the bend of the river trying to catch the granddaddy of all catfish. You were crazy about that old man. Just like Caitlin and our other kids are going to be crazy about you."

She sounded so sure, so indignant that he could possibly think otherwise, he couldn't help but grin. "You think so, huh?"

She nodded, her blue eyes dancing. "Of course, I'm a pretty terrific mother, too. Between the two of us, our kids can't lose."

"No, sweetheart," he murmured, lowering his mouth to claim hers. "Between the two of us, *we* can't lose!"

* * * * *

A Note from Cait London

I thought readers would enjoy sharing Irish Dalton with me. She's a perfect earth mother: soft, generous, sensing needs and caring for each person who comes into her loving realm. Yet Irish is strong, as well. I ached to create for her a man so special that he would be her perfect reward. Enter Maxwell Van Damme. A perfectionist, used to traveling in his unemotionally attached lanes, Max is instantly drawn to Irish, and she responds on an unfamiliar, greedy level. They are opposite personalities faced with the challenge of their lives—a pregnancy.

I wanted to present in the story a triumph over struggles and the characters' dedication to building a strong foundation for their baby and their relationship. Max's pursuit of Irish reverses the role of caring and nourishing and leads to new experiences for them both. The message of "The Daddy Candidate" is one I strongly believe in: that love at first sight does occur, and that life's challenges can be met with dedication and a love that never stops growing.

Cait London

THE DADDY CANDIDATE

Cait London

To the men who open their hearts and find joy in the special creations of life called "babies." We love these precious men, and pray that each boy will grow into the perfect Daddy Candidate.

One

"Maxwell Van Damme. Systems Warrior. I'll bet Madame Abagail LaRue Whitehouse wouldn't invite him into her bordello for a fun time," Irish Dalton muttered, replacing the updated antique telephone in its cradle. Irish forced herself to breathe calmly, inhaling the fresh air flowing in through the open window. She waited for the Colorado breeze, filled with scents of May and pine, to calm her. Not even the aroma of whole-wheat cinnamon rolls wafting from her kitchen could take the edge off her temper.

Tapping her fingers on the windowsill, Irish surveyed her TLC kingdom and thought of Van Damme swooping nearer. She'd been expecting his call, but nothing could have prepared her for the raspy, clipped and arrogant male voice informing her that he would be arriving in one hour and twenty-five minutes.

From the sound of his voice, Irish expected Van Damme to be cut from the same mold as Mark, her ex-fiancé. Unshakable, even at emotional moments, he'd have wires for veins, electronic impulses for heartbeats. A child playing with puppies couldn't warm the steely cockles of his heart. Kittens would scamper to safety in his wake. Wood violets and mountain daisies would wilt as he passed by; bees wouldn't make honey...

Irish frowned, vowing to protect her vacation health spa and inn. Originally a bordello, for years the inn and surrounding ranch land had provided rest and care to those with troubled hearts. A hundred and thirty years ago, Colorado miners knew they could come to Madame Abagail Whitehouse's bordello for understanding and care. Abagail had stepped between her two lovers in a duel, taking the deadly bullets and expiring in her elegant, red velvet boudoir. But somehow Irish doubted that even Abagail's loving heart could cherish a Maxwell Van Damme.

Irish liked to think the madam still inhabited the inn, drifting through the restored rooms in a cloud of lavender scent. One of Irish's TLC theories was that romance was good for the soul, and it was her duty to perpetuate the memory of the madam in a ghostly manner. But with Van Damme on a calculator rampage....Irish shuddered.

"A regular profit-and-loss hit man, and he'll be here for a week, no more than two," Irish repeated Van Damme's estimation through her teeth. "He thinks he can systemize and flatten my TLC business, does he?"

Standing in her large sunlit kitchen, Irish impatiently tapped her sneaker against the restored and varnished boards of her inn.

"My sister is at the bottom of this," Irish accused as she glanced through the window of her bed-and-breakfast health farm. "Katherine 'Angel' MacLean, attorney for the underdog," she muttered over the morning call of the mockingbird sitting on her picket fence. "I've always had the feeling that she wants revenge for my matchmaking—and now it's payback time."

Six years ago Irish had decided that her sister, Katherine, and J.D. MacLean, with whom she'd had a disastrous affair many years earlier, needed each other. Irish had set herself up as bait by allowing J.D. to help her out of a financial bog. Actually a few financial debts hadn't worried Irish, but Katherine had been incensed when J.D. reentered her life via her sister. Their rematch had equaled a shoot-out, and now the MacLeans had two children: his orphaned grandson, Travis, and a beautiful daughter, four-year-old Dakota. The MacLeans were impressive, tough and invincible when they worked together on a project.

J.D., the lean dark foil to Katherine's blond elegance, was also Irish's business partner. In the five years since he'd married Katherine, J.D. had continued to hold off his wife's instincts to take over her baby sister.

Then two weeks ago, J.D. had called. "The business is too big for your bookkeeping system. The winter ski season is showing as much profit as the summer. You've got repeat guests and an exclusive waiting list."

"So?" she had asked, trusting him. "We've always managed, haven't we? Red-apple cookie jar for big questionable bills, and the shoe box for lesser ones? And now that Jeff is perking things up..."

The name of the inn's manager had hung in the static silence for a moment before J.D. answered. "I think Abagail's is at a crucial turning point. It has exceeded my limits of time. When the bookkeeper untied the knot on the trash bag holding your receipts and bills, she fainted and threatened to sue for mental cruelty. We need an efficiency expert, and I've already called Maxwell Van Damme. Max knows how to cut the flab...."

Flab? Irish had remembered something Katherine had said. "Wait a minute. I remember something about flab, as in Kat's reference to my people." Irish had sighted down on J.D. "You're sending a hit man in here, aren't you?"

"Max or Katherine. Take your choice."

"Some choice. Send in your hit man. Anyone would be better than Katherine when she starts nitpicking."

Now, expecting Van Damme to arrive shortly—in one hour and seventeen minutes—Irish muttered, "Just knowing that...that man is invading my home, jamming his sneaky little nose into my business and messing with my people is enough to turn a chili pepper cold. Nod and smile, that's what I'll do. Then put everything back just the way I like it after he's gone. He's not going to efficientize one single little peony petal," Irish growled, glancing out the window. "I will not use prepared mixes and canned vegetables."

Granny, stooped with age, moved slowly through the field of sweet corn inspecting the green shoots. Granny and her husband, Link, were rest-home runaways who'd arrived at the inn the day after Irish. "We're here to work, missy. Link and I are too young for any old folks home. Besides, it ain't fittin' for a pretty unmarried thing to be here alone," she'd said, eyeing Irish up and down. Then her wrinkles had shifted into a wary smile. "We'll work for our keep. Think we can stay?"

Now the inn was their home. Nadia was the next addition to Irish's family. A recovered alcoholic, unemployed fortune-teller, Nadia's bus fare had run out in Kodiac. The ex-nightclub performer had hated fresh air and people in general. Now Nadia ate an apple and chatted pleasantly with a middle-aged couple debating divorce. Beneath the shade of the maple tree, she plucked coins from behind ears and pried smiles from their tense faces. Nadia knew what soothed aching hearts, and she applied her fortunes like a sweet healing balm.

Irish firmed her lips, wondering if hit men smiled. "Van Damme," she muttered, inspecting the new erosion cutting down the ski slope. Looking over the newly plowed fields and the rows of sprouting plants, she mumbled, "Sounds like a Great Dane. He probably never heard of eating alfalfa sprouts or hugging. A workaholic numbers person who thinks profit is more important than caring."

The calculator-for-a-heart image slid into another man's face, and thinking of Mark, Irish sighed and closed her eyes, ignoring the chug-rattle rhythm of the new water heater that threatened to expire with its warranty.

Seven and a half years ago she'd walked out on a five-year relationship with Mark. Looking back, their stark personality differences stood out like granite tombstones. Her degree in home economics hadn't prepared her for the office position that he had insisted she accept. While Irish had filed and typed and dreamed of a home packed with children, Mark had been perfectly happy. But when he had ordered Irish to have a sterility operation, she took one long gasp and decided she'd opt for a house filled with children. Then she'd packed her favorite cookware, her pots of herbs, and walked out.

Irish had bequeathed Mark her exercise mat and videotapes for trimming hips. He'd have to find someone else to be his willowy delight. Whatever lay ahead for her, it wasn't a nightly battle to keep the inches off her rounded posterior.

Wrapping the shreds of her heart in her forgotten home-economics degree, Irish had marched off to find her special niche.

She'd fallen in love with Abagail's house from the moment she'd first seen it. Deserted, staring at her with broken windows, the inn shimmered in the dry Colorado sun. Graffiti had been scrawled across the siding's peeling paint, and the orange neon hotel sign swung in a creaky tune.

Plopping her tiny savings and an amount from a bank loan down in front of the owner, Irish had purchased Abagail's. Now the restored rooms were filled with antique ornate furniture, and Abagail's Inn rated stars across the health-spa catalogs. Since she'd bought the former bordello, she'd shored up sagging hearts with large doses of TLC. Restored by her care and healthy food, her recycled, revamped and happy people returned to their individual worlds.

Unable to hold her dark mood, Irish smiled at the sight of a husband and wife, both stressed-out executives, kissing and whispering like teenagers in love for the first time. The couple sat on a wooden bench, holding hands and snuggling.

She grinned impishly as a young couple kissed in the shadows of a weeping willow. Later in the season, the inn would be filled with couples recapturing their love. When the Romaines had stopped at the inn to ask for directions, Mrs. Romaine mentioned that they needed time away from their three small children but couldn't afford the lovely spa's fee. Lacy and Nigel, now wrapped in each other's arms, had been ecstatic to discover they were the winners of Irish's new one hundredth customer-free-vacation prize.

Wrapping her arms around herself, Irish gave herself a hug. People needed hugs, she thought, tucking Maxwell Van Damme into a "later" pocket with the lawn mower that had died.

Maxwell Van Damme glanced in his rearview mirror, then shifted into a higher gear to pass the pickup truck. On the winding uphill curve, he allowed himself to enjoy the sleek sensuous power of the Porsche gliding over the Colorado Rocky pass. He shifted again, easing the engine for a smooth stretch of highway. On either side of the road, the one-o'clock sun tangled in the vivid sweeps of May foliage. Shadows hovered in the ravines, melding blues and purples with browns and ochres.

Running his palm around the steering wheel, Max savored the responsive powerful engine. Stretching in the low custom seat, he eased the drive from Lake Tahoe from the cramped muscles of his six-foot body. He appreciated good machinery and neat business systems tuned to perfection. Max's life-style reflected the same streamlining, free of attachments and clutter.

A doe and her fawn watched the car from the protection of a sumac stand, and Max smiled. Protective of her fawn, the doe reminded him of Katherine MacLean's description of her sister. "By nature, Irish is so loving, she doesn't see that the people she's collected at her bed-and-breakfast are using her. At thirty-three, she hasn't got a selfish bone in her body."

Glancing at a passing road sign, Max slipped a Bach cassette into the Porsche's sophisticated sound system. The town of Kodiac and Abagail's Inn, his destination, lay twenty-two minutes away. Settling comfortably into the customized seat, Max allowed the classical music to pour into him.

He liked fine music, good wine and gourmet foods, and had planned to enjoy all three after streamlining the sales and reservation systems of a popular resort chain in Tahoe. He'd discovered the perfect rental condominium, stocked with all the copper pots and chef's knives an experienced cook could want. Max had relished diving into his favorite recipes, cooking his favorite gourmet dishes.

But J.D. had requested a favor, and Max had agreed. He smiled quickly, the movement not reaching his eyes behind the mirrorlike sunglasses. J.D. was the closest thing to a friend and family that Max had ever had. The senseless brawl was years ago, but Max remembered vividly how J.D. had fought with him, back to back, against eight angry men.

Max slashed a glance at an elaborately scrolled sign that read: "Abagail's Inn. Health Spa and Inn. Let us take care of you. Tender Loving Care is our middle name."

He shifted briskly, rounding a curve shaded by stately firs. At forty-two, he'd long ago learned that love wasn't designed to mesh with his personal systems.

Max switched his thoughts to the task waiting for him. Apparently, Irish Dalton, a natural earth-mother personality, ran her inn with all the business aplomb of a child sucking her thumb and picking tulips. Concerned about her, J.D. and Katherine had asked Max to structure a fail-safe business system for the inn. The MacLeans had agreed that it wouldn't be easy. Irish had different ideas about the people she had tucked beneath her protective wing.

He took a deep breath, absorbing the mellow music as he thought of Irish Dalton, J.D.'s partner and owner of the health spa and inn. Sorting what he knew about the situation into neat labeled mental boxes, Max remembered Irish's lilting happy tones when she'd answered the telephone. Those welcome tones had changed abruptly once he informed her that he was Max Van Damme.

"I know who and what you are, Max," she had said tightly. "You're expected. You're welcome to stay and rest here. You're even welcome to snoop around. We only have a few guests so I suppose you can't do much damage. But you will not—I repeat, not—even suggest to any of my people the reason for your visit here. If you do, you're out on your ear," she had finished lightly before the line went dead.

Max slowed the car at Kodiac's city limits, quickly noting the typical Western setting, described by J.D. as "a wide spot in the road." He noted the gas station, the customary truck-stop café and grocery store, and a few houses surrounded by large gardens and picket fences. He slowed the

Porsche even more as a child rode a horse across the road, followed by two smaller children, who watched him warily.

Glancing at the rugged soaring mountains cradling the valley, Max hoped the inn was quiet and childfree.

A butterfly drifted across a flower bed, reminding Max of Dakota, who never stayed long in one place. Unaccustomed to children, Max had found himself anticipating her swift, moist lollypop-flavored kisses. The MacLean children reflected their parents' love and gave hugs and kisses unreservedly. At first Max had been uncomfortable, but now he looked forward to visiting the MacLean household.

Though he enjoyed J.D.'s children, Max didn't fit into the parent mold. The Van Damme genes didn't contain a loving nature. He hadn't seen his parents for years. Elena and Franz Van Damme, genetic scientists, hadn't missed their son from the moment he was born.

He smiled again tightly as he remembered himself at nineteen, responding hotly in the experienced hands of an older woman. After a series of teenage encounters, he'd been ripe for the situation. Starved for affection and deceived by his hormones, Max thought he'd found love; but Natalie was merely between husbands, and young Max didn't qualify.

On the rebound and out to soothe his damaged masculinity, Max had married Jennifer, a stockbroker. For seven years, she had been supportive of his studies and his budding career. His needs had appeared to be hers, and neither one of them had wanted children. She had been the young executive's perfect wife and partner. Max had thought the marriage would last forever.

But Jennifer's needs had been greater, and when he'd returned home unexpectedly one night, Max found his wife wrapped in the arms of her lover, his best friend. In the scene that had followed, Neil had suffered a broken collarbone and two cracked ribs. Max had been stunned by the emotions spewing from him—he hadn't liked them. He'd spent a year getting over the pain, trying to block out the scene and pasting himself back together.

Rounding a curve, Max spotted the rambling bed-and-breakfast, circled by a white picket fence that badly needed painting. The blurred image of Jennifer and Neil, wrapped in damp sheets, clicked off as Max surveyed Irish's property.

The hundred acres of fields and ski slopes sprawled around Abagail's, enfolding it like a dollhouse set on a colorful patchwork blanket. The house seemed to twist at odd angles, blending old cornices and wide porches and high pointed roofs with newer practical additions. Absently noting the rocking chairs lined across the front porch, and the elderly couple occupying two of them, Max parked his car by the front gate.

Through the Porsche's window, he noted a man dressed in work clothes leaning against the trunk of a maple tree. The man glanced at Max, then continued to watch a woman kneeling on a spot in a freshly plowed garden. In her wake, tiny green shoots formed an uneven line. When the man said something and eyed Max, the woman stood up. She dusted her hands on her dirty jeans and looked at Max. Framed by green fields, the young woman fitted Katherine's description of Irish.

Irish said something to the man, then carefully picked her way over the maze of zigzagging garden rows toward Max. In midstride she hesitated, glanced down at a new plant bed and bent to tend it.

Max placed his glasses inside his dress shirt pocket. She wasn't happy; she looked like a mother tiger stalking a predator who had come too near her cub. Irish didn't look particularly good-natured, nor susceptible to leaners-on.

She looked very hot and very passionate.

The thought startled Max, tightening his taut stomach. These days, wrapped in the comfort of his experience and age, he rarely thought of women as hot and passionate, nor soft and sweet. She reminded him of Tchaikovsky's passionate strains, rather than Bach's smoothly integrated chords. Max stirred against the leather seat restlessly, uncomfortable with his comparison of Irish to his favorite composers.

But as she walked toward the front gate, the late afternoon sun caught reddish sparks from her short curly blond hair. Max had a quick image of animation and light, sunlight and smiles, all at the same time. Her T-shirt and jeans had seen better times, though Max reluctantly admired her soft curves.

His gaze returned to her face. Irish had an all-American face with wide blue eyes and a strong jaw. Her pert nose suited her freckles, and a soft vulnerable mouth caused Max to think of California strawberries—not the large, too-sweet variety, but the medium size with the interesting tart flavor.

He glanced uneasily away from her T-shirt as she hopped over the row of peonies lining the brick walkway to the house. She moved like an athlete, the inn's TLC logo flowing over her quivering breasts. Distracted momentarily, Max thought they were nice breasts. Not too full, nor too slight.

His hands tightened on the steering wheel. In his palms, they would feel exactly right. About the size of succulent Valencia oranges, though the tips probably would have the slight nuance and mellow bite of a fine French wine.

Startled momentarily by the turn of his thoughts as he compared Irish Dalton to a gourmet's delight, Max swallowed to moisten his unaccountably dry throat. There were always reasons behind his emotions, and he suddenly remembered he hadn't been sexually active for quite some time. Irish Dalton, walking barefoot through the early-afternoon sun with the sprawling ancient house behind her, caused him to be uneasy. Max almost discarded the thought, but then Irish lifted her hand to brush away an errant reddish-gold curl. The movement brought her short T-shirt higher, revealing a smoothly indented waist that emphasized her rounded hips.

They would be soft hips, cushiony hips with the bones moving smoothly beneath the surface. A man could settle within her deeply and bask in the undulating warmth...

Max frowned, sliding out of the low-slung car to stand his full height. He shifted restlessly, stretching cramped muscles. Tuned to the needs of his lean body, Max perceived a definite sexual tension running through it. The thought made him uncomfortable, like systems with funny little imbalances. Since Jennifer, Max had exerted perfect control over his emotions and his body.

He pressed his lips together grimly. Evidently fatigue and truck-stop food had taken their toll on him.

Irish Dalton had that round soft look that his parents had classified as good potential childbearing material. And then Max tucked a third, nonlogical thought into his mental-Irish box: he wondered, with quick intense emotion, if Irish Dalton had a lover to kiss the freckles dancing across her nose. And taste the sunlight caught on the silvery tips of her reddish-blond eyelashes.

The man who had been lounging in the shade sauntered off, and the movement brought Max back to his purpose. He rubbed the taut muscle at the back of his neck, uncomfortable with the knowledge that he'd been distracted by sunlight on a woman's eyelashes.

With customary discipline, Max forced his attention back to the inn.

As she watched J.D.'s hit man survey his intended victim—her beloved inn—Irish firmed her lips.

Van Damme will not touch, systemize, nor dispossess any of my people. He will not change one hardwood floorboard, nor gossamer rose curtain. If he inoculates Abagail's with electronic room service, I'll rip out the whats-its. I'll...

Irish smiled tightly and glanced at his immaculately polished car, nesting under her shade tree. If Van Damme parked under that tree for an evening, he'd have a polka-dot, bird-decorated car.

"Get ready, Madame," she whispered to the resident ghost as she moved toward Van Damme, the systems warrior. "You and I have a mission. There's a carpetbagger approaching at high noon."

The black Porsche well represented the man, Maxwell Van Damme. The Black Knight on a mission. He looked sleek, and honed to suit his purpose. An efficiency expert with dark thick brows and a hard unsmiling mouth. As he moved around the car to meet her, she resented his height, resented his presence and the hard I'm-taking-charge way he walked toward her.

She gripped the mud ball in her hand more tightly. Van Damme's purpose was to mess with her land, and she intended to give him the feel of it immediately.

He looked exactly like what he was—a businessman, cutting the warmth and affection from his life by hurrying through all the whimsies that make life enjoyable and make people lovable, Irish thought sadly. She noted the hard well-shaved face, the slashing dark brown eyes that estimated and dissected everything in their sweep. His skin lacked laughter lines, and a taut muscle moved in his jaw as though he couldn't wait to accomplish his mission and soar out of the wilderness in his shiny car.

Irish glanced at his car. He probably loved it as much as she loved her inn. After all, hit men/systems warriors deserved their special loves, too.

She sensed that Maxwell Van Damme had never known real love.

She doubted that his auburn hair had ever been mussed by the wind, that its tendency to curl had ever been freed; she doubted he laughed easily or exclaimed with delight.

She wondered who and what would make him smile, lighting his cold dark eyes with warmth.

"Hello, Max," she said quietly, returning his stony unreadable gaze evenly. "Are you hungry?"

He flicked a wary look down his nose at her, as though she were a wrinkle that needed ironing. Though Max probably never experienced a wrinkle or a gravy stain in his life, he needed attention, just like a little lost boy, she thought whimsically. She allowed her lips to curve with the thought.

Instinctively, Irish placed her clean hand on his forearm and felt the ridges of muscle contract beneath the warm hairy surface. He withdrew fractionally from her light touch, and then she knew with certainty that Maxwell Van Damme was hers to take care of—even if he was on a devastation mission.

"I'm fine, thank you," he returned with a curt dip of his head. Irish noted the deep rough texture of his voice. Max hesitated slightly, then formally extended his hand. Max was a cautious man, moving through life by picking each step carefully, she decided, and smiled gently up at him.

But he'd stepped onto the lily pads of her precious pond, and Mr. Van Damme was on his own.

When Irish stepped closer, she caught the masculine scents of expensive after-shave and soap. And when his hand wrapped around her smaller one, flattening the mud on it, she felt safety in his touch. He released her hand immediately, and Irish stepped back, wriggling her toes in the sun-warmed grass and clasping her hands behind her innocently. Van Damme's hand was large; the broad palm had aligned neatly with hers, his fingers strong as they'd curled around her hand. She had the impression of controlled power, self-confidence and efficiency all at the same time. Of course there was disdain, too, as if his hand had never touched mud.

Impishly Irish wondered if Van Damme ever let his control slip. Would he take a second piece of her special deep-dish Dutch apple pie?

She glanced at his flat stomach and decided Van Damme never exceeded the proper limits of anything.

He looked down at his palm and frowned slightly, then extracted a carefully folded monogrammed handkerchief from his pocket. She felt a guilty twinge about her mud-ball revenge. "I hope you enjoy your stay, Max. I'll show you to your room so you can rest before dinner. We're having apple pie for dessert, and one of the guests is churning the ice cream now. The recipe uses fresh cow's milk and brown farm eggs. If you have any dietary restrictions, please let me know," she said, watching his quick assessing glances dart over her beloved inn as he wiped his hand dry.

"That would be fine," he said in that get-away-from-me tone, noticing the lawn mower that Jeff had left in pieces two days ago.

While Max thought he was setting up an efficiency system for her, she would be giving him the warmth he so badly needed. Plants, animals, humans and Travis MacLean's guppies had responded to her. Max would, too. She'd put him back in his shiny sleek car with a warm feeling, and her TLC business would continue on its original loving course.

"Laundry service is free," she said, taking the handkerchief from him. "I hope you like health food."

As Max swung his leather bag from the Porsche, Irish continued. "It's our specialty here at Abagail's Inn. Although it's mostly just-like-mom-used-to cooking."

Irish winked, impishly testing Max's formality. "Let me know how your mother prepared your favorite dish, and I'll give it a try."

"Whatever is on the menu will be fine." Max rounded the car and slashed her a grim look, then glanced suspiciously up at the rustling in the tree boughs. He had just the right stay-away-from-me look to intrigue Irish. The look made her want to stroke his darkly tanned brow, pet his tense neck and ease his...

Irish swallowed, caught by the sunlit patch of hair exposed by his opened collar.

As Max turned to survey Abagail's and the surrounding fields in the dusky light, Irish was presented with a full magnificent view of Van Damme's elegant backside.

From broad shoulders to trim waist and taut buttocks, Maxwell Van Dame seemed...touchable. She pondered the thought, flicking a curious and, she admitted, a slightly naughty glance down the length of his long legs clad in dress slacks. She knew without a doubt that the first free moment he had, Max would polish the Colorado dust from his Italian loafers.

Despite Max's occupation, his body seemed very hard and fit, she decided analytically. Not that she was really interested in him as a, well, male person. Good heavens, she'd had enough problems after the breakup with Mark.

Irish shrugged mentally, thinking of the wide variety of men who occasionally foraged through her affections. She liked a dinner date or a movie now and then, sprinkled with light hand-holding and a fond good-night kiss. She liked the scent of after-shave and a hot round of dancing to rock and roll.

Max looked more like the tango-type: smooth, stylish, unruffled, and structured down to his Italian loafers. Yet something pulsed beneath the surface, maybe a fiery flamenco with riveting guitars and castanets.

Max rolled a shoulder to ease his muscles, drawing the expensive wrinkle-free fabric tightly across the hard contour. Irish's fingers twitched just once with the urge to stroke it.

Mimi, a tiger-colored barn cat and a mother several times over, loped from the porch to Max. She stopped and leaned against him. Weaving happily around his legs, the feline hussy rubbed and purred as though she'd found her heart's delight.

Max shot Mimi his get-away-from-me look, and the cat grinned hopefully up at him, twitching her tail. Max nudged her away slightly, and Mimi leaned against him in a rhapsody of purring and rubbing.

Irish enjoyed the scene of a wrinkle-free perfect hit man waylaid by a cat. Max hesitated, bent stiffly and unerringly scratched the spot behind the cat's ear. Mimi pressed against his hand for a minute and licked it fondly. Then she lifted her tail high and sauntered away from him like a lover after a satisfying romp.

"Mimi's friendly," Irish offered, amused as Max's gaze warily tracked the cat into the snowball bushes. Actually Mimi never lowered herself to brazen seduction, preferring to let the guests seek her ears and tummy without invitation.

"Come along then, Max. I've prepared a lovely room for you," she said lightly and watched with pleasure as his head went back as though he'd taken a slap. Max wasn't accustomed to being patronized, nor to taking orders. She'd have to remember that if he tried to flatten her TLC policies with profit-and-loss statements.

Irish turned and began walking up the brick path to the inn, leaving him to follow. She waved to a passing neighbor child and fought a smile. Maxwell Van Damme would keep his hands off her business, and he would enjoy his stay, she promised herself. J.D. and Katherine had sent her someone to care for, because if ever a person needed her care, it was Max.

Max walked behind Irish, drawn to the buoyant confident stride and the intriguing softness of her hips. Instinctively Max calculated the amount of sway to a fraction of an inch. He reluctantly enjoyed the feminine flow for an instant as though it were the strains of Bach. A familiar scent followed in her wake, of cinnamon and freshly baked bread, and an elusive, enticing scent of warm womanly skin lying on cool sun-dried sheets.

Startled by the flow of his thoughts, he forced his gaze upward, noting the indentation of her waist and the soft curve of her shoulders.

The late-afternoon sun caught and played in her riotous curls, and he had the impression of gold dust on dewy strawberries. As she'd stood beneath the sunlight and maple-tree shadows, Irish Dalton had caused Max's body to harden sensually.

He frowned, remembering Katherine's description of her sister—*Irish is magic; she gets inside people and makes them feel good.*

His frown deepened; no one had really gotten inside or to him since his childhood. He could almost feel her wrap around him, the softness and the warmth.

Why did he want to place his mouth on her soft one and take all she could give?

Why did he want her softness enveloping him, keeping him warm and soothing the tense years away?

Dammit! Why was his body hard, honed intensely to the moving softness of Irish's?

For just that fraction of a second, Max needed what she could give....

Then Irish paused, looking at him over her shoulder, her soft lips parted to say something. Her blue eyes were warm with laughter, and Max fell straight into them.

Their gazes held momentarily, then Irish's widened. Max stepped closer, wanting to inhale the meadow-flower scent, wanting...

He could feel his passion snake through him, leaving heat in its wake. He hadn't felt stark desire for years, and now it tugged sharply at his lower stomach, the intensity painful and unyielding.

Beneath his shadow, Irish's face paled. Her eyes flickered slightly and darkened to cobalt blue. Max knew Irish felt the intensity, the smashing heat driving him.

The tip of her tongue flicked moisture onto her bottom lip, and the wild surge of desire riveted Max beneath the sunlight and shadows, intertwining him with a woman he very much wanted to explore. He wanted to lay her down on the lush spring clover and grass....

In that instant, he knew her skin would be dewy fresh, soft as rose petals. She'd taste like sweet mountain air and exotic sensual mists. In that same instant, he knew he wanted her as he'd never wanted another woman.

She shivered despite the warm day, easing away from him.

Head back, the sunlight twisting through her hair, her cheeks flushed, Irish shot him a look of queenly distaste.

"No, Max," she said quietly, turning away.

Two

Seated at the family-style dinner table that night, Max dutifully answered the questions he was asked. In his experience with groups, especially those of the relating and happy type, curiosity about him lasted until dessert. Then he could distance himself from the necessary chatter and begin sifting through the guests and staff. And in this instance, a cowboy who showed signs of territorial rights around Irish topped the list.

Max allowed himself to enjoy freshly baked whole-wheat bread and a rice-and-broccoli-and-chicken dish with delicate seasonings. The plain, tasty and healthy cuisine suited the country atmosphere.

He glanced at the whimsical garden salad. The chunks of crisp greens had obviously been savaged by a mad strangler. Reluctantly Max approved of the herbs drifting in the various fresh salad dressings. Except the vinaigrette dressing, which lacked Dijon mustard.

Max forced himself away from the tempting dissection of Irish's freestyle cookery. And the fact, of course, that he hadn't noted one copper pot, nor chef's knife in the kitchen. In a San Francisco gourmet shop, he'd spotted a beautiful knife, with a wide blade just right for smashing garlic cloves—but he'd always traveled lightly, unable to collect gleaming copper pots and a proper selection of knives. The antique oak chopping table in the sunny kitchen was magnificent....

Max frowned, realizing that the friendly atmosphere and savory aromas had momentarily seduced him. Setting himself back on track, Max sorted his thoughts, avoiding the mental controversy of Dijon mustard.

Max pushed the sliver of Dutch apple pie through the creamy ice cream, savoring the delicate sweet-and-tart taste of the fruit. Baked in a quiche dish in lieu of a proper pan hadn't changed the flavor. An apple chunk reminded him of the cookie jar and the shoe box he'd found placed on the bed in his room.

Stuffed with receipts, the shoe box, which contained Irish's notorious bookkeeping system, created an instant headache for Max. Irish kept scraps of paper that had obviously been through a washing machine. The blurred totals on the receipts were like something from *The Twilight Zone.* Irish's rounded script, listing denture polish and Dr. Seuss books, appeared on the tax assessor's statement. An outrageous tractor-repair bill, spattered with a raspberry stain, lacked a breakdown of labor and parts. Ditto marks covered the guest register, which was stuffed with pressed dried mountain flowers and assorted food-stained recipes.

Several unopened and outdated notices from major companies proved that she'd accepted credit cards as blithely as freshly baked sugar cookies. Various lists scrolled down the envelopes, one of which read: "Leta Jones cat—three whites, four calico. Order Dutch tulip bulbs. Bake chocolate cake for school supper. Bake cookies for Beth's seventh-grade class."

Concealing his mental shudder, Max allowed the dinner conversation to flow around him as he settled into his thoughts. Irish had also thrust a huge box of letters at him, her eyes dancing with mischief. The letters, as frazzled and spattered with cooking stains as the bills, swelled with gratitude. Max had thrown these thank-yous into the category of paving the way for further nonpaid visits.

He'd glanced at the papers, then decided to walk around the immediate grounds before tackling the project with the help of classical violins and oboes. Mimi had attached herself to him the minute he opened the back door. With the cat on his heels, rubbing and purring against him when he paused, Max had taken a cursory tour of Abagail's.

At first the ranch manager had been friendly, tossing off quick and indefinite answers to Max's questions. Then, when forced to answer specific points, Jeff had clamped his mouth shut and walked off into the fescue fields. After taking notes, Max had returned to the inn.

He cut through the second piece of pie Irish placed in front of him. It was delicious pie with a flaky crust; he found himself enjoying the lattice crust sprinkled with sugar.

Twenty-three people appeared to be just where they wanted to be—seated around the immense cherrywood table, which was draped with a lacy cloth. Irish treated each person with a touch, a smile and a personal comment. Without the bonds of blood, she had formed a family.

Feeling chilled despite the comfortable temperature, Max finished his pie. Throughout dinner, Max had followed the relationships and had cut the paying guests aside, leaving what Irish referred to as her "people." He had them pegged now—persons without financial means. He doubted that the elderly couple, Granny and Link, who helped several of the guests serve food, really justified the good wages, bed and board that Irish paid them.

Beside him, Nadia's bangle bracelets jingled. Nadia was fiftyish, plump, wearing a loose Gypsy blouse and skirt, a shawl and a head scarf, and she didn't like him. She fingered her ornate rings and the tarot cards evident in her pocket and stared ominously at him. Nadia had been laying out her cards constantly since he'd arrived. She had invited him to a tarot session, and Max mentally tucked the offer away. Max guessed that her purpose at the inn—if she had one—was to provide background for the madam's ghost.

Recently Nadia had undergone an operation, and Irish had paid the bill. She'd also paid for Link's hearing aid.

Max sipped the excellent freshly ground house coffee slowly, replacing his cup on the rose china saucer carefully. He glanced at Jeff, who, besides being the ranch manager, was the general repairman. Jeff's signature had been on the repair bills and questionable machinery purchases. Max had jotted down figures for payment of such things as workmen's wages, garage bills and a variety of contract work.

Irish wrote checks for the bills, which she indicated by drawing a smiling face on the receipts. Remembering the checkbook, from a joint account with J.D., Max shivered mentally. He preferred dates, check numbers, payee and amount, to *Flowers. John. School drawing. Tube of cerulean blue for Jonathan.*

Jonathan, the inn's artist, shook aside a wedge of long spiky hair to stare at Max. Jonathan's canvasses, stacked in a side parlor were good, capturing the Rockies with the softness of a Renoir. By wedging himself beneath Irish's protection, Jonathan didn't have to keep himself groomed, pleasant, nor did he have to worry about sales. In Max's opinion, Irish's cushiony nest did nothing but hinder what could be a soaring career.

As Irish poured more coffee into Max's cup, Boonie Riggs shot him a dark look. Apparently this cowboy type frequently placed his dusty boots beneath Irish's well-laden dinner table. Max returned the stare coolly as Irish moved around the table to refill Boonie's cup. Around the toothpick lodged at the side of his mouth, Boonie leered up at Irish. "You're looking pert tonight, honey. Just right for a ride in old Boonie's pickup. Want to go over to my place and watch some television? We'd be alone," he added in a lower suggestive tone that raised the hair on the back of Max's neck.

When Boonie's hand slid around Irish's waist possessively, Max thought fleetingly about placing a painful karate chop on Boonie's wrist. Instead he ran his thumb along the tablecloth, steadily mashing a whole-wheat bread crumb into the lace.

The other guests missed Boonie's low insinuation, but Max did not. Irish smiled softly and bent to whisper, "Don't come here after you've been drinking, Boonie. I know you've had a bad time lately, but you'll just have to manage better—"

"Hell, I could if you'd just spend some time making up with me. Is that dude over there—" he nodded at Max "—the reason you're avoiding me?"

Max glanced at Boonie's jaw and decided the cowboy would understand a fist better than karate. The thought of Irish's soft body nestled against the rancher's made his body tense. Trying to distance himself from such unsettling and unfamiliar emotions, Max stared out the window to the Hereford cattle grazing peacefully in the fields. He rummaged mentally for the soothing strains of Bach—

"Would you like to walk after dinner, Max? You've already walked over the grounds, but I'd love to show you our TLC center. It's so much fun sharing the farm with a first-time guest,'' Irish invited softly beside him, startling him with those wide vulnerable blue eyes.

For an instant, Max had an image of a clear snow lake in the high mountain country, then he caught a hot menacing look from Boonie. He returned the stare evenly for a moment, allowed a corner of his mouth to rise mockingly. Boonie's scowl darkened, and Max accepted the blatant male challenge with a nod. It pleased him to give the cowboy the wrong impression.

Irish's blue eyes lit up, and she patted his shoulder. Beneath the light touch, Max tensed. *No adult had ever touched him lightly or affectionately.*

''You've been a good boy, Max,'' she whispered into his ear. ''I'm so glad you recognized Jonathan's sensitivity. Not a soul here knows your real mission. Except maybe Nadia, who is a supreme fortune-teller,'' she added, kissing his taut cheek. ''Thank you. Just for that, you can churn our next ice cream.''

Placing his silverware exactly one centimeter apart, Max fought the urge to place his hand over his cheek to trap the kiss.

Dusk settled over Abagail's with the nuance of a delicate lace doily. The mountain chill slid down into the valley, bringing with it night sounds and the heavy scents of freshly tilled earth and pine trees. In the distance dogs barked, and cows called to their calves.

As Max walked beside Irish, his dark brown eyes slashed the grounds and swept up the erosion on the ski slope. As he took in the broken white board fence surrounding the cows, Max's expression was unreadable. Irish decided he was calculating losses in big dollar signs.

Then he reached out to pat Morticia the mule. The momentary gesture was more of a brisk tap than a stroke, as if Max wasn't used to giving any part of himself away. When

Morticia lifted her head, Max reached out to scratch her ears. Morticia blinked her long lashes at him flirtatiously, lifting her nose for a brief pat. Of course Max was forced to oblige; Irish had noted that Max was very well mannered, if distant. She wondered briefly what Max's grim face would look like sheathed in a genuine smile. She toyed with the idea of his tickle spots and remembered her fleeting but sharp response to his hard body earlier.

She forced herself to stop thinking of Max's hairy chest, his lean stomach and the taut curve of his buns beneath the dress slacks. She preferred to skip through certain sensitive areas in her life, and sensuality was smack in the middle of the briars. His tickle spots were not her concern.

But it wouldn't hurt him to smile, she thought rebelliously as Max glanced around the barn and said, "Needs a new roof and the clutter picked up." He nodded at a dust-covered saddle riding an unpainted fence. "Don't you have a tack room?"

"Why Max, I didn't know you were an authority on barns." Irish teased, wanting to dislodge his grim expression. Max didn't the smile. Irish really didn't like the little quiver of anger that went scratching through her when she smiled again, an expression he met with a cool look down his nose.

Morticia nudged him, begging for another pat, which lingered into an ear-scratching session. Max obviously was an obliging gentleman when it came to mules.

Max had a nice face, Irish decided when they walked through the peony gardens to the herbal ones. His jaw was tense and darkening, promising an evening beard. Irish looked away. Her fingers had just flexed with the need to stroke the taut cord running downward from his jaw to his throat.

She glanced uneasily at the wedge of hair at the base of his throat. It reminded her of Mark's chest.

She felt herself tighten, forcing away the memories of her one affair. In their modern glass-and-chrome apartment, Mark had scheduled lovemaking in the systematic manner he prepared his reports. She plucked a stalk of fescue grass and ripped the head away, tossing the seeds into the evening breeze.

No one could accuse her of not trying to fall in love. She'd dated and tried a variety of kisses. She enjoyed dancing close and feeling feminine; it was just that the special click she wanted hadn't clicked yet.

"The outbuildings are in need of repair, Irish," Max stated in an adult-to-child tone. "J.D. was right to be concerned about his investment here. By the way, I can't find receipts for additional billing charges—room service or the items a guest might require. Where are they?"

"There aren't any. People come here to rest, not deal with business. I try to provide everything they might want, and they have only to ask."

Irish's steamy temper returned when she remembered his reason for visiting Abagail's. "I'm sure you'll rake and gnaw until you get to the bones, won't you, Max? I suppose your real name is the Cruncher?" she asked sharply, surprised at her unusual flare of temper with a man she had just met. "You'll take all the beauty out of TLC and push everything into computers or whatevers. You think in numbers, not in care and love."

A dark brow lifted arrogantly as Max quietly looked down at her. "Do I? How interesting. In what terms does Mr. Riggs think? Or does Mr. Riggs indulge in the process of thinking at all?" he amended coolly, widening his stance as if he'd wait forever to hear an explanation he didn't deserve.

Irish held his stare for a moment and decided that humor couldn't possibly be glinting in the dark depths of his eyes. She bent, plucking a stalk of purple wildflowers and bringing them to her nose. "Be careful, Max," she warned quietly, watching the Romaines stroll off into a stand of isolated pine trees. Nigel Romaine had tucked a blanket beneath his arm. "I could fire you. I'm an equal partner."

Irish rarely argued, and she didn't like the feeling that she was about to jump into one. She could see that her threat hadn't frightened him; his long legs weren't exactly shivering in their locked stance.

His hard mouth moved into a mocking half smile, as if he wanted an out-and-out argument. "Your ranch manager should be fired," Max continued evenly, the gleam in his eyes deepening. He reached down and scratched Mimi's ears. "I'll start computing his figures tonight and will have a report ready for you in the morning. Tomorrow I'll order a computer unit that even a child could understand. *You* might even be able to manage it."

While Irish dealt with her rising anger, Max nodded toward the Romaines. "I doubt they can afford the fee here. There was another couple and the older woman with arthritis—"

"The Smythes and Edith Milway," Irish said between her teeth, glaring up at him. "They received giveaway vacations—you know, for advertising purposes. I've done well here, Max. The inn is always full, except in the worst weather when people don't feel safe making the trip—"

"Charity doesn't equal profits," Max stated in his cool clipped tones. Irish ignored the flickering lights in his eyes. "By the way, do you have qualifications for running this bed-and-breakfast?"

Curling her fingers into her palms, Irish narrowed her eyes at him. "It's a health-care farm, Max—carrot juice, sprouts and lots of smiles, hugs and kisses. We offer humanity, not charity. And I have a degree in home economics," she managed to answer, considering walking back through the cow pasture. Watching Max squish his Italian oafers through fresh cow patties might ease her need for evenge.

Irish didn't like the angry emotions Max could ignite within her. "Do you have a problem with that?"

Max shifted on his legs, crossed his arms and stood regarding her with unnerving patience. "Evidently you opted o skip the accounting classes. Can you use a basic adding nachine?"

Irish had the impression that Max was baiting her as punishment for a crime.

"By the way, a vet should be called for your stock," Max added in the same cool tone. "Morticia has dental problems, and several horses could use reshoeing. Their grain isn't quality, and the water trough needs a thorough cleaning."

"Jeff's men take care of those things..." Irish began hotly, then watched Max's arrogant eyebrow lift slowly. "They don't?"

When his other eyebrow lifted, she took a deep breath and said, "I'll look into the matter."

"See that you do. Neglect is animal cruelty, too. I can't abide poor upkeep," Max stated as he neatly sidestepped a cow patty on his way to the tractor parked near the barn lot.

Irish followed, casting a sympathetic look back at Morticia. In two minutes Max had insinuated she wasn't fit to run her business and had thrown in an animal-cruelty charge. Now he was meticulously picking through the entrails of the inn's tractor like a surgeon on his way to a ruptured gall bladder.

He thrust a black oil dipstick beneath her nose as though it were a murderer's bloody blade. "This oil is old. It's starting to turn solid. Upkeep makes equipment last longer, Irish," he added, replacing the dipstick. "I'll want the maintenance schedule for every piece of machinery."

Irish blinked, ignoring his tiny but pleased smirk "Schedules?"

"For your new computer system," he said slowly, carefully, with a movement around his lips that served as a smug smile. "I'll have you up and running in an efficient system in no time."

Perched on her high four-poster bed, Irish flipped through a magazine and muttered, "Data banks... systems... computers...."

Normally at eleven o'clock she'd be asleep, but Van Damme had intruded into her happy TLC kingdom, slashing his calculator sword through the magic. She took a deep breath, adjusted the twisted T-shirt covering her body and turned off the lamp beside her bed. She tried to push Van Damme into a night closet for Abagail to torture until dawn. Since Mimi's purring and rubbing caused him discomfort, she'd throw in the cat for free. She'd release him in the morning, check his fingers for calculator burn and send him on his way.

Irish punched her violet-patterned pillowcase, then rolled over and jerked her sheets up to her chin. She scowled at the pine-bough shadows sweeping across the tiny rosebud design of her wallpaper.

Max had prowled through the house after their walk, then returned from the basement holding a dusty bottle like a prize. His strong hand had grasped the neck of the bottle as though once he had something or someone in his grasp, he'd never let go. Strolling up to her, he'd lifted the amber bottle and a singular mocking eyebrow. "My favorite. If you're not saving it, I'll add it to my bill at a good price."

She hadn't resisted throwing darts at him. "You see things you actually like?"

His smile hadn't been nice. More like showing teeth before he used them. "I enjoy the finer things of life, and this wine is one of them. I've promised myself a treat after examining your cookie jar and shoe box. By the way, some customer credit-card numbers were expired."

He'd settled into his room with the bottle of wine and her receipts to systemize Abagail's.

Irish kicked the bed in a series of fast one-two's. "Ohhh!" She twisted again, turning onto her stomach, and felt the elastic on her worn briefs tear. Squirming out of them, Irish looked at the Colorado moonlit night beyond the inn. She found herself thinking of the dark lights in Max's eyes as he'd sliced away at her ability to own and manage Abagail's.

When Max baited her, those dark eyes almost had a glint of humor.

"He's out to get me, "she whispered to the great horned owl soaring across the silvery moon. Inhaling the fresh air touched with scents of lavender, peonies and pine, Irish tried to pry Van Damme from her thoughts.

The roof outside her open window creaked. Then a man's shadowy body slid into her room. "Hello, little lady," Boonie rasped, the scent of whiskey clinging to him. "You waiting for me?"

"Boonie, you get out of here!" Irish tried to keep her voice low as Boonie sauntered to her bed. Though Irish knew she could manage him, she didn't want her guests disturbed.

"No city dude takes Boonie Riggs's woman away," he whispered drunkenly as he leaned over her head. "I saw the way he looked at you. I suppose that little walk to the barn had a real hot reason."

Irish took a deep steadying breath. Van Damme had looked at her as though she were unable to tie a bow, let alone run a health spa and inn. He'd drained a large amount of her patience. But her guests needed quiet, and Irish snagged the strength to deal with Boonie. She tried to remember that this neighboring rancher was a nice man, battling a series of bad financial and personal times.

She slid across the bed from him and stood. "Boonie, I've enjoyed our talks, and you've been welcome to come to the inn. But I'm not your woman."

Boonie lunged and sprawled across the bed. When he moved to come toward her, Irish backed toward the door. "Boonie Riggs, you get yourself under control," she managed shakily, spotting his drunken leer. "I'm just going to open this door, and you're going to walk out of the inn. You come back when you feel better. I'll bake your favorite gooey hot fudge cake—"

Boonie stepped toward her, leering full force. "I got better ideas for dessert, honey."

When he reached for her, Irish opened the door and stepped through it. Closing it, she gripped the crystal knob with both hands just as Boonie tried to pry it open. "Hush, Boonie. You'll wake up the guests."

Max frowned at his closed door; he wouldn't allow the hushed demanding noises beyond it to wrench him from Rachmaninoff. He turned up the volume on his cassette player slightly. "Big mice," he stated tersely, wanting to ignore everything but the excellent bouquet of the fine wine and the wholesome scents of the Colorado night air. Rachmaninoff's movements wrapped around him soothingly, a Band-Aid on Irish's financial nightmares.

Not that Irish cared about profit statements.

Max scowled at the dark red wine, thinking about Irish. A rhapsody in smiles and sunlight, an upbeat personality who drew people to her without trying. J.D. had said that if Irish's TLC could be bottled, it would solve the world's problems.

Irish Dalton was an element Max did not want in his life. Maybe that was why he'd baited her earlier.

Lounging in his untied short satin robe, Max allowed the cool air to drift over his body. He swirled the wine thoughtfully, then rested the glass on his bare chest. He didn't like the sexual tension in his body, and he didn't like knowing that Irish had been the woman to fire it. He didn't like remembering how he had slashed at her about the conditions of the inn. And he didn't like remembering the vulnerable expression on her soft face when he'd mentioned animal cruelty. He'd felt as if he'd deliberately squashed a fluffy soufflé. Or a woman with a very tender heart.

Irish probably didn't have any idea about the animals' condition, though she obviously loved them.

Sipping the tart wine, Max rolled the taste on his tongue, savoring it. Glancing at his microcomputer on the antique cherrywood table serving as his desk, Max inhaled deeply. He'd filed Irish's bills and receipts away in a box beneath his large brass bed. With any luck, he wouldn't have to open that blitz of horrors again.

Another crash sounded in the hall, and Irish's muffled voice hissed, "Boonie, now I mean it! Be quiet! You'll wake up the guests. What about poor Mr. Essery who's recovering from a heart attack?"

Boonie returned something in outraged tones. Apparently his current problems overrode Mr. Essery's.

Max sighed and tried to place the feuding lovers at a distance while he enjoyed the sensuality of the cool air drifting over him.

Lovers? Max repeated mentally as the scuffle in the hall continued to grow louder. Max frowned, gulped down the wine he had been savoring and quickly tied his robe.

Startled to find himself jerking open his door, Max stepped into the hall to find the back of Irish's soft warm body thrust against his cool one.

With both hands grasping the knob to her bedroom door, Irish looked over her shoulder at him. Her eyes were wide and vulnerable, and Max reacted instantly. He took hold of the doorknob with one hand. To hold the knob and keep danger from Irish was instinctive. In that instant, she was his to protect. He circled Irish possessively with his free arm, drawing her into the protection of his body.

In the firm grasp of his hand, the doorknob rattled and shook while Boonie's muffled curses sounded on the opposite side. From Max's room, Rachmaninoff's romantic movements poured into the hallway. The ebb and tide of the emotional music wove around them, creating an intimacy Max hadn't experienced for years.

But Max couldn't move.

Max couldn't breathe.

Max couldn't think about anything but Irish looking up at him. A purple pansy nuance shaded her dark blue eyes, and a thick fringe of golden lashes framed the rounded shape. *An innocent,* Max thought absently, free-falling into a field of soft purple pansy petals. At odds with Irish's virginal expression, the sweet flow of her round body down the hardening warming length of his triggered an anticipation of melodious slow passion with incredible heights.

Her hands gently parted the gape of his robe and fluttered on his bare chest.

Violins quivered delicately in the Rachmaninoff strains, wrapping Max in Irish's magical soothing warmth.

Irish needed protection and care, gentleness and understanding. Yet at the same time, he could feel a passion within her that could melt away his emptiness.

Max instinctively drew her tighter against him. Opening his free hand to fit into the neat curve of her waist and hip, Max savored the rounded feminine line with a slow caress. His fingers smoothed a bare soft hip, splaying gently across the satiny skin.

"Oh," she whispered, her fingers widening on his chest.

Locked together, Max felt her every breath. Felt the rise and fall of her breasts against his stomach, felt himself being absorbed by her scents of lavender and mountain meadow flowers. Of sunshine and warmth.

Pressed intimately against her thighs, Max forgot about the rattling noise. He lowered his lips to fit slowly, carefully over her parted soft ones and felt himself slide into a lush field of clover and daisies and Irish.

As if testing his favorite wine, Max nibbled slowly at the delicate curve of her mouth, savoring the fresh sweet taste. Like buttery croissants with strawberry preserves. . . .

She moved against him slightly, lifting and parting her lips, and Max widened his stance to support her weight, drowning in the sensations her response aroused. Gathering her closer, Max slid his hand higher under her T-shirt until he found her breast.

The delightful nub responded to his circling fingertip. So soft, he decided distantly, smoothing the satiny skin. Soft and warm. She'd give him everything. He'd give her more.

Aligned with her body, Max deepened the kiss, lowering his hand to press her hips nearer. He absently let go of the doorknob and wrapped his free hand around the back of her neck.

Then Boonie jerked open the door.

"Now ain't this nice?" Boonie asked, leering at Irish's flushed and confused face. "Hey! What's that funny music?"

Gripping her possessively closer, Max was stunned by the hunger and anger washing over him. Boonie's leer needed to be shoved . . .

Max hesitated for a fraction of a second, torn between cramming the leer down Boonie's throat and lingering in Irish's warmth and softness.

Then he moved quickly, thrusting Irish behind him as he grasped Boonie's wrist, levering it behind him. "Come along," he gritted between his teeth. "Anyone who doesn' recognize Rachmaninoff needs to say good-night."

Boonie managed a "Hey!" before Max clamped his han over the cowboy's mouth. He moved Boonie through th hallway, down the stairs and out the front door without a sound.

"Oh, my," Irish said softly, placing her fingers over he well-kissed lips as she watched Max move Boonie quietl down the hall. Max's mouth had tasted of pungent swee wine. He'd kissed her with tender hunger, exploring an examining every texture and flavor as though her mouth wa a delicate aperitif.

Irish swallowed, remembering how his body had fitte intimately to hers. Wrapped in his arms and the beautifu music, Irish had felt as though she were in the arms of he beloved....

"Oh, my," she repeated as her other hand flattened lov on her stomach to control the warmth surging there. Sh closed her eyes, trying to dislodge the memory.

Boonie's truck sputtered and lunged out into the quie night as Irish moved into her room and closed the door. Sh crawled into her bed, arranged the sun-scented sheet safel over her and crossed her folded hands upon her chest. He heartbeat would eventually return to normal. Maybe.

She turned to stare at the moonbeams slipping throug the pine boughs outside her window.

Max had wanted her desperately. With tenderness. Wit consuming passion. As if she had been made for him alone. As if she was uniquely his to care for.

Breathing quietly, she relived Max's every touch. The slow warmth of his safe hands exploring her curves as if he found her exciting. She touched her breasts with her fingertips, remembering how he had gently caressed and supported their weight. She found tears creeping down her cheeks and she sniffed, wiping her eyes with a corner of the sheet.

A hallway board creaked, and her door swung open. From the hall, Max asked huskily, "Are you all right, Irish?"

"Fine," she managed, wishing her voice was more steady.

"Fine," he repeated grimly, closing the door and walking toward the bed. "Boonie is gone. Did he hurt you?"

The edge to his low voice reminded Irish of Max's savage expression as he'd leveled his attention on Boonie. "Did you hurt him?" she asked, drying her cheek on the pillowcase.

"Let's say I gave him something to think about." Behind her the mattress gave way to Max's weight. His hand found her shoulder in the darkness. "He won't be back. Did he hurt you?" he asked again, more urgently this time, his voice slightly rough.

"No." She was suddenly cold, and startled to find herself longing for the warmth of Max's arms.

Max rubbed her shoulder awkwardly as though he wasn't used to giving comfort. When she turned to him, the moonlight slipping through the window outlined his harsh expression.

He looked so worried, so alone in the silvery light. So angry and primitive. "I'm fine," she murmured again, after a tense moment when Max's fingers strayed to her collarbone, tracing the smooth skin.

He inhaled, his fingertips trembling as they passed over her arm. "Should I call Granny or Nadia for you?"

"I'm really okay, Max. You can go now." She didn't want him to see her cry, and his uncertainty had brought her to the brink.

"I suppose we'll have to deal with what happened earlier," he began roughly, searching her face in the square of moonlight lying across her pillow. "Look, Irish, I don't grab women in the middle of the night...."

Irish found herself placing her hand behind his neck. For a moment he resisted the gentle tug, then allowed himself to be brought gently down to her. Irish smiled softly. Against his cheek, rough with evening stubble, she whispered, "Don't worry so, Max. I wasn't hurt. Thank you...."

Max's head turned slightly until their lips barely touched and neither could move. "Look, Irish...I was out of bounds," he said huskily after a long moment.

"Stop apologizing, Max," she returned softly, stroking the taut back of his neck. He wasn't as cool as he appeared. A thrill soared through Irish. Max, it seemed, was not exactly in control of himself.

Rattling Max's perfect image and discovering his wonderful kisses had inflated her ego. Irish hadn't seen herself as a desirable woman. She smiled against his mouth, kissing him delicately. "Are you going to kiss me back?" she teased after a moment.

Max shivered. His breath was ragged, his skin heating to her touch. "Poor Max," she soothed, meaning it as she rubbed her cheek against his. "You've had a bad day, haven't you?"

He swallowed at that, muttering darkly, "I should be getting the hell out of here before it's too late...."

Because he needed her touch, Irish locked both her arms around him and drew him down against her. She loved the hard steely feel of his bare chest. She loved the rapid thumping of his heart and the way his mouth moved cautiously against her temple.

She rubbed the ridges of his back muscles, kneading the tense line of his shoulders.

Then Max kissed her fully. When the steamy sensuous kiss ended, he braced his hands on either side of her pillow and whispered roughly, "We should..."

In the shadows above her, Max looked distracted, hot and rumpled. And very much in need of her. Irish felt the answering heat race through her and she reached for him.

For an instant he rested against her, tense and trembling. "You're so soft, Irish," he said unevenly, levering himself onto the bed slowly. He lay full length against her, his hand running lightly over her body covered by the sheet. His touch trembled and sought, leaving her wondering....

"Come here," she whispered back, knowing he would.

"Irish," he protested in a low rough tone, just before settling his mouth over hers.

When Max lifted the sheet aside, and his trembling hands drew her against him, she could stop him with a touch, with a murmur.

When his robe followed Irish's shirt to the floor, Max knew he should stop. There was danger in relationships, pain in wanting to be needed and healed and caressed. But her warmth tangled like sunlight in the shadowy ache he'd carried for years, and he found himself seeking more.

Sliding into her heat, Max found what he had wanted, what he'd needed for a lifetime. She took him deeper, settling him into a soft tangle of arms and legs.

Max gave himself to her keeping, swept by the need to cherish and bind her to him, to care.

When their passion deepened, Max found her soft cries snaring him deeper, melting something long ago buried. Trapped on a heated pinnacle, Max gave himself to her.

An instant later, with Irish's body trembling beneath his, he realized she'd found that same desperate pleasure.

The second wave of passion caught him unprepared, washing over him before the first had allowed him to settle. He caught Irish to him, knowing that nothing else mattered but this moment of heat and softness.

Max's last thought before he drifted off to sleep, tangled in the warmth of Irish's scent and softness, was that he'd entered a magical kingdom of whimsy, tenderness and fire.

In her arms, he'd experienced a moment in time so fragile and wonderful that he didn't want to dissect it.

Three

Just before dawn, the soft coo of a dove drifted through the open window of Irish's bedroom.

Morning floated around Max like a silken feather, dusting, brushing, tantalizing. The cool air toyed in the folds of the lacy sheer curtain and slid through the hair covering his chest like a lover's seeking fingers. Keeping his eyes closed, Max allowed himself to drift in the moment and in the scents of mountain pine and lavender. Upon waking, his body was usually tense, ready to spring into the day; but this special morning, a lazy contentment spread throughout his muscles like a warmed berry syrup over fresh crepes.

Max slid his hand to caress the long smooth warmth curled next to him beneath the sheet. The night and the woman had become one—soft and powerful, magical and passionate—wrapping him in an ecstasy he'd never experienced before. He'd found the softness as powerfully exciting as the driving hot need she'd answered. The night had been a Tchaikovsky overture, pacing slow sweet desire into a rising demanding passion filled with husky whispers and sighs.

Max stretched, smiling as his palm found the smoothly rounded feminine thigh and slowly, luxuriously, traced the contours.

He wanted to loll on the sheets, to wallow in the lingering sweet taste of the night—now that he had found what he wanted.

Feeling pleased with himself, Max turned his head on the pillow. He nuzzled the silky strands clinging to his morning beard, inhaling the tantalizing scents as his hand leisurely explored the smooth curves shifting comfortably against his side.

Max turned slightly, adjusting more fully to the breasts settling softly against his chest. Their bodies folded together naturally, fitting perfectly.

He drifted along drowsily, clinging to the enchantment and knowing that he had never been more satisfied than at this moment. Smiling lazily, Max caressed the gentle indentation of a woman's waist. The soft thigh draped across his moved, sliding experimentally as her insole caressed his calf.

Max sighed, grinning slightly while he lingered in the elusive fragrance of the night's lovemaking. As he lingered in his pleasure, his grin widened. It would happen again. He knew in another moment they would be exploring each other tenderly; her sweet kisses would cause the fiery hunger, and the muffled startled sounds she'd make would storm his senses.

Exploring fingers toyed with the hair on his chest, smoothed it as though she were stroking a kitten. And Max thought of his youthful dream to spend a week in bed with a woman. Somehow he never had. Now the possibility seemed likely—

Max inhaled sharply, his heart beating more quickly. Her fingers skimmed his shoulders, and her breath swept across his nipple, sensitizing it and stirring other sensuous realms as she sighed in her sleep.

He shivered slightly, wrapped in the knowledge that Irish was the most responsive passionate woman he'd ever known. She'd given him honesty, a seductress who snared him with her magic and held him in her power.

Irish?

Max's lids opened, the sunlight blinding him just as a rooster crowed in all his male glory.

Who the hell was Irish? He'd only met her yesterday.

Fully awake now, Max forced his fingers to still just before closing possessively over her breast. He frowned and lifted his hand away as an enticing hardening nub brushed his palm. Trying to calm himself while her fingers were skimming the hair on his chest, Max replaced his hand carefully on the sheets and gripped them for an anchor. He tried to place himself into the *now* time zone.

He forced a hard swallow as the rooster crowed again, boasting his male powers. Max inhaled sharply, catching Irish's scents. They'd made love three times, *and he hadn't used protection.* He'd acted like a hot-blooded boy, hungry and careless of the results.

Max shut his eyes against the sight of the morning sun tripping across the tiny roses on the wallpaper. Last night, Irish had taken him into a tenderness he'd never experienced and into equatorial passions he'd never had stirred.

Max scowled at the gay rosebuds. He didn't want his passions stirred. A woman like Irish was trouble.

Chancing a glance at her, Max winced slightly at the sight of her well-kissed mouth. On her throat were tiny marks caused by his beard. She looked soft and loved—and inviting. The need to wake her with a kiss rose wildly in him, almost frightening in its power.

The morning breeze swept across his sweaty forehead, cooling it. He closed his eyes, fighting off a whimsical plan for the next time they made love; it had everything to do with changing positions on the sheets scented of the Colorado sun. Of fitting silky skin and freckles over his body in lieu of a sheet.

Of finding that sensitive spot just behind her ear and waiting for the delightful silken quivers....

A dull headache began to throb at the back of his head when he remembered Irish's breathless startled cries blending with the soft sound of his laughter.

The vein along Max's right temple pounded. *He'd never chuckled in his life.*

Max's fingers curled into fists. Irish wasn't a well-integrated business system; she was magic and softness, like an iridescent soap bubble flying high on the mountain winds and catching the sun.

A relationship would be disaster for them.

Slowly, carefully, Max eased his body away from her care. Then he stood alone in the cold morning air and shivered.

Placing the unbaked cinnamon rolls on the cookie sheet, Irish avoided Nadia's curious glances. Irish flushed each time the fortune-teller looked her way.

This morning wasn't filled with loving promises and sweet nibbling kisses. Things just weren't perking along like they should be after a wonderful night, and Irish resented the emptiness she'd carried since Max had uncoiled himself from her side. She ached in unfamiliar muscles, and her heart felt as though it had been sliced.

Boonie had called earlier, apologizing in muffled tones. With one blow, Max had given the rancher black eyes, a swollen nose and a split lip. According to Boonie, Max lacked "good-old-boy class" and was a "city animal from hell." In lieu of a legal suit, Boonie had settled for his favorite hot fudge cake, delivered to his doorstep safely away from Max.

Max.

She nibbled at her lip, wincing at the tenderness. Max had stood over her in the dawn, watching her for an eternity as she'd feigned sleep. His hand had trembled when he'd stroked a tendril away from her cheek, and she'd wanted to open her arms to him again.

She'd wanted to feel the safety of his strong arms wrapped around her, the husky low intimate sound of his voice soothing her again. Shy of him in the cool morning, Irish had waited for the moment when he'd kiss her. Max's kisses were startling—reverent, magical, lazy, hot and hungry.

Instead he had covered her bare shoulder with the sheet, smoothed back a curl from her cheek and had slipped from her room. Like a night shadow sliding from the reality of dawn.

Clinging to his scent, she had moved into the warm space he had vacated. *Max.*

In the kitchen, Irish opened the oven door to check the temperature. Satisfied by the heat swirling around her, she closed the door and thought of Max's cold scowl.

How could Max love her so tenderly in the magical night, then scowl at her over the rim of his morning coffee cup? His dark glance had not missed her flushed face as she'd passed him with a tray of blueberry muffins. He'd been lounging against the kitchen door, dressed in Armani slacks and a matching shirt. He'd slipped back into his calculator-for-a-heart image, and his hard expression had made her ache. "I'll need to wash my car. But then you probably know that," he had said ominously.

Remembering the tender night heat, she'd wanted to fold herself to him, kiss the tiny razor cut and offer to help wash the bird droppings from his car. But Max had looked as thunderous as a high mountain storm, his mouth grim. "Can you fit me into your schedule? We need to talk."

His impersonal tone had scraped on her uncertain nerves like a nail drawn down a blackboard, and she'd found an excuse to move away from him.

In her usual morning scramble to prepare breakfast, Irish resented the happy chatter around her. Granny and the guests moved comfortably between the kitchen and the dining room, serving themselves blueberry pancakes, fruit and bran.

Irish experimentally probed her sensitive lips with the tip of her tongue. She felt coiled like the cinnamon rolls she'd just thrust into the oven. She wanted to pommel Max with blueberry muffins at five paces.

A musical jingle of bangle bracelets signaled Nadia's arrival at her side. The fortune-teller nudged Irish. "Ah, the black knight who protected your honor arrives with his notebook. His face looks like cold steel."

"I didn't need protection from Boonie," Irish muttered, ignoring the amused slide of Nadia's eyes down to the whisker burns on her neck.

Max walked into the kitchen as Irish was scooping brown sugar into a bowl, and she steeled herself to look up at him. She shivered, reminded of the way the hair on his chest had tickled her bare back as he'd drawn her tightly against him.

She shivered again as she remembered Max's tongue tracking a spot he'd discovered just behind her ear.

"Interesting," Nadia murmured lightly before drifting away in a tinkle of bracelets and charms. "I shall ask Madame Abagail's opinion of the event...."

Nadia's voice was overlaid by Max's impatient growl. "Well?" Max demanded coolly. "When can we schedule a conference? Nine o'clock?"

Irish plopped the lid on the sugar bowl. Max's businesslike tone had ignited shimmering little sparks of anger.

Maybe he could stuff the magical night into a briefcase, but she couldn't.

Irish didn't like feeling angry. And she didn't like the quick efficient way Max checked her name on his notebook's list. *Why wasn't he holding her and kissing her with those tender rough hungry kisses and touching her with trembling hands and growling contentedly in her ear, and—*

A new wave of anger crashed over her. The night-after equation called for Max's tongue seeking that excitable spot behind her ear.

Her ex-fiancé hadn't discovered that spot. She hadn't known it existed. If Max was going to discover her sensitive responsive areas, the least he could do was to use them....

"I have enough notes to lay out a sensible system," Max stated. "If you can schedule—" he glanced at his wristwatch "—twenty-five minutes, we can discuss an efficiency system. You need an alarm unit. I'll contract people to instruct you on the fine points. I can point out a few discrepancies in Jeff's receipts, then you can find the rest of the errors yourself." Max's firm lips pressed together for an instant before he continued grimly, "And the other *matter* needs to be clarified, too."

His eyes drifted over her flour-dusted T-shirt, and Irish returned the cool look, crossing her arms protectively over her chest. Tuned to Max's hard length, her body ached to throw itself into his arms. But Max's scowl wasn't welcoming; Max-in-the-morning—the morning *after*—wasn't exactly a sweetheart.

Something dark and nasty roamed in the depths of his eyes, accusing her of seduction. Irish wanted to sling the accusation back at him. How did he explain the husky encouragements he'd murmured against her skin? Feeling betrayed, Irish acknowledged the basis of her newly discovered temper. Max had no business ruining something so beautiful.

Looking at the open collar of his shirt and allowing her gaze to stroll down, then back up the neat crease in his slacks, she said, "You're referring to last night as the 'matter,' I suppose? Is last night on your checklist, too?"

Max seemed to grind his teeth momentarily before he said tightly, "You're going to be difficult, aren't you?"

Irish's eyebrows lifted, her cold smile concealing the emotions racing through her. Max might slip from night lover to morning beast easily, but not without a tap on his arrogant nose. "You want to tear my business apart and suck the juice out, Max. What do you expect?"

"Be reasonable, Irish," he snapped after inhaling sharply. He glanced at Nadia, who was nibbling on an orange slice. When the fortune-teller smiled benignly back at him, Max lowered his voice. "You're emotional, and that's not good business—"

"Outside," she ordered, wondering how Max would look floundering fully dressed in the cold green clay of the beauty bog. "You have until the cinnamon rolls are done."

Irish wiped her hands on a dish towel and tossed it onto the counter. Max glanced at his watch. "Twenty minutes?"

"Does your heart run on a clock, too, Max? When the rolls are done, I'll take them out," she snapped, startling herself.

Stepping into the morning sun, Irish realized she had never been so angry. For once she ignored the scented herbs along the bricked pathway. She shook off Max's hand as it cupped her elbow, only to find her wrist encircled by his unrelenting fingers. "Irish," Max said under his breath, "emotion does not help the situation."

At the beauty bog, Irish jerked her wrist free and glared up at him. "Emotion? Now why would I be emotional?

Because I find myself in bed with every man who stays here? Do you think I'm under Abagail's lovemaking-versus-stress influence?"

A tinge of red moved upward from Max's throat, staining his dark cheeks. "Don't. Just don't," he ordered tightly.

He shifted uncomfortably as Irish tried to continue glaring up at him. It was difficult to do with tears burning her eyes and a sob clogging her tight throat. Cupid's arrow did hurt, she thought wildly, bracing herself as the chubby little winged monster started a flurry of painful little pings into her heart.

Max glanced at her face just as a tear oozed from the corner of her eye. He swallowed, then looked away, scanning the grassy foothills of the mountains. He shifted restlessly, locking his legs in an uncompromising stance, then pinned her with his stare. "If it's any comfort, I didn't expect last night, either. Sex isn't something I jump into lightly. But it's been a long time—that and the wine—and because you'd just had a frightening experience . . . Maybe it was a reaction on both our parts."

"Sex?" Irish repeated blankly and wondered how something so beautiful could be jammed into three letters. She swallowed, mentally tossing the poetry she had expected into the trash basket.

So he wanted to rationalize and dissect every beautiful moment they'd spent in the night, did he? She'd known exactly what she was doing—caring for him. And he'd merely needed someone for a midnight aperitif? What was she, the maraschino cherry on top of a sundae? A shell plucked from a sandy beach? A . . . Irish blinked against the tears misting her eyes. "So I had a reaction from a frightening experience," she repeated carefully through her teeth. "Or overdosed on that classical stuff coming from your room. Whatever happened to old-fashioned rock and roll? And of course I jump into bed with every Tom, Dick—"

She wasn't prepared for the savagery in his expression nor the quick way he moved to draw her into the shadows of the weeping willow and away from curious eyes. "You're not making this easy for either one of us," Max said roughly, scanning her swollen lips. "It happened and that's it."

"You practically broke poor Boonie's nose," she accused, struggling against him.

"That idiot," Max snapped. "He's damned lucky I didn't break his legs."

"Boonie is a friend!" Irish began hotly, ignoring the way Max tenderly brushed her hair away from her cheek. His eyes narrowed, tracking the whisker burns on her pale throat. She swatted at his hand as it lingered over her hot skin, testing the tiny evidence of the long sweet night. "You're not going to interfere by setting up computers beeping and blinking all over the place. And I won't have people run down for unpaid bills when they're dealing with enough stress. You're not dragging in gizmos and systems and trained staff to strip everything away... So you hadn't had sex for a time and you decided—"

"Irish, if you want to argue, do it logically. Stop skipping all over the main points and stay on track. You've got a houseful of people who don't pay their way. Jeff is playing you for a fool, and Jonathan needs to be thrown out on his ear. Nadia could use her spare time doing maid work. You need a computer system for record-keeping and credit references. You need an office with a resident bookkeeper to handle invoices, and a telephone linkup with credit-card companies to check your guests' credit."

"And you need a heart in there," Irish interrupted hotly, jabbing him in the chest.

"I have a heart," Max said carefully, looming over her. "You're too emotional."

"You don't scare me, Mr. Whizmo-Gizmo," Irish said just before she thrust her open hands into his flat midsection. Max's eyes widened in surprise; his Italian loafers struggled for a firm spot on the cusp of the bog just before he sprawled backward into the green clay.

Irish dusted her hands together and smiled down at him. "You're fired, Max. You can wash your car elsewhere," she said cheerfully and, in her opinion, quite elegantly. Then another tear slid down her cheek and she sniffed.

Walking back to the inn, Irish slashed the back of her hand across her damp cheeks and muttered darkly, "I don't know, Abagail. Men just aren't what they used to be. What happened to poetry and violet nosegays and compliments and morning-after hugs?"

She hadn't sensed him near her, but suddenly, Max's goo-covered hands were gripping her upper arms, holding her still.

His lips drew back from his teeth in a smile that did not suit the fiery anger in his eyes. A drop of goo clung to his cheek. "If landing me in that mess made you feel better, I'm glad. It was childish, but knowing your logic, it's understandable," he stated tightly. "I'll clean up and have a summary file prepared for you within one hour and fifteen minutes. Try to concentrate on the differences in the bills Jeff has signed—he's skimming a neat margin from you. I'll send a copy to J.D., and he can reach me in Tahoe if he has questions."

He paused, deepened his scowl and added quietly, "If you have any problems because of last night—"

Fighting for her pride, Irish lashed out shakily, "I won't have problems from last night—I'm an adult. I can deal with a one-night stand just the same as you."

"I said it was a moment in time, caused by special circumstances—not a one-night stand," he stated darkly, anger flaring in his dark eyes. "I didn't use protection, Irish,"

Max reminded her quietly, watching the red heat crawl up her face. A muscle worked in his jaw as he continued, "At forty-two, I've never experienced a ticking biological clock, Irish. I'm usually very careful, but the circumstances—"

"Usually?" she repeated blankly. "So you aren't in practice and you goofed?"

The harsh lines bordering Max's mouth deepened, and his lips pressed together. "Don't worry, Irish. Chances are you aren't pregnant. According to my parents who are genetic experts, the likelihood of pregnancy the first time are fifty to one."

Releasing her carefully, Max reached to remove a clinging leaf from her hair. He slipped off his muddy Italian loafers, and a moment later, the Armani slacks clung to his backside as he walked stiffly into the inn carrying his shoes.

When Irish finally recovered from Max's quiet implication that she could be carrying his baby, she shivered. "Not a chance," she whispered unevenly to the light breeze. "This isn't Las Vegas and I don't have to beat fifty-to-one odds."

Irish eased out of bed. She hadn't slept well since last week's enlightening experience with Max and his morning revelation that she could be pregnant. Her breasts were tender, and unable to sleep on her stomach, she'd tossed about restlessly during the night. Forcing herself to her feet, Irish heard the rooster crow. "Oh, shut up," she muttered, padding to the bathroom.

On her way back to bed, she glanced at Max's summary file lying unopened on the cherrywood dresser.

Max hadn't called, she realized wearily, as she put on her jeans. So much for the second romantic interlude in her life. Maxwell Van Damme was probably in Tahoe, puttering with gizmos.

She closed her eyes, shutting out the image in the bureau mirror. She looked just like she felt, aching and tired, her soul bruised. She'd reacted shrewishly to Max, and that knowledge hadn't helped her temperament.

After her affair with Mark, she'd managed to salvage her pride and dignity. Max had stirred her temper, and she didn't appreciate it.

Drawing on her bra, Irish loosened the clasp from its usual setting to ease the tightness. She frowned, studying her mirrored image. She'd lost weight in the past couple of months; the waistband of her jeans had been steadily loosening. Yet her bustline— "It's not possible," she said firmly, shaking her head and returning to the bathroom.

Later, Irish stood at the kitchen window and studied the dew clinging to a spider web. She held a bowl of pancake batter against her, whipping the mixture with a wooden spoon and staring intently at the tiny watery jewels.

She missed Max.

Irish absently traced the spider's path, bypassing the droplets on her way to the center of the web. Without a backward glance, Max had swooped out of Kodiac in his gleaming bird-spotted car. In his wake, clouds of dust had billowed, then settled slowly.

She gripped the big mixing bowl tighter, thinking of the possibility of a baby—a tiny reminder of Max, tucked safely away....

"Not a chance," she whispered uneasily as she set the bowl on the counter.

But then she remembered that night and the way Max had loved her—repeatedly. As though he needed her to live. Counting carefully until the next month, Irish marked a big red X on the kitchen calendar.

In the safety of her room three weeks later, Irish stared at the positive results of her home pregnancy test. She tilted the tube and blinked. "Well, maybe," she whispered. "Just maybe."

The next week, Irish marked a steady line through the second week on the June calendar. The inn was filled, and while she dealt with the needs of her customers, she thought about the reality of having a baby. She wanted one desperately, and now the idea had been presented to her à la Van Damme. All the forgotten dreams of children came dancing back on the wisp of a fifty-to-one chance. "Mommy? Mama?" she tested while grinning happily at the children racing through the meadow.

The baby was hers alone, she decided firmly. Max, who'd zoomed out of the Rockies in full regal male potency, had gifted her with the possibility of a child. In the privacy of the morning, she lingered in bed and dreamed about the tiny life within her. Max had a unique part in the conception, but he didn't need to know or feel obligated. Since she'd gotten him out of the dugouts and back into the game, he was probably practicing his batting average *with protection.*

She deeply wanted the baby. Wanted to love him and watch him grow. She grinned, running her hand over her abdomen for the hundredth time.

Then Irish's first wave of nausea swept over her.

Max parked his Porsche a safe distance away from the birds' roosting tree. At seven in the morning, the July air was cool and filled with enticing scents of freshly baked bread and coffee. He ran his hand through his hair and muttered, "What the hell am I doing back here?"

Irish had been dancing through his mind for two months; he didn't like the coldness shrouding him since meeting her. Pushed to the edge, Max had had enough. He'd driven all night to the passionate strains of Tchaikovsky's *Romeo and Juliet* overture.

Max ran his hand along his unshaven jaw. He wasn't used to sleepless nights and dreams of sweet loving impish blondes. During the days, Irish in the sun, Irish in the sensuous night skipped happily through his thoughts. She'd destroyed his concentration, entering his systems layouts for the Tahoe resort project. His assignment was a success, but Max wouldn't be able to work on another high-tech project until he put Irish in her proper place—well away from his emotions.

If only he could stop seeing her pansy-blue eyes filled with tears...

Mimi came running out, purring and nuzzling his legs until he stopped to rub the spot behind her ears.

When Max entered the foyer, Nadia smiled widely, as though she knew something he didn't, and pointed a ruby-encrusted finger toward the dining room. Max nodded grimly at Granny and Link, who looked at him as though he were a suspect returning to the scene of the crime. Then he spotted Boonie, seated at the breakfast table and buttering a fluffy biscuit just past a bouquet of daisies and delicate bleeding hearts.

Max stopped in midstride, fighting his rising anger as the rooster crowed outside in the July sun. The tiny red bleeding hearts shimmered quietly in a patch of sunlight as Max thought about the satisfaction he'd gotten from dealing with Boonie. "Hello," he said quietly, pleased that Boonie paled and touched his healed nose.

The new guests smiled, welcoming him as Irish entered carrying a platter of sourdough biscuits. "Max!"

Max glanced at Boonie who was excusing himself, then he smiled at Irish. Dressed in jeans and a tight Mickey Mouse T-shirt, she looked as inviting as the freshly baked biscuits. Max forced down the whimsical thought of how he'd like to honey and butter her. "Irish. I came back to check on your progress with my recommendations. How are you?"

She'd changed, he decided as she stared back at him. Those wide blue eyes had darkened, their depths mysterious. Her mouth, caught in a wide smile, needed to be kissed.

Max's gaze slid unerringly down her body, lingering on her breasts. Fuller now, they thrust against Mickey's ears.

"I thought I fired you," she began hotly, just before the biscuits slid to the floor and she fainted into Max's arms.

Granny plucked the platter from Irish's limp grasp, muttering, "Happens like that sometimes, I guess. First time for her... Don't just stand there—carry her on upstairs, Max. I reckon you two need to be alone."

"Get a doctor—" he ordered.

"Huh! *You* may need one. Irish will be fine."

Nadia winked as Max carried Irish's limp body past her. "Ah, love," she sighed in his wake.

Running up the stairs, Max took care not to jostle Irish. Lowering her to her bed, he placed a cold wet cloth on her forehead just as she began stirring. "Irish?" he heard himself say just as her eyes opened and she stared blankly up at him.

"Max, what are you doing here?" she asked huskily.

He brushed a curl away from her cheek, noting her pale color and the damp sheen of sweat on her forehead. "You're not well, Irish. Have you seen a doctor?"

She stared blankly at him for a moment, groaned, then turned on her side away from him. The cloth on her forehead slipped, and Max sat on the bed, holding it in place. "Irish?"

"Go away," she said unevenly. "Go back to your gizmo kingdom. Get lost... the birds are circling your car... Morticia's teeth have been cleaned... 'Bye."

"Try that rubbish on Boonie. He's dense enough to buy it," Max said just as unevenly and wondered when his heart had started beating again. He rubbed her back and found the muscles tense beneath his hand. "Irish, have you seen a doctor?" he repeated.

He couldn't remember terror and now it had found him, impaling him on the point of a giant cold knife.

"I'm not up to a Maxwell Van Damme moment just now," she whispered brokenly, and Max's stomach lurched. "Go bother a computer or something."

After a brief knock on the door, Granny entered the room carrying a glass of milk and a plate of crackers. She placed them on the bedside table, then scowled at Max as though he'd axed her favorite rooster. "Men. They get off easy. It's us womenfolk that bear the burdens. Have her eat the crackers and lie still for a minute. Morning sickness usually passes fast enough."

"Morning sickness?" Max rapped out sharply, his eyes slashing down at Irish. "Morning sickness as in *you're pregnant?*"

Irish groaned, pulled a pillow over her head and groaned again. "You should know, young man." Granny sniffed airily, then glared at Max and marched stiffly from the room.

Max stared at the crackers, then back at Irish. "Granny wants you to eat the crackers," he said, feeling a little woozy. Max chalked his unsettled nausea up to the long drive and the passionate strains of *Romeo and Juliet.*

He found Irish's limp hand. Fitted within his, her hand seemed small and fragile. "Morning sickness?" he repeated shakily as a cold damp sweat broke out on his forehead.

Max calculated quickly backward while his stomach threatened to lurch again. "Irish, you're pregnant...."

"Isn't anything private? Suppose I'm high on cinnamon fumes or catnip?" Irish returned shakily, turning her head toward him. Her eyes widened, searching his face. "Max? Are you sick?" she asked as he stretched out beside her, his free hand resting on his forehead.

"Just a little upset stomach...no, I'm hot...no, I'm cold," he said raggedly, turning his head to her.

Irish was beautiful, he thought hazily as she patted the cold damp cloth around his face. And worried about him. Her blue eyes were filled with concern, her fingers cool on his sweaty brow. If only the mushroom-and-bacon omelet he'd eaten earlier this morning wasn't rolling around in his stomach, he'd... Absently Max wondered what he would do. Somehow he seemed adrift in a soothing warm joyous pansy-petaled lake.

No one had ever really worried about him. "You're pregnant," he said quietly, letting the cool shadows of the room absorb the wonder he had begun to experience.

"Max, *I'm* going to have *my* baby," Irish said softly, reaching for a cracker.

He shivered, trying to dislodge the woozy clammy feeling. "Stop rocking the bed," he ordered, then attempted a smile as he explained, "I've been driving all night and I'm a little bit off balance.... You'll be a perfect mother, by the way."

Irish didn't return the grin. She glared at him warily while she nibbled her cracker. "Don't get any big ideas, Max."

He blinked, noting with satisfaction that his weak moment had passed. He wanted to nibble that tiny cracker crumb from her lips. "As the father, I have a certain interest in the matter. Have you seen a doctor? I'll have him checked out."

"Max," she warned, rubbing her hand across her flat stomach. "When I choose a doctor, you are not included in the decision. No one is asking anything of you. You have no obligations. I can manage."

Max replaced her hand with his, easing up under her T-shirt and beneath her jeans. Between them and the magical night, they had created a tiny life. It lay vulnerable and sleeping within Irish's soft body. She'd kiss every bruise and play games on rainy days. She'd be perfect while he... Max frowned, thinking of his childhood. *Would he be able to give a child the love it needed?*

Max grinned sheepishly, feeling as though he could leap over the Rockies like Superman. "I'll work up a Mendelian—a genetic chart. I'll need facts about your family. I'll set up charts and do probability sheets on the new computer—"

"I haven't ordered a new gizmo, Max. Back off," Irish ordered fiercely, easing herself from the bed to stand looking down at him.

Max wanted to tug her back, to hold her against him and kiss the strawberry taste from her soft bottom lip. He wanted to say just the right things to soothe her, to tell her of his fears and the wonder bubbling inside him, but right now he couldn't find the strength. He placed the cold cloth back over his forehead. "We'll talk later, Irish."

"Maybe we will, and maybe we won't. You can stay until you feel better, Max, but then it's checkout time for you. Do you understand?"

Max took her tightly closed hand and brought it to his lips. He had other plans, but just now Irish wasn't feeling well. He turned the cold cloth over and wondered why the bed was swaying like a hammock. He blew a bothersome lavender pillow ruffle from his cheek. "Maybe I do, and maybe I don't."

"Ohhh!"

"The one thing that I do know, Irish," Max said solemnly, closing his eyes and holding her hand like a lifeline as the hammock swayed and the ruffle bothered, "is that I have no intentions of checking out of the scene. I'm responsible for the baby and you now. And I intend to be right here through everything."

"Max..." Irish had paled during his declaration, and she'd sat down on the violet-patterned coverlet. "You're not invited to the party. There is no need..."

But her fingers tightened within his, and Max took that as a small comfort. "Are you sick every morning? When did it start?" he asked, remembering that human pregnancy was divided into three parts called trimesters. "You'll need to write the sexes of the children in your family as far back as you can remember. I'll call Katherine to confirm.... Aren't you feeling well again?" Max asked, just as Irish lay down carefully beside him.

She took the cloth, placing it back on her own forehead. "Shut up, Max."

Max drew her limp hand to his chest and smiled serenely. "Daddy," he whispered aloud.

Irish groaned quietly beside him and Max grinned. "Daddy," he said again.

"Max . . ." Irish protested weakly.

He patted her hand as tiny happy pongs shot off in the region of his heart. Suddenly Max wanted to boast to someone, anyone. He wanted . . . he felt . . . Unable to dissect his emotions, Max settled for a big grin and gave Irish his first spontaneous hug. "I'm very happy," he whispered humbly against the softness of her hair.

She stiffened instantly, and Max fought the panic clawing at him. The words tore at his throat, tasted bitter on his lips, as he asked, "Do you want the baby, Irish?"

She ran her hand lovingly across her stomach. "More than I've ever wanted anything. Thank you, Max."

When Irish had thanked Max for blessing her with a baby, his smile had reminded her of a wolf coming to dinner. She'd thought of how he'd looked at Abagail's that fateful day—as if he'd lay out systems and lives to suit him. "You're welcome, Irish," he'd said. "But you're not thanking me politely, then shutting the door on me."

He'd eased from the bed to stand over her, and she'd had the fierce premonition that Max wasn't going anywhere.

For the rest of the day, she waited for Max to return from his appointment in Denver and in the late evening, the black Porsche soared out of the dusk and slid into an empty cattle-loafing shed.

Mimi came running around the corner of the house, racing toward the shed.

Irish stopped watering the hanging parsley baskets on the back porch when Max emerged from the shadows of the building. Dressed in a cream-colored cotton sweater and tight worn jeans, Max glanced at her, then began emptying the car. Mimi trotted along beside him, and at each pause she rubbed sensuously against his leg, then flopped on her back exposing her stomach to be scratched. Max stopped and obliged. Carrying bags and boxes to the small cottage behind the inn, Max ignored Irish's "Hey! What do you think you're doing?"

The cottage had served as Abagail's private love nest, and J.D. had used it while pursuing Katherine. The intimate mirror-lined house had occasionally been used by honeymooners, but now Max obviously intended to stake his claim. He unlocked the door, glanced at her again, then held up the key. His teeth shone in the shadows, his wolfish grin widening.

"Oh, no." Irish dusted her hands on her jeans and tugged down her Mickey Mouse T-shirt. Mickey's huge ears had settled exactly over her breasts like big signs pointing out the promising milk factories. "I don't have time to deal with you now, Mickey," she muttered. "Van Damme is squatting on my land, and he needs to be dealt with."

"Move aside, will you, Irish?" Max ordered when she came to the doorway. He walked through the rooms and returned to her. Placing his hands in his back pockets, Max watched her closely. "Anger isn't good for the baby."

She held out her hand. "The key, Max. Then just pack up your—" she glanced at the assortment of electronic doodads sticking out of boxes "—stuff, and mosey on down the road. You're not staying."

"The hell I'm not," he said quietly, handing her a note. Max's hard jaw was covered with an evening beard and his hair was slightly rumpled. He looked very tough and determined. Not at all a likely daddy candidate. Or a gizmo guy.

Carefully unfolding the note, Irish read J.D.'s bold scrawl: "Irish. Max has just signed a year's lease for the cottage. If problems, call—J.D."

"I'll call J.D.," she said, refolding and sticking the note in her jeans pocket. "What's the big favor you did for him?"

Max arched an eyebrow. The gesture made him look like a certified, very tough hit man. "I'll tell you someday when you're not wearing that frown. I intend to be a parent to our baby, Irish. Fight me, and I'll cause hell. There are such things as paternal rights."

"You wouldn't dare, Van Damme," she began hotly, fiercely protecting the new life within her. Before she could move, Max's big hand slid out to gently grab Mickey's innocent face. Max tugged her near him, watched her for a heartbeat, then carefully, possessively placed his mouth over hers.

The long sweet kiss left her hungry and limp, melting against him. When his head lifted, his features had softened in the dim light. "I told you my biological urges hadn't been stirred, and now you'll have to suffer the consequences for opening the door. At my age, it's not likely that I'll get another chance at parenting, and I intend to enjoy every minute of our pregnancy."

The wolf's grin came and lingered. "I'm putting down roots, sweetheart," he murmured in a Humphrey Bogart imitation, his humor startling her.

While she tried unsuccessfully to counter his statement, Max kissed her again lightly. "I suggest you get used to having me around. By the time the baby comes, we should all be well acquainted. Don't worry, I'm going to be lovable and understanding. Right through the mood swings and the postpartum depression."

He punctuated the statement with a kiss that shattered Irish's last attempt to collect her thoughts. "There's no denying that you're carrying my child, Irish."

Max's lips roamed across her cheek to a spot that waited hungrily behind her ear. He kissed it lightly and she shivered in response. Unerring, the firm shape closed over her lips and she found herself answering helplessly....

A moment or a century later, he smoothed Mickey's ears back to their respective breasts and brushed her lips with his. "I've just realized that I've waited a lifetime for you and this baby. My biological clock and nesting urges are thoroughly stirred."

Four

"Daddy," Irish repeated darkly the next morning when she entered the kitchen and watched Maxwell Van Damme swing fully into his new role. She'd overslept again, trying to escape the fact that Max had installed himself in Abagail's hideaway. When she felt up to it, she'd call J.D. and bribe him with the promise of cinnamon rolls, big fat ones with raisins and oozing with frosting. Max's roots needed transplanting.

Max was standing in her kitchen whipping up a frothy batter. Lined up in groupings of spices, grains and flours, just like toy soldiers ready for war games, the contents of her kitchen cabinets filled the countertop.

Granny sat on the back porch, rocking and muttering as she knitted. Her needles clicked frantically while the purple snake-thing growing from them slithered into a heap at her feet. Occasionally Granny looked through the screen to scowl at Max. Link sat with her, nodding frequently while reading his morning newspaper and sipping coffee.

Dressed in a "Bach Is Beautiful" T-shirt and worn denim jeans, Max padded comfortably around the kitchen in his stocking feet. He tossed a quick efficient smile at her over his shoulder. "I have everything under control," he said in his clipped businessman tone. "We're having raspberry crepes. Of course we don't have the framboise to flambé, but sifted confectioner's sugar will do. Don't worry, I've placed a special-delivery order with a Denver grocer. We're going to set up a computer link for orders later this morning. Like I said, everything is under control. All you have to do is rest for your doctor's appointment. By the way, we have an appointment with Denver's finest obstetrician at one o'clock. Katherine recommended him."

"My sister is in this...?" Irish floundered, trying words from plot to takeover.

Max slipped a spatula under the crepe and lifted an edge. "Damn it, Irish. An iron skillet just isn't a crepe pan. It's a wonder you've managed so far without one—or an omelet pan."

"*By the way,* you don't have me under control," Irish said quietly, firmly. A Maxwell Van Damme in her kitchen was something frightening. And Kat really had messed in the wrong lily pond this time! Irish frowned. Max with a lease wrapped in his fist confirmed that Katherine was out for revenge. A payback for playing matchmaker with her and J.D.

"Out, Max," she managed, suddenly ravenous for raspberry crepes.

"Mmm?" Studying the crepe clinically, Max slipped it on a plate and poured batter for another one into the pan. "Oh...can't. Sorry. I've signed a lease and there's this biological clock thing," he returned absently. "I couldn't possibly leave before the birth of my first child."

"I said," Irish enunciated slowly, distinctly, "that I wanted bran muffins, prunes and raspberry syrup over pancakes this morning—not wimpy pancakes."

Max turned to her as though he'd just remembered something. "Ah, of course. Stewed prunes for the traveler. I started marinating them last night with whole cloves and oranges. Irish, you don't have a decent set of measuring spoons or cups in the place."

"I serve them plain," Irish said, tapping her toe. Until now, no one, not even Granny had challenged her rights in the kitchen, and she didn't intend for a Van Damme to go tromping through her private territory. "I use scoops, pinches, ordinary spoons and coffee cups to measure, Max."

He nodded absently, then dipped into her rearranged refrigerator to extract a crock. Max emptied the spiced prunes into a cut-glass serving dish and inserted a proper spoon. He handed the prunes to a passing guest with instructions to place them on the breakfast buffet next to the orange soufflé omelet. Then he returned to making crepes, filling them with thickened raspberries, and rolling them neatly.

"So in keeping with the healthy inn picture," he said to Irish over his shoulder, "we present prunes every morning. By the way, Jeff's connection with the grocery delivery boy is amazing. Has to do with charging and splitting the fee for delivery.... I'll have to brush up on prune cookery. The house-brand-mineral-water idea is great."

"Not 'we'—me. I serve plain prunes, Max, available dried throughout the day and offered stewed in the morning," she insisted, willing to duel with wooden spoons if necessary to uphold her rights for serving plain prunes. "And stop throwing around accusations about Jeff. There wasn't a problem until you showed up."

Irish walked to the spice soldiers, took a deep breath and traced Max's alphabetical line up. "My most-used spices are placed forward and the least-used ones in the back," she said slowly as Max guided her over to the kitchen table. "This is *my* kitchen. You have to be certified as welcome to enter it."

"Uh-huh," he agreed absently, lifting her chin and inspecting her face clinically. He eased her into a chair with elaborate patience, making Irish's temperature rise. "You look better this morning."

"I'm not." Irish glanced at his discarded eggshells and stood. "We have guests who are watching their egg intake...."

"Ah, oatmeal, then," Max said, pivoting toward the canisters as though planning an attack.

"... and we use the eggshells for lime," Irish finished as Max selected a battered pan for heating water. He carefully measured four cups of water, covered the pan and measured two cups of oatmeal into a side bowl. The way he had leveled the cups of oatmeal by scraping a knife across the excess made Irish want to scream. Her kitchen had been invaded, violated, by a measuring fanatic, while she puttered along the merry taste-and-season route.

"Max, get the hell out of my kitchen," she said in a quiet yell as he began washing the eggshells. He dried and stacked them neatly in sets of four. Then he re-sorted the arrangement, placing the tops and bottoms together.

"Can't," he answered. "You're going to need a cook later and I'm getting the lay of the land, so to speak. The rest of your mob can't boil water."

"We'll try to manage without you. Why don't you just putt out of here in your little car?"

He stared at her, his hard mouth fighting a smile. "You mean the Porsche? Sorry, can't go. I never leave a job undone."

"I suppose my baby is *the job?*" Irish wanted to throw something, anything, at him.

"I started the whole event. Me. The father of the baby you're carrying. There's no reason for you to get upset about this, Irish."

Upset? she repeated mentally. The word was mild for the emotion she was experiencing.

After calmly ladling the thickened raspberry mixture into a crepe, Max rolled and sprinkled confectioner's sugar over it. When he had completed another tray of the crepes, he motioned a guest to add it to the buffet. Max poured the oatmeal into the boiling water, covered the pot with a lid and placed it on the cool rear burner.

Then he turned to her slowly. Slit at the neck to expose a small wedge of dark hair, the T-shirt added to Max's ultra-masculine kitchen image. The pastel flower pattern of the kitchen towel draped across his shoulder contrasted with his dark skin, a stark male beast bathed in posies. Unwillingly Irish took in the neat tight fit of his jeans.

Max, while not a lean man, didn't have an ounce of flab clinging to him. This morning, his body had a sturdy look to it, as though she could lean against him and wilt comfortably.

Lifting a thick brow, he looked down at her while he methodically dried his hands with the flowered towel. Finger by finger. Recognizing The Look—methodical and in charge—Irish groaned.

Then he hung the towel around his neck. "Irish," he said in his extremely patient tone, "last night I did a quick computer linkup with a medical library and scanned the library's banks on pregnancy. You're in the first trimester—three-month period—of pregnancy. You're easily upset, moody, and you may sleep more than normal. Last night you slept nine hours and fifteen minutes. Added to the nausea and the fact the situation isn't routine, you are also emotional. Nothing like the postpartum—after the birth—depression can be, but you need care."

"You scanned what?" Irish had always waltzed through the weeds in her daisy fields alone. Max had ventured to stick his crepes and omelets into her picket-fenced privacy. She grabbed a wire whisk stored in a pottery bowl and wondered about the penalty for kitchen abuse.

Max leaned his hips against the counter and crossed his arms over his chest. He shrugged, and the terry-cloth flowers seemed to curl lovingly around his strong neck. "I've never been a parent before and needed briefing. You need understanding and affection in this trimester, as in all of them." A muscle contracted in his jaw, and he lowered his brows. "If you need support, you're getting it. From me. I want to make it clear that any conferences with Riggs won't be acceptable from this point on."

"I can see who I want, Max. The baby hasn't anything to do with that."

"Boonie Riggs isn't playing father to my child," Max stated flatly. "I discussed the matter with him this morning. He understands. Make sure that you do."

"I understand that you're interfering with my life, Max," she threw at him. Despite her anger, the ruffled male image combined with the workman's clothing had strongly affected her. She wanted to throw herself into Max's arms and kiss away his grim expression. Irish remembered reading something about the possibility of a pregnant woman's increased sexuality. She groaned and closed her eyes, aware that Nadia had stolen a stuffed crepe and was making away with it.

"In keeping with your needs—until we can see a qualified doctor—were you sick this morning, and did you find the crackers and milk by your bed?" While Irish dealt with learning that Max had slipped into her bedroom and watched her sleep, he added, "I picked the flowers myself. I hope they meet with your approval."

His Italian loafers had been waltzing through her elegant rose bed, too. Van Damme's invasion had to be stopped. "I'm the flower picker around here, Max. Stay out of my beds."

He mocked her usage of beds with a lifted eyebrow, and Irish blushed.

Max ran his fingertips across her hot skin. "Fine. But you deserve someone else taking care of you. From the way things have been running—" Max emphasized the past tense "—it's easy to see that you do all the catering. From now on you save your strength." He held up his hand as Irish parted her lips to argue. "You should have fresh flowers beside your bed every morning. Just because you're pregnant with my child doesn't mean that you can't have all the little perks you deserve."

He glanced at Granny who was staring through the screen, then lowered his voice. "We want our baby's mother to feel loved and pampered, don't we?"

Before she could place Max, the kitchen beast, alongside Max, the father of her baby, he sat on a chair and eased her onto his lap, holding her stiffly and carefully. After a second in which Irish fought her need to be close to him and to thump him with the whisk, Max eased her head to his broad shoulder and placed his arms lightly around her. "There," he said, evidently proud of himself. "I am determined to coddle you, make you feel secure. What do you think?"

With her cheek riding the uneven rise and fall of his chest, and her body warmed and comforted by Max's larger safe one, Irish couldn't pinpoint any problems at the moment. "About what?"

Max smoothed her hair. He bent to speak quietly in her ear. "I'm not what you might prefer, Irish. But I intend to be a part of the pregnancy and, thereby, a part of your life."

"You have no obligation..." she began.

"What you need to know, Irish," Max continued, nuzzling her hair and holding her more tightly, "is that I'm rather awkward at showing affection. But our baby should experience affection now. Don't you agree?"

Max tensed and Granny turned her back to them. The lines beside his mouth deepened, and Irish found herself exploring them and his bottom lip. It appeared to be more touchable than his firm upper one.

Max kissed her fingertips before frowning and murmuring, "I couldn't find a really good reference in the computer for giving physical comfort to babies, in or out of the womb. But there has to be some sort of manual on it."

He paused, swallowed and took a deep breath as if to steady himself. "I'm forty-two, Irish. And I don't intend for my only child to lack anything. Right now I'd like to place my hand over our baby. May I?"

"Didn't anyone ever cuddle you, Max?" Irish asked. How lonely, she thought, grieving for Max as she moved his large warm hand to her abdomen. He should have some warmth, she decided as the lines on his face softened and the tension around his mouth eased.

"My pet boa constrictor tried," he returned, watching her expression with flickering dark eyes as he traced her flat stomach. The naughty-boy look fitted Max well, Irish decided when she realized he'd been teasing.

"Poor Max," Irish soothed, kissing the rough line of his jaw and running her palm across his chest. She ached for him, settling more comfortably into his lap.

Max stared down at her for a moment, then slid his hand beneath her cotton shirt, cupping one of her breasts. He trembled, gathering her nearer as he ran a thumb across the sensitive crest.

Irish breathed lightly. Against her throat, Max's rough face was heating, and she recognized the instant tenseness of his body. She inhaled sharply as his fingers edged beneath her bra, caressing her. "Oh, Max!" she breathed, aware of his hard body against hers and remembering the passion they'd shared.

"Hmm?" he asked, distracted by her other full breast. "My God, you're perfect, Irish—"

His hand stopped, and flushed Max leaned back to look at her closely. "That's right," he said, as if just remembering her pregnancy. "You're probably extremely tender, and here I am—" he broke off shakily, stunned by the sensuous moment.

Because she wanted to soothe him, Irish kissed his mouth lightly.

The kiss was meant to stay his fears, but somehow Max's mouth caressed hers gently. He lingered over her lips, brushing them and kissing the sensitive corners as his hand again settled gently over one bare breast.

"Max," she protested in a breath as he ran a possessive hand down her body. "Max, this won't do at all...."

"Mmm?" he asked, carefully fitting his palm over the new life within her. He watched his hand for a moment, then leaned his forehead against hers. His skin was slightly warm and clammy. When Irish tested the temperature of his cheek with the back of her hand, Max paled slightly and attempted a lopsided smile. "I'm just not used to the altitude yet. I'll get over it."

"Max, you are banned from my kitchen," she ordered as gently as she could while smoothing his damp brow. "I'll finish breakfast if you want," she said, sliding from his lap.

Max paled and placed a cold bottle of buttermilk against his cheek. "Ah...that's right. We're having raspberry crepes, aren't we?"

He closed his eyes, and Irish wondered if she'd really seen a shudder cross his wide shoulders. Or was it just the posies sliding over the terry cloth? Max patted the kitchen towel across his damp forehead. His dark face paled again when he glanced warily at the crepes. "Ah...maybe you could finish...just for this morning. I still have some layout plans to go over."

Walking quickly to the door, Max shuddered again and ordered, "Don't forget to enter what you had for breakfast in the notebook lying next to your handbag. Keeping track of the four food groups is important. This morning you can have a half cup of orange juice, a half cup of oatmeal with brown sugar and a cup of milk."

After Max's color returned, Irish allowed him to push her around. She realized he might be fragile, since his biological clock had just started ticking. Max seemed to send off good-natured laser beams, and she didn't have the heart to strip his new father mood from him. She even felt like patting his head when he began installing a computer system in a large closet. When he was gone, she'd close the door and nail it shut.

In the late morning, Irish snipped fresh chives from the herb garden and plotted to snip Max from her inn and her life. Along the way, it was necessary to show her big sister that she could manage her life. Irish had just placed the basket of freshly harvested herbs on the kitchen counter when Katherine called. "So what's new?" Katherine asked in the cool legal-smegal lawyer tone that Irish recognized immediately.

"Nothing," she answered cheerfully and listened to the heavy silence stretch from Denver. Irish swept a sprig of peppermint around her chin, sniffing it appreciatively.

"Nothing?" Katherine asked, and Irish smiled, feeling righteously wicked.

"Well, the Romaines are leaving today. I told you about them. You know, the young couple needing just a breath—"

"Irish!" Katherine demanded, the cool tone gone. "I want to know everything about you and Max, and I want to know now."

Sniffing the peppermint sprig again, Irish grinned. "Max? Max who?"

"Max, the father of your baby. Do you want me to come down there and pry it out of you? I can, you know. And while I'm at it, Max deserves to be cut down to size..." Katherine pushed.

"But J.D. told you to butt out, right?" Irish finished for her. Katherine's silence proved her theory right.

"J.D. has nothing to do with this. Max called me last night wanting to know the name of my obstetrician. I had no idea *you* were the expectant mother and *he* was the father—until he informed me that he was taking time off from his career to spend time with you and his child. Okay, I admit J.D. had a little to do with throwing Max at you, but Max did need to relax...er...ah..." Katherine struggled for the right phrase. "You do have a loving touch. Ah...Irish, I really think you should consider a paternity suit and support."

Irish stopped playing with the peppermint. "Kat, you and J.D. sent him here to devastate my management systems. You'll have to swallow the results and the way I deal with my problems. Your niece or nephew and I can get along just fine without Max's ...contributions or interference."

"Your management whats? Where is Max? If he's there, I want to talk with him," Katherine said hotly in her out-to-get-justice tone.

Irish took a deep steadying breath, placing her hand over her flat stomach. Max's excitement over the baby had surprised her. She hadn't realized the Armani-Porsche scientist-type could be stirred, nor that he was so cuddly, or so lonely. If she didn't have the feeling that he was such an orphan needing a home and a hug... "Max is leaving shortly.

It's his nature to finish loose ends, otherwise he'll stew and fret and get ulcers. I know the detailer personality. I've let them putter around before—it's good therapy. Oozes out the stress and they go away satisfied. A guest who likes to do carpentry once remodeled the parlor after I'd just had it done. Max is installing a computer gizmo in the closet. I'll listen to his plans, keep him from disturbing the other guests, and then he's out of here."

"Max putters?" On the other end of the telephone line, Katherine was quiet. Irish waited. In the background, Dakota yelled and Travis called to his dog. But Katherine's silence continued. Finally she said, "Irish, Max doesn't have stress. He creates it. He's infallible and as deadly in purpose as J.D."

"I just talked with J.D. this morning about the lease. He thought Max needed the rest and quiet for therapy. J.D. is sweet," Irish tossed back.

"Max isn't."

When Irish replaced the phone, she found Max snooping through her basket of herbs. "Where's the sage?" he asked. Then, turning toward her, Max's gaze caught and lingered on her tattered floppy straw hat studded with fresh daisies.

Dressed in a business shirt and slacks, Max had returned to his computer-for-a-heart image—except for the sexy gleam in his eyes.

Irish stood still, feeling as if she were being absorbed into Max, as though he were taking her apart piece by piece and stuffing her inside him. Max stepped closer, and the scent of his newly bathed skin caused her to shiver. He'd smelled exactly that way the night they...

She blinked, trying to keep her bare feet on the linoleum squares when the rest of her body wanted to drift against his. In the distance, wind chimes tinkled and a calf bawled for its mother. Link's hammer tapped, and Irish's heart thudded quickly to the beat.

Max's long slow look flowed downward, touching on the yellow cotton sun top with tiny straps. He searched the crevice between her abundant and tender breasts. Beneath the fabric, her heart had decided to turn flip-flops.

She wasn't prepared for his lazy smile, nor the prowling finger running across the ruffled low-cut bodice. Her freckles seemed to dance and threatened to jump from her skin into the palm of Max's warm hand.

Max's gaze traveled farther downward, heating the small tanned expanse of her waist before moving on. Unable to move away, she forced herself to breathe. Her image of "poor Max" had changed to that of a hungry Rottweiler circling a tray of savory hors d'oeuvres and debating which morsel to taste first. And second.

He lingered on the denim fringe of her shorts, running the prowling finger down her breast and hooking it on the waistband. He tugged her toward him experimentally, and Irish resisted as Max took in her soft tanned thighs.

The finger hooked into her pocket and tugged twice. As he looked down at her, the gleam in his eyes caused her to shiver, her temperature rising.

Then he smiled—softly, sexily, intently. Tiny laugh lines appeared around his eyes, which were sending messages directly into her disturbed pregnant-woman hormones. Irish wondered distantly why she wasn't moving away. She wondered if Abagail had anything to do with the way Max affected her. Or was it the baby playing with her heart?

Max tugged again, looking very wicked and sexy and hungry.

"Max..." she heard herself protest breathlessly as Max's large hand spread across her lower hips. He fitted her against him intimately, and Irish trembled as Max nuzzled her cheek.

His other hand slid around her back, easing her full breasts against his chest, and Max breathed unevenly, his 'istful sigh sweeping across her hot cheek. He stood still, olding her gently to him.

Against her ear, he whispered roughly, "Do you know 've never held a woman like this before?"

Irish wondered frantically why she couldn't force her feet ɔ carry her body away. Max continued to hold her, his arm hands caressing her back. "This feels so good," he aid unevenly. "You're so soft, Irish. You'll know exactly ow to give our baby what he needs, won't you?"

"Max, we shouldn't be..." she managed after forcing a wallow down her dry throat.

"We could go upstairs and lie down," he offered in a low oft tone that made her skin heat and her freckles dance.

He nuzzled her temple, kissing it as his hand wandered up er spine to caress the taut back of her neck. "Irish, please. 'm experimenting in affection," he murmured huskily. "I'll eed someone to practice on before the baby comes. You're he likely candidate. Just hold still. Or you could help by olding me," he suggested, his hands caressing her.

"Max," she returned in a whisper, forcing herself to stand still. It wasn't easy when her mother-to-be hormones were acing wildly and screaming that she hold on to him. 'You're not a candidate for a daddy."

He smiled against her hot cheek. "I've already passed that est, remember? You really could cooperate better, Irish."

She shivered, trying to quiet her seething hormones. When she turned to protest, Max's mouth fitted tenderly over hers.

His kiss searched and warmed—a gentle brush of lips over hers, his breath entering her parted lips. Max nibbled on the corners of her mouth, then ran his tongue across her teeth. His hand supported the back of her head, adjusting her mouth to his as though he could taste her until eternity.

Her hat slipped, falling to the floor as the kiss deepened and heated.

When it was finished, Max looked into her drowsy ey and smiled sexily. He patted her bottom, issued a fru trated male groan and murmured softly, "Wear somethin comfortable for the ride to Denver. We'll leave at ten fort five. Allowing for two rest stops, we should be at the do tor's office at twelve fifty-five."

Still wrapped in the need to hold Max tightly, Irish looke at him blankly. "Denver?"

"Mmm." Max's dark sexy eyes stared down at her wel kissed mouth as if he'd like to enter a marathon kissin contest. "Your first doctor appointment?" he reminded he Looping a curl around his little finger, Max turned it to th light and studied the glistening strands intently. "If we'r lucky, my dark genes won't override your lighter ones. I' love to have a little girl with gold-and-strawberry hair. An big sky-blue eyes."

He kissed her nose lightly. "I didn't get a chance to fin out—do these freckles cover your entire body?" he aske huskily.

When she didn't answer, Max gently patted her bottor again. He grinned sheepishly when she glared at him. "I lik this demonstrating-affection thing. The benefits are great."

"Don't get used to it, Max," she said fiercely, steppin away to calm her stressed hormones. "You won't be her long. A systems warrior isn't on my Santa Claus list."

Max's expression stilled, his grin replaced with a frown o determination. "Of course you see me that way—now We're in this thing together, Irish. Remember, a pregnan woman needs attention. I'm going to give it to you."

"You shouldn't feel obligated," she began, startled by th raw savagery of Max's expression.

"Obligated? I'm not that noble." He paused, his flick ering eyes pinned on her face. "You're delectable, Irish pregnant with my child or not. If you think that my...hono has anything to do with my feelings for you as a desirabl enchanting woman, you are one hundred percent off-track."

"Max," she tried gently, "you're confusing the father role you feel obliged to play with how you feel about me."

"The hell I am," he stated low in his throat, anger swirling around him. "Try again."

She thought better of arguing when Max stepped nearer. She wanted him to hold her, she realized suddenly. Wanted him to kiss and soothe her. Badly frightened by the need to step back into Max's protective arms, Irish placed her hand over her tender lips and fled the room.

The remnants of Max's leashed anger seemed to cling to him like a dark swirling cape, despite his grim attempt to make light conversation on the way to Denver. Glancing periodically at his profile, Irish was uncertain how to soothe his ruffled Rottweiler image. Was it possible that expectant fathers needed care and affection, too?

Tormented by the thought that she had actually hurt Max, Irish allowed him to hold her hand. To ease his wounded pride, she might let him arrange an easy system for bookkeeping—before she sent him on his way.

She glanced down at his hand, laced with hers on her lap. Max's restless fingers rubbed her skin lightly, turned and fitted her palm against his. He toyed with the third finger of her left hand. "I've been married," he admitted cautiously. "Affection wasn't a part of that relationship. I want it to be a part of ours, Irish."

Unable to respond, Irish looked away. She'd given her heart away once, and now she needed to hoard it for the baby. Max glanced at her, his knuckles turning white as he gripped the steering wheel. He stared at the winding highway, the shadows of the pines slipping across his grim face.

In the doctor's parking lot, Max eased Irish out of the car with care. Just before entering the elegant building, Max paused and turned her to him, scanning her blue gingham cotton blouse and slacks. "You really look beautiful today. . . sweetheart."

While Irish dealt with the stiffly given endearment, Max guided her to the doctor's office.

Pacing restlessly and flipping through a magazine in the waiting room was Katherine MacLean. The elegant long-legged blonde glanced up when she saw them enter, her smoky eyes dark with fury. "Max, you should be ashamed of yourself," Katherine said tightly, furiously, then turned to her sister. "Irish, I don't know what to say."

"Say you're happy for me," Irish returned uneasily, sensing Max's tension. Katherine could be an imperial terror when tossing her big-sister image around, and suddenly Irish didn't want Max hurt. Tension ran through him like a live wire; she could feel it tingle in his fingers. She squeezed the hand that held hers. "Don't be afraid, Max. I'll protect you," she whispered in an aside to him.

Katherine glared at Max. "I want to see you in my office, Van Damme. Make an appointment. You're not walking away from this easily. I'll slap a paternity suit—"

"I'm not walking away from Irish," Max answered quietly, tightening his fingers around Irish's. "You checked Dr. Williams's calendar to see when her appointment was—I expected that much."

Katherine wasn't satisfied; she glanced at Irish, then glared again at Max. "Why Irish?"

"Because she's special," Max returned after a long moment as he searched Irish's expression. "I want her in my life."

"Yes, a baby would do that," Katherine said slowly, thoughtfully, after a moment. Her smoky eyes slid from Max's determined expression to Irish's face. "I had to see for myself."

Suddenly Katherine moved into Irish's waiting arms, and they hugged. "J.D. will be mad as a hornet that I threw my weight around, Irish. You'll calm him down, won't you?" Katherine whispered after a suspicious sniff. "Bake him something sweet and oozy. Put extra nuts on it. Have it special-delivered immediately—to his office."

Irish kissed her sister's damp cheek and whispered back, "Stay out of matchmaking technology, Kat. It takes a master's touch." Then she stepped back to find that Max had never released her hand.

He bent stiffly and kissed Katherine's other cheek. "I'll take good care of her."

Because Max looked so uncomfortable and Katherine needed a taste of humility, Irish grinned and demanded, "There, that was nice. You're doing fine, Max. Kat, you hug him and make up. His feelings bruise easily, and no matter what happens, don't hurt him. I won't have it."

Katherine's eyebrows shot upward. "You're protecting the deadly Maxwell Van Damme? The hit man you accused us of sending down to plague you?"

"Well—" Irish glanced at the nurse waiting for her "—he's that, too. But don't hurt Max, Kat. Hurry up and hug him, so I can go in. I won't budge until you do. Hug Max, Kat."

"Nobody ever hugs Max. Except Travis and Dakota." But Katherine grinned and hugged Max, who responded with a sheepish delighted grin. Somewhere at her feet lay her stiff resolve to boot Max out of Abagail's and her life. All the funny little hormonal disturbances were gleefully rioting, and she wanted a big dish of yogurt and olives.

After her preliminary examination and tests, Irish returned to the waiting room to find Max surrounded and chatting with three women. In varying stages of pregnancy, the women instructed Max on the role of father-to-be. Max nodded solemnly, asked questions, and took notes. In the corner of the room, a huge panda lorded over a realm of sacks and boxes bearing a toy-store logo.

Irish groaned silently, recognizing Max's absorbed expression and warned the women, "Don't give him any ideas. He has enough of his own."

"Wow. Is he yours?" a blonde in her ninth month asked wistfully.

Max smiled devastatingly. In fact, Max glowed. "Yes, I am," he said slowly. "Aren't I, honey?" Then he beamed as if he'd just mastered a new language. "Katherine had to leave for a court case. But she left me a list of be-good-to-my-baby-sister things. She thinks you need coddling."

"Oh, she does. Absolutely. Amen to that," the three women agreed in unison while Max intently shuffled through the bag of information booklets about pregnancy and childbirth.

Irish firmed her lips against her thoughts and pushed her lips into a tiny movement she hoped would pass for a smile.

Irish managed to stay calm as Max sat by her side during the doctor's instructions. Afterward, she was patient as Max packed the toys into the Porsche. "Katherine helped me pick them out in the store downstairs while you were with the nurse. She thought I was nervous, but she threatened me again—something about extended jail sentences and bread-and-water diets. But you'll protect me, won't you?" he asked smugly, sliding into the car.

Guiding the car into traffic, Max glanced at Irish. "You haven't said anything since the doctor's consultation. What's wrong? Don't worry, I'll be right with you all the way. I can't wait to begin the prepared-childbirth sessions. You could start exercising now—I like the idea of coaching my child into the world," he stated proudly.

Irish frowned, disliking Max's preening in the father role. She slid her hand from his and crossed her arms. "Max, *you* and the doctor had a consultation. *I* wasn't allowed to speak. Except to answer ways of childbirth and if I intended to breast-feed."

"Oh. Was there something he didn't answer? Are you having problems that we should know about?" Max was genuinely concerned, nudging the panda's furry paw from his ear. A yellow rubber duck worked its head out of his shirt pocket. "Irish, the first trimester is very dangerous. Katherine said your great-grandmother—who had wicked pansy-blue eyes, too—turned moody in the first stages of pregnancy, just like you."

"Me? Moody? Wicked eyes?" she asked, feeling distinctly prickly. "Max, everyone loves me. I'm adorable. There must be something wrong with you—"

"Irish, once we get through this stage—"

"Damn it, Max. Will you stop saying *we?*"

He shot her a long cool level look. "I'm in this, Irish." He placed his hand over her abdomen and caressed it briefly. "We're in this together. The three of us," he added, warmth returning to his dark eyes. "Just leave the details to me," he ordered mildly before Irish groaned, closed her eyes and slid lower in the luxurious seat.

Max took her limp hand. "That's right, dear. You need rest. Did you know that every woman in the waiting room was married? We might start considering..." he was saying just as she fell asleep.

In the next few days, Irish didn't have the energy to confront Max. But when she was feeling better, Maxwell Van Damme would have to install his gizmos, new kitchen appliances, utensils and himself elsewhere.

If only he weren't so obviously satisfied. Glowingly content.

Delighted to have her under his thumb, Max puttered, ordered new gizmos and cooked for the guests. He'd taken over her specialties with delight, such as mixing the nightly egg-and-oatmeal face masks with crushed cucumber base and sitting in the kitchen with the female guests, drinking herbal tea. He straightened her rows of aloe-vera sprouts and devised a body wrap using the plant pulp. Max meticulously measured alfalfa seed and water in his sprouting jars and the results were perfect.

That grated. Before Max's interference, she'd been the champion alfalfa-sprout grower. She'd been the one passing out the facial masks and listening to troubled guests beneath the maple tree.

Somehow he found the time to pamper Irish, seeking her out from her hiding places and following Katherine's request for coddling. Irish didn't think she liked being coddled; her patience wore thin each time Max placed his arms around her and held her lightly. She was too busy dozing and wondering about when her breasts would stop inflating.

While she took naps, Max deposited bouquets, milk and crackers on her bedside table. He seemed to know instantly when she was nauseous, urging her to rest before he lay down beside her. "High-altitude problems," he would explain again weakly, holding her hand, "something I picked up in the Himalayas.... Where do you think we should put the nursery?"

In the hot afternoons, Max maneuvered Irish into elevating her legs by lying down and napping. In the rocking chair near her bed, he studied the doctor's pamphlets and splashed his thoughts about their combined genetic traits in his growing notebook. Then he managed to stretch out for a nap at her side, and sometimes, when she awoke...

Irish wanted to make love to him. She wanted the sweetness and the delight of having Max's gentle trembling hands moving over her.

Reluctantly she would force herself away, fighting the urge to dive on top of Max's delectable body. After all, she wasn't Mimi.

Five

"This time your man is building a helicopter pad, Irish," Jeff said, leaning against the laundry-room wall. He tossed a long roll of paper at her. "Check it out. Van Damme has plans for sticking an airport right in the middle of the north field. Looks like he's got plans for a hangar, too. What I want to know is, who's the boss around here? You or him?"

"Where did you get these?" Irish spread the blueprints over her folded bed sheets. At four months into her pregnancy, Irish had wilted under the August heat and the fact that she was losing control over her life.

She needed to call her parents about the baby. But what would she tell them about the father? She hated feeling like she'd trapped Max and that he felt obliged to blend into a rustic boring life-style. That he felt duty bound to put on a happy face when he could be systemizing Tahoe or Switzerland. Or discussing classical music with other highbrowed buffs instead of reading volumes on pregnancy and baby care.

On the other hand, Max's gentle rubbing hand was heavenly when the yogurt and olives decided to roll around uncomfortably in her stomach.

Irish forced a smile, remembering Jeff's presence. "Well? Where did you find the plans?"

He shifted restlessly. "I found 'em.... Van Damme has been all over this place with a fine-tooth comb. He's jumped me and my men once or twice, but I handled him. And I've turned in the bills to him just like you said."

Irish remembered Boonie's nose and wondered how Jeff had managed so easily. "How did you handle him?"

"Just told him that it wasn't good for you to get upset and that he was disturbing you plenty. Anybody can see that you're not as perky and happy as you were before him. Took the air right out of him."

"And he let it go at that?"

Fury leapt in Jeff's expression. "Hardly. He's a cool one. All business. Seems he's keeping a list on me. Let me know he respected your decisions about the running of the place. Told me to watch it and that he wanted 'any personal differences settled between us' away from you."

Irish scanned the blueprint, defining the plans and thinking of Max's noble efforts as the pleased father-to-be. He was protecting her, backing off from a situation that normally called for sharp Rottweiler teeth.

She frowned at the plans, thinking of Max's detailer personality. It must have cost him to avoid a confrontation with Jeff, who wouldn't disappear quietly.

Her own scene with Jeff wouldn't be pleasant. She didn't want her overstimulated emotions affecting a man who supported an elderly mother and disabled daughter. When she felt up to dealing with him, she would.

Despite the situation, a warm little leap of pleasure went through her. *Max respected her business decisions.*

Jeff continued, "He's got some idea that you'll handle things when you can. Says he's got confidence in you." His face twisted with anger. "We can do without him. He'll be on his way soon enough when he figures out that we're a penny-ante hotel."

"That's enough, Jeff," Irish said softly, glancing up at him while she rolled up the plans. Jeff had been needling her since Max's arrival, and she didn't like defending herself, nor Max. "Abagail's may be small, but we give our guests quality care. Remember that. And by the way, while you're working here, don't charge guests for minor car repairs or for any of the services they should have free. The Obersons didn't really have the fifty dollars you charged for chauffeuring them to the airport."

Jeff's mouth tightened, his eyes narrowing at her. "They're rich. They can afford it. Van Damme has you jumping through hoops. Anyone can see it. Before he came, you always let me do my job how I saw fit. No need to jump me because you're prickly, Irish."

She arched an eyebrow at him. Challenging males weren't her favorite animals this morning. "Make sure you get the field crews started on changing the sprinklers in the clover. We'll be harvesting the honey soon, and the clover flavor sells well. The carrots and tomatoes need more water...and the raspberries. Then check in with the Langtrees—they want to try out the horse-and-buggy moonlight ride this evening."

Irish continued to rap out orders, disliking her rising temper. "And by the way, don't ever call Max my 'man.'"

"You're having a baby by that—" Jeff glanced at Irish's flushed face, then clamped his lips closed. "Irish, Van Damme is nothing but trouble. He's interfering with the way I do business. He's asking for receipts and checking every penny. Wanting things 'itemized.'" Jeff's mouth curled distastefully around the word. "Don't like everything being changed. Whatever he's got going with you, he isn't my boss, is he?" Jeff demanded sullenly.

"He doesn't have anything going with me now." Irish faltered, thinking of the way Max's eyes tracked her. Like a wolf waiting for a lamb to weaken. Like a man eyeing a deliciously slim sexy beauty dressed in a tiny bikini.

Irish wasn't ready to deal with Jeff, but Max was another matter. She said goodbye to the sulking man and marched off to find Mr. Van Damme.

"Where's Max?" Irish demanded a few minutes later as she tapped Link's fishing newspaper with the roll of blueprints. The August heat had settled heavily on the inn, and the guests were nestled in their cool rooms, waiting for Max's promised Baked Alaska that evening. Max could bake the state of Alaska for all she cared, but he couldn't build helicopter pads at Abagail's.

Continuing to rock in the shade of the back porch, Link peered over the top of his newspaper, flicking an appreciative glance down Irish's loose peasant blouse and denim cutoffs. "See where the brown trout are biting over at Newman's Spring… Max is puttering at the barn. Now that he's got the solar-heating panels installed and adjusted for heating water inside, he's building an automatic gizmo to dispense Morticia's and the horses' grain. Looks like a good system—grain comes down the main chute, then goes into each stall when the animals need it…"

On a course set to destroy Max's latest plans, Irish absently returned six-year-old Patty Shoemaker's wave and toothless grin. She ignored the sweeping fields baking in the heat and the new Hereford calves playfully butting their heads together. Max had to be stopped.

She marched through the barn, nodding politely to Morticia as she passed. Following the sound of Max's hammer,

Irish emerged on the back side of the barn. Shading her eyes against the early-afternoon sun, Irish spotted Max and his project.

On a bale of hay was an empty yogurt carton and a can of black olives. Mimi lay on top of another bale, watching Max intently and twitching her tail. The barn cat was heavily pregnant and craved Max's attention, which he supplied by rubbing her tummy and sweet-talking her until she grinned and purred sumptuously. Irish frowned, regarding the cat as a traitor to her sex. The soothing strains of Bach swirled around the barn, and she remembered Max's statement that music was good for animals, too.

Irish swallowed, trying to ignore the sight of his tanned broad rippling back tapering down to the strip of pale flesh above his low-cut jeans. She didn't want her eyes strolling down his backside and long legs. But somehow they did anyway.

Fighting to keep her emotions in line, Irish tapped him on the shoulder with the roll of plans. "You blueprinting macho dictator. You low-down city list-maker."

Max placed the hammer aside and turned slowly toward her. A wild daisy was tucked behind his ear. He took the blueprints from her and placed them beside the hammer, then looked down his arrogant nose at her. "Is there a problem . . . sweetheart?" he asked coolly.

"Bingo! You've got it!" Irish fought studying the effect of fragile white petals against his darkly tanned skin. With new laughter lines radiating from his eyes, Max's face had taken on a lived-in quality. Irish fought the wave of sensuality washing over her. Her fourth month of pregnancy was not the time to discover how badly she wanted to dabble in Max's lovemaking. She shivered, trying to avoid remembering their first episode. If only she weren't in tune with Max's sexy new Western look; he had no right to be so devastatingly appealing. "Just what are you doing wearing a daisy?" she demanded.

"Nadia said I'd need it today—a good-luck charm. Cool down and tell me what's bothering you."

Cool down? Irish thought wildly. She didn't want the hot look in Max's eyes to set off tiny electrical charges and an instantaneous need deep in her body.

She didn't want to need Max, daisy behind his ear or not.

But Max's hand was tunneling beneath the weight of her hair to rub the back of her head. The gentle caress stilled her as effectively as his strong arms. Irish's body melded with his instantly, startling her. She wasn't prepared for the swift hunger racing through her, the stark desire written in Max's intent expression. Against hers, his body hardened, the denim jeans chafing against her bare legs.

While she managed to inhale, Max's dark eyes were skimming down her body, lingering on her full breasts. He lifted the heavy curls from her neck, allowing the breeze to cool her skin. He crushed the strands, watching her intently. A flush ran along his cheekbones, his expression darkly intent. "Do you have any idea of how much I want you?" Max asked through his teeth. His fingers edged up under her denim shorts, tugging at the elastic of her briefs. "Why the loving names?" he asked, sliding his fingertips along the rounded softness of her hips.

Irish's brain scrambled to remember the reason for her anger. Somehow Max had defused that anger, splintering her emotions into a devastating heat. "You're plotting to build a helicopter pad, Max."

A bee droned nearby, sashaying past them on its way to a field of clover, and Max eased her into a narrow slice of shade, concealing them from the inn. "Jeff's been snooping where he shouldn't be. He'll have to stop that. The pad is a practical idea, since Colorado is famous for snow-blocked roads in early February—your due date. A helicopter would be dependable transportation."

Max leaned against her, foraging for that sensitive spot behind her ear, and Irish's resolve to step free slithered away on the soft pine-scented breeze. "Max..."

"You are exciting, Irish," he whispered against her damp skin. "Do you have any idea how you can stir me?"

Of course she knew how Max had been stirred! She had been just as stirred! Irish closed her eyes, trying to lock her knees to keep them from giving way. Max's arm looped around her waist, scooping her to him just as he stepped backward and fell into the soft fragrant hay.

Lying on top of Max's aroused body, Irish trembled with the need to hold him. She didn't want to reach out and stroke his cheek, to savor the rough stubble chafing her palm. If only he didn't look so intent, so needing of her touch. Max needed to be stroke and loved, she thought dreamily, lightly kissing his lips.

She trailed kisses over his face, finding his cheekbones and pursuing them down to his mouth. Did Max have the same sensitive spot behind his ear? Would it ignite with her kiss? she wondered.

Beneath her, Max lay perfectly still. "God, Irish," he murmured quietly. "I thought I was past needing a woman like this."

Blueprinting scoundrel or not, Irish thought, Max could do marvelous things for her ego.

"Did I ever tell you how much I like your hips?" he asked huskily on cue, caressing said parts in a movement that brought her deeper into the cradle of his long legs.

"My hips?" Irish managed blankly, remembering all the hours of inch-reducing exercises she'd logged in with Mark.

"Mmm." Max's teeth tugged at the elastic bodice of the peasant blouse.

"Oh, my," Irish whispered as he found the tips of her reasts through her cotton bra. She wanted Max and it rightened her. "You're not stuck with me."

His head came up, his expression intent. "What if I want o be?" he asked softly, his thumb gently rubbing her inner lbow.

While her body wanted to respond, Irish fought to keep er thoughts stacked neatly, like Max's spices. "I undertand your need to set up college funds and financial trust whatzits for the baby. And I understand why you're conerned that our baby have the best of care, the best diet, the appiest mommy-to-be. You're an honorable man, Max. But we're not anything alike. In fact you drive me batty. But don't want pity or honor to keep you here. And I don't vant you acting as though..."

She couldn't meet the dark mocking humor in his eyes nd looked away at a doe grazing in the meadow. "You lon't need to pretend you really want me, Max."

Irish closed her eyes slowly, helplessly, when Max found hat traitorous spot behind her ear. "You are so delectable," he whispered in a low rough tone.

"I'm not a roast-beef sandwich...." She ran out of breath s Max's hard body leaned over her.

"Mmm, with enticing hints of spicy mustard and orseradish."

After her freckles had been individually charted by Max's ips, they began walking back to the inn. With his slightly vilted daisy behind his ear, Max strolled beside her whisling *Bolero.* On the back porch, Irish tried not to crush the arge bouquet of daisies that Max had picked for her.

Burying her face in the blooms, Irish hugged the thought hat Max was the first man ever to pick flowers for her.

When she blushed and looked away into the zigzaggy peony fields, Max tipped her face to his and kissed her nose. He grinned rakishly. "I've traded the Porsche for a station wagon. It will arrive sometime tomorrow. After all, we need more room when you expand, won't we?"

Carrying her hand up to his lips, Max nibbled on th center. He smiled wickedly, smugly. "Will you marry me?

Irish stared at him blankly, her emotions playing tug-o war as they ran wildly through her. Her lips parted to say n but her heart cheered yes, yes! and did joyous flip-flops.

While he waited, Max's confident male expressic reached right inside her, and sensitive little chords all we *whang!* at the same time. Then Irish began to cry.

Because she was crying and didn't know why, she look up helplessly at Max's taut, yet vulnerable expression. Sh sniffed, fighting the tears. "Don't look so frightened, Ma I...just...want...to...cry...."

"Look, Irish," Max began uncomfortably, shifting on h long legs. "Maybe I didn't pick the right time or the rig way...."

She looked up at him helplessly, the harsh angles of h face softened by her tears. "I can't...stop...crying. Yo haven't done anything wrong...but I just can't marry yo today," she managed between sobs. "Lora Canfield is cal ing to let me know how much money the tooth fairy le under her pillow.... It's her front tooth and she's expec ing the fairy to be generous."

Max ran his fingers through his hair and closed his ey briefly. He looked like a swimmer caught in a crosscurren trying to find a safe bank on the shore. Irish tried for dig nity and failed, the tears running down her cheeks. "Oh Max, please take me to my room?"

Max muttered something ominous beneath his breat before he swept her up in his arms.

Beside them, Link rattled his newspaper. "Don't jus stand there, boy. Take her to bed. Nadia can bring up th olives and blueberry yogurt."

"I hate crying," Irish managed weakly against the security of Max's strong shoulder. Because Max was so competent, so safe, Irish gave herself to his care. When she was better, she'd fight his takeover and convince him that he really didn't want to marry her.

Three weeks later, the strains of Rachmaninoff flowed around Max as he lay in the madam's opulent mirror-lined boudoir. Uncomfortable with the sensual need riding him, Max ran a hand across his bare chest, wishing Irish's inquisitive fingers were there in lieu of his. Dammit! He loved Irish's sunshiny smile, his name on her lips. But she was keeping him at arm's length.

Max slung his pillow at the wall. He'd slid away from relationships for years, and now when he wanted to wrap up Irish in legalities, she wasn't buying.

Maybe her loving instincts were right.

Maybe he wasn't worth taking the risk. The Van Damme dominant genes weren't affectionate ones. He shuddered slightly, remembering the way his father had shaken his hand when Max the child needed a hug.

Max studied the photograph Nadia had slipped him as a reward for letting her tell his future with tarot cards. Circling her, he'd endured Nadia's clucking and nodding; he'd discovered that Nadia wanted to write the story of her life from Romania, to New York, then to Kodiac. Forty-five minutes of crystal balls and cards had been a good investment, and at the end Nadia had rewarded him with a photograph of Irish.

Standing in front of a trellis dotted with crimson roses, Irish smiled back at him, sunlight dusting her hair with gold. In return for the photograph, he'd let Nadia use his computer in the cottage. Pecking away in his study, the fortuneteller was too busy to interfere with Max's plans for Irish.

Irish never turned away orphans, and Max counted on Nadia's presence in the cottage to support his homeless look.

He turned his head slightly to view the painting hanging above the fireplace mantel. Jonathan had captured Irish's loving sweet innocence perfectly in his soft Renoir style.

Jonathan was Irish's pet, Max thought darkly. But the artist fed upon his fears, turning to Irish for comfort. Max's fist tightened on the delicate crystal stem of his wineglass. Jonathan overcharged the guests for his landscapes and portraits, reveling in his starving-artist role.

Max scowled at the portrait of Irish, which had cost him enormously. He ran his hand across his flat abdomen, rubbing it tentatively. The muscles were taut, his skin seemed stretched over them. Max continued rubbing as he thought about plucking Irish from Jonathan's clutches. The young artist's pictures should be hung in galleries around the world and sold for top prices. But fear kept him clinging to Irish's soft secure nest.

Jonathan should be ripped from the inn and tossed into a den of hungry critics. Critics went for the jugular, and if he survived, they'd put a fine salable edge on Jonathan's talent.

After mentally dealing with Irish's beloved mob, Max had headed straight for Jeff. Jeff had been skimming major amounts from Irish's operation for years. At first the amounts had been small, but in the past year they'd soared to thousands of dollars.

Overpaid and lazy, the ranch manager had Irish's sympathy. According to Irish, Jeff mailed every paycheck to his elderly mother and disabled daughter. According to Max's investigation, Jeff didn't have a family, other than a girlfriend he liked to squire to Cancun. Several choice pieces of farming equipment were mysteriously missing, and Max suspected Jeff had profited from that.

Max ran a hand across his jaw. Jeff needed to be handled delicately and away from Irish's soft heart. Right now, she needed confidence, and exposing Jeff's activities could possibly harm her.

Trying to ease the tension in his body that thoughts of Irish aroused, Max lifted the decanter of fine wine next to his bed and poured more into his glass. He lifted the drink to toast the many mirrors reflecting his lonely bed, then emptied it. Pouring still another, Max thought of their baby. Babies needed love, not nannies and laboratories. Irish would be a perfect parent. But would he?

Irish's discomfort showed more every day. *How could he tell her about the guilt that plagued him?*

And how could he find the words to tell her of his unshakable fear that something might go wrong? He shuddered each time he thought of childbirth complications. With the baby due in early February, Irish's contractions might start when the snow had blocked the passes....

She'd filled the emptiness that had haunted him all his life by wrapping him in her warmth and care, and he wanted to protect and cherish her. Why couldn't he tell her how he felt?

At four and a half months into her term, Irish stood in front of her bedroom mirror studying the edges of her unsnapped jeans' waistband and hoarding the house's quiet.

The late-afternoon air had stilled, promising a storm later. The guests were off on the annual September trail ride and would camp that night in a neighbor's huge barn. Granny and Link were spoiling their latest great-grandchild in Denver, and Nadia had locked herself in the cottage, writing frantically. Jonathan had suddenly received an offer to present his paintings at a art gallery and had left within two days. Max knew everything about shipping paintings and had helped extensively with the arrangements.

Jeff, scowling and snarling, had taken two days off to recover from Irish's recent discovery. The manager had chosen cheap paint for Abagail's siding, and after a month, it had begun to peel. He'd blamed the vendor, but when Irish called the store she'd learned that Jeff's order had been filled properly.

Irish tugged on her waistband, frowning as she thought of Jeff. A veteran with a steel pin in his hip and a plate in his head, he wouldn't find employment easily. As the only supporter of his elderly mother and handicapped daughter, Jeff needed understanding. Not the harsh treatment Max had suggested—an embezzling charge wouldn't help Jeff's dependents.

Accommodating Nadia's need for privacy during her final draft, Max had moved into a vacant room for a few nights—one he was considering for the nursery—and locked himself away in his closet-computer room to itemize, vandalize, and systemize.

The baby's kick startled Irish and she placed her hand against her side, awed by the tiny life within her.

The first time it had happened, she'd caught her breath and looked helplessly at Max who had immediately rushed to her. "What's wrong, Irish?" he'd demanded urgently, his expression taut.

"The baby just moved," she'd whispered helplessly just as Max picked her up in his arms, carrying her to the stairs.

He'd stopped in midstride, stared at the steps and had swallowed slowly. "Moved?"

She'd nodded and smiled, watching him slowly absorb the wonder with her.

"Our baby moved," he'd repeated, placing her to her feet. His hand had caressed her abdomen gently as he'd begun to grin widely. The next few days, Max had explored the tiny life almost hourly until he was rewarded by a movement. Tears had come to his eyes although he'd turned away.

But Max's scrutiny wasn't always welcome, Irish decided firmly.

She frowned and ran her palm across her abdomen. "You'd just better not be as methodical as your father," she informed the baby, patting her tummy. "I've had enough measuring, weighing, dieting and diagrams on how your growth is progressing to last a long long time. I'm fed up with genetic charts and chromosomes. Searching out the best hospitals for maternity care isn't my idea of a fun time."

She listened to the mellow chords of Bach winding up the dumbwaiter chute Max had just installed. "I could live without classical music, and the first word you say better not be computer," she warned.

The freshly baked aroma of Max's morning croissants mingled with Abagail's lavender scents. "Max might be under stress caused by his feelings of honor and obligation, but I could live without a resident chef."

But could she live without Max?

Irish shook her head and eased a length of clothesline through her jeans' belt loops. Tugging on a large T-shirt, she studied the effect in the mirror.

She'd been too busy fighting Max's menus and plans for the baby to notice the way she had changed. Her hair had grown longer, framing her face in ringlets as bright as the aspen leaves. Surrounded by the shining mass, her face was fuller.

There was something softer moving in her. It touched her mouth and deepened the color of her eyes. It was as though she had a wonderful secret and was hugging it to herself. Irish ran a finger across her bottom lip, testing the sensual contours. Of course, any woman's lips would seem sensual with Max exploring them frequently. Max seemed to love to taste her.

Irish studied the mirror. Thoughts of Max made her blush; the reflection's eyes shone warmly back at her. Wrapped happily in his father-to-be role, Max created lists of appropriate baby names on his closet computer. He installed an intercom in the nursery—once the madam's immense closet—and tested the sound system piped into the tiny room with classical tapes. Max's Himalayan nausea had eased. His drowsiness due to an old ear infection—also triggered by Colorado's high altitude and chill in the early fall breeze—had stopped.

A quick one-two knock on her bedroom door signaled Max's arrival. She jumped, feeling guilty that she had been thinking about the culprit. "Honey?" he said in a low intimate tone that caused her skin to tingle and her full breasts to harden.

Irish glanced down at the twin nubs thrusting against the faded cotton T-shirt. "Traitors."

She glared at the door that had caused everything. If she hadn't been fending off Boonie's advances by holding on to the crystal knob, Max's measuring spoons and cups wouldn't be in her kitchen. Max's protective streak would never have surfaced.... "Go away, Max."

"Amore," Max murmured beyond the door, and Irish winced. He'd been snatching Granny's romantic paperback novels and experimenting with endearments. Every time he tried a new foreign version, Irish's whole body went limp. Except her inflated sensitized breasts.

Irish threw up her hands, then opened the door slowly. Leaning against the wall and holding a cardboard box in his arms, Max stood looking down at her. "Hi, beautiful."

Longer and riffled by the autumn wind, Max's hair softened his face. The sun had lightened the auburn color; the new length waved deeply and rummaged down the back of his tanned neck. A skiff of curls played at the collar of his faded pink shirt. He'd just showered, and tiny beads of water clung to his hair and chest.

Hanging loosely down his stomach, the shirt was unbuttoned, exposing an exciting wedge of dark hair covering his chest. Irish fought the urge to nuzzle that gleaming curling wedge by gripping the crystal knob with trembling fingers.

His jeans dipped low on his hips and fitted snugly down the length of his legs.

Max grinned, a flash of white teeth in a darkly tanned face, and Irish's baby kicked her again in response. Unable to look away from his sparkling brown eyes, Irish placed her hand on her side, quieting the quarterback's running legs.

Max kissed her forehead. "Are you feeling all right?"

The movement presented her nose with an enticing whiff of newly showered male body and tangy after-shave. Irish closed her eyes against the impulses tugging at her to press her nose into his gleaming damp hair.

"It's my private time to relate to the baby, remember?"

Max straightened from the door frame and padded into the room. He dropped the contents of the box—an exercise mat, books and his white boxer shorts—on her bed. Then he drew a plastic tube from his back pocket and tossed it onto the bed. "We need to start working together, Irish. Exercising now will help us later."

Picking up the tube of cocoa butter, Irish leveled a stare at him. "What's this?"

"To aid skin elasticity." He glanced at her abdomen. "On our next checkup, we need to shop for maternity clothes. Or we could order a personal showing...."

His eyes lingered on her burgeoning breasts and he added softly, "You might want to try the cocoa butter—"

Irish held up her hand, pointing to the door. "Enough. Out. I'm having a conference with my baby. My...chest is my business and the baby's."

"What about exercising? You need to tone up your back Irish. Preparing for childbirth is necessary and you are approaching your fifth month—"

"I'm not flabby, Max. Besides I've been exercising."

His eyebrows went up. "Did I say you were flabby? Irish if we're going to work together, you've got stop being so touchy."

His eyes lingered on her endowed chest, and the reoccurring nubs responded happily. When Irish blushed, Max relented and tossed the boxer shorts to her. "Here, these will do for now. Put them on."

Irish placed her hand against her hip. Max's eyes had that challenging twinkle, his mouth curving with sensuous expectancy. She tilted her head, eyeing his lazy stance. "Max I really don't like the feeling that I'm being hunted or pushed. Just because you feel you need to stick around and take care of me..."

His hand caressed her cheek, and Max moved nearer leaning down to nuzzle her throat. "You'll have to start learning about accepting someone else's care, Irish. Namely my TLC. By the way, Katherine is concerned. Your parents haven't been informed of becoming grandparents again Don't you think it's about time—"

Irish jumped back, rubbing the spot his lips had found She glared up at him. "You stop that."

"Start exercising with me and I will," Max threw back smugly, flicking a glance at the books on her bed. "Then we can pick out names over my chicken Kiev. What about Shawnee or Sasha? Then there's Abagail, Tyree, Sloan Sam..."

Irish lifted her chin, sensitive to Max's probing gaze, which always returned to her chest. But then again, how could he miss it? "I'm not into games today, Max. Torment somebody else. You have parents—go explain fifty-to-one odds to them."

When she mentioned his parents, Max's face stilled. He leveled a stare at her and said quietly, "This is not their concern."

Beyond the window, lightning lit the clouds racing across the sky, and Max frowned immediately. His gaze traced the dark clouds over the Rockies, and his face hardened. "I hate lightning," he said in a low tone. "In Missouri, thunderstorms can be hell for a kid."

A gust of autumn wind slid into the room, and his head went back as though taking a blow. Irish touched his cheek, smoothing the taut muscle there. Instantly Max caught her hand, bringing it to his mouth. He closed his eyes and she felt him searching his thoughts. "Max?"

When his lids opened, the fear and desperation in his eyes made her ache. He swallowed the raw emotion beating at him, his shoulders tense as he watched her warily. Whatever had caught him in its midst had made him vulnerable, and Irish had a glimpse of his internal scars. Max's pain needed tending and she instinctively reached out to him.

Looking fiercely alone, ravaged by something she couldn't fathom, Max picked her up and carried her to the bed.

Six

Held aloft in Max's strong arms, Irish absorbed the tension flowing through his taut body. The air crackled with the emotion driving him, as though the faraway lightning had splintered into the room. Thunder rolled in the distance, and Max's heart pounded beneath her palm. Framed by the window, his face was outlined against the gray clouds skimming across the late-afternoon sky. The breeze riffled his hair, and each time lightning shot silver fingers across the gray sky, Max's arms tightened around her.

Another stroke of lightning etched Max's harsh face against the shadows of the room. His loneliness reached out to her. She felt his ragged breathing, as his fingers pressed almost painfully into her.

His eyes were wary as her hand moved slowly around his face. She traced the hard jaw, the slashing cheekbones and the firm set of his lips. Beneath her touch, something desperate and vulnerable shifted, seeking her. Then it scurried away, shielded from her as Max looked out at the storm. She'd had a piece of him then, touched it and cradled it in the palm of her hand.

"Max," she murmured softly, caressing his shoulder with her other hand. She felt his muscles ripple and shift. "What is it, Max?" she said, trailing her fingertip across his lashes. His eyes closed as if drawing the moment and her presence into him, and he breathed sharply.

"Sweetheart," Irish murmured, placing her lips lightly against the grim line of his mouth. Her fingers soothed the tense muscle in his cheek and came away damp. Was it the mist of rain, or was it the sweat of fear?

"This is the wrong time, Irish," Max warned when her lips slid along his cheek. "Control isn't something that I've got to spare right now."

"Sweetheart," she persisted in a whisper, knowing she was pushing him to the edge.

"No one has ever called me that," he murmured shakily, emotion darkening his eyes.

Whatever bound Max to the savagery of the storm, she would fight it with him. Unbuttoning his shirt and caressing his hard chest, Irish wanted nothing between them now.

Beyond the inn, the wind tore against the corners of Abagail's and bent the trees in its path. Lightning sent out silvery fingers to dance along the starkly outlined Rockies. Rain moistened her cheek as Irish wrapped her arms around Max's shoulders and held him tightly. "Come to me," she murmured against the rapidly pounding vein running down his throat.

"Irish, I'm warning you. This isn't the time for discovery games," Max said against the strand of silken hair tantalizing his skin.

But his arms had tightened around her—as if he'd never let her go.

She kissed the hard line of his chin lightly. "You're going to tell me about it later, aren't you, Max? But right now I want everything you want."

"What I want..." he said urgently. "Oh, damn..." Max shuddered, easing her to the bed. His hand slid down her arm to find her wrist, linking her to him. The gesture symbolized the new life within her and the strong bond between them. Irish wanted that—the knowledge that Max would fight to stay in her life. Max wasn't the type to run away in hard times.

He'd caught her hair, sending his fingers through the heavy mass and crushing the curls. Passion ran across his taut expression as he lifted her face to his.

Meeting his searching stare, she wanted him to know that she could match anything he could throw at her, the good or the bad. And when he was ready, they'd walk through the scars tormenting him together.

"Now, Max," she said as cool mist blew into the room, riffling the curtains. Taking her time, Irish slid her T-shirt up and over her head, then dropped it to the floor.

Max's gaze fell to her shoulders, flowing down her body to the baby. "Irish," he murmured huskily. "The baby. This isn't the time, Irish. You don't know what you're asking of me," he finished roughly.

She undressed slowly, and Max's face darkened with heat, his eyes following her movements.

Early-evening shadows slipped intimately toward them. Then distant thunder skimmed into the room. Max stiffened, shuddering; something hot and fearful raced across his expression, a desperation reaching out to her. Aching for him, needing him, Irish linked her fingers with his.

"Don't think about anything but now, Max," she whispered, looking up at him.

"Only now," he repeated, searching her eyes as she loosened his clothing.

The next time the lightning sliced across the Rockies, Max lay on the sheets with Irish.

His mouth ran hungrily down her, and she lifted her body to his lips, answering the mood driving him. When he returned to her mouth, Irish parted her lips for him, and wrapped him tightly in her arms.

Max moved swiftly over her, his mouth hungry and demanding. She answered his demands, taking him deeper. His urgency became hers, the hunger and the stark passion racing over through them with the intensity of the storm raging outside.

He wasn't tender; she hadn't expected anything but honesty.

Where she led, he followed. When he demanded, she gave. Tangled with the past, new passions and new discoveries soared between them.

Turning, blending, angles, softness, heat. Irish gave Max her pride, her past.

He took her into his pain, his desperation, his need to be consumed by her.

Riding the stormy passion, Irish held him tightly, absorbed him into what she was, what they could be....

Max's desperation spread through her and became her own. The eloquent pleasure sharpened, coming quickly now, and Irish placed her trust in Max to carry her safely through the stark passage.

At the crest of the flight, he waited for her. Then as she found him in that special place, Max gave everything, crying out her name softly. Spiraling over the silken edge, Irish paused in the strength and the glory, fought to linger in the joy they'd found, and heard Max's distant voice unevenly repeating her name as she dissolved into tiny quivering pieces.

Max found her mouth, kissing her and whispering to her. Over the sounds of the wind sweeping through the pine trees outside, the sweet urgent words were indistinct, yet comforting. Irish lazily returned the light kisses, running her palms down Max's broad back. She tried to open her eyes and couldn't. She wanted to remain where she was, warm and snug under heavy, dependable, huggable Max.

Keeping her with him, Max shifted slightly to draw a sheet across them. With an enormous effort, Irish tugged it up around his shoulders. She smiled drowsily at this new Max, this part-of-her-body Max. He'd given her a part of himself in the savagery of their lovemaking, some treasure she had yet to explore. With his hair mussed by her fingers and his eyes shining softly down at her, Max was cuddly.

Against the window, the rain fell softly, skipping into the room on the light breeze. Wrapped in warmth and wallowing in a pleasure she'd never experienced before, Irish wanted to keep Max with her.

Smiling wickedly back at him, she stroked the cooled contours of his shoulders and traced the cords running down his arms. Max did such wonderful things for her ego. "Maxi. Sweetheart. Sugar pie," she murmured against his mouth, teasing him.

Max's kisses had changed from sweet and lingering ones, to careless lighthearted ones that tasted of new passion. "Passion pie," he returned, and she felt his grin against her shoulder.

"Ah...Max?" she asked as his kisses trailed upward.

"Mmm?" Max found the spot behind her ear, and another round of fluttery little quivers shot excitedly through her.

"Max...the spot," she managed in a gasp as his tongue took up the search and his hands slid downward to cup her hips. Irish tested the spot behind Max's ear and he tensed.

"Again?" Irish asked, moving with him into the heat.

"This time we'll take it slow," Max said against her throat.

* * *

Later, Max tucked her against his side and they watched e lightning shimmering in the distance, its power spent and thering away into the soft rainy night.

He held her hand on his chest and breathed quietly. "No e has ever seen me like that, Irish. Not since I was a child. y parents couldn't bear that their perfect child, the prod-t of perfect genes, was terrified of storms."

Then she understood. "So you fought the storms alone."

"Crying and huddling away from the sounds. When I was ght, the housekeeper said I disturbed her favorite pro-am and she locked me in a closet for the duration." Max rned his head on the pillow to stare fiercely down at her. I don't ever want our baby to be alone and afraid," he hispered urgently.

"He won't be, Max," she soothed.

"What if I can't give him the love he needs, Irish?" he ked rawly, the pain shimmering in his eyes. "My parents ere just my age when I was born. They'd already formed eir life before I arrived. In a clan of genetic doctors, I was e only child. Apparently, I was an experiment that my ints and uncles hadn't wanted to try. The Van Damme mily trait doesn't lean to hugs and kisses. Children can nse when a parent doesn't care. They feel... I don't want y parents coming close to you or our baby."

Sharing his pain, Irish smoothed a curling strand of hair om Max's temple and traced a heavily beating vein in his roat. "Later, when you were old enough, did you tell them ow you felt?"

Max tensed, his eyes fierce. "I was too busy trying not to sappoint them, excelling in private schools."

"You could ask them here and—"

"No." His statement was flat. "They're not involved in y life. Especially now."

He paused, then softened the harsh statement as added, "You have a loving heart, Irish. But you don't u derstand my parents. Don't ask me to invite them into c relationship or the baby's life. I want them away from h and you. I'll deal with them—by myself, away from here

Irish placed her fingertips over his mouth and snugg close to his warmth. "Shh. Don't worry, Max. Everythi will be fine. Our baby will have everything he needs...." S hesitated, startled by the quick kick against her side.

"He kicked me," Max murmured, reverent pride threa ing through his deep uneven voice. Spreading his hand o the spot, Max waited and was rewarded by another delic kick. "Hello, baby. I'm waiting for you," he whispe softly.

"Daddy," Irish murmured, watching his eyes light w pleasure and a grin slash across the shadows of his face.

Max rested his chin on her head, and she was comfor by the rise and fall of his chest. He continued to look c into the dying storm, searching out the lightning dying in t mountains.

"Call them, Max," Irish insisted softly, smoothing frown with her fingertips. "Or go see them. They sho know—"

"Let it go, Irish," Max ordered curtly. "They're no part of this."

To let him sort out his thoughts, Irish remained silent a waited.

After a long while, Max turned his face from the wind to her. "I'm staying the night," he murmured against l lips. "Tomorrow I'd better move back to the cottage wh I can."

Snuggling back against Max's warm chest as she doz Irish thought she heard him murmur, "I never liked bei an only child. We've got time to go for two...."

* * *

A few days later, Irish and Katherine watched Max re-aper the nursery wall.

"Max is such a sweetie," Katherine said. "He's designed he traffic-flow pattern of the nursery, and he's refinishing randma's favorite rocking chair. And he cooks, too. What lse could you ask for, baby sister?"

"He's a prince," Irish returned darkly, her gaze skim-ning the baby's toys and returning to Max. Dressed in tat-ered jeans and a flannel shirt, he looked delicious. As if e'd been waiting for her to wrestle him to the floor, roll him nder the crib and have her way with him. "See if you like im checking ounces and calories on your dinner plate. Kat, 'm not used to being cuddled and tucked under anyone's ving—Max can be pretty overpowering."

"I know. You like to do the tucking. Maybe you should earn to accept someone else doing it for you. Sharing isn't n easy lesson to learn—I had to work very hard at opening p to J.D. You've escaped the tyrannies of a well-meaning pouse long enough, my dear little sister. Don't tell me ou're deprived of the essentials. Max is taking good care of ou. I saw him slip you that second helping of olives and ogurt. And this morning when he thought J.D. and I veren't watching, he burned and peppered your eggs just the vay you like them. Max is spoiling you and you know it."

"He's just feeling obligated," Irish returned, catching Iax's intimate glance at her. "The burned eggs are just ayment for what he feels is a debt."

"Ah, that's why he can't keep his eyes off you. Of course. That's why he keeps touching and hugging and kissing you."

Irish blushed and looked away. "He's read about bond-ng with the baby. Right now, he has to deal with me."

Katherine laughed, running her hand down Irish's hot heek. "Give up. The man's got a thing for you. Your fran-hise on loving has been sliced to ribbons. J.D. said that

Max has laid out a flowchart for your lives, and accordin to it, you could be expecting again in two years. He's starte hunting likely churches for a full-scale wedding—"

"Expecting again?" Irish ignored Katherine's giggl moving past her into the cheerful nursery. Max's takeove had to stop. Nothing had been on an even keel since h broke the fifty-to-one odds barrier.

Holding aside a strip of wallpaper decorated with tin smiling bears, Max dipped to kiss her nose. "You were righ The teddy bears with the pink ribbons are really better tha the ducks and the cats—"

"Don't patronize me, Max. Kat said you're planning ar other baby—" Irish stopped in midsentence, watching Ma blush. The red coloring moving beneath his dark skin caugh her broadside. "You can't have your way all the time," sh finished limply.

"I'm late realizing my goals in life, dear heart. My bic logical clock just needed you to wind it up," Max said wit a sheepish grin. "A second baby would be just perfect. Af ter we're married, we could adopt—"

"Now, Max," Irish interrupted earnestly, feeling a though she'd been pushed into the number-one priority slc in a series of takeovers. "You're running a little fast here don't you think?"

Max patted Irish's abdomen proudly. "We started ou that way, but everything is in sync now."

"Marriage," she repeated carefully, trying to herd th king of the teddy bears back onto the current subject "Max, as far as I know *we* have no plans for marriage an none for a second baby. Right now coping with you i enough."

"I know," he returned smugly. "But you do it so nicely."

His dark eyes shaded with a gee-isn't-this-great look, an Irish found her anger sliding out the open window.

Max kissed her on the nose. "My studies show that healthy reproduction at our ages is a possibility we shouldn't overlook."

Irish stared at Max's wide grin and wondered if she had heartburn, or if her heart had just caught another Cupid's arrow. Just then Max frowned. "What's wrong, Max?"

"Uh. Nothing is wrong. Must have been too much spice in the manicotti sauce at lunch."

In the background, J.D. chuckled and Katherine giggled. Dakota ran into the room, throwing herself into Max's arms. When he picked her up for a kiss, Dakota beamed. "Uncle Max says that Aunt Irish is gonna have a baby with black hair just like mine. He says Travis and me can baby-sit while he's out—" Dakota struggled with the word, then grinned as she found it "—dating Aunt Irish."

Irish stared over the little girl's shining black curls to Max's haunted eyes. "Dating me?" she asked huskily. "Why?"

"Figure it out," Max murmured, bending to brush her lips with his.

"She's five months along," Max told the nurse at the hospital's main desk. "Dr. Williams has set up a tour for us."

The nurse's sharp gray eyes peered over the top of her glasses to Irish. "Yes, Dr. Williams said that since he lived within an hour of Kodiac, you might want this hospital rather than Denver's. With Mrs. Dalton's due date in February, this hospital would be the better choice and she can start having her checkups here at the doctor's rural clinic. We may be small, but we have all the necessary equipment and a very good staff. Mrs. Dalton will have the best of care."

At Irish's waist, Max's fingers tightened slightly. His Rottweiler look had returned. "We're not married."

The nurse's white eyebrows shot up, her gaze shootin over Irish's loose yellow overblouse and black harem pant "Oh, I see. Then we'll proceed on the basis that Ms. Da ton's wishes alone will be considered. You realize that sh can demand that you be barred from the birthing room."

"In a pig's..."

The nurse pulled her lips back from her teeth, daring him She'd obviously backed down bigger men, standing tiny an pristine in her white uniform and noiseless shoes. "Yes Mr....?"

"Van Damme. I'm the baby's father. And I will be at *Ms* Dalton's side when she gives birth to *our* baby."

"Hmm, we'll see. Dr. Williams wanted me to arrange th tour for several couples due at the same time, and they'r waiting for you in the family room. Shall we go?" sh asked, swishing silently ahead of Irish and Max.

Taking Irish's hand, Max muttered between his teeth, " could tell her where to go."

"Max, be nice," Irish urged. "She won't invite us to th Pickles and Peanut Butter tea later. You'll blow your chanc to meet the other fathers."

"She's a bully," he muttered in an aside as the nurs looked back at them. But he smiled at the nurse; a disarm ing devastating male grin that most women returned with out hesitating.

Unmoved by Max's attempt to make nurse points, sh peered at him over her glasses. "Five couples are taking th tour and attending the Pickles and Peanut Butter party late Two months from now, you'll probably all be taking La maze classes from me. No chatting during the tour, excep for questions. You can visit freely at the party."

When they entered the room filled with couples of as sorted ages, Max stopped midstride and stared at the othe women. He gripped Irish's hand tightly. "I don't like this," he stated ominously as though they'd just entered a den o man-eating tigers. He scouted the room carefully, his click-click-I'm-computing expression intent. "They're all wearing wedding rings," he noted, the quiet statement dropping into the silence of the room. "You're the only one who isn't wearing maternity clothes, and the only one who isn't married."

At his side, the nurse smiled quickly and warmly at Irish. Then she looked up at Max's guard-dog expression. "Dr. Williams told me that you were a tough commando in our overseas troops. Remember, Mr. Van Damme, that those techniques have a time and place. Cooper General Hospital is my turf," she said, then smiled. "I think we'll all get along if you remember that, don't you?"

Max held Irish's wrist throughout the tour as though she might escape him. In the birthing room, his fingers trembled on her skin. In the delivery room, Max paled when the nurse described cesarean sections. When they came to the nursery with six babies wrapped tightly in flannel blankets and in rolling cribs, Max began to perspire.

He leaned his forehead against the nursery's glass window and closed his eyes, explaining that his stomach was just a little upset. The nurse patted him on the shoulder briskly and grinned. "I haven't lost a father yet, big guy." Then she plopped a Lamaze booklet in his hand and ordered, "Better study up. I'm the instructor, and when I say hop, you hop, mister."

Irish treasured the thought that Max could be bullied.

While Irish stood on a low ladder to wash the inn's windows, she thought about Max's fierce scowl down at the tiny nurse and grinned.

"Oh, no, you're not," Max said in the vicinity of her chest. Lately everything seemed to happen around her chest, including food crumbs that honed in on the generous shelf her breasts provided.

Max tugged on her loose flannel shirt gently. "Get down now," he ordered in a tone that stirred Irish's unsteady nerves.

"I'm quite happy here, minding my business. But thank you," she returned, ignoring him and squirting cleanser on the glass.

"Are we in a perverse mood today, dear heart?" Max asked. Lifting her into his arms, Max held her lightly. "You're not climbing anything but stairs."

"It's October, Max. Window-washing time. We can't get help, Granny can't do it, and you're working on gizmos—"

"Those are computer linkups to the stock market. Granny is foraging through the morning report right now. She and Link have just discovered the bull and bear markets and have invested in pork bellies. Where is Jeff's cleaning crew? They can handle windows, and if they can't, I will. They need caulking, too."

"You're a bully," she tossed at him, shaking with anger. "Barging in here, getting everybody to wait on me hand and foot. . . ." Max was either too understanding and sweet, or demanding and arrogant, when she did something he considered taboo for pregnant mothers. The combination was upsetting. Lately, Max had been backing off from her brief but undeniable temper. It wasn't that she was moody with hormones swishing up one side and then the other. It wasn't that she'd toss at night, wishing for Max's arms to hold her. And she didn't like greeting the morning with a groan.

Irish frowned. Things just weren't perking along her way, and it was Max's fault.

She'd asked Jeff to paint Abagail's front porch for the group of "spit and whittlers" arriving in two days. The elderly couples traveled as a group to Abagail's each fall and pursued their cherished activities: the husbands were deposited on the porch with pocket knives and sticks, while the wives swarmed Irish's kitchen to make jams and jellies for

Christmas gifts. Using frozen fruits and canned juices that had been stocked away for their visit, the women preserved and sealed hundreds of fancy jars.

Irish hadn't told Max about the wives—ten women who didn't like men in the kitchen. During their stay, they would hand Irish grocery lists and shoo her from their realm. Wearing huge aprons with pockets, they'd serve the guests "down home" meals until their bus arrived to whisk them back to their condos.

"Do you realize how dangerous a fall would be to you or the baby?" Max demanded, carrying her along the wide porch. "Irish, Jeff has a highly paid maintenance crew." He paused, nudging aside a huge potato that had rolled from a gunnysack propped against the wall. The scent of fresh apples rose from the two bushel baskets near the potato sack, blending with the pungent odor of big sweet onions in another sack.

Irish gritted her teeth, brushing a long winding curl from her throat. Max's eyes darkened when she tucked it into the ponytail, and Irish suddenly remembered that the first button was missing from the shirt she had borrowed from him. "If anything happened to the baby, you'd really feel obligated to me, wouldn't you? Max, we're expecting a houseful of people in less than a week for Abagail's Fall Fiesta."

Max's mouth tightened grimly. "Shouldn't you be showing off new maternity clothes? What are you wearing to the Box Lunch social? This?" He hooked a finger in the worn flannel shirt and tugged.

Settling down in his arms, Irish tried to minimize the deep cleavage soaring up from her neckline. "It's never been a problem before."

Max lifted one eyebrow, bleached by the sun, and glanced at her chest. "You've changed, heart of mine. Though you always were delectable."

"Max..." Just then Max sat slowly, easing himself and Irish into her grandmother's refinished cherrywood rocker.

"Shh," he said against her temple, gathering her closer and beginning to rock.

Mimi wandered lazily across the porch in front of them, holding her tail high. She twitched the tip, and a parade of scrambling mewing kittens followed in her wake. Plopping down on a sun-warmed board, the barn cat meowed and rolled on her side, exposing the kitten's dinner. In a flash the kittens found her milk, their tiny paws pushing against her stomach.

Licking the kittens as they nursed, Mimi then stretched out to luxuriate in motherhood.

Unshed tears burned at the back of Irish's lids, and she allowed them to flow down her cheeks. The baby kicked pleasantly along her side, wanting more rocking, and Irish sniffed. "I hate being a weepy wimp," she whispered, admitting it aloud to Mimi—not to Max.

Max eased her head to his shoulder and continued rocking slowly. Being the tired limp-wimp that she was, Irish let herself slide into the security of Max's comfortably padded body.

Tucking his chin over her head, Max murmured, "If anyone calls you a wimp, leave them to me."

Irish swallowed and sniffed, fighting the smile toying along her lips. The image of Max dressed for a duel was impressive. As he had been when he'd kissed the head nurse's cheek after the Pickles and Peanut Butter tea. Ms. MacMannis had actually blushed. "Did you ask her to marry you?" the nurse had asked after tugging Max down by his collar to her level.

When he'd nodded, the starchy little nurse had patted him on the head. "Good boy. You'll do."

A serene delight had slid into his expression, and the nurse had nudged Irish. "We call that the 'new father glow.'"

Rocking in his arms, Irish wiped her cheek with the collar of his shirt, and Max lifted her palm to his lips. "Protection from wimpdom comes with a marriage certificate."

"Stop pushing, Max. Shotgun weddings aren't my favorite subject right now," Irish returned too quickly, instantly regretting it. But she wasn't comfortable with the situation. She just couldn't manage to tell her parents; once they knew, Max was in danger of extinction. He really hadn't done anything wrong—he, his potent genes and chromosomes had just come swooshing out of the Rockies at the wrong time. Now Max loomed at her side, pampering and understanding—a tower of strength.

He made her feel like a real wimp.

She'd never needed anyone really, just fluttering along through life passing out hugs and kisses. When she'd needed to be strong and fight for a cause, she had. But now Max was scooping everything away from her and replacing it with something else.

While Irish dealt with role reversal, a muscle moved in Max's hard cheek as he pressed his lips together. "A shotgun wedding—I don't like the sound of that. No one is forcing you to do anything."

Swept by the light breeze, a huge dry maple leaf rattled on the porch boards. Max rocked her slowly, locked in his thoughts, and the baby settled peacefully into his warm nest. Irish wanted to know more about Max. His warmth contradicted what little she knew of his past. She'd hurt him just then, she knew, aching for whatever Max kept wrapped so tightly inside.

She'd had a glimpse of it during the storm and hadn't liked what she'd found.

Max shifted her slightly, arranging her legs across his—the elevated-leg remedy. The rocker creaked steadily, the same noise at the exact place, and Irish relaxed against him. The peaceful moment stretched, running along into the autumn air as though it could last forever.

Then he said, "Marry me, Irish," and destroyed the first peace she'd felt since Max had stepped into the hospital's room of married parents-to-be.

Seven

The small room was soft with October light filtering in through the window. Max adjusted the shelf he'd made against the nursery wall. The baby's eye-coordination muscles would strengthen when he looked at the objects Max intended to place on the shelf. Smiling to himself, Max mocked the use of *he*. Irish didn't want to know the sex of the baby and neither did he.

Gauging the distance from the crib to the shelf again, Max stood back to view the effect of the maple wood against the tiny dancing bears.

Since the bus had arrived with the "spit and whittlers," Max had sought privacy in the greenhouse and Link's cluttered woodworking shop. The maple shelf was his first project from scratch, his gift to the baby. Max eased the shelf an eighth of an inch higher on the right side, leveling it. With the installation of humidity and temperature controls, the nursery would be perfect.

The aroma of apple dumplings and plum jam rose up the stairway, and he sniffed appreciatively. From the cassette player on the dresser, Brahms's violins floated over the nursery. Machine-gun sounds from Granny's printer in the computer room shot from the intercom, punctuating the classical movements. Max turned up the volume on the wall unit, listening to Granny mutter about the "damned bear market."

"What's the problem?" he asked, then bit into the zucchini bread a jam-making guest had slipped him out of guilt. After all, they had seized his new copper pots and owed him the tasty rental fee.

"Pork bellies are down a quarter. Stock in communications rising. Don't people know what's important?" Granny demanded hotly. "Pork bellies are where it's at."

Another refugee from the kitchen, Granny had attached herself to Max's computer room. Under Max's direction, she'd taken to stock indexes like the proverbial duck to water. With a grade-school education, the elderly woman had raised eight children and now looked at a promising future in stocks and bonds. Her portfolio was tidy and growing, and Link called her "The Whiz." Link had a promising future of his own. Max and Link had talked with a local radio station, and now Link's fishing reports were carried after the morning news.

Following Max's text for computer bookkeeping, The Whiz had started logging in payments and receipts. With that skill under her massive apron, she'd moved on to the guest register and payment system.

Granny could be a nightmare when she wanted to evict Irish's nonpaying guests. Recovering from a wayward husband and debts left in his wake, Liz Fredell had received a free pass from Irish. While the woman was on a mountain trail ride, Granny had packed her bags and cleaned the room. "Fredell is out of here," the farm woman had told Max, crossing her arms.

Realizing how Irish would react—citing him as a bad, negative, money-picking influence—Max bribed Granny with a new stock-communications computer system and had supplied payment for Liz. When the elderly jam-makers migrated back to their tour bus, Max could have his kitchen back and revert to swaying Granny with pâtés, stuffed grape leaves and anything with nuts floating in a flaming brandy sauce.

Granny continued muttering through the intercom, and Max interrupted, "Check the penny stock. You might be encouraged there," Max said.

"Hey, Max, I got a lead on some hot stocks. Stop in when you get time—tell me what you think. I scanned Jeff's figures on labor and repair to the combine—they don't jibe with the mechanic's bill. Looks like the numbers have been doctored with carbon paper."

Max's mouth tightened. A tracer on the manager had turned up a tidy rap sheet, including a sentence for check forgery.

He watched the bear mobile dance over the crib. A confrontation with Jeff now wouldn't help Irish. He'd pushed Jeff just enough to let him know that he was being watched.

The Whiz repeated his thoughts over the intercom. "Don't worry. I remember what you said about not upsetting Irish, but she knows a scam is up... Nadia left a message for you to call her at the cottage.... My broker's morning report is coming in. Catch you later, 'gator."

Switching the wall unit to the cottage intercom, Max waited for Nadia to answer. A storm of Gypsy curses—Nadia had gleaned them from a textbook—crackled over the intercom. "*What!*"

Max dusted the last of the zucchini-bread crumbs from his fingers. "You wanted me?"

Turning down the volume, he waited until she had paused for breath. Then she began again and Max felt obliged to say "uh-huh . . . uh-huh . . ." in the proper places. According to Nadia, the latest research on crystals and the psyche must have been written by a baboon dining on funny weed, not a true medium. She intended to call out the author for a crystal and tarot-card showdown.

"Uh-huh," Max agreed dutifully as a movement beyond the window caught his attention. "In your book, why don't you list the author as a source, then go on to contradict him with your personal experiences, Nadia?" he suggested absently, moving the curtain aside to watch Irish below.

As Irish walked to the barn, the slight autumn wind caught the dark gold fields sweeping out behind her and rippled through them. Aspen leaves trembled, shimmering and riding the breeze as it swept upward to the mountain pines.

The breeze lifted and tossed Irish's hair; the bright reddish gold mass caught the sun and played with it. A long curl blew across her cheek, and she carelessly brushed it aside. Pasted against her body by the wind, her denim coat outlined the gentle mound of her stomach.

Dressed in jeans and joggers, carrying a small basket of apples for the horses, the mother of his child fitted beautifully into the timeless rustic scene under the shadow of the majestic Rockies.

But he was running out of time.

The mother of his child, Max repeated mentally as maple leaves skipped across the lawn to riffle at her feet. She was more than that. She was the warmth of his life, a combination of sunlight and flowers.

The Van Damme loveless hearts wouldn't touch her or his child.

Max's hand tightened on the back of the rocking chair; he realized suddenly that he'd been gripping it tightly, the wood cutting into his palm.

Fate had given them a child. Max swallowed the dry wad of fear in his throat. Dangling just beyond his experience, a tiny word—love—taunted him.

He hadn't known love. How would he recognize it? How would he give it?

Irish and the baby deserved to be wrapped in love, given by a man who knew how to love. *Could he?*

Fear, unbidden and wild, went slithering through him. Tucked into Irish's TLC domain, Max was a trespasser without credentials. He slowly uncurled his fingers from the chair. Degrees in loving weren't handed out easily, and he might not qualify.

Max had never waited for anything; he'd plunged through his career, methodically lining up the facts and getting results. Experienced and skilled at his work, Max had never relied on his loving instincts, and now Irish needed them.

He'd never been vulnerable and helpless in his lifetime. And he'd never felt more inadequate to a challenge.

In the autumn sunlight, Irish ran her hand over her stomach and smiled softly, talking to the baby—his child.

Max's mouth tightened. *How badly he wanted that tiny part of himself.* The fierce need to hold Irish, sharing the baby, ran through him like warm pungent wine.

Closing his eyes, Max ignored the burning behind his lids, the dampness oozing out to his lashes. Emotion sliced through him, and his hands trembled. He leaned back against the wall and listened to the uneven beat of his heart. He'd never listened to it before, never felt the hard lonely thud in his chest.

He didn't want to be alone again.

Max ran his hand across the antique dresser he'd just refinished. Carried upstairs from the basement, the cherrywood had responded to tung oil and hand rubbing, and now it gleamed richly in the muted light. He smiled slightly, warmed by the gift from the past.

Since he'd met Irish, he'd developed a feeling of belonging in this special place. With Irish.

Outside, the whittlers had started a musical-spoon symphony. Oddly enough, the beat seemed to blend with the sounds of Brahms.

Sitting on the rocker, Max listened to its comforting squeak-squeak noise. Then he leaned his head against the back of the chair and watched the bears dance and thought about Irish.

In her sixth month of pregnancy, she was more delicious than when he'd first met her. Irish's fresh-faced, all-American look had been replaced by a sultry exotic beauty that could stun a man at fifty paces. Beneath a mass of curls, her eyes had darkened to a luminous blue, and her lips had taken on a dewy softness. Max didn't want her stunning men without him at her side. The thoughts of another man parenting his baby caused Max to break out in a cold sweat. But if Nadia's predictions were on course, Irish should be weakening soon.

He rubbed his stomach uneasily. Lately it had had a tight uncomfortable feeling as if he'd eaten too much. Maybe it was all that sexual energy wadded into one tight ball.

He'd kept his distance, giving Irish the breathing space she needed. But space between them had cost him. Max smiled grimly at the huge panda lounging in a corner. In trading his Porsche for a station wagon, he'd picked up values he'd once considered old-fashioned. Sleeping alone in the cottage wasn't easy, but Irish had been compromised enough.

Lounging amidst the cottage's bedroom mirrors, the madam's portrait reminded him of Irish—sexy, warm and knowing how to love. Lying across her pillows, swathed in a transparent scarf, the madam mocked his celibacy. Once he'd found himself standing in front of the climbing rose trellis leading up to Irish's room.

Max reached for a flannel receiving blanket and wrapped a fuzzy blue bear in it. Holding the bear against his stomach eased the tight empty feeling.

Max traced the bears dancing from the crib's tiny mobile. He'd been like that, never touching the ground or staying in one place for long. He'd never wanted the white picket fence, the American apple-pie dream. Nothing but his career had mattered. But now lying within his grasp was a life with Irish, and Max wanted it desperately.

As owner of the inn, Irish could toss him out at any time, and the thought terrified him. Max had grown to like the shotgun-wedding idea; writing Irish's parents that he intended to marry their daughter was a stroke of genius.

Ida and Ruben Dalton, Florida retirees, had once owned a small vineyard. Katherine had tossed him the idea in an offhand remark about how her parents would love immediately any man who knew how to make wine.

According to his research, a small winery near the inn was possible with irrigation. Granny had located an acreage bordering Abagail's and had gotten Max a good price for the land.

Rocking slowly, Max thought of holding his baby in the middle of the night. Patting the bear's bottom, he thought of holding Irish anytime he could.

She fitted into his life with a softness that filled his heart.

In the room next to the nursery, Irish stripped in front of the full-length mirror. According to Max's chart, she'd gained twelve pounds. All of them pressed tightly against her white cotton briefs and bra.

She ran her palm over the small mound and was rewarded by a small kick. Turning to the side, Irish studied her body. She'd always been . . . rounded, she decided benignly and hoped that the cocoa butter helped freckles stretch, too.

"Pudgy," she muttered, turning her back to the mirror. Her breasts ballooned over the edge of her bra, which had been loosened to the last loops.

She'd never been interested in fashion or investing time and energy in getting the "right look." But Max hadn't seemed to mind; of course he was obligated to compliment her—a happy mother's disposition was good for the baby. Those fond pats to her bottom when no one was looking were designed to make her feel feminine—another part of Max's expectant-mother program, added to the blood-pressure and diet charts. As the responsible paternal party, Max cheerfully monitored her body systems, poking a thermometer into her mouth if she sneezed and measuring her waist every two weeks.

She didn't want those brotherly kisses he'd been serving.

She turned her back to the mirror in a Betty Grable pose and tried her sexiest look. She wet her lips, parted them and leaned her head back, fluttering her eyelashes. A plain old earth mother stared back at her, rounded from shoulders to thighs. If ever she'd wanted to wear fancy black lace panties and bra to excite a man, it was now—when she felt like a potato and Max wasn't giving her those seductive kisses. In fact, Max was keeping his distance. She sniffed, ignoring the lively music of fiddles, and spoons clicking to the beat, beneath her window.

Max said he wanted to marry her. Good old Max, trying to make her *feel* as though she was beautiful, spreading his compliments around like Granny's favorite pâté. Good old Max, squiring her on medicinal twenty-minute walks every morning and evening. In another month, he wouldn't be able to stretch his arm around her waist. Max's hand always seemed to slide lower, riding her hips and smoothing them. Irish frowned at that rounded curve, suspiciously spotting what she thought was another fleshy inch.

She did like those walks, being tucked close to the safety of his chest and the scents of his after-shave caused little excited tremors to race through her—or was it her disturbed hormones? She wanted to wake up to those scents and tremors every morning and pat his freshly showered back dry. Irish closed her eyes, remembering Max's back—wide shoulders with muscles that rippled beneath dark skin, tapering down to the cutest little dimple....

Sleeping wasn't easy in an ex-bordello, she'd discovered. The nuances of past lovers clung to walls, steeping her in restless wistful dreams. Before Max had zoomed into the valley in his Porsche she'd slept marvelously well. She'd practically dozed through the early part of her pregnancy, but now the nights were endless—even with the baby's comforting kicks. She'd begun to think of ways to seduce Max back into her bed—just to have him near her. "Oh, spare me, Irish. How low can you get?" she asked the reflection. "You've never played the femme fatale, and now your equipment isn't exactly in champion shape."

She turned to the side, viewing her eggplant shape intently. "I miss sleeping on my stomach," she muttered, remembering cuddling to Max's sturdy back. She'd tried the giant panda in the nursery, but somehow fuzzy cloth wasn't like rippling muscle and warm skin.

Max's reverent kisses may have slipped over the edge to sensual once or twice, but for the most part, he was keeping his distance.

No one was letting her do all the things she loved—cooking special dishes, serving apple cider to the guests, cleaning and freshening the rooms. All those little cherishy things she loved to do for her guests were outlawed, tabooed and generally dismissed. "Put your feet up, rest awhile," she repeated darkly. Link's comments were always prime—"Take some weight off your feet."

"Hell's bells, stop whining, lady." Irish scowled at the mirror. She wasn't into scooping up sacrificial males, no matter how well they carried off the attentive father-to-be role.

Obligation now wouldn't keep Max happy later, she reminded herself again. Nobility could be stretched only so far, then it would snap, and Max would find himself in a situation he wouldn't want for a lifetime.

A long curl slid across her cheek, and Irish blew it out of the way. She'd meant to cut her hair, but somehow never found the time. Irish thrust it into a ponytail high on her head, tied a blue ribbon into the wild curly mass and studied the effect. She didn't look like a woman who would suit Max—sleek worldly Max. She looked like a freckle-faced young girl with huge eyes and a soft vulnerable mouth. Or like a woman who didn't have a clue in the world how to appeal to a man like Max. Of course he tried to make her *feel* as if she were a crepe instead of a pancake. But then there was that obligation thing of his. "The old ball and chain," she muttered.

While she struggled to keep from waddling, Max had begun to swagger just a tad, she decided moodily. Shielded in his new rugged Western look, he'd developed into a warm friendly person with a sense of humor. Those laughter lines were deepening beside his eyes; his mouth had lost that flat hard edge. And the cutest little twinkle flirted with her from his dark brown eyes.

She rubbed her stomach, easing the tightened skin. When Max did laugh, the rich genuine sound warmed her clear through. Last night Link played his harmonica, and Max had instigated a kitchen hoedown with the ladies from the bus, and Granny and Nadia. The impromptu dance squashed a hot skirmish over paraffin options for jars of apple butter. When he'd spotted Irish, his eyes had darkened and he'd swung her gently against him. His kiss had been long and searching, so intensely hungry that she'd barely heard the ladies' wistful oohs and ahhs.

Max had traded in his calculator-for-a-heart image for... the happy-daddy look that tracked her every movement.

How was she going to manage watching Max hold the baby, caring for him when he grew? What if Max found someone else?

Someone lean and stylish who wasn't shaped like an eggplant.

Irish sniffed again and turned toward the bed. Strewn across it was an assortment of new maternity clothes, from casual to dressy. Across one T-shirt, big wide letters screamed, "Baby Cargo."

Caressing the baby, Irish whispered, "Don't get the wrong idea down there. You're wanted very much. It's just that your daddy isn't obliged to marry me. I can putt along without his sympathy."

Allowing herself one more sniff, Irish began trying on clothes. Katherine had sent boxes from Denver's exclusive shops, a sisterly gift. While Irish preferred T-shirts, sweatshirts and jeans, Katherine's taste ran to sweaters and jumpers, trim business suits and designer jeans. These clothes however, ran to frilly lace, ruffles and tiny splashes of nosegays on blue and pink backgrounds.

Irish lifted the pink maternity jumper to study it, then she frowned. Katherine, a sleek blonde, wasn't the type to choose the old-fashioned country-girl look. Nor was she likely to buy jumpers with bears scooting around on tricycles, or fluorescent maternity sweatsuits with "Call Me Mommy" in big letters across the chest.

Irish held up a lacy white dress. Cut in a simple princess style with a wide collar and long puffy sleeves, the dress was exquisite right down to its big satin bow at the bodice. Katherine had pinned a tag on it—"From me to you." Another tag slithered from the folds of the next box from a lingerie shop—Katherine's elegant script read, "Go get him, sis."

Carefully folded between sheaths of tissue paper, a pale blue teddy with an expandable front panel rested in all its transparent glory. "She's certainly picked the wrong time to develop her sense of humor. Max hasn't even come close to me."

Irish lifted an immense bra to her chest and groaned. "Great. Just what I need—room for expansion."

Taking a deep steadying sigh, Irish grabbed a dress, took a courageous breath and dived into it.

Tiny white sprigs danced around the loose blue cotton, and white lace skittered around the wide collar and sleeves. The tiny pearl buttons on the puffy sleeves matched the buttons at the throat. The bodice clung to her chest and draped loosely down her legs. The bow stuck out from her chest like a pom-pom.

Irish sniffed back a sob, smoothing the strings of the pom-pom. Max, in his obligated kindness, hadn't mentioned her breasts or parts south. But there they were, like two huge balloons.

In fact, Max hadn't touched her anywhere but at her back. He probably couldn't find her waist. Oh, he may have sighed a little when he gave her an obligatory hug. And no doubt his uneven breath was from the effort. And the trembling, too.

Irish blinked back a tear. She couldn't blame him for not wanting her. She'd grabbed his fifty-to-one chance of pregnancy and run with it like an experienced quarterback with a football.

She didn't want to answer the knock at her bedroom door.

"Honey," a woman's voice called softly.

"Mother!" she exclaimed just as the door swung open to reveal her parents.

"My little girl!" Her father's outraged tone swept into the room.

"Baby," her mother cried softly, her eyes widening on Irish's maternity dress. "My sweet little innocent baby girl..."

Max entered the scenario, standing a head above her parents. In the shadows of the hallway, his expression was grim and his body rigid. "Irish is having my baby."

Much shorter, her father pivoted slowly as though at any moment he'd reach for the nonexistent six-shooter at his hip. "*You* sent the letter. You're Van Damme. I'm Ruben Dalton, Irish's father," he said in a deadly tone, spelling out his parental rights to the usurper. "Irish Serene is my daughter."

"She's my baby girl," Ida added in a righteous tone to the seducer of her child.

Max smiled his warmest, most devastating new-father best down at her parents. "I want to marry her. She isn't buying."

A collection of the tour couples had gathered in the hallway. "Marry the poor guy," an elderly gentleman leaning on a cane called.

"The baby needs a name," a dignified gray-haired giantess added.

"The baby has my name," Max said, smiling benignly in his supreme confidence. "It's a formality that the baby takes the father's name."

"Try again, son," a retired attorney stated quietly. He nodded toward Irish. "Mama there holds the reins."

"My grandson deserves the best," Ruben began huffily, turning to his wife. "Ida, make plans to move from Florida. My grandson needs someone to raise him and I guess it will have to be me," he ordered, glaring up at Max. "A boy can't just be tossed into the world. He needs to know how to catch trout and slide into first base..."

"I know how to fish and play ball," Max said between his teeth, returning the glare.

Ruben looked up Max's tall body, then back down. "Bet you can't slide into base worth a hoot. You're a damned foreigner to this grand state of Colorado. A city slicker to boot. Throw in making your living with a computer and what do you get?" he asked, his face coloring with anger. "Some fly-by-night yahoo—"

"Pop," Ida interrupted softly just as the tears came to Irish's eyes. "Look how pretty she is in a dress and her hair in a ribbon. Our little girl—"

"She's the most beautiful woman in the world," Max stated emphatically. Then he loomed down over the smaller man and ground his teeth a moment before saying very quietly, "Could we continue this later? The guests are here for peace and quiet."

"No, we're not," three of the grandmotherly types returned. "Go right on ahead. I know a lot about this situation—went through it with my daughter, and her marriage turned out just fine."

Ida moved into the room and smiled at Irish. "Hello, honey," she said, brushing a curl back from her daughter's hot cheek.

The two men, keeping a wary distance between each other, stepped into the room and closed the door.

Max stopped, shot a hard assessing glance at Irish, then moved swiftly to pick her up. Too tired to deal with a full-fledged Dalton-style hullabaloo, Irish simply leaned her head against Max's safe shoulder as he lifted her into his arms. He tensed, holding her tightly against him. Then he kissed her cheek once and her lips twice in short bits of care that soothed her rumpled nerves. Max moved to an old rocker and sat in it, still holding Irish. Ignoring her parents, he kissed her a third time, more slowly, tenderly.

Irish found herself responding, lifting her lips to receive his kiss. She cradled Max's jaw with her palm, soothing him. "I'll protect you," she offered, kissing his hard cheek.

In the background her father moved restlessly. *"Protect him?"*

Her mother pushed aside the maternity clothing on the bed and sat watching them closely. "I'm really good at putting on weddings, Max," she offered quietly. "With all my experience, I could throw one together in half a day—a day at the most—with everyone's help."

Irish let herself fall into Max's warm gaze; Max looked at her as though he'd just discovered ice cream—the interesting double-dutch-cherry-nut kind. She saw herself in his eyes as they moved over her face and hair, taking in the jumbled curls and the feminine lacy collar. His gaze swept slowly down her loose dress, his mouth beginning to curve in a wolfish smile.

In another instant, they were alone with Ruben's muffled outrage and Ida's soothing tones coming from the hallway. When the lock clicked, Irish whispered shakily, "She's locked us in. She used to do that to Katherine and me when we fought. We made up just to see daylight again."

She blushed as Max's fingers found the bow and prowled around it. "I've never seen you in anything but pants—or nothing but freckles," he added naughtily. "Don't be shy, Irish," he said in a low hungry drawl that deepened her blush.

"I'm bosomy," she said.

"Mmm, sexy." Max stood and carried her to the bed.

"Max..." she protested weakly as he placed her on the bed and stretched out beside her. "Max..." she whispered shakily as his eyes darkened to silky black, his expression intent as he leaned over her. His fingers played with the bow and the lace, tormenting her sensitive breasts.

"Marry me, Irish," he murmured, lowering his head to kiss her lips.

While Irish hazily tried to find reality, Max's lips were building his case. They slid across her hot cheeks and down her throat where he had just unbuttoned and exposed new grazing area. She swallowed, trying to keep her traitorous senses on a level keel, but they kept shifting and heating.

"You're beautiful," he murmured in the proximity of her collarbone, his hand slowly lifting the hem of the dress to find her thigh. His mouth found hers again, brushing tempting little unsatisfying kisses across it.

Her fingers had somehow found all that nice hair covering his chest and were rummaging through it. Somehow her other hand was trailing through his crisp hair, mussing it and finding the way it curled to the back of his strong neck. Between kisses, she looked up at Max's flushed intent face and whispered, "You don't have to do this, Max. My parents will migrate back to Florida when they see they can't have their way."

Breathing heavily, Max ran his hand up her thigh and across the baby nestling in her. When he rubbed the small mound, the kicking movements stilled. "I put him back to sleep," he whispered proudly. "I've got the daddy touch. I could put him to sleep every night if you'll marry me," he whispered, foraging with tiny kisses a direct trail toward the spot behind her ear.

But Irish wanted his lips on hers, wanted the taste of his hunger. Max allowed her to draw him back, to nibble on his lips while his fingers eased open her tiny pearl buttons. When he held back the kiss she wanted desperately, Max ran his finger around her sensitized lips, tugging at the bottom one. "Marry me," he urged, the dark passion in his eyes igniting her hunger.

"No, Max. Marriage for the baby's sake or mine isn't necessary," she managed huskily.

"It's necessary for me," he stated roughly, just before his mouth took hers fully.

The kiss was long and devastating. Her theory that she could manage without Max shot out into the sweeping autumn wind. When she tugged him closer, Max resisted.

When she moved to pull him back, he whispered, "Marry me."

"Yes, Max."

After a deep kiss that stoked their hunger, Max forced himself away from her. Irish snuggled to his side, the eggplant and balloon syndromes kissed away. When she pressed a kiss to his damp chest—his shirt had been opened somehow—Max groaned shakily, stilling her wandering fingers. "How fast did your mother say she could put a wedding together?"

Eight

"What am I doing?" A week later, Irish gripped the stairway handrail tightly with her left hand, the one with Max's heirloom-style engagement ring on it. The afternoon light coming from the stained-glass window caught the heart-shaped diamond and sent out myriad colors. Through her wedding veil, the expressions of her family and friends looking up at her ranged from wistful to delighted. The inn's antique organ played the "Wedding March," and the white dress Katherine had given her slid silkily over a lace maternity teddy.

Irish listened to her heart beat heavily. She gripped the frothy bouquet of pink roses and white daisies tightly and swallowed. The movement lifted the antique sapphire necklace Max had sent to her just before the wedding. She blinked, fighting back tears. Sapphires and roses weren't her style, more fitting for a model on the cover of a bridal magazine. Yet the stones matched the current shade of her eyes, bringing out the dewy dark blue color, and the pink roses were exactly the color of her cheeks—beneath the freckles. Piled high on her head, her long curls danced when she turned, tiny tendrils fluttering at the back of her neck. Taking a last look in the full-length mirror earlier, she'd realized she looked radiant beneath the bridal veil.

In the past week she'd been pampered and shushed and shooed away from anything that resembled work. Katherine, her mother, Granny and Nadia had jumped into action, inviting neighbors, relatives and a collection of her favorite guests. The ten couples had stayed past their checkout date; the women bustled through the house making tiny candies and comparing cake, punch and groom's-cake recipes. The men, including J.D., had equaled the tasks under Ida's and Granny's direction. Katherine had been placed in charge of Irish's uncertain temperament and had advised Max to keep his distance.

Throughout the hectic week, Max remained serene, his checklists thrusting from his pockets, and his eyes tracking Irish. Her father grumbled that the cart had been placed before the horse. But he liked Max—who had apparently passed the "What're your intentions for my little girl?" test.

The full-scale wedding was the combined effort of the two males. Her father was adamant about escorting his baby girl down the aisle, and Max couldn't be swayed into a practical civil ceremony. He wanted a traditional wedding: ribbons, baskets of roses and daisies, beeswax candles and French champagne served in long-stemmed crystal glasses. He'd insisted that a seamstress add another lacy tier to the dress.

Tonight she'd share the cottage with Max; her parents would use her room for the duration of their visit. No doubt Max had been properly threatened by her father and Katherine. Everything was arranged.

There was no going back. *Did she want to?*

Somehow she'd jumped through time zones, shucked her jeans and T-shirt and slithered into bridal white lace and a coronet of pink baby roses and daisies. Her wedding would serve as the kickoff to Abagail's Fall Fiesta.

Irish couldn't worry about Abagail's now; she had to think of herself. And Max. And the baby.

Poor Max. Pressured by his own code of ethics, he was obliged to marry her, a temporary patch on a bad situation. He couldn't possibly love her now, just at the waddly-pudgy stage. Max was gallant; he wanted to shield her from gossip and protect the baby, too.

But that wasn't love.

Max was performing exactly like he thought he should, right down to the wedding.

When would he discover his mistake? He'd wake up one morning and wonder why he'd been so noble.

At least he hadn't lied by telling her of a love that didn't exist. Max was too noble to lie, too upright to leave her in a maternity bridal gown.

Frantic, Irish shivered, looking down at her father who waited at the bottom of the stairs. Without Max, she could have managed her life and the baby's....

The minister waited in the parlor. The matron of honor, Katherine, and the best man, J.D., stood beside him.

Max needed someone to really love. Not a marriage trap.

He couldn't say he loved her—because he didn't.

One day he'd hate her....

Irish swallowed again.

As if reminded of his father, the baby kicked impatiently against her side. Then Irish started slowly down the stairs to take Ruben's arm.

Max waited with the minister, Katherine and J.D. Her mother sniffed from the rows of folding chairs, and her father's hand gripped hers tightly. Dressed in a gray tuxedo, Maxwell Van Damme was elegant, and the sight of him made her heart beat faster and the baby kick frantically. His eyes flickered over her, and his harsh features seemed to soften. She met his eyes, holding them as she walked slowly to his side, leaving her father's hand.

The wedding vows were spoken, her voice husky as she answered the minister's questions. Then Max was lifting her veil, taking her gently into his arms and kissing her sweetly as though she were his heart, his love.

Oh, he had to do that for appearances, she thought distantly. When his arm kept her close, Irish ached with the bittersweet pain. Ached for Max and the charade she'd put him through. She almost sobbed when he kissed away a tear.

Nadia caught the bouquet. Rafe, J.D.'s handsome brother, caught the blue garter from her leg, and Jonathan had arrived to take formal wedding pictures. Mac, J.D.'s other brother, and his wife, Diana, helped Granny and Link serve the guests at the reception.

Later, alone in the cottage—he'd insisted on carrying her over the threshold—Max's kisses changed and became filled with an immediate hunger she returned. "At last," he murmured softly, lifting the rose buds from her hair. Max carefully removed the pins holding her ringlets on top of her head and dropped them to the floor.

Finding the teddy beneath her gown, Max's darkened gaze caressed the lace slowly, intently. "Cute," he said softly, slipping a finger under the strings and tugging them free. "But freckles are better."

During the long exquisite night, Max kept her close and kissed away her tears.

Two days later, Irish tidied up the cottage, left a note for Max and set out for her favorite thinking spot in a stand of aspens. Max, Ida and Ruben were off to his "vineyards," leaving her to sleep. She'd badly needed the time alone. Somehow no one needed her anymore. The guests were fiesta-ing themselves silly with barbecues, whittling contests hoedowns, and had generally run over the inn.

Irish walked through high dry weeds, gathering her coat around her. Clouds skimmed the sky, sweeping shadows across the craggy mountains. A deer leapt gracefully over a bubbling stream on its way to a field. A hawk soared high in the sky, screeching, and aspen leaves crackled beneath her feet.

The arrival of her parents had tripped off a fast pace, and Max hadn't given her a quiet moment to think.

Max was acting exactly like a new bridegroom should—if only she didn't feel that he was only trying to reassure her parents.

On the ski slope, workmen were testing the lifts.

The new cables were to have been installed and running properly for guests who wanted to take in the panoramic views. Irish paused, brushing a curl back from her face as she watched the laborious climb of the empty seats up the slope. The movement was jerky, the machinery fighting the cables.

Picking her way across a rock embankment, Irish headed toward the small shed housing the motor. Jeff met her at the doorway, wiping his oily hands on a rag. "Hi, Irish."

His eyes ran down her body like slimy hands, and Irish suddenly remembered his furious expression at the wedding. Then she'd been too wrapped up in her own emotions, but now seemed a perfect time to talk with him. "Hello, Jeff. How's it going?"

"Going fine. The men have just put in the new cable...." He paused when Irish's gaze skimmed the rusty worn cable. Before Max's precise notations, she'd left the machinery and fields to Jeff while she'd maintained the inn and near grounds.

"A new cable?" she repeated, running her fingers along a length and looking down at the rust on them.

Jeff's hard face flushed, and his eyes brightened with anger. "Look, you just keep Van Damme happy and keep him out of my business," he snarled, shifting into a defensive stance. "You get pregnant—the guy naturally feels obligated to stick around until the kid is born. Hell, he even does his duty and marries you, but that isn't any reason for me to put up with him. He's been sticking his nose into my business. That's why I got those blueprints from his house."

"You went into the cottage?"

"Damn right. Got worked over for it, too. Van Damme wouldn't have touched me, but he's got these foreign moves. The guy's not human, except when it comes to you. A regular machine. Keep him away from me."

"Max had a right to protect his privacy, Jeff. You had no right to pilfer."

A cold wind swept up her neck and she shivered. Jeff's angry accusation mirrored her thoughts while she'd walked. With her parents arriving on Abagail's doorstep, Max was compromised into marrying her. Of course, he hadn't wanted her to be uncomfortable, and the wedding solved everyone's problems but hers. She didn't want him trussed and stuffed and serve up into a marriage without... without what Max deserved most—lots of love.

She crushed a thistle stalk in her hand, ignoring the tiny thorns prickling her skin. Max had been forced by his personal code to stand before a minister and promise to love her.

What did he really feel?

Max hadn't said he loved her; she hadn't expected it.

Irish shivered, realizing how deeply Max had infiltrated her heart.

The cable creaked loudly, bringing Irish's thoughts back to Jeff. Suddenly all the discrepancies in Jeff's stories about his needy family fell into neat little shards at his feet.

She hadn't seen Jeff's livid anger before and now that she had, Irish didn't like it.

She touched the cable, and when she held up her hand, the rust color was evident. Jeff scowled and tossed the rag aside. "Yeah, so what?" he asked belligerently. "I've been running this place pretty damn good for years, and you're not ruining anything I've got going."

The game warden had come asking questions about Jeff's trips into the mountains with a group of male guests. Trophy deer had been drugged and staked out for hunter's bullets, and hearsay had brought the law to Abagail's. Irish thought of the tractor, dying just past its warranty. Rather like a marriage after a beautiful wedding... "You're fired," she said quietly, looking up at him. "Leave your forwarding address with Granny—she'll see you get paid what's due you."

"The hell I am," he muttered, reaching for her. Then a shadow moved across Jeff's face, and Max stepped into view.

"That's enough," Max said quietly, placing his arm around Irish's shoulder and easing her aside.

Irish shook loose. "Stay out of this, Max," she said between her teeth, glaring at Jeff.

"Fine. When you cool down, you can handle it any way you want. But not now," he added, glancing at Jeff. Max took her hand in his and looked at Jeff. The air stilled between them; Max loomed dangerously over the smaller man. A taut muscle moved in his cheek. The veneer of civilization slipped from him, and he stood like a gunfighter, long legs locked and his hands hanging loosely by his sides. "You heard her. Go on."

In that instant, Irish thought of the mountain men and pioneers who had stood their ground, defending what was precious to them against enemies and the elements. The same fierce savagery, barely trimmed, skimmed along Max's hard face.

She swallowed, remembering all the gentle times. The same harsh dark eyes flickering dangerously at Jeff who had warmed her with tenderness.

Then she knew that Max had not revealed himself like that to anyone else; he'd kept that loving part of himself for her. Whatever it was that Max hoarded for her alone, she'd treasure.

After Jeff had skulked off, thinking better of tangling with Max, Irish shivered, suddenly realizing the dangerous position in which she'd placed the baby and herself. For a moment Jeff had terrified her and now, knees shaking, she felt the full impact.

"You came after me," she whispered, wrapping her arms around his waist.

"I'll always come after you." Taking her into his arms, Max held her quietly. Against her temple, he spoke in an uneven low raspy tone. "Dear heart, promise me you won't face anything or anyone in a situation like this without me. I couldn't bear losing... Just don't."

After a long while, he tipped her chin up. "Hey, we're partners, remember? Like Bogie and Bacall, Roy and Dale, the Marx brothers—"

She couldn't help grinning, wrapping her arms tightly around him. "There's three of them."

"And three of us," he murmured before kissing her.

"Psst. Max, are you busy?" The Whiz whispered from the intercom.

Max opened one eye, pulled Irish's warm soft body closer and nuzzled the jumble of curls lying across the pillow. He noted mentally that the next time he had Irish in his arms, there wouldn't be an intercom or a telephone in the room.

Irish mumbled about obligations and anchovies on whipped cream, rummaging for a pillow to put over her head.

"Psst," The Whiz insisted. "Got a glitch in the communications systems. Can't find out whether pork bellies are up or down. Think you can spare a minute to come over here?"

Shifting his thigh aside to allow for Irish's comfort, Max closed his eyes. "Do I have a choice?"

"Pork bellies are important, Max," The Whiz reasoned. "Tell you what. I'll cut you a deal you can't refuse. After the baby is born and Irish is back to feeling pert, Link and I will run the inn for a solid month while you hightail it out of here with your family. When the baby is old enough, we'll baby-sit while you..."

At the inn, Max quickly answered The Whiz's questions, then started working on a breakfast tray for Irish. He'd wanted to serve her breakfast that first morning. Now three days later, he hadn't managed to leave her until it was time to have lunch with the guests and her family at the inn.

Her family. Irish had been raised in the warmth of a loving family. Ruben and Ida's love filled a room when they entered it. Katherine and Irish bantered, giggled and hugged.

Stirring the wooden spoon in the copper pot as the mixture thickened and ignoring the ringing telephone, Max wondered if Irish knew what she had cried out in the night. *Oh, Max, I love you... love you... love you.*

The soft passionate cry had gripped him in fear. He didn't want to hurt her. But he might. Irish needed everything a man with a loving heart could give.

Staring at the hot mixture, Max sorted methodically through his emotions. When he'd been alone, the absence of love in him hadn't mattered. But she needed to know that he cared. That she was the one shining thing to happen in his life.

Granny's voice slid into the kitchen from the intercom just as Max was flipping a crepe. "Personal call from Geneva on the line, Max. Sounds important."

He picked up the kitchen telephone while thickening the raspberry sauce. "Van Damme here."

"Max. This is Elena. How are you?" The voice of his mother caught Max in the stomach, reminding him that his world before Irish had been a cold and painful one. He placed the raspberry mixture aside and turned off the burner.

"I'm fine. How are you and Father?" A muscle tightened in his cheek and ran into his throat; Max rubbed his palm across the burning pain in his stomach. He didn't dislike his parents, but if Irish glimpsed the prominent Van Damme family trait...

"Excellent. Our genetic report on familial associations was well received. What projects are you working on? According to your message center in New York, you've been tied up on some rural Colorado project." Max frowned, noting that this was his mother's expression of caring—a periodical progress report that she could file under "Van Damme, Maxwell—Male Child."

At his side, a soft fragrance and a softer touch told him that Irish had entered the room. He couldn't hide his uneasiness that his parents might ruin the one relationship he wanted most in the world.

The Van Dammes weren't vicious people, but their lack of warmth could cut a loving heart to shreds; no one knew that better than he did. Placing his cheek in the curling reddish blond hair, he gathered Irish's softness against his side, shielding her. Or was he shielding himself?

Irish's comforting arms wrapped around him while he completed the necessary report. He omitted Irish and the baby as her hand gently rubbed his stomach. Then, when he replaced the telephone in its cradle, he realized he'd been trembling. "You're not going to tell them," Irish said quietly, her dark blue eyes looking up at him.

"No. Not now."

"Max," she whispered, leaning against him, "everything is going to be just fine."

"I don't want them near you. Or the baby," he said finally, realizing how poorly equipped he was to fight fear.

"Sweetheart," she murmured, resting her head on his shoulder. "Haven't I protected you against the Daltons?"

He wanted to smile, but the past lurked too near the treasure he'd just found. Irish leaned back and the bright jumble of her curls spilled over his arm, warming his flesh. She ran her hand down his cheek, caressing and soothing him. "Time to let go, Max," she whispered finally.

"No, I can't afford them touching my life now," he managed huskily. "Not even for you."

Once her parents had left for Florida, Irish was at Max's mercy again. Her father had gotten her a brief respite, claiming Max's attentions for the new vineyard partnership. They bickered pleasantly about top billing on the sign—Van Damme versus Dalton.

Her mother had offered brief protection when she'd snagged Max for an afternoon of creek fishing. Ida thought of Max as "just a little boy, cute as a button when he catches a fish. Can't wait for my grandson if he's anything like Max."

But now he was back in charge, discussing her examinations with Dr. Williams and making certain that she'd remembered her specimen jars.

At the evening organizational meeting of prepared-childbirth class, Max snarled at Nurse MacMannis, "No, I'm not going to drown the baby. Pick on someone your own size." The rubber doll he'd been bathing and diapering for twenty-two minutes squeaked, protesting his tight hold. J.D.'s gift to Max, the deluxe model of Baby-Wetcakes, promptly dampened Max's jeans in an inappropriate place.

"Get used to it. Comes with the territory," MacMannis crowed, shooting Irish a conspiratorial grin as Max frowned and dabbed at the wet spot. She nudged Max with her elbow. "It's November—she's in her seventh month, Max. Two more months and you'll be putting all this good training to use. You'll want to kiss me when it's over."

Max muttered a dark phrase about her kissing something, and the nurse grinned up at him. "Boy, do I love to get big macho guys like you in my childbirth classes. I can usually crack the cool prepared ones on the first night. Takes the starch out of 'em so they make better coaches."

Max shot Irish a look of pure fury.

She blew him back a kiss.

MacMannis kept the pressure on Max during the orientation session, and Irish kept on blowing him kisses. Caught between the curt demands of the starchy little nurse and the promise of Irish's kisses later, Max was delightfully confused.

When he botched a session of "slow deep chest breathing" with an improper count, MacMannis resorted to tapping him on the head. "Bad boy."

Later that night, Max threw the crumpled practice schedule onto the four-poster bed. "MacMannis is an animal. In the morning, I'm checking out her credentials as a qualified leader. Even her toenails better be squeaky clean. I think we should consider an apartment in Denver just before the baby is due. This whole thing needs a good working system."

Irish sat on the bed, propped up with pillows, and enjoyed the delightful sight of Max, rumpled and outraged, stalking across their bedroom floor. His fingers rummaged through the hair on his bare chest as he thought about ways to systemize MacMannis. The white boxer shorts set off his dark skin, fluttering against his hard thighs when he moved.

Running his hand across the stubble covering his jaw, Max paused. His gaze skimmed Irish's face, hesitated as though caught in the act of boiling the nurse in oil, then ran leisurely down the T-shirt covering her body to her legs. He returned her grin slowly. "You like her, don't you?"

"Uh-huh. It's been a hard day, hasn't it, Maxi?" In the hospital, he had paled and leaned against the wall when they'd passed the birthing room and a woman's high-pitched scream shot out into the hallway. First-time fathers-to-be were given a tiny newborn to hold, and Max had actually shuddered. He'd held the infant clumsily, letting the baby nuzzle on his shoulder. Just when Max had begun to relax, the baby had burped.

Walking slowly to the bed, Max looked down at her, his face in the shadows. "Irish, I'm not about to let anything happen to you. I'm serious about the Denver apartment. Or we could stay at your sister's. A hospital is just two miles from them."

She took his hand and drew him down beside her. Max had grown so necessary in her life, she thought, placing her cheek over his heart and listening to the comforting steady beat. She smoothed the hair on his chest, patting him. His fingers tangled in her hair, finding her scalp and rubbing it gently.

Foraging in the night, coyotes howled. Irish closed her eyes and drifted with the luxurious caress; no wonder Mimi ran to Max. "Everything will be fine, Max. You'll see. But if it makes you feel better you can have your helicopter pad."

He kissed her forehead. "Thanks. Can you promise me better treatment from MacMannis?"

The baby kicked against him, and Max placed his palm over it. His awed expression tugged at Irish and she stroked his hair.

"The doctor said the baby is fairly small but healthy, Irish. He thinks you'll make it through without a cesarean delivery," Max stated quietly. "I don't want anything to happen to either one of you."

"Nothing is going to happen, Max. You'll be there, remember?"

Max looked at her, his dark eyes flickering. "Such trust. What if I come apart? What if I faint?"

She ran a finger down the groove next to his mouth. "Then MacMannis will toss you over her shoulder and carry you off."

Max caught the finger in his mouth, nibbling it. "Did I ever tell you how much those exercises you do turn me on?"

"Nah. No way."

"Wanna bet?" Max murmured, drawing her into his arms.

In the kitchen, Max retained his image of a swashbuckler boarding a new prize ship.

"Back off, Max," Irish ordered as Max checked his grocery list. "We are not having truffled capon for Thanksgiving. We're having turkey, turkey, turkey. Plain old turkey buffet with pumpkin pie and whipped cream. With mashed potatoes and green beans. With apple pie and Waldorf salad. Plain stuff the guests count on year after year."

Living with Max wasn't easy, she decided, watching him digest the thought of "plain stuff." On Max's "Wednesday Night" she allowed him to cook to his heart's delight. The guests picked suspiciously at the food while Max hovered with the perfect wine to compliment the dish. His selection of dinner music drove most of them to the local tavern where they could dance to country tunes, drink draft beer and eat stale pretzels.

He arched his left brow, the disbelieving one. Then he leveled a contemplative look at her. "Turkey—with oyster stuffing?"

Irish leaned against the counter and placed her fist on her waist—what she could find of it. "With giblets," she said tightly, rubbing her lower back.

Max's hand found the matching spot in his spine. "What about truffled turkey? Or I could..." Max sifted through an immense collection of recipes, all of them untried. Jabbing his finger on a prize, he said, "There. You couldn't ask for anything better than a ham in decorated crust."

Riffling through the recipes, he snatched another treasure. "*Pintades au champagne*—stuffed guinea hens. The guests will love them...." He stopped in midsentence, his eyes flickering as he rubbed his back and stretched painfully. "Damn! My back is getting ready to go out. Aches. Old soccer injury."

Irish rubbed her lower back and scowled at him. "Max, you know what's happening, don't you?"

He scowled back, rubbing the injury. "Yes, damnit, I do. You're not receptive to new foods. I want stuffed capons for Thanksgiving."

She stared at him and took a deep steadying breath. "I refuse to argue the point. Abagail's is having turkey and pumpkin pie made from fresh field pumpkins. The tom is stuffed with natural grains and all dolled up. You put anything else on my table and I won't be responsible for the guests. You may be invited to a tar-and-feather party." Just then Irish had a magnificent stroke of genius. There were more subtle ways to pay Max back for invading her kingdom, for wrapping her in cotton wool so tightly she couldn't move without him at her side.

That evening, Max knelt beside Irish in the dimly lit room of the hospital. According to him, the peaceful background music lacked technique but was just MacMannis's style.

He held Irish's hand and counted her slow deep chest breaths; she found his soft male chanting almost seductive. Max would look delectable in hospital scrubs, Irish thought while he coached her calmly à la MacMannis. "The contraction is ending...take a deep cleansing breath. In through your nose, now let it out...slowly...let it all out."

Concentrating on his wristwatch, Max frowned and glanced down at her. "Breathe, Irish. This is not game time, you know. We're not having the turkey-versus-capon debate now. MacMannis said sixty-second contractions—that's the deal. If we can pass these, we'll move on to the fast chest breathing. Remember, you take deep cleansing breaths before the contraction starts and when you feel it leaving..."

She looked up at him, straightening her red cotton knit maternity top over the baby who tried to kick it off. "Max, are you sure you want to interfere with Abagail's traditional turkey buffet?" she asked carefully while Max checked his watch to prepare for a new sixty-second contraction.

"There are some things a man just has to do," he muttered, getting the go-for-the-gusto look on his face. "Now you remember the uterine stroking, don't you? Get ready..."

Irish thought about her plan through the fast shallow "hee... hee..." breaths at the peak of her sixty-second contraction. The slide into the second stage of labor, "transition," had totally absorbed Max.

"Turkey," she said after the last cleansing breath.

"Capon. Shh. MacMannis is talking about dilating and centimeters. All this information is really going to be helpful. Everything is going to be systematic, running on a schedule. A piece of cake. The monitors will track the baby's heartbeat and your contractions. A surgical crew will be standing by... but you won't need them... there's nothing to worry about." Max adjusted the pillow under her back and rubbed her tummy absently as though she were Mimi. "Dr. Williams asked me to stop by the delivery room after this session. He wants The Whiz to check out some transportation stocks...."

Practicing controlled breathing while driving home wasn't easy for Irish. If Max wanted to play hardball on her side of the street, or bake capons in her oven, he'd have to be able to stand the heat. She had Max's payback waiting at the local tavern, Big Jakes.

Of course Max would stop at Big Jakes. He was always very understanding and patient about her frequent visits to the washroom.

In front of the tavern's neon sign, Max buttoned her coat and tucked her collar high around her throat before he let her out of the station wagon. Irish kissed him, almost feeling guilty that they had now arrived at the scene of her intended crime. Patting his cheek, she smiled. "This won't take a minute."

Big Jakes was a classic tavern. The stereotyped dress code was cowboys in pearl-buttoned shirts, jeans and boots, and women wearing the same. Smoke and cooking grease swirled around the tables. Sad songs about love-gone-wrong drifted over the noise. In a corner, a cowboy's tears dripped into his mug of beer.

Max sheltered Irish with his body as a burly man wearing a cowboy hat with a band of pheasant feathers staggered by them. Over the entire scene floated a marvelous aroma of "the best dad-gummed chili dogs ever made." Served with chopped onions and cheese, the foot long 'dogs were served on freshly baked buns and accompanied by batter-fried, baked-potato wedges.

After her visit to the ladies' room, Irish caught sight of Max leaning against a wall. Wearing a shearling coat and jeans, he blended with the Westerners.

Easing past a couple two-stepping to a fast country-and-western tune, Irish touched Max's arm just as a loud burp roared toward them. Wrapping his arm around her shoulders protectively, Max started toward the door.

"Oh, Max," she cooed, digging in her heels. "Wouldn't you just love a Big Jakes 'dog?"

His arm insisted gently and Irish grabbed the back of a chair. "I want one, sweetheart," she stated flatly, dragging the chair with her for a few inches.

"A hot dog. I'll make you one at the inn. Let's go."

"But, Max. I'm craving one of these."

Max's patience lasted until she ordered a banana split, pickles and chips. He rubbed his flat stomach, eyeing the food before her.

The trick was not to have the beer, Irish thought, watching him slowly pale.

And while he was watching her, Max had sipped a tall mug of draft beer with an inch of foam.

"I think I have heartburn," he admitted slowly when she crunched on the last pickle.

"Max, I've been intending to talk with you," Irish said, leaning back in her chair and nibbling on her last chip. "You're much too serious—lighten up. Remember that childbirth is going to be a piece of cake. Want to dance?"

Max's heavy brows shot together, his eyes narrowing at her. "Just what are you trying to pull, Van Damme?"

Irish grinned, feeling for once that she had the upper hand. "Daddies need to know they haven't lost their touch, don't they? I mean, just because you're expecting doesn't mean you're totally over the hill and unappealing."

The dark flickering dangerous light in Max's eyes promised her an experience she wouldn't soon forget.

"Dance? Where?" he asked, scowling at a couple laminated to each other and swaying to the beat of the music.

Later, swaying to the beat and placing her cheek on Max' broad chest, Irish was totally happy. Because Max had bee such a good sport, she rubbed that aching place low on hi back while they danced a slow sensuous two-step. Becaus Max reacted so wonderfully and did enormous things fo her ego, Irish placed her lips against his warm throat an nibbled just the way he liked it.

His long frustrated groan preceded Max's hot sweet kiss Always proper, Max's response startled her into locking he arms around his neck and returning the kiss. When it wa finished, they stared into each other's eyes, breathing hard

"Must be love," a cowboy said in a whiskey voice besid them. "I heard this guy's too stiff-necked and tough to hea up a dance floor. Sure doesn't look like a block of ice t me."

Max's blush preceded a good-natured sheepish grin as th cowboy clapped him on the back. "Congratulations, Pop Irish is topnotch hereabouts. If she can kiss you like that you're okay with us."

Nine

In her last month, Irish surrendered her kitchen to the measuring maniac. She'd completely lost control of Abagail's under Max's fruitcake-and-Christmas-cookie siege.

While managing the ranch with The Whiz backing him up, Max nurtured and hugged Irish. He watched her like a hawk and handled all the little niceties of Christmas. Like strudel and dough baked in the shape of Christmas trees. Like filling the guests' stockings with dainty little cookies and candies.

Irish exercised, rubbed Max's aching lower back and watched her TLC kingdom continue merrily along without her.

The chilled skiers delighted in challenging Max on the slopes. They relished his clove-and-orange-juice grog, chicken-noodle soup with chives, and hot cider with lemon wedges. The Whiz, Link and Nadia played poker with Max until he won all their frosted fudge nutty brownies. Jonathan sent a card he had designed, inviting them to his first rave showing.

Tonight, at Abagail's New Year's Eve party, Max dressed in a cotton ski sweater and jeans. He glowed and threw off sexy laser beams that attracted women of all ages. For Max, Abagail would have gladly taken a deadly bullet in her bosom without regret. Women—unpregnant and lithe—tossed passes at him.

Across the parlor from Irish, Max winked at her. Irish lifted her nose and looked away; she knew he was trying to worm his way into her affections when he'd just served a dish outrageously scampied and truffled. Not down-home seasonal cooking at all. His clam chowder was delicious, she admitted reluctantly. So was his French bread, baked over cornmeal in special pans instead of her cookie sheets.

Seated on a comfortable overstuffed chair with her feet propped up as per Max's instructions, Irish thought of the way Max's kisses had changed in the privacy of their bedroom.

Long sweet kisses, dipped in a tasty dampered hunger and sprinkled with rewarding frustrated male groans.

She rubbed the baby, easing the tightness just under her diaphragm. Max called the baby "Jones" after a cabaret dancer he'd found listed in the madam's memoirs. Nadia had completed her first manuscript, tossed it out to the publishing wolves and had zeroed in on developing a biography of Madame Abagail LaRue Whitehouse. Apparently, Jones, a tiny Frenchwoman, could kick the hat out of a tall cowboy's hand.

Jones, Max said, was also a famous football player who kicked the winning ball in some obscure game. Cabaret or football kicker, Max didn't care.

Irish noted a long lithe brunette with a tiny waist and snaky hips making her way toward Max. Carefully arranging pâtés, canapés and quiches away from the eggnog and cracker-and-cheese trays, Max barely seemed to register the brunette's hot-pink fingernails on his cream-colored sweater. The nails traced his broad shoulder while Max slid the smoked salmon nearer the cheese-ball side.

Irish wanted to waddle over and snatch him from Snake Hips. But instead she practiced her candle-blowing breathing exercise and concentrated on willing one part of her body to relax at a time. She'd been exercising muscles she hadn't known were available, preparing for the birth, and now they started constricting rhythmically.

After all, Max wasn't a brunette's oyster Rockefeller waiting to be plucked from a serving tray. He was happier than a clam in lemon dip. Or was he?

Max glanced at Irish. She was curled in a huge overstuffed chair, looking small and very pregnant in her pink maternity overalls.

His stomach contracted sharply, fear tearing through him. Irish needed to be loved, really loved, by a man who knew all the right things to do. But Irish didn't have a man who knew how to love; she had him, he thought as he walked toward her.

"Hi, beautiful," he said, kneeling at Irish's side.

Misty pansy-blue eyes stared up at him and the single tear coursing down her cheek caught Max broadside. His heart beat painfully in his chest, his throat drying. "What's wrong, Irish?"

She sniffed delicately and another tear slid down her cheek. "You should be skiing in Switzerland. Not stuck with me in the middle of dull Colorado. Max, I want you to start thinking about an annulment. Just because I trapped you doesn't mean you have to spend your life paying for it...and...you'd have visitation rights, too," she finished on a sob. "We're adults. We could manage...."

"What?" Without thinking, Max scooped Irish up in his arms and carried her upstairs.

After placing her on the bed, Max locked the door. "I don't want any interruptions for this discussion. To set the record straight, I wouldn't be here if I didn't want to be. Got it, pansy-eyes?"

God help me, he thought, watching the tears skimming down her cheeks. Clinging to her silvery-gold eyelashes, each shimmering drop wounded him. *He had to convince her that he cared. That he loved her.*

Instead Max sat on the bed and took her hand. "This isn't a temporary affair, Irish. I thought you knew how I felt."

"I'll never be anything like you need, Max." She sniffed, turning away from him. "Go away. Go play with the brunette with the hot-pink fingernails."

"What?" At a loss, Max shook his head and ran his hands through his hair. "What are you talking about?"

"Sex. Here you are, duty bound to a pumpkin." Irish's muffled voice was ragged, drenched in unsobbed tears.

Max blinked, feeling as though he'd just stepped into a world of fairies and gnomes with no road map. One wrong word could land him in the toadstools-and-snakes section.

He filtered through the right things to say, dismissing most of the list as clichés. What he needed for Irish was new and fresh—a genuine mix of words that had never crossed another lover's lips. "I'm married to a sexy pink pumpkin whom—"

Irish's frustrated wail squashed his brief glimpse of success. "See? *A pumpkin!* You feel obligated to cater to me, but you really think I'm a pumpkin. Go pat Mimi. Go rub Morticia's ears."

Whom I love, he'd been about to say. Mimi and Morticia were pushovers. In comparison, Irish was a hard-nosed brute.

And she held the key to his heart, his future.

Downstairs someone started playing an old Sonny and Cher tune to bongo drums, and Max found the erratic rhythm matching his heartbeat. If romantic whimsy was what Irish needed to convince her of his affections—his love—she'd have it. Max rubbed the back of his neck, foraging for just the right words.

After carefully removing Irish's sneakers, he removed his loafers and lay down beside her. He nudged the pillow's pink ruffle aside and studied the antique chandelier overhead. Relating to an emotional pregnant wife wasn't all that easy, he decided as Irish kept her stiff back firmly turned away from him. The nuances of a bordello madam clung to the room; in the past century a cowboy had managed to sway Abagail with romance. Max frowned, concentrating on the brass cupids hanging from the chandelier and trying to draw from these nuances, which Nadia vowed inhabited the room. He tried to tap into that long-ago lover's sweet talk.

The cupids grinned contemptuously down at him.

Irish sniffed again and Max shuddered. Logic wasn't the answer, and whimsy wasn't his style. He'd told her with his body, but now she needed more....

Max ran his fingers through his hair. Telling a woman you love her shouldn't be that difficult, he thought. They'd broken the rules when they started, but he wouldn't have Irish pay for his inadequacies.

Then Irish sniffed again and Max found his fingers smoothing the soft mass of her hair. The curls wound around his hand, clinging to him as softly as Irish had captured his heart.

Coyotes yelped on the mountain and the lonely sound penetrated the room, carrying over the howling winter wind. Snowflakes dusted the windows as Max turned Irish carefully to him.

He blotted her lids with the ruffle, kissing away the tears. Holding her, Max stepped cautiously into whimsy, testing the treacherous waters. "Once upon a time," he began, stroking her hair, "a cowboy came riding out of the West. A wild range rider, a hired gun, bent on suiting himself and—"

"Riding a black Arabian stallion with a silver-studded saddle," Irish interrupted between sniffs, her cheek riding his shoulder.

Max blew aside a reddish-gold tendril. "Hmm?"

Irish nuzzled his shoulder, finding a comfortable spot while Max stroked her lower back. "At least make him sexy, Max."

"Ah... the wild range rider and hired gun rode a black sexy stallion. Is that better?"

She shrugged, slipping an arm around him as the bongos started throbbing. "Uh-huh. This should be interesting, Max. A change from your lists and orders."

He smiled, placing his chin comfortably on top of her head. "Okay. But there's a moral in here. You just have to let me forage for it."

"Hmph! Go ahead...." Irish rubbed Max's stomach and he closed his eyes. She always seemed to know the best spots to pick.

"The cowboy parked his horse under a tree—so the birds could dive-bomb his expensive polished saddle and sexy black horse with droppings."

Encouraged by her slight giggle, Max continued, "Then, sashaying her rounded hips and bouncing full bosom across the lawn, this blue-eyed vixen with sun-kissed curly locks met the cowboy, stopping him in his tracks—"

"—boots."

"Stopping him in his boots. The cowboy's lecherous hungry eyes drifted down the fair maiden's luscious body, coveting it with evil plans—like counting freckles."

Giggling openly, Irish slipped her hand lower on his stomach and stroked. Max sucked in his breath and fought to continue his tale. "The cowboy had known many women, visited many bordellos in the West. But this bodacious lady offered sweet delights he hadn't yet sampled, and the cowboy needed to indulge…refreshing himself in her four-poster bed."

"After disposing of the villain. Practically breaking his nose."

"Ah, yes. Ever after, the cowboy was grateful to the blackguard. You see, the cowboy—"

"The sexy range rider with the big dangerous gun…"

He chuckled at that, leaning down to kiss her lips. Turning her more fully to him, Max kissed her again, enjoying her slow delicious response. Then, smoothing his hand along her hips, Max continued, "Ever after, the range rider never wanted to roam again. The lady had lassoed his hard heart and tamed his restless needs. He fell beneath the spell of her strawberry kisses."

Irish's arms went tightly around his neck and Max gathered her close to him. "Was the cowboy happy forever, Max?" she asked quietly after a moment.

He kissed her damp cheek. "He never knew he could be so happy. Because every day the lady made his life better. To make his life even happier the lady gave him a baby cowboy."

She lifted her head, propping herself up on an elbow while stroking him with her free hand. "Is that really how you feel, Max?"

Max tasted the lusciously soft strawberry lips of the lady, turning her on her back.

Reaching for him, Irish held him tightly and returned the kiss with all her loving heart.

"Oh, Max," she murmured in a distressed tone just as he was working up to telling her he loved her.

"Mmm?"

"Max, my chest..."

He nestled against her, luxuriating in her lush softness. "Oh, Max, I've dampened myself," she whispered shakily, her pansy-blue eyes staring up at him helplessly.

The tiny twin spots darkening the pink cotton top reminded Max of the baby. Of the love he had yet to profess and the doubts that he needed to waylay for Irish. "I think," he said slowly, running the tip of his finger across her full breasts, "that this may be the loveliest, most exciting sight in my life. Your body preparing for my baby. The baby we made together because we cared..."

"Oh, Max," she cried achingly, throwing her arms around him tightly. "You say the sweetest things. Even if you're just trying to make me feel better."

While he held Irish, Max stared at the mocking cupids on the chandelier. Before the baby arrived, he had to convince her that his love would last.

The next morning while Irish was sleeping, Max saddled a powerful black stallion, Guy de Charlemagne. The horse matched the sexy-stallion description in the range-rider story. Tugging up his shearling coat against the biting Arctic wind, Max nudged Guy's side with his boots. The horse responded in a powerful surge of muscles under a sleek coat, picking his way through the snow-covered peony fields and the zigzagging rows of dead cornstalks.

In the snow and the pines, Max prepared himself for what he must do. *His only chance rested in the thing he least wanted to do—invite his parents to the inn, exposing himself again to their cold hearts. Exposing his wife and child. Yet it would please Irish. And just maybe...*

He shivered and huddled beneath the warmth of the shearling coat, the yawning white abyss in front of him no colder than his past.

Max drew the brim of his Stetson lower, protection against the biting winds. *For Irish's love, he'd walk through hell or into his past.*

Irish looked in the mirror, hating her freckles and heavy jumble of curls. The navy jumper and cornflower-blue frilly blouse didn't hide Plain Old Irish. She looked like a pregnant Raggedy Ann doll. In half an hour the Van Dammes were arriving to meet their daughter-in-law and mother of their coming grandchild.

Since inviting them to Abagail's, Max had suddenly lost his devastating sexy smile. The naughty-boy twinkle was gone.

Tucking a wayward curl behind her ear with Abagail's tortoiseshell comb, Irish smiled brightly into the madam's boudoir mirror. "This is all going to turn out just peachy," she told her reflection. "Max didn't want to do this—but he did. He did it for me, and everything is going to be fine. Jones has a right to know his grandparents on both sides."

She patted the baby who kicked back at her. "Isn't everything peachy in there?" she asked. When Jones kicked again, Irish grinned. "There. Let's go find your father. He's in a snit and playing with his gizmos because he's frightened. We'll protect him, won't we?"

Holed up with The Whiz, Max propped his boots on a desk, and leaned back on the chair's hind legs. Looking lean and cowboylike in his flannel shirt and jeans, Max had never been so appealing.

When he looked at her, his eyes lit up and his hard expression slid away with the sounds of Granny's computer printer. He held out his hand and Irish took it, sliding onto his lap.

"Jones and I had a talk, Max. He's worried about you," she said, smoothing the taut muscle at the back of Max's neck.

Granny muttered that pork bellies had dropped in the stock market, grabbed the computer printout and ran to ask Nadia's opinion of the future stock picture.

Irish leaned her forehead against his. "Max, why don't you whip up something gooey and sinful while we're waiting for your parents?"

His eyebrows went up and the hand caressing her stomach stopped. "Are you feeling all right? The last I remembered we were having a battle over whether pecans were legal in fruitcake. I only agreed to walnuts because you said Jones wanted them."

Irish fluttered her lashes, prying a grin from him despite his tense mood. "Please, Maxi?"

When he chuckled, easing her to her feet, Irish knew that the Van Dammes would be pushovers. Because he walked through perilous times, Irish framed his rugged face with her palms and urged him down for the sweetest kiss her heart could manage.

When the kiss ended, Max hauled her close and stood holding her for a long time.

His parents arrived promptly, taking a taxi from the nearest airport.

Max, dressed in a maroon ski sweater and jeans, greeted them at the front porch. At his side, Irish held his hand and swallowed the last of his honey-coated walnuts.

Elena Van Damme was tall and rawboned. Her eyes were the same shade as Max's; they penetrated as they touched Irish, flowed down the navy jumper and blouse, measuring and predicting everything about the baby. After being seated in the parlor, Elena's movements were efficient, her hands carefully folded on her lap. She looked as though she could remain in the same position forever.

With stooped shoulders, Franz sat carefully beside his wife's stately erect body. Though graying, his hair was the same auburn shade as Max's. When he talked about his latest research, his eyes lit up behind his glasses and his hands were beautifully expressive.

Seated at Irish's side, Max held her hand on his hard thigh. He talked quietly, responding to his father with the same reserve he'd shown when first meeting her. Only his fingers and the hard muscle beneath their hands showed the strain.

Isolated from the scientific discussion that Franz began immediately, Irish studied the Van Dammes. Their relationship was tense; Franz shifted restlessly as he glanced at Elena. The only movement the elder Mrs. Van Damme made for half an hour was to pat her husband's hand just once. Irish and Max shared a long stare of understanding, and then Max inhaled sharply, holding his breath. His hand tightened on hers and, without hesitation, Irish reached up to kiss his cheek.

Immediately his expression changed, his dark eyes lighting as he looked into hers. Abagail's tortoiseshell comb began to slip, and before she could replace it, Max had carefully tucked it back into her curls. His fingers lingered, testing a soft strand. When she began to smile up at him, Max briefly kissed her mouth.

Franz shifted uncomfortably. "Ah, Max. Elena and I thought a fully researched genetic chart for all the families involved might be in order."

Instantly Max turned toward his father, his face hard. "No... thank you," he said with the force of a slammed door.

Elena's head went back slightly, and Franz swallowed with apparent effort. A muscle contracted in Max's cheek; the tension crackled around the room.

In that second Irish ached for Max and his parents. The distance was years deep and would stretch into the future if not stopped. Max needed her help, and from their anxious expressions, so did his parents.

"I think a genetic chart for the baby would be lovely," Irish said, patting Franz's hand as she stood. "My family would just love to help out. Elena, would you like to help me in the kitchen? Max has made some cakes—we can have them with our tea."

Leaning down, she whispered in Max's ear, "You are to show him your computer setup, explain the gizmos and return back here in exactly half an hour. Got it, Maxi?"

When he looked like he might rebel, Irish kissed his hard mouth and treated his parents to Max's naughty-boy look. She flashed the astonished Van Dammes a wide smile and found Elena warily returning it after a moment.

In the kitchen, Elena stood aside while Irish prepared the tea tray. His mother toyed with Max's petits fours, rearranging them on the tray into exact rows. "Max made these?" Elena asked carefully, tracing the delicate pink frosted flowers decorating the tiny cakes.

When Irish nodded, sensing that the older woman wanted to talk, Elena said slowly, "They're lovely. He was such a beautiful little boy."

The wistful aching tone caught Irish and she took Elena's larger hand. "Max is a beautiful man."

Elena's eyes darkened with emotion; her fingers clung to Irish's. "Is he truly happy at last? How I've wondered about him. We haven't been close, you see."

The personal admission had cost Elena, her eyes bright with unshed tears. "Franz and I were too engrossed in our careers when Max came along."

She looked away from Irish, her voice raw with emotion. "We regret our mistake. He was just a baby, and then suddenly he was a young man. He was loved, but I'm afraid that Franz and I aren't very demonstrative. . . ."

Without a second thought, Irish reached up to kiss the older woman's cheek. "The wonderful thing about the past is that it is past—the future and your grandchild is waiting for us. The baby and I will need you to protect us from Max. He can be such a tyrant."

Slowly Elena turned to Irish, smiling softly. "He does make lovely escargot.... Then we're welcome to visit again?"

Irish hugged her, and after an initial stiffening, Elena carefully returned the embrace. "Franz will be elated," she said formally, but her dark eyes were shining.

When his parents left for their home in Missouri, Max turned to Irish. "Wonderful, aren't they?" he asked coldly.

She kissed his cheek and hugged him close—as close as the baby would allow. She definitely had plans to narrow the gap between the Van Dammes, but right now Max needed cuddling. "*You're* wonderful. And now you're mine, not theirs."

Max's naughty-boy twinkle sprang back into his eyes. "You mean you're not offering me an annulment?"

Tracing the firm line of his mouth, Irish leaned back in his arms. "Of course not. Without me, they might never know their grandchild. Without their grandchildren, they might never know love."

She kissed him, slowly, carefully. "Thank you, Max. Meeting the grandparents of our baby meant very much to me. And I know how difficult it was for you to see them under the circumstances."

Max shuddered, gathering her closer. "You have no idea."

"Poor Max. Poor Daddy," she said, meaning it and cuddling nearer to him. "He's going to be fine. We'll have fantastic family reunions with Pop teaching Franz and Jones how to play football. Mother and Elena can fish in the creek while you and I—"

Max's hard kiss stopped her from finishing.

* * *

By the last of January the baby had lowered into birthing position, allowing Irish to breathe easier.

Max seemed to be constantly tired, tense and anxious while Irish felt great. She began freestyle cooking again and helped Nadia with the last stages of her manuscript. Plotting her successful future on tarot cards and confident of a sale, Nadia sailed off to New York.

The first week of February swept into the valley on an unexpected blizzard. The fierce storm stranded Granny and Link in Denver. Maudie Kleinhauser had been offended by Nat Johnson, who said women couldn't manage without men and had rallied the support of Kodiac's "womenfolk." Lizzie Caulder's husband didn't act as romantic as Max, and she added to the mutiny by ordering that all the children be left in charge of the "menfolk." The hostile women had barricaded themselves in a neighboring town's high-school gym and were having a glorious time despite the weather.

Alone with Max, Irish watched the snow fall softly across the fields. The weather prediction was for several inches; the mountain passes were already blocked by heavier snow. The storm hovered over the valley all day, and on the second morning, Irish padded around the kitchen, making Max's favorite pancakes—lumberjack buttermilk pancakes with tiny bits of apple in them.

With just the two of them, Irish had chosen to use the old wood cookstove. The electricity had been chancy since early dawn, and cozy warmth added to Irish's happy mood. While Max was busy with the outside chores, she arranged the spices her way.

Jones hadn't kicked all night, and Irish felt as if she could clean Abagail's from top to bottom by herself. Because she felt so wonderful, Irish had showered and dressed in Max's favorite blue frilly nightgown. The granny-styled garment never failed to rate a magnificent, ego-building, first-class seductive kiss.

Max had developed a sexy Western look that could take her breath away at ten paces; he looked like Abagail's handsome cowboy lover. Alone with him, she discovered that he liked nothing better than watching old movies while eating popcorn.

She plopped a spoonful of batter onto the griddle and grinned. She'd introduced Max to a marvelous game of drive-in movie. It had to do with snuggling on the couch, and Max, though careful of the baby, delighted in playing sensual games with her. He said he didn't mind the cold showers and he'd started lifting car bumpers for a hobby.

He didn't appear to feel trapped by impending fatherhood.

Bringing in the wood for the day, Max tromped the excess snow from his boots on the back porch and entered the kitchen in a flurry of snowflakes.

He placed the wood in the box, dusted his leather gloves and tucked them in his pocket. Shrugging off his coat, he leaned down to kiss her, his face cold and ruggedly appealing. "Dear heart," he murmured in the raspy steamy voice that warmed her as his eyes took in the gown.

Setting out to earn the nickname, Irish put her heart into the long slow kiss.

"Oh, Max!" she exclaimed a moment later when warm water trickled down her legs.

He looked at the puddle forming at her feet, frowned and yanked a towel from the rack. Lifting her gown, Max tucked the towel between her legs and carried her to a chair. "First stage of labor. The baby is coming," he announced grimly, picking up the telephone receiver.

Max's face darkened, his eyebrows drawing together in a single line and his lips pressed together as he listened. "Lines are out."

He frowned at her, then down at Jones. "Are you having contractions?"

Irish's eyes widened as she realized that all morning she'd been getting warning signs. There was just that slight tightening across her stomach and… "My back hurts," she said quietly, watching the fear leap in his eyes.

"We're here alone, Irish," Max stated, moving toward her, his expression grim. "There isn't a chance of anyone coming in or us making it to the hospital."

He shivered and Irish placed her palm on his cheek. "Don't worry, Max."

Gripping her hand and bringing it to his mouth, Max frowned. "Irish, I'm going downstairs to switch on the electric generator and then I'm coming back."

The pancakes began to burn. "Max, the pancakes—"

"Pancakes, hell," he muttered, flipping them expertly and placing the griddle aside. Checking the antique stove's water reservoir and finding it filled, Max ran down the basement stairs.

In a matter of seconds the generator thudded comfortably below them.

"Oh, Max," Irish managed as he ran back up the stairs and scooped her up in his arms.

Carrying her to the couch, Max placed pillows behind her back and stripped her briefs from her gently. His hands moved on her carefully, tracing the baby's arrival.

Wiping his hand across his brow, Max took her hand. "Lady, you and I are in love," he stated roughly. "I've been wanting to say it in pretty ways, ways to make it new and special to you. But now the baby isn't waiting for anything, and I want you to know you are my life and more to me. There isn't going to be an annulment and we're going to raise our baby together. I love you. Got it?"

She inhaled, fighting the urge to cry. "What a time…" When Max's face paled, she gripped his hand. He needed everything she could give him and she gave him her love. "Got it."

Gathering her to him, he kissed her hard. "You've got to trust me now, Irish."

"Max . . . don't debate the point . . . I love you," she said as his hands moved over her, seeking the baby.

He frowned, arranging the towel beneath her. Taking a deep breath, Max attempted a carefree grin. The one that could make her melt—at other times. "Actually, I've talked to MacMannis and Dr. Williams about a home delivery, and they made me a list. Dr. Williams gave me his favorite stethoscope—a thank-you for connecting him to The Whiz who's been busy researching library banks. He's been hoping that he could fly down in the helicopter, and now he's going to get his wish. While he's taking care of you, I'm going to stuff him with German and French dishes."

She caressed his cheek, loving him. "Always prepared, Max."

When he grinned sheepishly and kissed her hand, Irish grinned back. "Get your notebook, Max."

"Well," he said, standing slowly, "this is where the sturdy foldaway bed and the portable radio system to MacMannis is important. I designed a special beeper for her and it will only take a minute to set up—she'll talk us through this. Then with the generator working we can use the home contraction monitor. . . . "

"Hurry, Max," Irish gritted between her teeth as another contraction hit her.

He placed his hand over the baby, read his watch, timing the contraction while he coached her breathing. After her cleansing breath, Max swung into action.

Two hours later the snow kept falling outside and the pains began coming closer together. Lying on clean sheets on a comfortable cot in the warm kitchen, Irish watched Max talk quietly to MacMannis. "Three minutes apart and lasting forty-five seconds—yes, of course I measured. She' up to eight centimeters—yes, I know it's coming fast, dam it."

"Max, be nice," Irish urged softly, listening to Max stor quietly at the nurse.

"She's in transition, dammit," he snarled impatiently glancing at Irish who had just begun to feel another shar contraction. "Yes, I know they get nasty and I'm pre pared—"

"Max, dammit, get your buns over here," Irish snapped.

His eyes widened momentarily as though she'd jus slapped him. Irish began breathing desperately, feeling a though she'd *like* to slap him. "Max, get your lists and ge the hell over here," she managed, breathing heavily. "Or th deal is off."

While he stared blankly at her, Irish glared at him. "Tha does it," she muttered, struggling to rise from the cot. "I'v changed my mind. I'm going upstairs and forgetting abou you forever. You pop in here loaded for bear..."

"Irish," Max finally said, moving swiftly toward her "Honey, lie down—"

"Yes, I did lie down—with you. Hell's bells, now I know what can happen when a range rider shows up at my door step," she managed as another contraction zigzagge through her.

Max held her hand and coached her through the painfu interval. When it was finished, Irish was sweaty, lying back to doze momentarily.

Max's hands moved over her, his paper lists shuffling in the notebook. Adjusting the speaker to his head, he spoke quietly to MacMannis. "She's nasty-tempered. Yes, I know the snow has stopped...where is the helicopter now...okay, yes...easy, Irish...MacMannis says you deserve a medal for putting up with me...."

Rolling Irish gently to her left side, Max used the base of his palm to rub her back. "You're doing great, sweetheart. That's right, take a rest. Remember on our next contraction, we're breathing hee-hee-hee, who-who-who-ing...."

Irish glared at him. "What do you mean, *our* next contraction?" she managed just as the pain began. Max talked calmly into the mouthpiece, flipping his manual with one hand and holding her hand with the other.

"Yes, Irish is beautiful...yes, dammit, I love my wife...no, I haven't told her enough.... Irish, I love you," Max stated flatly. "I love you. See, MacMannis, I told her...the storm's over...he'd better get here fast...now, shut up...of course I won't stop saying it when the baby is born...yes, I see your note about crowning in paragraph five...."

Irish began working hard, concentrating on breathing, concentrating on her love for Max, and resting. When the contractions began again she pushed, squeezing Max's big secure hand and obeying his commands.

Max loved her; the lines on his face deepened with concern, his kisses punctuating the easier moments. After a heavy contraction, he attempted a lopsided beguiling smile. "Still want to change your mind and go upstairs, sweetheart?"

"Tell me you love me. Now," she demanded when he wiped her forehead with a cool cloth. "And what happened to 'dear heart'?"

Max's hands stopped moving over her. "You are the sunshine of my heart. You took me from the cold and made me yours," he said in a deep tone of raw emotion, tears coming to his eyes.

Another pain peaked and Irish pushed against his hands. "You can do this, Max.... Hell's bells," she gasped. "You can love this baby. You'll give him every drop of love he needs...."

Irish closed her eyes, working with the contraction. In the distance, a door opened and closed and a burst of Arctic air entered the room.

When she opened her eyes, Dr. Williams stood near Max, drawing on his gloves. He held them up for Irish to see. "Baby time," he said cheerfully, stepping briskly into position. "You owe me some fancy cooking for that helicopter ride. But right now, give Mama something to push against and let's get that baby here in time for supper."

"Dear heart..." Max began, leaning over her.

"That's it, talk to her. Irish, let's go. We can do this in just a few minutes. We're practically home free...."

"Ah, Max," Dr. Williams said a few moments later. "You've done a fine job, followed my orders perfectly. Now how about holding your daughter?"

Irish had a glimpse of Max's astonished expression, the tearful joy filling it before he handed the tiny squirming baby to her.

Max wiped away a tear running down his cheek, then dabbed Irish's tear trails. "She's beautiful," he managed raggedly as the baby nuzzled at Irish, seeking nourishment. "Perfectly beautiful," he repeated in an awed tone.

Dr. Williams's firm order cut through the moment. "Max, you're woozy. If you're going to pass out, sit down. Now."

For once, Max obeyed and poured his tall body into a kitchen chair.

Irish's love for him rose, trembled on the afternoon air and filled the room. Looking helpless and vulnerable, Max continued to stare blankly at her and the baby. "Daddy, we love you," she called gently.

He grinned slowly, sheepishly, responding to her. "Say hi to Daddy, baby," Irish whispered to her daughter nestling against her breast.

When she waved the baby's tiny hand at Max, he waved back, grinning widely. "Hi, Jones."

"I'll want lasagna tonight," Dr. Williams said, taking the baby.

Ten

"Boonie's hot fudge cake is classless," Max stated flatly. He dropped walnut halves onto the cake's thick layer of chocolate frosting with an air of disdain. The halves hit the frosting to the beat of Beethoven's Fifth Symphony, Max's after-dinner music, which played through the kitchen's sound system.

"See Daddy grumble, Abagail," Irish teased as she held four-month-old Abagail against her shoulder for a last burp. She rubbed the baby's back and kissed the small head covered with a cap of black curls.

Max turned to her, his frown sliding into a warm delighted grin. "Abagail, Daddy's happy to bake Boonie's favorite chocolate cake. Boonie deserves it. See Daddy smile?"

Abagail Serene Van Damme accommodated her parents with a loud but feminine burp. Her head bobbed toward Max and she cooed, blinking pansy-blue eyes.

Standing in his stocking feet, wearing a T-shirt and jeans, Max looked as delicious as the gooey double-chocolate nut cake he'd just created. His auburn hair had caught the early evening June breeze, and the mussed waves caused him to have that living-on-the-edge dangerous-cowboy look that always excited Irish. Abagail LaRue Whitehouse's sequined and lusty heart would have quivered at the sight of Max's cowboy image.

With laughter lines radiating from his dark exciting eyes and his skin weathered by the Colorado sun and wind to a texture that tempted her fingertips and lips to explore, Max was the perfect daddy candidate.

Irish had definite plans to explore Max's lean and accommodating body later in the evening. The Whiz owed Max a debt, and payback involved baby-sitting for a whole night and the next day. Irish had plans that involved slow two-stepping at Big Jakes and... She could almost feel her fingers rummaging through the tuft of hair escaping the neckline of Max's T-shirt.

Abagail Van Damme blew slobbery bubbles at her father and blinked her wide eyes again. "Daddy's little girl won't like gooey fudgey cake, will she? Say 'Abagail wants crepes, Abagail loves crepes,'" Max cooed, his deep raspy voice causing Irish's breasts to peak.

Motherhood had pounced on Irish's breasts as though making a proud announcement to the world. Though the rest of her body had trimmed, her breasts retained a lush contour. This instigated Max's fascination with the precise construction of bras, ballast and support, and caused The Whiz to invest in a special line of lingerie.

Boonie's short rap on the back door signaled his arrival, and Max let him in. Shaking the rancher's hand in genuine warmth, Max said, "Your weekly cake is ready. How are you doing?"

"Doing fine. Been seeing Dortha, but she can't cook. Sure appreciate this cake, Max. I'll have the campsite set up when you and Irish are done at Big Jakes. Don't forget, that will cost you two cakes for three weeks."

Boonie walked toward Irish, totally ignoring her in pursuit of Abagail who reached out a tiny hand. "How's Boonie's peachy-pie little sweetums?" he asked, taking the hand and kissing it gallantly while Abagail blinked and blew bubbles at him.

Then he noticed Irish and grinned shyly. "You okay, little mama?" When she returned his grin and nodded, Boonie said, "Got plans for my own family if everything works out right. But since I figure Max owes me, I'll still be coming in for my cake, okay?"

"You're welcome any time, Boonie," she returned. "Even for Max's Wednesday Night dinner."

Boonie shuddered and released Abagail's hand. He backed toward the door, holding his precious cake as though fearing Max would retrieve it. "Yuk. The French snails and smothered-tongue delight," he muttered before slipping out the door.

"There is nothing wrong with my escargots," Max muttered while drying the kitchen counter. With his nose definitely out of joint, he padded into the laundry room and returned with an overflowing basket of clean diapers. Sitting down at the table, he grumbled about low-class no-taste cowboys while he methodically folded Abagail's diapers.

Precisely stacked, the mound of fluffy diapers grew quickly. When he moved on to the bibs, gowns and jammies, Irish handed Abagail to him. She'd found that contact with Abagail sweetened Max's rough edges instantly.

Max cuddled the baby to him, his large hand supporting her bottom while he grinned and toyed with her tiny hands. The baby cooed and waved her fists around, and Max chuckled, lifting her for a kiss. She blinked her eyes at him and he held her close, rocking her slightly and humming a movement from Bach.

Irish finished the laundry and glanced at him. "Abagail can't come camping, Max. Don't give her any big ideas."

"Definitely not this time, Abagail," he agreed, tossing a wicked grin at Irish. Max cradled Abagail on his thighs and deftly unsnapped her jammies. In less than fifteen seconds he had replaced her diaper, exactly matching the angles of the diaper pins. He snapped the jammies and held Abagail aloft, playing with her.

Watching Max loving Abagail with such delight and pride, Irish caressed his shoulder. "Happy?"

Max's dark eyes swung to hers as he cradled the baby against his chest. "Dear heart, I didn't know there was love until you filled my life," he stated simply in the rough tone she'd come to know as deep emotion.

For that instant, their eyes met and held. Love coursed through the moment like a heavy sweet rhapsody, timeless and strong.

Max's expression when he rocked Abagail was one of absolute peace, of contentment and love. He no longer doubted his ability to love; it radiated from him, spilling into every touch, every quiet sharing moment.

Each night when he at last took Irish in his arms, it was with reverence and love.

Abagail interrupted the long meaningful look when she investigated Max's ear, her cheek gently bumping his, and Max sent Irish a hot promising look that she answered with her own.

"Our first night out," he murmured, lifting her palm. His tongue flicked the sensitive center. "I've got big plans for our date. After Big Jakes—when we're camping."

Irish traced his lips, grinning impishly. "Be careful. I've got some ideas of my own."

* * *

Later at Big Jakes, Max surveyed the smoky interior with the air of a range rider scouting for a lookout post. "Our first night out," he said between his teeth, "and you pick a place that smothers chili dogs in fried white onions. There's a place in Denver that knows how to parboil shallots with white sauce—"

"Maxi," Irish cooed, fluttering her eyelashes at him. She loved how he always stared at her for a moment blankly, as though all the click-click circuits had stopped momentarily.

Max took a deep unsteady breath, his eyes flowing appreciatively over the frilly eyelet blouse Irish had chosen for the occasion. The blue lacy-skirt-and-blouse concoction deserved a man who appreciated a woman—one with masses of curly blond hair. "I can manage," he murmured huskily.

Irish fluttered her eyelashes again. "I know."

Because everyone at Big Jakes knew it was the Van Dammes' first after-the-baby night out, Max and Irish received special treatment. Big Jake ladled more chili onto Max's hot dog, but slyly avoided the onions. Mineral water with lime filled their beer mugs and later a bottle of Max's favorite wine appeared at the table—with pretzels.

The Western band played two-step songs, and a cowboy stepped up to the microphone, wailing about his dying love and dying dog. Snuggled against Max's broad chest, Irish managed to find that tempting spot at his throat. When she kissed his warm skin, Max's hands wandered in the dark shadows of a favorite corner.

"We'll have to bring your parents here," she whispered against the spot, and Max's hands stopped wandering.

Against her ear, he whispered loudly over the bass guitar, "Irish, you've been pushing your luck about my parents. Sending them Abagail's picture was your idea, and now they want growth charts."

Irish's nose nuzzled the hair on Max's chest. Having her own range rider, dressed in a Western shirt, was definitely a perk for marriage. She slid her hands into his jeans back pockets to more fully appreciate the taut lean muscle moving beneath the denim. "We can never be one big happy family, Irish," Max managed huskily, his hands moving lower on her lips.

"Well . . . they are going to visit in the fall. Mom and Pop have agreed to come and run interference if they pick on you. But according to Nadia's readings, they'll enjoy their granddaughter so much that you won't have any problems."

She looked up into Max's dark flickering gaze. "Max, have you ever realized that your parents are the only people we know who truly appreciate your escargot recipes?"

He stopped swaying to the music. "You know, I think they do appreciate fine cooking."

"And fine wine. When I told them about Van Damme-Dalton vineyards and wine, they decided to research the genetic composition of the strain of grapes. Your mother asked about the soil composition and breeding for taste—" She stopped when Max's lips covered hers.

Max fitted her against his body as he had fitted her into his life, systematically and devotedly. With gusto supreme that Irish returned in kind.

Big Jake's ham-size hand shook Max's shoulder, interrupting the kiss. "Irish, the band wants to try out their first rock-and-roll session and need some dancers on the floor. How 'bout it?"

Still wrapped in Max's arm's, Irish gazed up at her husband, who looked as though he'd like to carry her out into the midnight air and kidnap her in his station wagon. Then he grinned slowly, devastatingly. "Clear the floor. I won a rock-and-roll trophy a few years back."

Irish stared up at him. "You?"

He led her on to the dance floor with the air of a knight escorting his lady to the cotillion. While the band warmed up, the lead guitar tossing out Chuck Berry segments, Irish tossed Max a challenge. "I'm very good, Max," she said, confident he would return the tease.

He lifted an eyebrow, his eyes daring. "Think you're hot stuff, do you?"

"Tops."

The band started playing, and Max took her hands. They began dancing carefully, following the hard beat and gauging each other's style. Tucking her against him, Max said, "Dear heart, you ain't seen nothin' yet."

"Take it slow, Pops," she returned just before Max flipped her across his back.

"Oh, my," she said, just before he picked her up at the waist and Irish found herself sitting briefly on his hard thigh. "Oh, my," she repeated when she slid through Max's long legs to emerge on the other side.

"Having fun, Mrs. Van Damme?" he asked as Irish stepped into the beat, and Max twirled her under his arm.

"Definitely, Mr. Van Damme," she managed between laughing. "Do you think you could squeeze some rock-and-roll tapes into the sound system—between Bach and Tchaikovsky?"

"Abagail needs soothing music now. But we could have it piped into our bedroom when we add those private apartments to Abagail's Inn."

When they danced later to a slow song, Irish snuggled safely against Max. "Thanks for sneaking those free coupons to the Hendrichs, Max."

"I don't know anything about it.... Okay, they needed to get away from their problems for a few days," he murmured against a curling wisp of her hair. "Ah, are we going to dance all night?"

* * *

Located miles from Kodiac, the campsite was in a mountainside clearing in the sprawling, rugged Rockies. In the starlit night, the Colorado moon hovered like an elegant silvery disk.

Boonie had set up a small tent, stocked with cassette player and tapes. Two ice chests were stocked with food, and an array of cooking gear waited near a camp fire that just needed to be lit.

Dominating the clearing was a solid brass four-poster bed covered by a sheet of plastic. Beneath the bed, a large shag carpet covered the pine needles.

Irish watched Max neatly fold and tuck the plastic away, exposing the red satin bedspread. "Nothing like planning," she said as he entered the tent to retrieve the battery-operated cassette player. The strains of Bach immediately flowed through the mountain air.

"Hmm, the old thee-and-me game, huh?" Irish asked when Max finally turned to her. She could feel the heat and the tension growing in the night, sending sweet expectations running along her flesh.

"I wanted tonight to be something you'd remember, dear heart," Max said, his voice deep and raw with emotion. An intense hunger filled his harsh features, the rugged planes and angles catching the moonlight. Max stood several feet away from her, and his tall body was rigid.

They shared the moment silently, thinking of their love. The future would be filled with Abagail and each other, every moment precious.

Then Max began to unbutton his shirt. Following his motions, Irish began loosening her blouse, her eyes holding his.

They undressed slowly, watching the moonlight spill between them, over them, like a silvery magical sheet.

Irish allowed her blouse and skirt to fall at her bare feet. Covering her pale shimmering skin were twin strips of black lace. He followed the curves of her body hungrily, this woman who had brought him love and taken his heart.

She lifted the heavy fall of her hair, the simple gesture seducing him instantly. Max traced the lush new lines of her body: her full pale breasts shimmering in the moonlight above the low-cut bra, and the delicate indentation of her waist flowing into her rounded hips; a thin strip of lace and shadows concealing the joining of her long tapering thighs.

He moved to her swiftly, trimming his passion for the moment and savoring the dark mysterious eyes of his wife. Tracing her hot cheek with his finger, Max bent his head and tasted her soft parted mouth.

Her scent filled him with joy; beneath the fresh daisy scent, her own seductive musk reached out to ensnare his senses. Irish's soft skin heated to his touch as he knew it would, her eyes widening with the emotions trembling on the soft still air. He nibbled her bottom lip, inhaling the soft gasp of pleasure. The movement brought his bare chest against her breasts, caressing him.

Skimming her body with the flat of his hands, Max smoothed her hips, treasuring the softness filling his palms.

Taking his time, Max slipped the lace from her. "Oh, Max," she cried out softly as he fitted his mouth over her breast. Lingering on the satiny skin, Max felt her heart pound beneath his lips. Her cries delighted him, heated his passions until he trembled, aching for her.

Max eased his fingers under the lace at her thighs and found the delicate heat waiting for him. Her hands skimmed over him, trembling, touching him intimately with an awe that always astounded him.

Their lips touched and hovered and fitted together as Max slipped the last shred of lace from her. The delicate play of their tongues tempted him to deepen the tantalizing kisses that never satisfied, yet offered more. Still, Max held back, savoring the fragrance and the gentleness of his wife, his mate, letting her set the pace.

Her palms slid over him as her breasts moved against his hard chest, the twin softness melding gently to him.

He caught her in his arms, lifting her to his chest. "My heart, my love," he whispered against the tumbling mass of her hair.

Irish's arms curved around his neck, her cheek resting on his shoulder. "My love," she echoed softly, stroking his taut chest and soothing the hot immediate hunger momentarily.

Then Max needed her desperately, and he lowered her gently to the red satin bedspread.

She found him waiting for her, his trembling hands and uneven breath exciting.

The satin moved smoothly at her back, and Max's hard thigh nudged her intimately, his mouth parted and moist on her skin.

His hands ran down her body, claiming, seeking. The fine trembling of his fingers heated her senses immediately, her own hungers stoked and waiting. Tonight while their daughter slept peacefully, they would renew their love and wonder.

Max's hand found her breasts, lingering luxuriously in the moment preceding the passion they would explore. His fingertips traced the sensitive nubs delicately, reverently. His lips followed his touch, tasting her with kisses that made her tremble.

Heating against the long length of Max's hard body, Irish moved swiftly, seeking and finding. She smoothed the rigid contours of corded muscle, tangling her bare thighs with his bulkier ones.

Max shuddered, his hands seeking her softness, his voice rough with passion. She cried out in answering need, her body aching with a poignant sharpness. Moving over Max,

Irish fitted their bodies together; they became one, just a their lives had merged.

Poised on the peak of pleasure and passion, Irish stilled taking into her the wonder of their perfect lives. Max caugh the precious timeless moment, held her body in his large saf hands and waited, savoring the very edge of the coming ecstasy.

The fiery peak grew, consuming and flaming on the edge then drew them down into the heat and urgency of passion Carefully lowering herself to him, Irish rested for an instant.

Closing her eyes and taking the intense pleasure into her she ran her palms down his damp hair-roughened chest.

"Dear heart," Max said roughly against her ear, nibbling on the lobe.

While Irish concentrated on his throat, dragging ho kisses along the taut muscular length, Max resorted t drastic tactics and sought her most vulnerable area.

Pressing her hips against him with one hand, Max opene his lips on the spot.

Irish reacted immediately and beautifully. For just fraction of an instant, Max felt guilty for disturbing he survey of him. Then as she moved swiftly and hungril against him, the soft cries startling and urgent, Max los himself in the experience of Irish's passion.

In the moonlight and shadows, she moved over him binding him to her with love.

He met the delicate savagery of her mouth with hunger her body flowing over his, taking and yielding.

Her hair caressed his skin, the silky strands binding then as closely as the child they had created.

The pleasure point held as Irish's body closed rhythmically around him, her soft exclamations of pleasure flowing over him, filling him.

He followed her immediately, calling out his love in the fierce driving pleasure.

The night was long and steeped in love, and in the morning, Irish lay snuggled in red satin while Max moved around the camp fire, dressed only in jeans. The morning birds flitted from tree to tree, and chipmunks raced up and down red-barked pines.

A gentle mist hovered in the clearing, and stepping through it, Max served Irish breakfast in bed. He carefully placed the tray across her knees, tugging the red satin bedspread up to her chin. He grinned, looking pleased and very rakish for a systems-warrior husband. "I've noticed that this portion of your anatomy is sensitive to temperature—cold and hot," he explained in the deep raspy tone she loved.

He bent to kiss a tender peak. "When you were pregnant with Abagail, your breasts were delightful."

Then, slipping off his jeans, he joined her in the brass bed. When Irish kissed him, Max lingered in the sweet kiss, tantalizing her. "This must have been Madame Abagail Whitehouse's camping style," she said, nibbling on the spot at the corner of his mouth.

"One learns from the past. According to her diary, the madam used this ploy a few times with her favorite lover," Max stated, nuzzling her throat with his new beard. "Do you like the omelet?"

Irish shared the golden brown mushroom-and-green-pepper mixture with him. "This is marvelous, right down to the daisy bouquet. Max, you are so romantic."

Leaning back against the fluffy satin pillows, Max lounged in all his masculine glory exposing a deeply tanned hair-covered chest. "I try to please," he returned contritely, his hand finding her thigh beneath the satin.

"Maxi, I do love you," Irish murmured, placing aside the tray and curling up to him. She walked her fingers up his chest, fluttering her lashes at him.

A chattering chipmunk ran up a tree, and a bird darted through the hovering mist.

He caught her fingertips, bringing them to his lips. "What's up, pansy-eyes? You've got that look."

Irish fluttered her lashes again, thinking that systems warriors made great husbands. "Hmm? Max, did I ever tell you the story about the fertile Van Dammes? The ones living in Abagail LaRue Whitehouse's bordello? The ones expecting their second baby?"

Max sat up, the red satin sliding downward. He turned her roughly to him, his dark face urgent. "Us?"

"Uh-huh. You do make such a wonderful daddy candidate, darling," Irish murmured before Max kissed her, sweetly and with love.

* * * * *